THE HEART OF THE OCTOPUS

Mariateresa Boffo

Makindo Press
Flat 4 The Red House
Hove BN3 1FE

Original text © 2019 Mariateresa Boffo
English translation © 2021 Mariateresa Boffo
Copyright © 2019 Enrico Damiani Editore 2019
ISBN 9798700039352

The Heart of the Octopus was first published as *Il Cuore del Polpo* by Enrico Damiani Editore, 2019

First published by Makindo Press in 2021

All rights reserved.. No part of this publication may be reproduced, stored in retrieval system or transmitted in any form or by any means, electronic, mechanical, photocopying, recording or otherwise, without price permission in writing from Makindo Press

To Declan

One of the commonest and most generally accepted delusions is that every man can be qualified in some particular way – said to be kind, wicked, stupid, energetic, apathetic and so on. People are not like that. We may say of a man that he is more often kind than cruel, more often wise than stupid, more often energetic than apathetic or vice versa; but it could never be true to say of one man that he is kind or wise, and of another that he is wicked or stupid. Yet we are always classifying mankind in this way. And it is wrong. Human beings are like rivers; the water is one and the same in all of them but every river is narrow in some places, flows swifter in others; here it is broad, there still, or clear, or cold, or muddy or warm. It is the same with men. Every man bears within him the germs of every human quality, and now manifests one, now another, and frequently is quite unlike himself, while still remaining the same man.

Resurrection, Tolstoy

Children begin by loving their parents; after a time they judge them; rarely, if ever, do they forgive them.

Oscar Wilde

CONTENTS

1	Prologue	1
2	Part I	Pg 3
3	Part II	Pg 124
4	Part III	Pg 223
5	Part IV	Pg 312
6	Part V	Pg 378
7	Epilogue	Pg 421

PROLOGUE

October morning, Castel San Gerolamo.

The house stands on top of the hill, zig-zagged through with vines. It is robust, has thick walls, and it is yellow. There is a chestnut tree in the middle of the garden. Its branches skim the upper floor windows. It has been uninhabited for a long time - the windows are barred. The interior is dark. The garden is a jungle of nettles.

There is only one chair where many years ago there had been two. The cloth has all but disappeared; the rusty metallic frame is what has survived. Next to the chair, under the chestnut tree, there is a fountain. It is accessed via three steps; on the top is the statue of an angel - wings open, swollen lips, eyes half closed, it seems intent on observing the tadpoles that circle the dirty water.

Giovanni and Bianca had remained here for entire afternoons sitting on those grey stone steps, fingering the water, locking up the tadpoles in glasses, watching them go crazy.

A sweet smell of rotting leaves rises from the water, and it mixes with that of ripe grapes that thicken the air and of the wild mint that Giovanni has crushed underfoot. The water is completely still. The silence is broken only by the rustle of the leaves that rub against each other, and by the mild *ploc* of chestnuts that occasionally fall into the water, shaken free by the wind. It is a morning in October; the air smells wet with the recent rain, with fog, with rotting fruit; the leaves of the tree are a crazy reddish-gold.

    Giovanni is alone. He's old; he walks slowly. He sits on the edge of the tub and plunges both his hands into the water, rippling the smooth surface with rippling waves. He observes his fingers move like fish in water, white and pink like petals, like flowers.

PART I

His name is Giovanni. He is sixteen years old – an impatient boy, handsome in a stringy sort of way, with luscious locks of dark hair and sage-green eyes that slant downwards, making him look sad. He is not sad: he is sixteen, and fed up. Tired. Bored by small life, by his school and his school friends, and his parents. Mainly his parents. Mainly, his mum.

He lives in Castel San Gerolamo, a pretty village in the Monferrato area, a northern Italian region famous for its beautiful churches, its fairy-tale castles and its vineyards that produce award-winning wines. A guidebook mentions it: "A quaint hamlet in the Monferrato, in the Piedmont region of north-western Italy. Worth visiting are the Church of Santa Liberata, with frescoes from the 1500, and that of St. Gerolamo, with a crucifix from the 1300s, and the nearby monastery."

The village unrolls between the soft hills around Piazza San Gerolamo, where the main church stands, not far from the southern bank of the Po river. This is also where you can find the café and the restaurant Da Giuseppe, managed by the same family, the chemist's, and the grocery store owned by the brothers Carlo and Mario, a shop that sells everything from matches to loo roll, from cheese to cold meats (prosciutto, bresaola, lardo) to cigarettes and alcohol (but only the wines produced in Piedmont). The house where he lives with his parents stands just outside the village, on top of one of the hills. It was built by his grandfather's, and is old, and it feels old. Giovanni hates it – the smell that lingers along its grand, musty, colourless corridors. He hates the heavy, dark-wooded furniture, the creaky chairs, the cold tiles under his feet. Most of all – more than the house, more than the village – he hates his parents. No: he hates his mother. His father, he can bear. Just. But Luigi's always elsewhere, either hidden away in his office or working in the small vineyard he cultivates with solitary obsession.

Giovanni is an only child, loved with fierceness, spoilt like all Italian boys and then some more, even if his Dutch mother Marieke thinks she is – and she *is* – hard on him. But the hardships she inflicts are symbolic: she sends him up to his room when he's rude, for example, without considering the fact that he's actually much happier sitting on his bed than downstairs with her. She'll ask him to read, or to do chores around the house, which he doesn't mind. But then she punishes him subtly, by withdrawing, and it works. Giovanni feels lost, without her approval. He craves her praise - it's been his nourishment for so long; his go-to fix when he's down, when he feels lonely. And when she withdraws – not talking to him, unavailable, unsmiling – he crumbles, reacting with anger. Until a couple of years ago, he had screaming fits, easily controllable. Since he entered the murky waters of adolescence, it has been a quiet crescendo of fury, followed by silence, and then slamming, silence, kicking, silence, breaking.

Giovanni hadn't been a difficult baby, or child - from an early age he'd followed the rules: he had always slept twelve hours, from seven in the evening until seven in the morning; he had never woken up at night. Never had nightmares. He'd been a great breast-feeder; later, never spitting out the disgusting mixture of rice and broccoli when he was weaning, never refusing porridge for breakfast, never asking for chocolate, snacks, sweets. He had eaten a whole apple every night before dutifully giving a goodnight kiss to his parents and retiring to his room. He'd always said yes thanks and no thanks with a smile, he'd always held an adult's hand before crossing the street, he had always addressed formally people he didn't know well, showing respect to teachers and adults. Until now. Until last summer.

A rip. A gash. An explosion. It is common to associate an unforeseen change of character to a loud, unexpected noise: and there you are: Giovanni's official entry in the intricate and toxic woods of adolescence is comparable to a thunderstorm. It shares the same violence, the same power, the same suddenness: it's as if he's gone from being a quiet and obedient boy to a young hooligan. Not that Giovanni is the kind who breaks windows, throws stones, vandalises: his, from the very start, is a subtle violence, made of silences and sighs that grow – the screech of chairs overturned by the energetic impetus with which he rises from the table; the slammed doors (a classic of the genre) paired with the shrill: "you don't understand!," with the variant: "nobody understands me," either shouted out loud or whispered at the moment that precedes his exit from the scene (scene three, act one). Precisely: it is as if Giovanni were both the actor on the stage *and* the audience; he looks at himself making gestures and saying things that don't belong to him but that inexplicably do come out of his mouth, or from his body, without him truly having made a decision to do so, to say so: spontaneously, like an explosion. Giovanni looks at himself from the outside, thinking: this is not him. He is not like that. Not really. He doesn't scream, he doesn't stamp his feet like a ridiculous toddler; his are not tantrums. But oh: yes, there he goes again: declaiming monologues, falling over onto his bed (with shoes!). And there again, this time launching into a frantic race that takes his breath away - at least his heart goes crazy for a real physical reason, not for incomprehensible ones.

Last summer he started feeling this - how to call it? – let's define it *impatience*, the feeling of being intensely annoyed by someone's mistakes or because you have to wait; wanting something to happen as soon as possible. Just like someone suffering from presbyopia moves the pages of a book closer to his eyes to read them, Marieke observes her child - but fails to see him with clarity. She looks at him without being able to focus because pure and simple habit makes her believe everything is as usual. But it isn't. Perhaps the hair on his cheeks has not yet grown as a physical manifestation of his inner torment, but it is there, it exists – Giovanni too is a prisoner of his habits, and it takes months before he realises and takes stock of his own discomfort and malaise, before he can give it a name, a definition.

What's up.

I don't know.

What's up.

I don't know.

There is something, but I don't know what it is.

What's up.

There is something, but I can't give it a name.

What's up.

There is that. That. That I hate my mother.

***

"Fuck Bitch Cunt

Cock Dick Fuck

Whore Whore Cunt"

As Timothy Jay, Professor at Massachusetts College of Liberal Arts, has written, swearing is a ubiquitous practice: we learn to say taboo words after we learn to speak and continue to do so even in old age; in cases of dementia or senile decline, we do it even more. We do so at a rate of about one every two hundred words, though this rate differs among age groups, with a high peak during adolescence, between genders (men more often and more offensively than women), and above all from one individual to another. Swearing is a practice that Giovanni's parents disapprove of, as do teachers, not to speak of grandparents, aunties, uncles, priests: adults in general frown upon it. And yet, and yet: what incredible satisfaction derives from the clicking of fuck and the aspiration of the h in whore, the sibilant of piss and ass, the nasal wickedness of cunt. It's such a joy: more: it's as liberating as a burp – yet another practice widely discouraged by adults and embraced by teens.

Giovanni recalls an afternoon at a friend's house. They were playing cards, and Riccardo, as soon as he realized he'd lost, had shouted: "Oh Sssugar!" Giovanni had enjoyed the novelty, the trick of turning a swear word into another word commonly used, but with the undertone, the aftertaste of the obscene one. Franco had laughed, teasing Riccardo: what, did he not dare say "shit"? "Shit shit shit," he'd said, bolder and bolder; and Giovanni whispered "shit shit shit," and then Riccardo had joined in, and "shit shit shit" they repeated and sang in chorus, temporarily uninhibited, free and proud. Not that the pride and freedom would last long: no one at home dared to openly use profanity. Giovanni had heard only once his father muttering "asshole"; Marieke said as much as *Godverdomme*, which means damnation; she had explained that most of the bad language, in Dutch, refers to diseases: *kankerlijer* for those who have cancer, *tyfuslijer* referred to those with typhus, *tering* for the tuberculotic. In short, to send someone to hell meant to wish them to contract incurable diseases. No, Marieke had reiterated: no, it is not done. And Giovanni – the only son, the good son, the son who wants to please, who needs approval compulsively – had never disobeyed: until last summer.

"Fuck Dick Cock

Pussy Bitch Whore

Cunt. Cunt Cunt Cunt," Giovanni repeats thoughtlessly, standing in his room, looking out the window.

"Fuck Fuck Piss Cunt

Fuck, Fuck. Yes: Fuck!"

He should sit down at the desk and finish translating Cicero, but: enough. He's had enough. He snorts, breathes a halo on the glass, draws a phallus with his finger, erases it with the sleeve of his jersey, repeats the process; this time, his finger goes around in circles: tits; two, as round as oranges. He deletes them, draws a heart, then a flower, his initial: G., and then wipes it all off again. He sits at his desk. He gets up again, walks to the bed and flops down, his mouth pressed against the brown crocheted blanket. Completely still.

A voice slips out of the kitchen, echoes on the stairs.

"Giovanni, Giovanni, where are you, come on, come here."

Giovanni – lying on the bed, his eyes closed—jumps up. His left leg snaps forward, hits a book that tumbles onto the floor. The woman's voice calls again, louder.

"Giovanni!"

Giovanni jumps up again, exaggerating every gesture. He can hear her heavy footsteps on the stairs. He sighs, stands up. His head peeps out into the corridor.

"Yes?" Silence. The steps retreat. She wants to win. "Mamma?" And then, louder. "Mamma?"

She won.

"Ah, Giovanni: there you are. Did you not hear me call you?"

"No."

Silence.

"What's up?"

Marieke stands downstairs by the kitchen, a hand on her hip, sleeves rolled up on her sturdy forearms, hair held up into a bun.

"I need to show you something," she says.

"What?"

"I'll show you. Come downstairs. In the kitchen."

"I don't have time." A pause. "Not right now." He looks at her and smiles. Christ, look at those teeth: no, not teeth: fangs, as sharp as a fox's. The woman smiles back. She can't not.

"I have to go into town. Am meeting up with Riccardo and Pietro. You can tell me later. This evening." Giovanni flies down the stairs and past her, brushing her arm with his hand.

"Giovanni, look, wait," Marieke cries, but he is already gone.

THE HEART OF THE OCTOPUS

Out. Outside, outside, air, wind, air. Breathe. In, and out, and again. He walks slowly at first, yes, that's it; but then he breaks into a run, faster, faster, yes—and as he runs, he counts his steps: ten, eleven, fifteen, sixteen, seventeen: and he runs even faster: one hundred and two, one hundred and three— faster, faster, yes, yes, until he feels a lump in his throat, and he knows he must stop, he must, he can't go on any more, not at this pace, not one more step, he feels sick, he must stop he must, he has to, now, and he does that, it's that easy, stop, now, yes, hands on his knees, the taste of blood in his throat. He spits on the ground.

"IhateyouIhateyouIhateyouIhateyou" Giovanni repeats. "Fuck, mamma. How much I hate you."

The countryside is green and red and yellow, the mist is fine and low like wisps of smoke. He can smell the soil, a rotten smell - summer is over. He used to love this season. When it signalled the beginning of everything. Back then. Promises, promises.

But now, no.

No, not now.

"I fucking hate you."

***

Giovanni lives with his parents in the house built at the top of one of the hills—you can recognise it because of the bright yellow of the external walls and for its unusual shape. His grandfather Ludovico had made several changes to the original structure; he had extended and widened the kitchen on the lower floor and built a bathroom of the same size – cavernous – on the upper floor; and then he had added a kind of turret to dominate the countryside all around. A 'folly': a whim: an extravagant, frivolous or funny building, designed more as an artistic expression than for practical purposes.

Ludovico Ferraro had been sent to a boarding school in Cornwall in the summer of 1918, at the age of thirteen, to remove him from his home after his twin Nino had become ill with the Spanish flu and had died within a few weeks. His parents had dispatched him away immediately to avoid contagion, directing him to the British Isles, which had appeared the safest haven. Ludovico had adapted quickly and easily; he had learned to speak English with public school pronunciation, to play hockey, and golf; he had visited London, Bath and Oxford; finally, he had embarked on a day trip to Doyden Castle, a nineteenth century tower on the north coast of Cornwall built by Samuel Symons – a wealthy man, a drinker and a gambler, who needed a space so remote that nobody would be able to spy on his vices. Perched on a small promontory, the castle was perfectly placed. It was a structure at the limit of the possible, almost at the end of the world: a place where one could do what he wanted, where one could be truly free. Ludovico had fallen so much in love with this idea of freedom that he extended in his mind to anything English. He was enthusiastic, adoring even the weather, even the rain, even the distance from his family, and in spite of the horrid beatings he had to endure from his fellow pupils, and occasionally from the teachers. The masochist Ludovico had not suffered much: as he liked to repeat, he had *adjusted*. In fact, he felt it was the spanking that made him "the Man I am today."

Many years later, Ludovico had decided to raise his very own folly as a tribute to the England of his youth, to Cornwall, with a nod to Doyden Castle. He had instructed the local builder to erect a hexagonal tower, with large windows on each side and a bizarre round porthole at the front to give a panoramic view over the surrounding vineyards. It was reached by thirty-six steep steps. After it was built it had become Ludovico's study, lined with shelves full of books, and a large wooden model of HMS Victory on the window sill. Against a wall, it even had a wooden helm ("this is a Captain's Cabin, after all"). After his premature death, it had become his son's, who had removed most of the furnishings, but after knee surgery due to a fall, Luigi had been struggling to walk up those steps, and it had finally become Giovanni's bedroom. He had enjoyed the old maritime theme so much that he'd asked for the walls to be repainted azure, and the bed a particular, darker shade of blue wood; he had painted all the shelves blue and white, hanging flags, choosing a wallpaper with a pattern of sailboats - it now looked like the cabin of a cruise ship, an illusion: maybe if you looked out of the window you'd see the ocean.

Giovanni loves his room, its irregular shape and the view

that he enjoys through the round porthole. He can see rice fields extending to the north and a sea of vineyards to the south. His parents sleep on the first floor, where there is the only bathroom, and two more bedrooms. On the ground floor, which has vaulted ceilings, there is a lounge, the kitchen and dining room, and Luigi's study. The general decor is heavy—furniture made of decorated wood, sofas upholstered with flowery, chintzy material, maroon carpets with elaborate designs. The walls are thick, the windows have shutters to protect from the cold in winter and the heat in summer. The interior, facing north, is dark. Outside there is a garden with a table on which they dine on hot evenings. The house is surrounded by a low wall and closed by an imposing wrought-iron gate; the driveway is lined with tall cypress trees. Beside the main building there is also another brick structure, formerly used as a barn, now a storeroom, and a vast wine cellar, divided into two smaller rooms: the first contains various barrels and the implements for the transformation of grapes into wine; the second compartment has a door that leads directly into the kitchen, and here are hundreds of bottles, accurately sorted and methodically catalogued by Marieke into vintages and varieties.

Giovanni used to like sneaking into the cellar, especially when the grapes undergo the transformation into wine, when they mutter and splutter like little old ladies on a cold autumn's day, and spread a unique, sweetish aroma. The harvest is held on the same day as the village festival, on September 30th (or the week after, if it has been too cold); the villagers attend church in the morning, to light a candle in front of the painting of the saint (hundreds of candles that illuminate the interior, as dark as a tomb), and then they open up their cellars to those wishing to visit them. At night, they celebrate the long sleep of the must in the barrels before turning into wine to be bottled. He knows the ritual since forever - ever since his grandfather Ludovico took him to the wine festival; now it's his father's turn. Giovanni enjoys the procession - that thick bearded, melancholic looking priest, the lit candles, the aroma of chestnuts in the clear and fresh air, the prayers of the women, a sad litany recalling the buzzing of mosquitoes, a whisper: "summer is over, summer is over, summer is over." His mother, who is Lutheran, does not take part in this pagan festival, as she likes to call it. "To celebrate a sad and celibate saint feels wrong; a terrible thing. I prefer to stay at home. You go."

Tomorrow: tomorrow is September 30th.

Giovanni knows that his father expects him to accompany him to church, and to the procession, and then go on to eat roast pork and drink the local wine: an annual ritual that father and son diligently follow every year. They have always attended: yes, even the time he had come down with chicken pox; even when he'd had the flu, aged nine. Luigi had taken him once with a broken tibia, hopping on the one leg.

But this year: no, Giovanni is not going. The smell of must feels sticky in his throat.

THE HEART OF THE OCTOPUS

***

Marieke, also known as Maria, has lots of curly hair, as wild as a lioness', blond-red like a mane, and a throaty Dutch voice, even if she has lived in Italy for twenty years and is completely fluent in the language.

She was born in a village in West Friesland near Medemblik, where her family had a farm. She grew up amongst cows and horses, in the flat countryside fractured into a mosaic of canals. A region still little known yet curiously recognisable, because the yellow landscapes, illuminated by the pale northern sun, seem to jump out of one of the paintings by Vermeer. They are the same landscapes that in 1871 Claude Monet described, during a journey: "There is so much to paint to last a lifetime."

Marieke is the great-great-great granddaughter of Antonio Monteverdi, a missionary in the late seventeenth century, who'd travelled to South America in the name of the Society of Jesus, which he belonged to, "in order to convert the poor people of the place." Monteverrrrdi, Marieke rolls, saliva covering the name. Monteverrrdi, she says, as if her tongue was sinking into a pool of melted chocolate. She rolls her consonants whenever given the opportunity, fierrrcely prrroud of her orrrigins. She left the flat, boring Netherlands too many years ago to count them – "to be among equally boring hills" - when she married Luigi, but still regrets her life - not the life she would have had, but the one she would have wanted. The one she believed she deserved. She thought she would be famous, someday, somehow. She imagined herself as head of a company, foreman, boss. It did not happen. "I became a stay-at-home mum, after Giovanni was born, and everything I'd learned, all those long hard sweaty years of study, well: I threw it all away." Regrets, regrets. Marieke is not bourgeois but petite bourgeois, no, look, worse: petite-petite bourgeois, a *Biedermeier* (which comes from *Bieder*, which means a simpleton, respectable and *Meier*, a very common German surname, as banal as Smith). One who loves doilies under gaudy ornaments, placed on top of mirror-polished walnut furniture; bedspreads and curtains with the same design, or colour – "matchy-matchy," as she puts it; she serves coffee in gilt-edged cups, on a silver-plated tray, with matching sugar bowl and milk jug. She wears slippers but with a little heel, and tight, nylon dressing gowns; she loves carnations with pink coral shades, lacey curtains. Marieke likes to think she is like a fairy-tale frog, hiding the soul of a princess – that's what her first boyfriend used to call her: "my golden princess." So long ago. It is so abstruse and sad to think that the Dutch girl with wild hair and farsighted ambition has become a sour, petty, country would-be lady, supporting a nasty ideology that is in fact a form of ignorance, as low as it is malignant. She thinks badly of everyone, she knows little of the world and doesn't want to learn more - she has not bought a new book since Nineteen-Seventy-Four, and dislikes those purchased by her husband; should she read them, they'd confirm how little she knows, how little she has learned, and how little her pathetic certainties count. If she were middle-class, that could be OK; working class, it would too. But petite-petite-petite bourgeois with the "p" as lower case as can be: there is nothing worse.

Having been unable to give vent to her personal, moral and social ambition, she has poured it all over her only, beloved son.

"Far, Giovanni. You'll go far. Like all the Monteverrrdis," she purrs.

Few of the objects originally belonging to the famous Great Uncle Monteverdi remain: a brass compass, that Marieke rubs with manic ferocity; a battered copy of the third edition of the *Dizionario della Crusca*, and a black leather notebook with fragile, brittle pages: a diary in which Antonio had described his early travels and adventures among the uncivilised. The dictionary and the notebook with wafer thin pages lie in a glass showcase in the blue living room, "the good one", where the family never set foot. Sometimes Giovanni frees them from the crystal coffin in which they are buried.

"I used to read for hours, word for word, dictionary definitions; sometimes they were illegible. I used to lose myself, in the definitions. And look: I have been hooked for life on dictionaries, as it is appropriate for the son of a bilingual person who is constantly searching for the right word, the one that is most appropriate to the context. I have become quite a collector of vocabularies - I like to compare them, observe what has gone out of use and which are the new entries, the subtle difference in meaning. But what I liked most, when I was a boy, what I spent hours doing, was looking at the pages of that diary, at the maps that my uncle had drawn. Rivers, lakes, mountains. Dots that were towns and cities. I used to dream incredible dreams, leafing through the pages covered with a velvety, indecipherable writing. Dust, dust, and more dust – but at times there was a page sublimated by the drawing of a butterfly or a flower, with a trace of colour, and away I used to go, away with the fairies, as they say. I imagined the lives of the men who lived inside those dots—the underlying promise of adventure. And I dreamed that one day, one day I'd find myself my own dot, my own home, my lair, the one that fits you like a shell.

From a very early age - Giovanni will write in his diary, years later - I wanted to go – away, away, away – far away from Piedmont and get on the road to the discovery of distant lands. When I was a child, the mere sight of the notebook of my great-great-great uncle, in which pages and pages were covered with drawings of exotic trees, tropical flowers, maps with details of mountains and rivers and lakes, moved me to tears. I never wanted, like my mother would have wanted, to have a career. The dream of my childhood was to find, somewhere, someday, the homeland of my soul."

***

"It flows through my veins," Marieke says. "It's in my blood. Even in yours, Giovanni. Glory – the Monteverrrdi's legacy," she says. "Like plant physiology: like a tree: from its roots to its leaves. Directly - dirrrectly (rrr). Tenacious roots that go all the way into the ground. Not like these little roots here of the vineyard that are tiny, so superficial. Like oil on water."

"Maria: can't you just leave him alone," Luigi says in defence of his son. He doesn't say much, his father; just few words, always carefully chosen. "Let him be, Maria, come on."

He is an accountant - the only one within thirty kilometres. His office, which stands in the centre of the nearest town, has been open for three generations: before him it was his uncle's, before him his grandfather's, his great-grandfather's; consequently, he knows everyone's business, in town - literally. The earnings of each, the good and the bad years of every profession; who did well, when, and why. He knows all the many mini laws of the complicated system of Italian taxation, taxes on waste materials, second home mortgages, VAT: they are documents that reveal all, like a strip tease. The receipts he has the privilege to see reveal unexpected aesthetic retouches, confess to dental implants, betray hair transplants, but also show unsuspected diseases, hidden accounts, secret families. It is a job that requires discretion, and eyes and ears that see and hear everything - but nothing. Luigi is good at his profession: he knows how to keep secrets; and he is also patient, methodical; he is friendly and warm, yet he keeps his distance. It is this attitude that makes him exceptional: he never takes sides, he stands above and beyond, and when he has to intervene, he does so with a light touch.

"It is only with my land, that I have a heavy hand," he says.

Luigi loves to cultivate the land – his orchard produces sweet tomatoes, according to him the best in the region, green beans, carrots, potatoes – but he especially loves the grapevine: a plant hard to maintain that steals away so much of his time. He owns just a few hectares of land, a few thousand vines, enough to produce a few hundred bottles a year. A ruby Grignolino, a sparkling Barbera, a few tens of litres of a murky Cortese. It's hard work, but a retired couple with the same passion help him out. Luigi spends every spare moment in there. He likes to drink his own wine, made by his own hands; he likes to give away bottles to special clients, in a reverse ritual. He likes to mess with the earth. He often sports dirty fingernails and is obsessed with washing his hands.

"There he goes again. Always in the bathroom to scrub his nails. As if he were the manicurist to celebrities. *Godverdomme*," Marieke complains. "Always there with his dirty little brush: scrape, scrape. I can hear the water running, Luigi," she cries from the ground floor. "*Basta*."

"Almost finished," Luigi says, scratching off the soil. "Almost," he repeats. He switches the tap off, he has a good look at his nails, switches it on again. "Almost."

Scratch, scratch. Scrape, scrape.

Luigi is a humble man, reserved, surprisingly well read – the many books he has bought lined up on the shelves of his studio, away from the eyes of his stingy wife. He is a man who listens without interrupting, always respecting the desires of others. "The fact is – he says – that nobody ever listened to me. I got it all wrong, in life. I shouldn't have become an accountant as my parents wanted me to. I read Kierkegaard, who said the most important thing is to clear one's head and find out what one should do, what he is destined to do; to find the real truth, the idea for which you are ready to die. I should have studied literature. I should have been a teacher. And of course in my spare time, I could cultivate my land. You see, those of teacher and farmer are not, in fact, such different professions: they both help a living organism, a creature, to grow. Yes: it was my calling, my vocation; but everyone insisted so much, rationalising my future with the knowledge of the past. They never asked me whether I had a dream, whether perhaps I had envisaged another career, if I wanted to exercise an art other than the obvious. In any case, I would never have said no, to my father. God help us: a farmer, his son? No, I was born into the wrong family. Too educated, too posh. Instead, I should have found a job that had something to do with working with my hands, with soil. But the fact I did wrong doesn't mean my son has to do wrong, too. That's why I want you to choose by yourself – if you end up making the wrong decision, it will be a shame, but it will have been yours. Your choice, your responsibility."

Giovanni is an intelligent young man. He studies hard, he has good marks. He adores Greek literature, reads the *Iliad* and the *Odyssey*, of which he knows long passages by heart.

"Passion is my passion," he explains to his father, who listens enchanted to every word uttered by his only son. "The idea to dedicate one's life to something, or someone – one's country, a woman, glory. With a capital letter: Country, Woman, Glory. I'd like to live my life with that clear and firm intention, printed on my forehead: to focus with all of myself on to one thing, unique and rare, that's worth it. And when I die, to think that it was really worth it."

Luigi nods. He always nods, whatever he's told.

***

"No! I don't want it!"Giovanni repeats, throwing the hat his mother bought for him on the floor. She picks it up.

"But I bought it for you. I thought you'd like it," she says. He laughs scornfully. "That?" he asks. "Do you really mean: *that* hat? You must be joking. Only a moron would wear it. Only a moron would buy it."

She raises her hand, aiming for his left cheek. He ducks just in time; her hand ends up hitting the cabinet behind him. Giovanni walks out of the room, slamming the door.

If only Marieke could take two steps back and re-examine the scene using a sense of perspective (or of time: if she could jump forwards and land in a few years' time), she would behave differently; she would try and pull her son closer to her, not push him away. She would see that the hat is a pretext – the same scene would have happened whatever she'd have chosen for him. The boy is angry: let the boy be angry. It's him, not you. But she is too busy with her role as wife-and-mother, too busy with being a housewife who cares excessively about the little things at home, which end up acting as quicksand and sinking her into the swamp of familiarity. She is constantly rushing around to tidy up, to clean, to prepare dishes copied from food magazines a neighbour passed on to her a couple of months after their release, to knit sleeveless jumpers and hats and scarves for her husband and son, made out of the bright, sad wool yarn she buys in one-pound-stores.

"You won't believe how cheap it is," she tells her husband, who shakes his head.

"You need not economise, Maria," Luigi says. "We aren't poor. Go and buy something nice, something you really like. Don't buy stuff just because it's inexpensive."

Marieke buys salad only at the market, where it's cheaper; she drives for miles to find something up on sale; she adores car boot sales. She hunches her shoulders and rubs her hands like a caricature, when she thinks she's made a good deal. Marieke recycles, mends, lengthens, shortens, knits and crochets. In her vocabulary: she gives things a new lease of life.

"Look at this dress. Looks like new. All renewed," she says. "Better than new."

Their house - the big house on the hill - is chock full of things that Marieke has bought over the years, for the sole reason of their being cheap. Stuff - sometimes useless, often without any good taste: vases and jars, doilies, pot-pourri, mirrors and rugs and sheets and tablecloths she found on sale for one reason only: their lack of marketability. Nobody wants towels of a pale hazelnut colour; nobody buys a frame that contains faded but somewhat broken dried flowers; a bedspread whose central embroidery is off-centre; tank tops with pulled threads. The truth is that Marieke has no taste, loves a good deal, and hoards junk. The anxiety of compulsive accumulation – and the opposite pull towards tidiness – causes her to lose sight of those around her. Now, Luigi has his life: that of an accountant, like generations of Ferraros before him, all taken up with the papers in his office, and the vineyard, and the garden. He is a busy man, who hardly notices what surrounds him. Giovanni, however, is a typical sixteen-year-old in turmoil, and needs several pairs of eyes focused on him. It is interesting to note that while Marieke suffocates him with care and attention, she treats him as if he were still her little boy. She doesn't seem to realise that even if there are, so far, limited external changes – a certain lowering of the voice, a cluster of pimples on his forehead – they actually and irrefutably correspond to an inner earthquake. The American geophysicist Charles Francis Richter gave the name to the well-known seismic scale that measures the magnitude of an earthquake, which is the estimate of the energy emitted at the point where the earth's crust breaks; the Mercalli scale, on the other hand, evaluates the intensity of an earthquake relying mainly on the damage caused to the homes of a city hit by an earthquake. The one that is shaking and placing the entire equilibrium that governs Giovanni upside down must be measured with the Richter system of measurement, because an earthquake in a deserted area according to the Mercalli system would have zero effect. The adolescent earthquake develops exclusively *within* its system - no shocks nor tremors are felt, no cracks can be seen. But inside, ah, well, inside, it's like the Valdivia earthquake of 1960, the most powerful ever recorded in history, with a magnitude of 9.5.

Inside Giovanni's thin body there is a red and angry magma that presses, and presses, that wants - needs - to blow up. There is a cry in his chest that takes his breath away and burns his lungs, that makes his heart burst with furious beats, that makes him itch all over – his hair, his biceps, his sex, his tongue, his brain. What happens when you can't scratch an itch? It explodes. Perhaps to become an adult means to keep that crazy itch at bay. But when you are sixteen, and you feel tough and invincible, and yet sensitive, a bit like a soldier hiding behind a white flag, you cannot do anything except, trivially, predictably, rebel against those nearest to you: brothers, sisters, parents. The best friend becomes a rival; yesterday's mates, competitors; teachers, saboteurs; one's father, an adversary; one's mum, a threat.

When he returns home from school, he slams the front door. He runs upstairs, in his tower-room, he locks himself in, throws himself on the bed, the heart that boom-boom-booms in the cage of bones that holds him prisoner; he feels as if he's going crazy, and while he tries to breathe more slowly, more reasonably, his mother's voice slips from the floor below:

"Giovanni?"

Not worthy of a reply. *Minus quam merdam.* What does *she* want, now. And the itching sneaks its way into his thoughts and between his legs and jumps like a nit in his hair, inside his ears, on his neck and it pinches him and yes, it is *she*, his mother – no longer: his mamma – it is she who wants to chat, "just a little chat," she says, feigning innocence, bitch, his mother who keeps calling his name, Giovanni, and he can't stand it, not any more, not now, not ever, bitch, and he gets up from the crumpled bed and runs downstairs and puts his shoes back on and says:

"I don't have time I have to go I have to go see you later," and runs out and runs and runs and thinks: "I hate you I hate you I hate you," while Marieke, unaware and plump and blonde like a Vermeer in the warm light of September, keeps peeling - unaware, blonde - potatoes for dinner.

***

It's the end of June. School has been out for two weeks, tests and quizzes are just a memory. The alarm clock, in the morning, stays switched off. Days and days of doing nothing stretch in front of Giovanni's eyes like route 66: thirteen empty weeks to fill up. There is a sultry heat, the sky is a grey and thick, mosquitoes stick themselves anywhere they can cling to – flesh, curtains – like leeches. Tomorrow they will leave for the holidays. Marieke has prepared their Last Supper. The table is laid with care, with an embroidered table cloth and the crystal glasses they use only on special occasions, a bottle of *spumante* in the fridge; strips of smoked salmon are laid on white stringy bread, a cold ripe melon is sliced and served with prosciutto, there is rice salad, fruit salad, a tart with apricot jam. Balanced on top of Luigi's plate, a new tie and a book of puzzles. On Giovanni's, a diary for the summer.

She has prepared the suitcases meticulously, as always – she compiles a list and then ticks each item off, with a pencil, like a schoolteacher: seven pairs of underwear and socks, dresses for her, both for the beach and for the evening, her beloved white blouses ("Really, that's all a woman needs to feel elegant: a crisp white blouse"), skirts and shorts and t-shirts, a couple of cardigans, two shawls, and shoes, many shoes. Three bags, beach towels, shampoo and conditioner and make-up and sun-creams. A bag full of stationary and books; a little radio.

She has spent the last few days in the kitchen to prepare a series of dishes ready for Luigi, and has frozen them, even if she is well aware that he would prefer to dine in the local trattoria each night. She's called the cleaning lady, and arranged for her to come two hours every day. She's put away her jewellery in the safe. She has locked the guestroom – although in truth nobody ever stays. She has written a long letter to her husband with all the latest recommendations: when to water the plants, how many degrees to heat the oven for lasagne, various phone numbers "just in case." All is ready for the long summer: a whole month at the seaside. Giovanni, such a good boy, had been a sickly child, prone to ear infections, bronchitis, laryngitis; Marieke loved to take him to the GP – she thrived under his attention, liberally bestowed on both of them. She loved to feel like she was taking good care of her son; she was a practical woman: she administered medicines, made him sit for his regular steam inhalations, forced him to drink two large glasses of freshly squeezed orange juice every day. A paediatrician once suggested he should spend some considerable time at a seaside resort, and she followed his instructions *verbatim*. Now Giovanni doesn't get sick anymore, but that month by the coast has remained a family routine. Luigi doesn't join them; he is not a beach type and has work to do. As always, it would be the two of them, mother and son. At Easter they tend to travel to Holland to visit the maternal relatives, but summer is *their* holiday- a few weeks in the exclusive company of each other. A ritual they repeat every year, with a few changes: they have been in Puglia, Sardinia. They were now exploring the Côte d'Azur - Cannes, Nice, Menton. This year they would return to that pretty seaside town; they'd found a central apartment with a large terrace near the beach, so Giovanni would be able to go out with his friends, in the evening.

It had been easy to make new friends, when Giovanni was a little boy – all the mummies gathered to exchange tips and disappointments whilst their children helped each other to build sand castles and play marbles, to swim, to play in the water. They would go home for lunch, and at times joined the other kids again in the late afternoon for an ice cream, or to go on the rides. It was easy. In more recent years, Giovanni struggled to create a circle of acquaintances, only to be stuck with his mother. Marieke enjoyed his exclusive company; they were always together, seven days a week. During the first few days, they would go to the beach early in the morning, whilst in the afternoon they'd visit the town, churches, museums - Marieke with the pretence of wanting to learn, to see more, to understand better, but then quickly her attention would turn to shopping. She'd start yawning, pulling him into the museum shop to buy tacky postcards, the cheaper ones. As the weeks went by, they remained longer and longer at the beach, even all day. In the evening, after a long shower, after they changed into more appropriate clothes, they would choose a restaurant and dine opposite one another, chatting amicably. Giovanni did not ask for more.

"What if we sent him to England for a study holiday?" Luigi had asked. "He's older now, he should be with kids his age. Maybe a sailing course? Riding? French?"

"Don't even mention it. He needs to rest."

"To rest? A boy of twelve?" (And then thirteen, fourteen, fifteen ...)

"Sure. He studies hard, he gets tired. He'll be just fine."

"If it's fine with him ..."

It had always been fine. He's not adventurous, he's not sporty; he's shy, and rather lazy.
Last year they'd stayed in a hotel a few kilometres from the centre of Menton; they had met a couple of nice families, with whom they had remained in touch during the winter, and had helped them to find a rented apartment near the centre so they'd be able to spend more time together.

"Are you sure you don't mind going back to the same place?" Luigi had asked her, knowing her restlessness.

"Of course I'm sure," she had replied. "There is so much to see and do. We won't get bored – although I wouldn't mind just sitting on a beach, doing nothing. I have seen such a fabulous beach, in a brochure. Much better than the Italian ones."

For Marieke, the Côte d'Azur represents the height of elegance. Chignon buns, pearl necklaces, 100% silk outfits. *Très chic.* She imagines herself on the marina admiring the luxurious yachts anchored in the harbour, or visiting the splendid villas of famous people, wealthy actors, sophisticated actresses. All winter she's been dreaming of the South of France, spying Brigitte Bardot topless on the beach or Grace Kelly, elegant in her wide-brimmed hat to balance the slenderness of her waist, accompanied by the impeccable Cary Grant. But *To Catch a Thief was* released in

1955, now it is 1983; Princess Grace will never be filmed again, because she died last September, at the wheel of her car on the road between La Tourbie and Monaco. Marieke had burst out crying when she had heard the news. She had watched the funeral live on television, read all the articles about the accident, cut out pictures of the princess when she was a young actress and glued them into a notebook, the one in which she keeps recipes and pictures of clothes, knitting instructions, as well as articles about celebrities, the British royal family and Princess Diana, a firm favourite of hers. Another reason to return to the South of France is to visit Grace Kelly's grave in the Immaculate Conception Cathedral in nearby Monaco. The tomb is simple and understated, almost hidden away inside the enormous church; Marieke finds it actually a little sad, not imposing, not quite enough to preserve the memory of her beloved princess.

In truth, the Cote whole d'Azur feels slightly disappointing: rather than exclusive boutiques and trappings of royalty, she discovers, there are only souvenir shops, with lavender and lavender and more lavender, used and displayed in every guise, hidden in small sachets, used to stuff cushions and cheap-looking dolls. Rather than the Negresco, the rented apartment looks like an overheated cube. Marieke tries to ignore the ants, which accumulate in creeping lumps around the tiniest breadcrumb forgotten on the floor, and the broken venetian blinds in her room, the shutters that slam when it's windy, the tap water that tastes horribly salty. Giovanni likes it, because it has a breath-taking sea view, and the beach is five minutes away, and soon he will meet last year's friends. Marieke can see something bright and glistening like pleasure in his green eyes - he had lost it, that smile, that brilliance; now it's back. She is grateful even though she knows it isn't for her; on the contrary. When he looks at her, he does so with resentment or pain, with irritation and feverish anxiety to get away from her, with indifference or ill-concealed resentment. Yet: yet: today Giovanni smiles and what felt like a stone on her chest rises and vanishes – perhaps it's because it's summer and it's sunny and it's hot and he's sixteen and he's bursting out of his own skin. I barely remember what it was like, Marieke thinks. Being sixteen. All that vitality, that vigour, that desire to do and to discover and that stupefying optimism.

She sits on the brown sofa trying to ignore the dubious spots on its cover, looking at her son who is standing on the terrace - thin and white and snappy, he can't wait to get out of here, to go somewhere, anywhere. To be going: pure and simple motion towards; full stop. Where exactly, to do what, with whom, why: questions that don't matter. So they go, mother and son, talking about nothing in particular. In fact, not talking for a while. They walk down the cool marble stairs, through the door that opens onto one of the main streets – it's hot – and stop on the sidewalk in front of the building, trying to orientate themselves, to give themselves a direction. It's too late for the beach, towels and swimming costumes are still buried inside their suitcase; it's too early to have dinner; but:

"Come on, let's take a walk along the promenade, let's see how it is," she suggests. She'd like to hold his hand but it isn't the right thing to do, with teenagers. There is a whole new way of behaving with them, especially regarding their body, which is clumsy and cumbersome - it has unlearned the carelessness of childhood and hasn't yet learned adult nonchalance. Giovanni seems taller and more awkward, wooden, ungainly. He stumbles onto the sidewalk, holds his arms at his sides, dangles them and slams against the corners of the tables and chairs. He's closer to things and further away from people - especially from her.

***

Walking along, Marieke tells Giovanni that her own mother – his Dutch grandmother - as a young girl had been a guest at the Chateau de l'Horizon, a villa situated between Juan Les Pins and Cannes, built in the Thirties by an American actress. It was a stunning building, with a swimming pool carved into the rock from which a long slide jutted directly into the sea. The villa boasted distinguished guests, Churchill and the Windsors; in the Forties it had been sold to the Aga Khan, who had bought it for his wife, Rita Hayworth; even the Kennedys had visited.

"Your granny! Can you imagine that? If only she had met a brilliant man, an aristocrat, or perhaps a writer, or a famous musician..." Marieke dreams. If only. Giovanni yawns. He knows he needs to show how delighted he is by the history of these places, by the adventures of his Dutch grandmother, the ifs and what ifs of her life. He knows that; but can't be bothered. He yawns again. On that first afternoon, Marieke and Giovanni walk around the medieval old town of Menton, up to the Saint-Michel Archange Basilica (which they do not visit).

"...Is a rare jewel of baroque art. Over 100,000 tourists come to see the site every year... The construction of the Basilica took several centuries to be completed. The façade was renovated in the 19th Century adding typical decor of the period such as smooth columns with Ionic and Corinthian capitals," Giovanni reads this in his guide book, sitting on a bench in front of the church. "And: the old city, here, where we are. Look. Founded by the Ligurians around 1200; passed to the control of the principality of Monaco in 1346. Blah blah blah. Then. Here it is. In 1861 following the Plombières agreements between the Count of Cavour and the Emperor Napoleon III, Menton joined Nice and passed to French rule."

Marieke isn't listening; history bores her, dates confuse her. She plays with the revolving display of postcards. She fishes into her bag, finds her purse, buys three.

"*Avec timbres, s'il vous plait*," she asks. She sits down, retrieves a pen, bends down to write while Giovanni continues to read. "Here, sign here. This one for dad, this one for your uncle," she says, waving a view of the harbour at sunset. That's what she always chooses: pictures of sunsets or sunrises on the sea, full moons on the ruins of ancient temples, dramatic storms on the mountains. And she always writes: 'Miss you! Wish you were here! So beautiful! We're having such fun!' as if the exclamation marks could act as a crutch for those who stay at home, supporting loneliness.

They retrace their steps until they reach the port. Tired, hungry, they stroll, dawdle, stopping from time to time to read the restaurants' menus.

"Mais non! Marià, Marià! Vous êtes arrivé, alors." They hear a voice behind them, and they are saved by Carla and Jean Claude, whom they met the previous year with their children, Marc and Manu. She can see the relief spread on Giovanni's face like butter on a slice of toast.

***

They have dinner with the Blanchards in a pizzeria al fresco, the adults sitting on one side of the table and the children on the other. At first they are quiet, almost shy, then less and less and so more and more boisterous until they end up, as Marieke says, in the realm of fools, each with a role (chamberlain, prince, jester). They laugh, they scream, they elbow each other between bursts of irrepressible laughter. The Blanchards live in Belgium, but Carla (Carlà, as they call her) is originally from Milan; they have a flat here, a second home, like the good bourgeoisie used to. They are sociable, cheerful, chic people but not stuffy at all, she tells Luigi later, on the phone. Normal people. People whom she trusts. During dinner, they invite Giovanni to join them the next day for a boat trip. He doesn't need to think about it or consult with his mother, or ask her permission to go: he says "yes," with a heartfelt, touching sincerity. But.

"And you, Marià? Would you like to come along?" Carla asks.

Allow me freeze this moment as if we were in *Bewitched*. Samantha has an adoring husband and a vicious mother, and the curious ability to make things appear with just a twitch of her cute nose. She can turn enemies into dogs or reptiles, or immobilise bystanders – to clarify a situation, to run somewhere else in order to remedy a mess previously caused, to cast a spell. And I – MTB, myself, the author of the book you are reading – am going to do that. Now: right after Carla's question. I freeze the scene and invite you to observe it. In cinematic film, static images are imprinted sequentially, giving the viewer the impression of continuous movement even if in fact it is a simple sequence of still photos. See what happens in our film, *Supper in Menton*. We are at the point where Carla is asking Marieke to join them on the boat. Stop, right now. And then start again, but only for an instant: look: Carla has closed her mouth; she and her husband look at Marieke, who looks at Giovanni, who a moment ago was looking at Manu but (as all adolescents do) has a radar in his ears, and while he eats pizza and drinks Coca Cola and laughs with Manu, he also eavesdrops on the adult conversation taking place at the other side of the table.

We leave the guests alone and focus on mother and child. Marieke hears the question; and she is pondering it, wondering what to do. She likes to go boating - not that she's done it all that often, in truth, perhaps three times, in all of her life. But the mere idea of a twelve-meter yacht embodies the essence of the perfect holiday on the Côte d'Azur. She will be able to boast with her friends, her husband, her sister-in-law. But: all mothers sacrifice themselves, if their puppy needs something; they are more than ready to give them the softest piece of meat, the juiciest pasta at the bottom of the pot, the only piece of cake left. They offer their offspring the ultimate choice: do you want this last cookie? If you don't it - and only if you are sure not to want it for yourself – then, may I eat it?

Marieke looks at her son, and in her gaze there is a question: "Do *you* want me to come along?"

I fast forward – a few frames, let's say seventy-two. I press play again, and there it is, in the cruelty of Giovanni's eyes, there is his answer: "No."

No, do not come, do not ruin this moment, do not embarrass me in front of my new friends, I've never had that many, we have always gone on vacation the two of us, just the two of us, but now I've had enough, I need to get away from you and enjoy my space, my things, my new life. I'm not your baby anymore. I'm becoming a Man. Back off.

I press 'play' again for a few more seconds - just two or three - and let the film carry on. Focus on the impact of Giovanni's silent reply on Marieke: she absorbs the no; she puts it in her mouth and swallows it whole, like a hard morsel; she takes a sip of water. Only then she raises her eyes again and responds to Carla's question: no, thank you; the thing is, she has so much to do - unpacking, cleaning the apartment, doing a shop for the next few days - and she is ever so sorry but no. She will definitely join another time.

"Giovanni, you go. You'll have so much fun," she says, and Giovanni, who had held his breath all this time, can finally exhale.

***

I leave mother alone, a fake smile curled on her lips. I go out with *my* friends. I'm back at a quarter past ten; and I am cheerful, and – what's that adjective that does not truly belong to me? – yes: *carefree*. Ah. Yeah, right. From the doorstep I spot her figure crumpled on the couch waiting for me, the book she is not reading open in her hands, the untouched glass of wine on the table; ad I offer an insincere hug to which she holds on, as if I had been a soldier at war, walking home from a distant battlefield. I see she is trying to smell my breath, examining me centimetre by centimetre to investigate what happened in the last two hours, grilling me on what I did, where did I go, with whom. Were there any girls. A full interrogation. What the fuck.

I'm sixteen.

THE HEART OF THE OCTOPUS

I've had enough. Last year I did it; the year before I did it. Now: *basta*. This summer, I cannot stay attached to my mother. I cannot go to the beach with her and have lunch with her and coffee and biscuits with her as if I were a baby. I am sixteen, for fuck's sake. I want to stay up all night long, I want to go out with my mates, I want to drink beer and laugh and dance till dawn. I don't want to go to bed at ten. I don't want cake. Ice cream. Sweets. I don't care for yet another chat about what are my plans for next year. After high school. After my A-levels. When I grow up.

You know what? I've had enough of fucking holidays with *mammina*. Enough. Enough. I've had enough of our little six o'clock walk, of my non-alcoholic *apéritif* as if I were nine, as if I were a boy scout. What the fuck.

***

Their suitcases are yet to be unpacked. Marieke pulls clothes out of her case, she tries on a turquoise turban she bought to hide her tousled hair, frizzy in the salty air. Giovanni has breakfast on the terrace, watching the shimmering Mediterranean Sea, which seems to invite him to join it. He is happy to be back here, to show off the few hairs he sports on his cheeks, which do not hide a sprinkling of pimples. He is in a hurry. He gobbles up his cornflakes, his caffelatte.

"See you later!" he shouts and runs outside. He does not have time to take off his T-shirt, that first day on the beach (while the painful awareness of his too thin, too pale body makes him curl his back) before he can hear the boys from last year call him. The awkwardness of the first moments – a few questions about the year just passed, how was your bac, did you have a good winter, any girls yet? - gives space to last year's camaraderie, to vaguely dirty jokes told in two languages mixed together, to general laughter. He meets others (they are a group of seven) and in the ensuing days the group thickens: they are seven, then nine and then eleven: boys and girls, French and Italian, between fifteen and nineteen years old. They meet in the morning, they laugh, they play in the sea for hours, they laugh, they joke, they swim, they remain in the water all afternoon. It isn't like when he was little, and while the children played their mums would stay nearby, to have a chat on the shore. Now their parents read the newspaper under the beach umbrella. Marieke is left alone. Giovanni waves her goodbye in the morning and returns at lunchtime for a quick bite, or to have a shower – quickly, quickly.

"See you later," he says cheerfully.

"I only ever see your back," she complains. "You are always going out. Away."

"Sorry. See you later!" Giovanni shouts from the doorway.

After the first week, it is obvious to Marieke that this is the summer of Giovanni's turnaround. The summer when he slips away from her fingers.

***

Days are repetitive. Marieke is bored tremendously, and wonders: but how: last year we did the same things, and the year before also; beach in the morning, a sandwich, a salad, beach in the afternoon, shower, dinner. Together. But while twelve months ago she felt herself to be the protagonist, the one who makes every decision. Now she follows; she tows along.

She waits.

She watches.

She waits.

Giovanni is the one who *does*, who performs actions that have consequences. He subject; she complementary object. He inside, she outside.

"I'm going out.

"All right. See you later. I'll wait for you."

"Don't stay up. I'll be home late."

"It doesn't matter. I'll be waiting for you."

She is alone, day after day, evening after evening. Inevitably, she takes refuge in memories, in the nostalgia for a time when Giovanni was hers, completely. She thinks of him when he was a child, but her memories are fake, pastel-coloured like Menton's houses, muffled and tidied by time - not: the endless afternoons at the playground, pushing him on the swing for hours; not: when her eyes were so tired they kept closing, and she could not wait for seven o'clock in the evening to put him to bed; not: sitting on the wet sand to build yet another castle, digging yet another hole; not: the boredom that darkened her brain, rereading the same book for the tenth time, singing the same song, playing once again Monopoly, or Scrabble, or hide and seek; not: the loss of her identity that so dangerously, so easily disappeared to merge into that of mother. Not: the boredom of being a parent. But: the sweetness of saying goodnight every night, the pure physical joy of holding her son's body against hers, warm like a fox, the sweet smell of his hair, his smooth cheeks. Purely physical sensations, yes, because her head was elsewhere. Where? She wasn't sure. Asleep, probably; resting. She needed to sleep, even if Giovanni never woke up at night. The tiredness that one acquires when one has a small child does not necessarily stem from sleepless nights, but from the exhausting, persistent, infinite weight of responsibility on one's shoulders and conscience.

Children are repetitive; mothers have little time, and that little time they have is never for themselves; and it's easy to look back to the past and re-imagine it as happy as an advert for Center Parcs, with a respectable white middle class family gathered around a table - all of them smiling, with perfect skin, dazzling teeth, shiny eyes. It was not like that: Luigi was always in a bad mood because he was working too much, Giovanni was an only child: such a colossal bore, to have to be his playmate all the time, getting dressed as a pirate at six in the morning, his hand clinging to hers as if his life depended on her. Which was the truth. And that constant tiredness that made her drag her feet, bend her back, that shadowed her eyes. But, as her mother in law never ceased to repeat, "mothers always sacrifice themselves for their children." Sacrifice: the act of giving up something valued for the sake of something else regarded as more important or worthy. Giving up, renouncing. Surrendering.

"Three pounds eight. Healthy. Male. Goodness, Maria, aren't you lucky. What else could a mother ask for?" her mother-in-law had said, when Giovanni was born. An unbearable woman. Marieke could not stand her; thankfully she had suffered a fatal stroke not long after.

"What a gorgeous little boy, what an incredibly cute baby, what a darling," everyone repeated: friends, neighbours, in-laws.

"A true wonder," sighed the unmarried colleagues of Luigi - well, not precisely his colleagues: we are talking about the secretaries, really, since the accountants were all men, and didn't care about children in general. Planet childhood was a completely female dominion until they reached seven or eight years of age, when father and son could kick a ball together, and only for an hour weekly. For the rest, from personal hygiene to food, talking to their teachers from kindergarten to middle school, for sports or homework, for any small or large medical emergency, to buy shoes or to teach how to read, in short: for all daily needs, it was mothers' responsibility.

"When you were a baby, you suffered terribly from colitis," Marieke used to tell Giovanni, who loved to be told stories of when he was a baby.

"Really? Did I cry much?"

"Oh, yes. And I used to hold you in my arms, all night long. Sometimes on my shoulder."

"On your shoulder? All night?"

"Yes. You'd immediately calm down. And I would walk up and down along the corridor, for hours - as soon as I stopped you screamed."

"Tell me again of when I was a baby," he begged her, again and again, as if the story could give him the eyes of time. Marieke repeated the whole story all over again, remembering. How exhausting, it had been. Giovanni can't even imagine all that effort, all that tiredness, all that attention. He can't, and won't, because he is still at the centre of his mother's attention even now, at the age of sixteen.

***

Next year Giovanni will turn eighteen, which in Italy is the age of majority, according to which the rights and privileges of an adult are legally granted. Giovanni will be able to take his license, and drive; he will be able to vote when there are elections; if he were in Holland, he could buy marijuana. He could smoke, get drunk, take drugs, do whatever he wants without restrictions, because he will formally be an adult. He could rebel when his mother tells him: no. Then again, he already does that now. His silence, his sulking - he looks at her with resentment, his eyes turning the dark green of mud, leaving behind a trail of nastiness that follows her everywhere, like perfume.

Marieke remembers when she had just arrived in Italy from Holland, years before, and a gypsy woman had stopped her in the street and had taken her hand, turning it over, and told her that she would marry a very rich man and have five children. Marieke, who wasn't remotely interested in marriage, had quickly turned away, and the woman had covered her with insults. She'd never again had her palm read. Not like her neighbours in the village, who like to consult psychics – yes, really - on a regular basis, and pay dearly in exchange for hope: because that's why one goes to see a fortune teller: in order to receive a dose of hope. To believe that this is not it, not all of it; to continue to be positive and optimistic, to convince yourself that you can count on a better future.

Marieke, on the other hand, knows that the present is all we have, that the future can't be known but will be roughly like the present, and that the past has passed; good or bad that it was, you just have to accept it and leave it well alone.

***

Giovanni leaves in the morning and comes back in the evening.

"It feels as if I never see you," Marieke complains.

"I know – I'll be home early, this evening. I swear," Giovanni says, but he comes home later and later.

"You had promised."

"I know, but I couldn't really leave before ten o'clock… The twins had just arrived."

"The twins, Marc, Annie, this one and that one, there is always someone else to blame."

"But we are a gang, mamma. A gang. A cool gang."

"And what do you do, with your gang?"

"Nothing much. We hang out. It's cool."

He's never been part of a group, before, and she is pleased for him, as if her son's popularity could rub off onto her.

"We are driving to Monaco."

"We are going for a pizza."

"We are off to San Remo."

"To Nice."

"To a barbecue."

"It is Luca's birthday; we'll be late."

Marieke smiles, opens her purse. "Have fun, honey," she responds every time, happy to see he has friends, to see him at the centre of the action. She'd like to be in his place – she's left behind – behind the shutters of the flat, behind a book, waiting.

***

"I'm going out," Giovanni says.

"Go and enjoy yourself, sweetheart," Marieke says, feeling as if a knife was cutting her heart into thin slices, like prosciutto.

When she thinks that this holiday can't get any worse, when she thinks she can't possibly get lonelier than this: Giovanni falls in love.

***

Giovanni is a handsome boy. Tall and slender and curly-haired, with those eyes whose colour changes according to his mood, meadow-green when he's placid and serene, swamp-green when he's nervous, ice-green when he's angry. Now they are veiled with a white patina like fog on the rice fields in November. Because he's fallen in love – yes, in love, for the very first time. Marieke is blind, Marieke is deaf, Marieke doesn't want to see what's happening. Giovanni goes out, he's never home, he is elusive and taciturn, and then suddenly smiles a smile that takes her breath away; and she still doesn't ask, doesn't wonder. Until, one day, she sees him with a girl – a pretty and *vervelend* girl, boring and irritating, with a French upturned nose and eyes of a very light brown. Giovanni blushes and stutters while the girl – relaxed, self-assured – introduces herself:

"*Buongiorno, signora.* I'm Julie," she says, squeezing her right hand with confidence.

"But I call her Amber, because of her eyes – look, mamma: they are yellow. Like a cat's."

"He is all over this girl," Marieke thinks, cringing; "and he stares at her all Bambi-eyed and tells me: but have you ever seen such a colour, mum, isn't it amazing, they are extraordinary eyes, mamma, aren't they; like honey; like amber – *Amber*, he calls her, Christ: Amber. Amber, he keeps repeating, as if he'd seen the Venus of Milo. Just like he used to look at *me* when he was little and I was a goddess, his goddess. And Julie ehm ehms with fake embarrassment and a frog in her throat, and he keeps staring at her with an idiotic grin; I would like to shake him until he regains his senses, his common sense."

Marieke has never seen him with a girl, in Castel San Gerolamo; when she'd asked him if he had a girlfriend, he had raised an eyebrow as if to say: "Who: me? Are you kidding?" And he'd smiled sweetly at his mother, as if *she* were his girlfriend. And look at him now, playing volleyball with a group of friends; but: he's throwing the ball only to *her*, and she – wearing a yellow bikini – jumps up and down trying to catch it and she hugs him and he lets himself be hugged, and they dive into the waves free like dolphins, and they swim together towards a buoy fifty metres away, fifty metres that seem the farthest, as far as the horizon, as far away as the moon is from earth.

"I think he's having his first crush," Marieke confides Luigi on the phone that evening, bursting into tears while her husband remains silent on the other side of the phone.

"It will pass, darling," he says.

"It will pass. You'll see," Carla Blanchard, in whom she has confided, tells her. "It will pass with the end of the summer, as these first loves always do. But get ready, my friend, because if it's bothering you now, ah, well. When love ends, and it will – well, it will be a tragedy."

***

Marieke decides not to mention anything, not to tell Giovanni she knows that she has seen him, them. She tries to act as if nothing has happened, as if she hasn't spotted Giovanni and Julie kiss passionately, in front of everyone, at the buoy in the middle of the sea. She tries to behave as she did before - getting up early, even if she went to bed late because he came back well after midnight. And after her morning coffee she tidies up and washes and irons, waiting for him to get up, and when he finally joins her in the kitchen he tells her that he is not hungry, that he feels nauseous, maybe just a cup of tea with lemon, thank you. And he looks at her and at the dressing-gown that she wears on holiday, and looks at her with a melancholy that she understands, and that clings to her throat. He remains in the bathroom for a long time; she can hear the water in the shower but doesn't say anything, doesn't knock on the door; she gives him privacy. When he opens the door a cloud of steam comes out, but: "Shhh, shhh, Marieke," she tells herself. "Shhh, don't say anything."

Giovanni goes to get dressed and she sneaks into the bathroom that is dripping wet, the floor is wet and even the walls look sweaty, and on the window panes there is a trickle of water that looks like rain. She picks up a pair of boxers from the floor and:

"I swear: I do not even smell them, I immediately put them in the washing machine, with the shirt he wore last night and the towel. Shhh, Marieke. I make him the cup of tea he asked for, but when he comes back into the kitchen he tells me that he has changed his mind."

He is starving, and wolfs down a bowl of rice crispies with milk and a banana and two biscuits. Wasn't he nauseous? But "Shhh, Marieke", she reminds herself. She asks him whether he has any plan for the day, for the evening.

"Oh, didn't I tell you?"

"You didn't, as a matter of fact," she replies. "I barely saw you, yesterday."

And he says he did, but she must have forgotten, and she says no, that's not true, and then lets it go. "Oh. Well: we're going out, we, the gang, Marc has his mother's Fiat 127 so we're going for a drive. Yes; we'll be careful, I promise. Yes, I'll tell him to drive cautiously, don't worry, I won't drink anything, no alcohol I mean, just a Coke, yes yes we are going to eat something. I promise. But that's tonight, now it's late, I'm going to the beach, with the others. Yes, see you later, ciao."

THE HEART OF THE OCTOPUS

One minute he's there in front of the bowl of rice crispies, and the next one he's at the door, no, he's already out. Marieke carries on tidying, she rinses the cup and the bowl, she dries them, she puts them away. She walks into Giovanni's bedroom and takes the sheets off the bed; she can see that they are stained but she pretends nothing – "Shhh, Marieke" – and puts them in the washing machine. She has a shower, smears sun-cream onto her shoulders, gets dressed, prepares a bag with a spare costume and a towel, and is ready to leave. She locks the door, goes down the stairs and out onto the road, walks to the beach, reaches their sunbeds, one of which bears the sign of Giovanni's earlier arrival: shorts and T-shirt and flip flops thrown carelessly onto the floor. She lies down and looks around; it doesn't take long before she spots the group of youngsters in the water. They play volleyball, again. She can see the Blanchard children, and some other face that has become familiar - but not her son. Nor Julie. She goes to the café on the first floor and orders a cappuccino and sips it at the counter. Still no sign of her son. She goes back to her sunbed, puts her bag on the hot sand, lies down onto her stomach, reading the magazine she's already read three times. And when she looks up again – there, there they are, the lovebirds, on the furthest buoy, a platform a hundred meters from the *Les Sablettes* beach. They are far away, of course, but unmistakable: Julie with her yellow bikini and Giovanni in red trunks, sitting with his legs in the water on the rocking buoy. They are kissing. They're kissing as if the air was unbreathable, in Menton, and they were oxygen for each other.

THE HEART OF THE OCTOPUS

***

It's awful to see him like this – thinner and paradoxically paler. He wakes up late (he couldn't sleep, tossing and turning for hours), he's never hungry, he's always in a hurry, he doesn't have breakfast, doesn't tidy up his room, doesn't comb his hair - he rushes to the beach to see Julie. Julie, Julie, Julie – he talks about her constantly, without even realising it. Marieke keeps her watch, in the following days, without saying anything – "Shhh, Marieke." Ah, Julie is so funny, Julie is so good at swimming, have you seen Julie dive. Marieke pretends she knows nothing, pretends Julie is another friend, one of the gang – but she watches his every move from behind her sunglasses, unseen.

"And she's not even that special," Marieke tells Luigi, who listens without making any remark. He never takes sides. "Giovanni looks at her in ecstasy. This is not love, I would like to tell him. You need to love with your head, not your willy. Don't go where your heart takes you. Listen to the frontal cortex, the one that makes decisions. *Think*, I want to tell him. Think," she carries on, breathless.

"But you fell in love too, long ago, for a foreigner, don't you remember?"

"Yes. Of course I do."

"And you were very young, too," Luigi says.

"Yes," she says. "I was."

"You followed your heart."

"Yes. I was so young. There were so many things I didn't know."

"You didn't know you didn't know. You needed to know yourself first," he says, quoting in a single sentence both Donald Rumsfeld and Socrates and Sun Tzu, but she doesn't know she doesn't know. All she knows is how angry she feels, how loud she'd like to scream, how hard she'd like to punch Julie in her amber-coloured eyes.

***

What could they possibly be talking about all the time. It is a mystery. I can see them. Yes, of course I'm watching – there they are, lying on the sand next to each other. I can't hear what they're saying but I see their mouths open and close and they smile and occasionally laugh. Julie speaks a good Italian, yes, but what can they talk of? They are only teenagers, they have had few experiences, they know little of real life. They don't have friends in common; they don't attend the same school; she is disenchanted, sure of herself. She lives in Paris. Giovanni was born and raised in a village, and shares the same characteristics: he's solitary, because he does not trust a large group; he's slow, because there is never any hurry; he is serious, and doesn't quite get irony; he is not gossipy but he knows what gossip is: rumour, reputation threatened by petty and jealous words. He knows what honour is: that it is everything one has, especially in a village. Yes: Giovanni is provincial; his world is completely different from that of a Parisian girl. Look at her clothes; check her hair, her shoes, her jewellery, her make-up, her hair-cut. Listen to how she speaks, the choice of every word, even if foreign; look at how she moves: loose, uninhibited, elegant, presumptuous. Like a woman; and now look at Giovanni, who is awkward, clumsy; he looks like an inflated child, not a man, not even in the making. He lowers his eyes, dangles his arms, drags his feet. Innocent, harmless, modest. They are two opposite personalities, and they attract each other like magnets.

Marieke spies on them, sees them as they kiss - maybe just a quick kiss, the quickest touching of lips against lips, and she can't help herself: every time her eyes flash downwards, to the front of his trousers, where she thinks she can detect a flicker of movement, a dart like that of a fish, and she drowns in an uncontrollable, uncontrolled rage. Mine, she thinks. My Giovanni, my son, mine.

***

Marieke is convinced she has succeeded to keep to herself the tsunami of love she feels for Giovanni by building a kind of moat around her. Updike would have said, elegantly: hopeful, deluded, docile. I say: fool. She doesn't know what awaits her. Because it's as if Julie took a run to attack that moat. Or, better: as if Giovanni, protected *and* prisoner inside the walls built by Marieke, was trying to take down the bricks that form the building around him. Julie hands him a hammer; no: a pickaxe.

Giovanni can finally get out.

***

A shitty vacation, Marieke thinks; she is furious. Furious, yes, but also depressed; angry but also sad, demoralized. Frustrated. And what is it exactly that's bothering her so much? That Giovanni ignores her, treating the apartment like a hotel, his mother as a maid? What is it that disturbs her the most: the waves of testosterone that are pouring out of him like sweat? Or is it the idea of Julie robbing him of his virginity? In short, is it simple self-pity resulting from loneliness or pure rivalry, jealousy of a woman towards another woman who is trying to rob her of her loyal, adoring man?

Marieke doesn't know that Giovanni and Julie's relationship is platonic. In her mind she sees hidden sex scenes - on the beach at night, among the trees of the park, on the back seats of the car lent by a friend. She imagines Julie as the Great Seductress: she who behaves like a man, who does not wait to be seduced by him but who seduces him first; a Circe, a Salome or a Judith by Klimt, her eyes lengthened by black kohl, her hands with rapacious fingers, her pupils widened by desire. A woman who hypnotizes, a witch who bewitches, who attracts and imprisons her victim. Marieke is certain of it: Giovanni was not chosen because he is special. If it had not been him, it would have been another. Julie is one of those who get fixated on a potential prey and circles around them like a vulture, a snake - all eyes and lips.

"I'm going out," Giovanni says.

"Where are you going?" Marieke asks, knowing the answer.

"Out."

"Yes, but where?"

"Just to the marina."

'For an ice-cream?"

"Yes."

"With whom?"

"With my mates. The gang. You know."

"What about Julie, your girlfriend – is she coming along, too?"

"What did you say?"

"Julie. I've seen you two together, at the beach. I know she is your girlfriend."

There, she said it. She didn't want to, but it came out. Giovanni stands still, unable to say a single word. He blushes with shock, embarrassment, annoyance. Darwin wrote a whole chapter about blushing in his book *The Expression of the Emotions in Man and Animals*; he considered it to be "the most peculiar and most human of all expressions." Giovanni reddens; the redness spreads from his forehead to his chin, to his neck but in that very moment the telephone rings. It's Luigi, who calls every evening at the same time. The telephone rings once, twice, three times, until Marieke breaks eye contact with her son and answers. Giovanni walks out of the room, his face in flames.

"Giovanni's having his first crush," he hears her say to his father.

His heart is crushed.

***

How can you describe the heart of a sixteen-year-old boy who has just tasted the first sip of love? Not a promise. Not hope. Real love, though just a sip. He's on holiday, he's enjoying the company of new friends, and: on the second week: Julie, from Paris, sixteen and a half, with the predictable upturned nose and dimples and almost yellow eyes - Amber, he nicknamed her on the first day, dazzled. Amber-Julie, who likes to wear floral print dresses and tiny sunglasses on the top of her head to hold the threads of golden hair cascading on her shoulders like a waterfall; her nasal vowels and her ripening breasts that Giovanni struggles not to stare at. And those two pimples, one on her chin and one on her forehead, under the fringe – there!, he has discovered her blushing weakness – the fringe obviously there to cover the spots and a deeper blush on her cheeks, oh so suddenly, when she sees him notice them, and a breath of tenderness in his heart. Love.

THE HEART OF THE OCTOPUS

Julie arrives after two weeks but she's tanned and knows everyone already – all but Giovanni. And he extends his arm to shake her hand but she laughs and pulls him towards her and kisses him on his left cheek, and says his name. Giovanni can feel her saliva on his cheek, just a trace, and he'd like to touch it but doesn't want her to think he's wiping it away, like he used to do when he was little and his great Aunt Ada used to leave a slippery snail-like trail on his skin that he'd wipe off with the sleeve of his jersey; he'd actually want to touch Julie's trail, Julie's slobber, he'd like to bring it to his mouth. Immediately. Because it takes just a few hours for Giovanni to fall in love. *Coupe de foudre classic,* Marieke would call it, because for her French is the language of seduction, and she's right: it is like a storm, like a lightning, that hits him like a dart. After meeting her, nothing else exists. She is the summer, she is the sea, she is the sand, tiny grains that sneak everywhere inside him, in his hair and in his nostrils and between his fingers and toes, in his pants. He can't see anything else, he doesn't hear anything else, he can't think of anything else. And he smiles constantly, like a fool, but he can't avoid it, he smiles until his cheeks hurt. And he looks for her, his eyes fluttering over her body like a butterfly, over her bikini as yellow as her name, like a cheesy summer song that doesn't leave your head. She invites him to play volleyball in the water: he runs along; she asks him to go with her for an ice cream: he runs along; she pats the fabric of the chair next to hers and he throws himself onto it, grotesquely grateful. He meets her in the afternoon, and in the evening, and the following day she is the first thing he looks for – the first star. There: his Venus.

Amber looks for him and flees, escapes, slides away like the tentacles of her blond hair, Amber, Amber who is always on the run, Amber who does not speak but whispers, AmberAmberAmber, he can't think of anything else, he masturbates for hours, all night long, Amber with skin as taut as an apricot's, her high arse, arse tits arse, oh fuck, Amber, Julie. Amber keeps teasing him, pushes him away and pulls him towards her, like table tennis, pingpong, Amber whose laughter is like an explosion, Amber whose firm breasts bounce, pingpong, pongping, Julie, Julie twitches her nose, Julie, she says that she'll come out in the evening for an ice cream and then doesn't show up, Amber who fools around with the beach lifeguard and looks at him sideways and flirts like crazy, curious to see what jealousy looks like on a boy who has a crush on her, Amber who touches his knee while playing cards, Amber who climbs over his shoulders in the water while they play volleyball, Giovanni brushes her left boob and she cries: "*Non!*" And he is ashamed, he apologises profusely, oh he is so fucking ashamed but she laughs, she laughs her extraordinary laughter, an incredible burst of dimpled air and those dimples laugh with her.

Amber at dusk sits on the cold sand and looks at the sea, lost in her thoughts, and he sits down by her side – it is a cloudy late afternoon, there aren't many people on the beach, his mum stayed home - and she rests her head on his shoulder and he remains motionless, tense, confused, almost not breathing, his heart crazy.

Do not breathe, stop, everything stops.

Shh.

***

And life changes, – that's how it happens, no?: dead calm, days that blend and merge into each other and then abruptly: here, look, here, now: everything has changed. Amber. His heart beating like mad and more and more, her hand on his arm, she's pulling him towards her, and at the last moment no, look, what, look: she isn't pushing him away, pongping, she is holding on to him, grabs him, wants him: Yes. Yes. Her hot hand clinging to the sleeve of his shirt, and on the back of his head, in his hair. Her hot hands and the surprise of her soft and warm lips, god, so hot. Yes.

Can you remember those kisses, the kisses you kiss at sixteen, those kisses that last for minutes, saliva dribbling on your chin and your tongue that almost hurts but kisses, kisses, kisses. Can you really remember when you have an erection for hours and do not know when you can take care of it, when it does not matter, when you stroke her side, her armpit, but don't dare go further, to her breasts, do not dare more, when you open your eyes and see her eyes closed, concentrated, tense but soft, as tense as infinity, soft like a wave, as warm as the warm sand, in the evening, and you take her face in your hands and nobody had e v e r seemed so - so so incredibly full of life.

You call it love because you do not know that it isn't love,

Or not only,

Or never again.

That night, that summer night when you are sixteen, that is magic like never again, the ice cream melting on your fingers, but so what, you leave in a few days, what, that's not possible, when will I see you again, I do not know, it does not matter, not now, now Sunday seems years away, now I want to touch you, you're as hot as the sun, then we'll see, I do not know, we'll see, give me your address, your number, but later, not now, now come here, if I don't kiss you I'll die.

The sea, the waves, the absolute and ridiculous love of a sixteen-year-old, but: it *is* love, as real as death, and it makes you feel light and heavy, it doesn't make you breathe, you close your eyes and roll your hands into fists, tight tight tight to hold on to something that can fly away at any moment.

***

And there: it happened. I feel like Rosemary when she falls for Dick Diver, on the beach. It takes a minute. A heartbeat, a fluttering of eyelashes, and everything changes. Julie, my Amber. Is it possible, can life really be like this, an unexpected and sudden change, and when you are on the other side, you turn to have a last glance at the opposite shore, far away. I was there - I've been there all this time, still, tied, hands and feet tied to her, and now I'm free. As if the capacity of my lungs had increased twice, three times. Now I can inhale and exhale, and I am no longer alone, and Julie, Julie, Amber, I want you, and I want to tell you 'I love you' but it makes me laugh, and you'd laugh too and it would be embarrassing but God I do love you to death. *Je t'aime-* no, no, I can't say that, but I want to hold you till I'll hurt you, I want to break your bones, I want to crush you, crush you, make you mine - Amber, you have the beginning of a pimple on the chin, and yet you have never been more beautiful.

***

Night, oh night: don't end.

***

I can't give it a name. Happiness? Yes; I do feel happy. Yes. A veil has been lifted. The numbness is over, as if – before – I'd had a plastic bag over my head, to deprive me of air; my heart beats, it beats, I can feel it, every single beat, deafening inside the cage of my ribs, and I'm breathless overwhelmed by pure happiness and full and crazy, I feel great and I feel awful, I'm not hungry - but I devour food - I did not sleep – but am not one bit tired - my body has lost its importance - and yet I am all body, only body - a mass of contradictions. And joy, joy, a joy that pours out of my thoughts my body my every pore and runs through my veins with blood, like music.

***

The next day everything starts all over again. He wakes up nauseous, full of dead beer from last night and the live fear of the possibility of not meeting his new friend ever again, her. It's nine o'clock, oh my God, how can it be nine already, quickly, quickly, there is no time to waste, a cool shower on his warm sleeping body, the hurried breakfast swallowed as fast as he can, the juice of the peach he's wolfed down that runs on his savage chin and he flies down to the beach out of breath, the flip-flops flying on the pavement, flapflapflap, the curls of his hair flapping in his eyes, he collapses on the deck chair, tears off his T-shirt, shoots his flip-flops in the air, and there it is, his triumphant body, perfumed with shower gel, bursting with youth in the scorching mid-morning sun. He closes his eyes, overwhelmed - by the heat, by this summer's turgidity, by this fullness that surrounds him like never before; that's in him; that is him. The flavour of the peach on his tongue.

"Giovanni!"

The smiles of his friends and: here she is, here, yes: she's here: her smile, honey, gold, yellow, golden, amber - her skin and her mouth and her hair in the sun. He brushes her mouth with his lips, again and again.

***

It is not sex. Not yet. It is more, less, but more, a young, *innocent* love.

Many years later, Giovanni would write in his diary: "I hate that word. In the common lexicon, it has a sweetish connotation, or religious - an innocent love becomes a love without malice; we are talking about candour, chastity. But it was not so. I know. I remember, I was there: it was happening to me. There *was* malice, complicity. And: desire. I am talking about innocence as a kind of interior situation, of a psychological state – innocence regarding her respect towards me, and mine towards her. I respected Julie, I wanted her desperately, but it had nothing to do with sex. I loved her more without having had sex with her that if I'd had. Holding her in my arms as if she were my little girl. Just holding her precious body in my hands. And yet not really possessing her."

Here, now. He squeezes her, strokes her, smells her hair, her neck, he gently touches her body - desire on each of his hot fingertips.

"I've never even tried," he'll confess, years later. "To go further, I mean. To really have her. But if I think back to the sweetness of that summer, I know with absolute certainty I've never experienced another love like that."

***

THE HEART OF THE OCTOPUS

Tonight is the night of the fourteenth of August - Ferragosto. The term derives from the Latin *feriae Augusti,* or festival of Augustus, which was used to indicate the period of rest established by Emperor Augustus in 18B.C.. It is a day of celebration in Italy, a Catholic festival, according to which the Virgin Mary, mother of Jesus on August 15th was assumed into heaven with body and soul. To celebrate, on this night, many Italian cities exhibit an event with fireworks. Marieke and Giovanni have seen them many times, during their summer holidays - Giovanni has always loved the fireworks, the colours that transform the dark blue of the night, their bang, pop, fizz, crackle and boom. This year his friends have decided to go to Sanremo, with Marc's car. Marieke holds her son's arm.

"Be careful, please," she tells him, while Giovanni, red with embarrassment, tries to distract his friends, to have them look elsewhere, not to stare at his mother dressed with an old crumpled linen shirt, what a shame, she who cares so much, who always wants to appear well groomed, at least outside the home, and instead: look at her: her hair dishevelled, her ankles swollen in the heat. And - goodness - in slippers. What a horror, what a shame.

"Don't come back too late."

"No, mamma, don't worry," he says, sliding inside the car. Julie presses her hot, naked leg against his.

"Put your belt on."

"Yes."

"I gave you money. Don't be too late."

"Yes. No."

"Don't smoke. Don't drink."

"No. Go home now, please," he begs her. But she stands at the side of the road until the car leaves with six laughing, impatient boys and girls inside. The white Fiat 127 hurtles into the clear evening. Two are sitting in the front of the car and four are behind, crammed, sweating despite the open windows, the smell of the evening and of the sea and of the wilted, tired flowers after a day glorious with sunshine, the smell of the night that is approaching, of the salt that encrusts air and hair and clothes, the smell of hot bodies, of the rubbery car seats.

Marc is driving too fast and too close to the car in front; next to him there's Anna, and behind them are Luc, Perry, Giovanni and Julie. At every turn they exaggerate the motion that throws them onto each other, they laugh, and Anna puts on the radio and they start singing Battisti and then *Enola Gay* and *Bette Davis Eyes*, and *Summer Nights* from *Grease*, in a crippled English.

Can you see them?

Happy to be there in this unrepeatable moment, because they will not be sixteen and seventeen and eighteen next year, it will never be like this again, never again, only this night, tonight, a night of fires and flames and as hot as a nest, like hot breath, never again, this carelessness, this lightness, never again, because now they have everything before them, all possibilities, all the optimism and hope and the future, and they don't know it yet but they will know it soon, when they will turn into adults; the future will be shorter and shorter and shorter until it will no longer exist, the choices will be made, decided, finished. And this is the real disaster, which is passed on from mother to son, from father to daughter; our true legacy, which is not of goods, or of money, of stuff: but it is human and only human – the awareness of everything that we have lost, of everything we are losing, and of all that we will lose.

The Fiat 127 glows white in the black sepia of the night, the windows open, the hot air, the hot seat, the hot breaths, the discordant voices, the young supple bodies full of youth, oh how I wish, oh Christ I do so, I do I do wish to go back to that moment, then, there, in the warm night of the coast road passed Ventimiglia, to see the fireworks that marked the fullness of summer, as gaudy and pink as the atrocious carnations Marieke adores, ah, my good god that feeling of freedom, of possibilities, of lack of accountability, that youth: they want nothing, seek nothing more, they do not think about nothing but:

Here.

Now.

***

Here.

Now.

THE HEART OF THE OCTOPUS

***

Today does not differ from yesterday and tomorrow it'll be the same: water and ball games, a quick dip in the sea, getting wet and then dry and wet again, lying in the sun and fleeing under the shade of an umbrella. The others have known each other for years. They have come to the same seaside place since they were children; a group of Italian and French adolescents, thin and worldly, well behaved. They aren't a chatty bunch, No one has asked Giovanni where he is from, why did he come here on vacation, how long he will stay, when he will leave, what he is studying, who he is. There is a general and rather vague acceptance of one another, no questions asked. It does not matter. *N'importe pas.*

"Come here," Julie tells him and behold: these two words contain all they have to say. Come here. You're mine, you're mine, I want you, I want you here. Here, now.

***

When it's too hot, in the late morning, they gather to play cards in the shade next to the changing cabins. They play Slapjack, Crazy eight, and Giovanni, who knows the games well, ends up winning. He wins once more, and he bursts out laughing, and Julie laughs with him as if they were at a Las Vegas Casino and he'd won a jackpot.

"You really are good!" She says, touching his arms, his hands. "My Jay Gatsby! *Enfin*, you're like a character in Scott Fitzgerald - as beautiful and as dangerous ..."

"But no," he parries, but right then Marieke walks by – peacocking, so proud.

"Interested in joining me for lunch, my little winner?"

"No, *madame*, I'm sorry, but *non*. Giovanni eats with us," Julie responds for him, placing a hand on his arm. Marieke looks down on the girl. Two seconds to decide: treat them as little kids or as grown-ups? She goes for grown-ups – there is less to lose.

"Of course. See you later,"

"Ciao, ma," Giovanni responds, shuffling the cards. Julie kisses him on the cheek.

"Sympa, la maman,"

"Yes. *Sympa*."

Julie gets up and he's straight behind her, always behind her, to admire her ass, to follow it step by step. They drop on their chairs as if they had been standing for hours. They join two tables together.

Marieke, who is dining alone at a table nearby, reads the paper trying not to stare at her son and his girlfriend - but he knows she is watching him from behind her dark sunglasses. The new waiter stops to talk to her, and she asks him a question, and another, and why is he staying so long by her table, what could they possibly have to talk about, thinks Giovanni, gloomily. What the fuck. What a nuisance. Yes: his mother causes him a sort of physical discomfort - the curly reddish hair like the mane of a lioness, the brown costume that seems to match the freckles scattered over her shoulders, like nests on her cheeks, the bracelets tinkling on her wrists. Like a cow in the pastures. Big boobs. He looks at her again and again, observes how she smiles to the waiter who smiles back. His mother smiles again. She looks at Giovanni and almost winces with pain as if she could read the disgust on his face. She grabs her bag and leaves without even saying goodbye. What the fuck.

He calls the waiter over to their table.

"A coffee for all of us," he orders, without even saying 'please'. Loud. None of them likes coffee, but it stinks of adulthood. Julie's foot climbs up on his thigh, hidden by a towel.

"Cappuccino for me," Julie says. Giovanni's heart is pounding under her foot. "How handsome you are," she says, her mouth so close to his ear he finds it hard to understand what she is saying, he can only hear her breath on him. Giovanni blushes, he can't swallow the bitter coffee, the desire to touch her rising from his throat like a burp.

***

They hold hands and jump into the sea - the water is as warm as a bath. They lie down to dry, they dive in again. The sand is fine, golden. They don't talk much; they don't know what to say and don't need to say anything. They want to be next to each other, hand in hand, side against side, swimming and getting out to dry in the sand, his skin hot from the sun and cold from the sea, then hot again. They come and go from shore to water, like waves. Giovanni doesn't think of anything.

"So you live in the countryside?"

"Yes."

"And how is it?"

"It's nice. There are hills. My father has a vineyard."

"Like the ones in Tuscany? I have been there."

"A little like in Tuscany," Giovanni smiles. He's never been there.

"How about you? You live in Paris, no? Is it beautiful?"

"*Un peu.*" They laugh.

"I live in the 16eme, near the Parc de Boulogne."

"Maybe I can come and visit you."

"Yes. Do. I'll show you around."

"Yes."

"Yes, you can see me, see where I live, my little apartment that I share with my mother and my brother."

Giovanni knows Julie's parents are separated, that her father is Italian (that's why she can speak the language so well); he had left her mother and returned to Genoa when Julie was four.

"Do you miss your father?"

"No, not really. I see him quite often. I was with him before coming here. And I have my friends. And you? Do you have a best friend, or a gang? Or are you always with your *maman*, just the two of you?"

"But no," Giovanni says. "There's my dad. And I have a group of friends I've known since I was little. Riccardo, Lorenzo, Pietro."

"Tell me. Tell me about them."

Giovanni is silent. "About them? I don't know what to say. They are there. They are just there, as they have always been."

He thinks about his friends; they meet every Saturday afternoon, every Sunday morning to play football. He has known them since primary school - Pietro, he's known since nursery. He doesn't know what to say.

"Will you tell them about me?"

He looks into her yellow eyes. Amber. What will he say? He knows they don't know what *this is*. They have never had a girlfriend. This kind of girlfriend. This love.

"I don't know," Giovanni says. Pietro, Riccardo, Lorenzo: three young skinny pimply boys that have never left Piedmont, and who regard Giovanni - with his Dutch mother, his foreign holidays, his house full of books – as an exotic person. "They are just there," Giovanni repeats. "Tell me about yourself," he asks. He closes his eyes and listens to the sound of her voice. Amber, Amber.

***

THE HEART OF THE OCTOPUS

To discover: Verb. [from the Latin *discoperire, dis* and *coperire* 'cover completely'].

1. Find unexpectedly or during a search.
2. Become aware of a fact.
3. Be the first to find or observe
4. Show interest in (an activity or subject) for the first time
5. Be the first to recognise
6. Divulge
7. Disclose the identity of someone
8. Display a quality or a feeling

I find I am feeling all meanings of the verb. I find, I become aware of, I show interest in, I display all feelings – for Amber, and Menton, France, the sea, love, desire, the burning desire to know everything about her. I find that I am good at listening, I know how and when to shut up and let Julie talk. I find that I know as if by instinct how to observe, the most minute and insignificant details - and then I can recall each detail of her conversation, and how she likes that, the fact that I remember, that I was actually listening and not just pretending, listening in an active kind of way and remembering what she says, so I intervene in her story and casually throw in: ah yes, your cousin Francoise, the one with the ginger cat. It is as if I recognised her: we are so different, she and I: she is a sophisticated, Parisian girl, a girl of the world, a fashionable, glamorous girl, and I am a little boy from a little village. But we are the same: she looks at me while I am talking to someone else, and I see in her eyes that she knows, she knows I know, and I know that she knows, we know. We discovered each other.

***

Giovanni is a strong swimmer and is the first to reach the platform, a hundred meters from the beach *Les Sablettes*. He helps Julie to get on it, and they sit next to each other, their bodies dripping. They look at the coastline before them, the colourful parasols and deck chairs, and behind, the pastel-coloured houses of the Riviera, pink and powder pink and light green and pale yellow. Today it's windy, it's less hot, the outlines of objects are sharp.

"September air," Marieke said when they got up. Late summer air. The end of summer.

***

And it is the 21st and then the 22nd and then the 23rd of August, and every day repeats itself like the beads of a rosary, one after the other. They slip through sweaty fingers, *Ave* Maria, *Ave* Julie, full of grace, the lord is with you, our lord our god Giovanni who divides his gracious presence between his mother Marieke - how appropriate - and the girl with golden eyes, between hatred and love, between the blue of the sea, now, and the brown of the

Monferrato hills, which are waiting for him like Penelope, in their flat and stable and infinite future.

Marieke surrenders to the softness of the last days of vacation, with that curious melancholy that precedes departures. Luigi calls her more often, knowing of her distress - Giovanni's first girlfriend ruining their holiday - stays longer on the phone. He finds it hard to do small talk, he never discusses his job, but does his best to distract his wife, bringing her up to date with the news about the village and the neighbours, the leaking tap in the kitchen that needs sorting, the plum tree that is making few fruits, this year, there won't be enough to make jam, never mind, and we need to order wood for the winter, make an appointment with the dentist, the ophthalmologist, the hairdresser, my hair is a mess, but no, I don't believe it, you will be beautiful as always, but no, but yes, believe me. I am here alone, it is so hot, you should see the size of mosquitoes. All so boring. Marieke listens, which is uncharacteristic, as she never does.

"Everything else alright?" Luigi dares asking; you have to be careful, Marieke, you have to kind of sniff around and try to guess what kind of mood she is in, adapt the questions to the answers and not vice versa.

"Yes. But. Uhm, I don't know."

"Tell me."

"It's Giovanni."

"Of course it's Giovanni. What."

"The girl."

"The French girl?"

"Yes. He doesn't see anything else; he can't think about anything else."

"It's normal. It will pass."

"You always say that: it will pass."

"I say it because I was young too, Maria. You too."

Too long ago, Marieke thinks. I can't really remember.

"Do you remember how easy it was, to get lost into something else? In a new hobby, in a sport, in a game. Especially when you're little, when the game is everything."

"Giovanni is not a small child."

"True. Also: this French girl is not a toy; but the game they are playing is called love. He never played it before. He doesn't know the rules. He's seen it before, but always from afar. He has read about it; he has watched dozens of films. But on his skin, no: he's never tried it."

"He can't play."

"Precisely. He'll need to learn. If you think about it, the first crush comes with a series of verbs - burning, getting hurt ... not for nothing. Because falling in love for the first time hurts, whatever happens."

Marieke sighs, says goodbye, puts the phone down, but doesn't get up. She stays still, sitting on the couch, gawping. After a while, when you think her stillness must be a sign for sleep, yes, you think, she will fall asleep, just then: she smiles, she smiles a smile that reminds me of Kevin Spacey in one of the first scenes of the TV series *House of Cards*: the actor, in the role of Frank Underwood, is rescuing a dog that has been hurt in a hit-and-run accident. The dog is laying on the road. Frank looks at it and at us, directly at the camera: he is looking at me; he is addressing me, speaking to me, the viewer. He talks about pain.

"There are two kinds of pain," he says. "The sort of pain that makes you strong, or useless pain. The sort of pain that's only suffering. I have no patience for useless things." While he kills the animal with his own hands, the camera lingers on his placid, pale face; the elegance of the tuxedo, jacket off, immaculate shirt that contrasts with the violent gesture. Spacey is calm, his movements contained, reserved; his sweet hazel eyes are full of a quiet, ruthless threat. Now: reader, my reader; imagine this scene: Marieke looks at you – yes, you - from behind the pages, with a straight and combative and sarcastic look, all together: a little knowing smile that you do not know how to interpret. With a banal phrase, we may say that she suffers, because she sees her own son suffer. But: take a good look at that grimace of disgust, halfway between pain and pleasure, which pulls the corners of her mouth. The truth is that she likes, right now, to think that Giovanni will get hurt. It gives her some kind of satisfaction. It happens to everyone. It happened to her, too. It is another of the things that are inherited. It's in the order of things, Luigi said. Then: let's allow for things to be reordered. Let's allow for a little pain.

***

THE HEART OF THE OCTOPUS

They dine on the terrace, Giovanni and Marieke, facing each other on either side of the plastic table. Salad, *pasta alle vongole* ("without garlic!" pleads Giovanni), peaches marinated in lemon and sugar. They speak – again - on the phone with Luigi; Marieke once more makes ironic comments on Menton, on the tourists, the shops selling tacky souvenirs, lavender everywhere - which relenting, she has bought for herself and her friends. Giovanni does not know if it's a tendency of his family, or something that everyone does: this constant teasing, talking badly of one another. His mother has two friends whom she often sees, in Castel San Gerolamo; perhaps she spends the whole morning with them: but then as soon as she goes home she makes fun of them, criticising their clothes, their hairstyle, the way they sit at the table, their gossipy conversation. Then she sees them again, the next day, as if nothing had happened. The same here; it's their second vacation in Menton, which means they liked the place enough to come back. Yet, there is always something wrong, a detail that must be taken and examined and made ridiculous.

"I saw the little *mesdames* with the designer scarves, along the promenade," she says. "I thought there would be more elegance, in France. Instead, here too: what provincials." Silence, while her husband speaks. "Yes. Yes, I know." Silence.

"I'll see you on Sunday then," Luigi says, and Giovanni - who knew, who has always known – realises there are just forty-eight hours left. Then they'll leave. He feels sick.

"Mamma. It's almost over. We are leaving," he says, tears in his eyes.

"Yes," she says, and hugs him. Mamma. Giovanni wraps his arms around her waist, leans his head onto her shoulder, starts crying. They are standing in front of a mirror and Marieke watches, observing the body of her son clinging to her, devoid of strength, like a Pietà.

"He has the body of a man," Marieke thinks, holding him – he has the compact, hard body of a man.

"And yet he's still a child."

Marieke had studied biological sciences in Utrecht, graduating with honours. A passionate researcher (and reminiscent of her uncle's travels) she'd continued studying, and had enrolled in a Master's degree on the animal biodiversity in Piedmont, focusing on animals in danger of extinction: rabbits, turkeys and guinea fowl from the Monferrato area. She'd spent several months on a farm in Moncalvo, where she'd met Luigi, who had started an immediate, irresistible courtship. Within four months she was pregnant, she'd left for good the studies and the Netherlands, and was married. "I did not know then I was leaving everything behind, for him: my family, my home, my country, my career. It seemed romantic and crazy – but good crazy – to live with a man I knew little or nothing of. Italy, back then, was considered exotic, idyllic. Lifeguards seemed princes, ski instructors paladins: pizza, Lambrusco and Dante and Pasolini, Sophia Loren and Marcello Mastroianni, the Dolce Vita, ah, yes, yes: the sweet Italian life, clichéd but also so romantic: even my mother smiled, recounting my deeds to her friends. No one tried to stop me. No one took me aside, to ask whether I was fully aware of what I was doing. I was blinded. I couldn't help myself. A few months later I woke up and realised the mistake - in the meantime, Giovanni was born. That mistake could have made me depressed; but I turned depression into a project: Giovanni became my life project. He must succeed."

***

It's the first time that he has truly, seriously fallen in love - a love that feels important, that's changed his life. Forever. Yes, he's had a few flirts, in the past, but each experience had felt like candyfloss. There has been Mariella, a classmate, whom he'd kissed on the back seat of the coach on a school trip to Florence, a few years before; Elena and Serena, sisters – he had kissed them both, at two separate parties; Ottavia, daughter of friends of his parents, with whom he had gone to the movies on a Sunday and whose hand he'd caressed in the dark for two hours - but then as soon as the lights had gone back on she had pretended nothing had happened; and finally the crazy Alessandra, Sandrina, a cousin twice removed, who was eleven and had beckoned him into the bathroom where she had proceeded to stick her tongue into his mouth, moving it with a desperate fury, and then had firmly taken hold of his hands placing them over her non-existent breasts, causing his first sexual arousal.

He doesn't sleep much, falls asleep late and then wakes up after ten o'clock, with swollen eyes and a sick head. No he can't have breakfast, he's late, and it is too late, he runs down to the beach with the urgency of the last hours. Everyone is there, all his friends, already in the water - Paul, Marc, Julie with a bikini as yellow as her name. Giovanni feels a knot in his throat, squeezing it tight shut. His mouth is dry, his eyes moist. And he gets angry: "Yes so angry, angry, angry with my mother who wants to leave, with my stupid friends who continue to play like idiots with the stupid ball, and my Amber there smiling her fucking smile with her fucking perfectly straight teeth. But what are you laughing at, you fool, now that I am about to leave? But what are you laughing at, you idiot, now that the world is ending? My world. And she smiles her sweet fucking smile and tells me: *partir est mourir* – a tiny pause and - *en peu* and her smile turns into a burst of hysterical laughter. I feel belittled. Betrayed."

Giovanni runs home, where his mother continues to tidy up – she always cleans over what's clean already, even though she knows the cleaning woman sent in by the agency is due to come tomorrow, but the idea that a common maid might set eyes on her dirty stuff fills her with shame. She dusts, sweeps, washes, cleans, shines. Giovanni comes in breathless and Marieke's febrile activity comes to a stop.

"What happened?"

"Nothing."

"You seem upset. It's not nothing. Tell me."

"Nothing."

"Was it Julie?"

"Julie what, Julie nothing, shut your mouth, leave Julie out of this, shut up," Giovanni says moving away from her touch. "I'm hot, I stink, I'm going to take a shower," he says, and slams the bathroom door shut. He opens the tap and sits on the floor, not moving. His mother listens to the sound of the pouring water, flowing like rain. Giovanni sits down on the wet floor, his heart pounding. How long does he sit there for? I don't know. But at some point he gets up, undresses, walks into the shower cubicle and remains under the running water until it becomes cold. Later, he goes back to the beach; he buys two ice creams and takes one to Amber as a gesture of reconciliation.

***

Surely someone has done studies on *kissing*, Giovanni writes in his diary.

Somewhere in the world, at some moment in history, a learned scholar must have completed extensive research on why and how we kiss, on the distinction between the different types, the kiss between friends or siblings or lovers or with children, and the rubbing of noses, on the function of the muscles of the tongue and lips. On how much saliva is exchanged and on the best positions for one's nose, that at times gets in the way. On what type of hormone is released by one's brain as soon as one opens his lips.

On the effect of germs when one's saliva mixes with that of another human being.

    I move closer to her face - we are sitting on the sand at sunset, there are few people around, the sea in front of us looks blue and flat and perfect, straight out of a postcard. I move closer and her features become larger and larger as if I was zooming in – I can see the dark dots where she plucks her eyebrows; the pores on the side of her nose, dilated by the heat; the fine blonde hair on her upper lip, a mole that I had not noticed, a crumb of a mole; her large pupils, dilated despite the light; the yellowish colour of her unbelievable eyes - sometimes they seem greenish, others hazelnut, such as the Russian amber necklace my mother wears, now as yellow as some cats' eyes; and her mouth, fleshy and pink, her lips parted, her lower lip with a fleck of flesh – she is constantly biting her lower lip, I can see a tiny lesion, drops of congealed blood - the slightly upward curve, that makes its way towards her upturned nose. She lowers her eyelids like a curtain on her amber eyes and I come even closer, I can feel her breath on me. We stand so, so still, my face a few millimetres from her face. Still, motionless. I close my eyes, too. I hear nothing, I see nothing. My breath is short. I smell the air: her smell: the smell of her skin, sour from the sun, and her saliva, that I know so well. I know what she tastes of: of what she's had to eat or drink, or of toothpaste or candy, but behind that there is another taste and smell, her own, a salty smell that feels exciting, warm and liquid, but it feels also kind of viscous, lukewarm. I brush her lips with mine, slowly, softly, barely. I can feel her holding her breath and she lets it go and syncs on my breathing. We remain like that for a very long time, attached to each other by nothing more than a caress, a touch as soft as the beating of a bee's wings. Inhaling and exhaling. Our beating hearts. Hush. The sea is so near. Amber is a restless creature, her concentration falls apart, she loses patience. The tip of her tongue opens a gap between my lips, insistent, curious, wet - and finally I open my lips too, my tongue meets hers and I feel a rush of electricity in the groin. My saliva mixes with hers - what do I taste of? - Julie moans a little, first we only move the tip and the whole of our tongues, saliva dripping out of our mouths, the deafening noise of my and her breaths, saliva, water, saliva, the sea, waves crashing against the shore, blood pulsating, running crazy.

***

Amber presses against him, to feel his hardness, and he presses back against her rhythmically, and stops. No, no, no: that's not what he wants, not like this, like horny dogs on the beach, under the disapproving eyes of the small French bourgeoisie on vacation. Sex has nothing to do with *this*, for the first and last time.

***

Giovanni returns home in the late afternoon, tired. Empty. And with a resolution in his heart: to impress every single instant to memory, to remember it all: he walks slowly towards their apartment and looks around with a different, piercing attention: he remembers that there is always an elegant lady who walks her dog; that the same bearded man sips a drink at the local bar. That the bougainvillea that covers almost entirely the opposite wall is wilting. There is a pot hole in the road. An aroma of lemons, lavender, soap. The road he needs to cross; the traffic lights are green. Twelve steps, and he reaches their door. It is made with a heavy, shiny wood. He slips the keys in, he walks into the marble entrance; into the wrought-iron cage of the lift, whose interior is covered in dark red leather. He looks at himself in the mirror while riding up to the third floor. He opens the lift doors; they produce a little clickety sound; the lift goes further up with a whirr. He has the keys, but presses the doorbell. Ding, dong. He can smell garlic, and onions. The window on the landing is open – it looks into the courtyard; he can see the sea, even from here. An infinity of sounds and noises and flavours and smells and gestures that are about to vanish.

    The steps of his mother. Marieke opens in a hurry, fretting, still busying herself with the making of their suitcases, with their departure in mind. Their departure. The scent of their imminent journey mixing with that of the small basil plant she has thrown away in the bin. The refrigerator stands open and empty. The kitchen cupboards lie wide open, and empty, like Giovanni's heart, wide open, and empty.

THE HEART OF THE OCTOPUS

***

It seemed the summer would last forever - those empty days of August, that time made of hot air - and yet here it is, the end has arrived.

Never was the perception of time so antithetical, for Marieke and Giovanni: for her it is as if every day was an old man who is dragging his feet, indolent, apathetic, too tired; he can't take another step, not even a metre, not even an inch. Marieke looks at the hands of the clock, tries to catch it off-guard, but it's not possible, the clock keeps ticking, the seconds move, tac tic tac, inflexible, unstoppable, but it's still ten o'clock, and eleven, and then it's still only three o'clock (four, five, six). In the evening she is exhausted. If only she could close her eyes and wake up on Saturday morning, the suitcases prepared, the shutters closed, the keys slipped into an envelope and popped into the mail box on the ground floor; the sandwiches in the fridge bag, the car that is driving closer and closer to the Piedmontese fog, ready to welcome them like a hug. She's had enough. Enough sea, enough sun, enough loneliness.

For Giovanni, every hour flies away like a swallow who has smelled autumn, like a cliché: it goes like a flash; in a moment; a beat of eyelashes, the time of a sigh, and - look - it is already afternoon; night; and another day, one less. Marieke watches her son lose weight and lose sleep and lose his head, eyes as wide as a fox that crosses the street in the middle of a city.

There is fear, in that look, illusion and ignorance. Poor Giovanni, thinks Marieke: he still hopes.

Six, five, four, three, two, one. Boom. The penultimate night offers a majestic storm, almost a divine manifestation: here, the summer was ending, almost, and now it's officially over. The next day the beautiful Menton looks fresh from the laundry, the dust has been washed away, the air is clear, the sky a deeper blue - September sky, says Marieke loudly, intending to hurt her son. She's had enough. Enough with the saccharine, enough with the sighs, enough with the suppressed sobs like a plum stone spat in one's fist.

"September!" Marieke says gleefully. "Tomorrow we'll have a nice rest from the long drive and on Monday we'll buy the last things for school; a new backpack; a new diary; your new shoes. I do love shopping for Autumnal bits and bobs," she says out loud, imagining herself tanned, her hair smooth and silky after her visit to the hairdresser, in simple pullovers and jeans - her tanned ankles still bare for a while - in the shops of Vercelli, or maybe in Turin, why not, or even Milan, with Giovanni (who's found his smile again, in her daydream) contentedly by her side. When she returns to reality, Giovanni is slamming the front door.

***

Last night. Last supper. Last sip of beer. Last pizza. Last ice cream. Old songs in the jukebox.

THE HEART OF THE OCTOPUS

Sitting on the rocking chair in the bar, bright neon lights, loud music, Julie's sticky hand tight in his sticky hands, her head on his shoulder, her hair tickling his lips. Every so often he moves apart, just a few centimetres, so as to look at her. Again and again. She is tiny, her arms two thin golden wires, and her hands, oh they are like those of a child, and her very thin neck, and that cluster of moles on her right shoulder, light as crumbs. Her enormous eyes, of that indefinable colour – yellow, golden, amber – right now, as green as a swamp. And I would love to dive right in that mud, deep into stagnant water, I don't care if there are alligators, if it's too deep, if there are corpses of pirates at the bottom. I'd happily dive in and die, in there, in her eyes. And her lips, how could I possibly forget her lips, which play a vital role - swollen, tired, swollen and painful lips, wet with and dried by wind and sun, lips that smile, even now, yes now, in the saddest moment of my life – these last few days we have been lips, only lips, and mouth, tongue, teeth, tongue, lips. It was a different world before Julie. Before Amber, my Amber. What am I going to do, how can I leave you. I can't, I can't leave, and she lifts her head off my shoulder and looks at me and smiles with her perfect mouth - her beautiful lips, magnified by the proximity, red for all the kissing, pink with modesty, oh god suck my lips as if you would suck on an oyster; take me away, do not let me go

And it's two in the morning and her mouth suddenly opens into a yawn. The first time she stifles it but it comes back, and god

I'm tired, too, and the night is over, the holiday is over, my life is over

And it comes, here it is, here it is, the inevitable moment I have thought of a billion times. The Last Kiss, the last hug. It passes in an instant.

"Write."

"Yes."

"Call me."

"Yes."

Nothing else. What can you say after one says: *Yes*.

Walking home, thinking about her

Yes

Climbing the stairs, thinking of her

Yes

Walking into the flat, taking off my shoes full of sand, thinking of her

Yes

A hum in my ears like an army of mosquitoes

Yes Yes Yes

Julie, Julie

And in my bed, my meagre baby bed, I stare at the ceiling and try not to close my eyes, convinced as I am that sleep will not come - how can I sleep? It seems absurd that my life could continue as before. I read, somewhere: you have experiences that serve as watersheds: there is a *before* and there is an *after*. One can have an experience, sometimes, able to change everything. Before. After.

Before Julie.

After Julie.

And tomorrow I'll be without Julie, and the day after too.

I fall asleep, my hands clasped together as if in prayer.

Yes.

***

The suitcase is on his bed, with his clothes well folded inside; swimming trunks, shorts, T-shirts, bathrobe, sneakers; the books that he brought along and never opened; the tourist guide to the Riviera. Marieke hears him move, in the bedroom, she hears the thud of the trolley pushed to the floor, the creaking of the bed when Giovanni throws himself on it. She'd like to open the door and ask if he is okay, if all is well, but doesn't.

Giovanni shows himself busy, so he doesn't have to talk. He takes the cases downstairs onto the street, loads them into the trunk, goes up and comes down ten times with their bags and sandwiches for lunch, water, shoes, and the many trinkets bought at the market for a few francs, lavender in many guises – sewn inside purple coloured cloth bags, in rag dolls, in puffy cushions. When all is loaded, he and his mother take a coffee and a croissant at the café nearby. They both think "for the last time." Giovanni continues to glance around, then back, this way and that, hoping to see someone, a friend. Her. His Julie. From the back pocket of his jeans, he takes out the photograph she gave him the night before. Marieke almost snatches it from his hands.

"Let me see," she says, and he entrusts it to her, proud. "Pretty, well: yes, she *is* pretty,"
Marieke says.

"I miss her already," Giovanni confides, putting the photo back in his pocket - all day, he pulls out that rectangle of paper and puts it away, consuming it with his greedy fingers, his hungry gaze. They leave; the journey is long, slow, monotonous; an accident on the Savona-Turin motorway slows them down even further. Giovanni after a while climbs onto the back seat; the headphones cover his ears, a shirt on his face shields his eyes. Marieke thinks she can hear a sob, but maybe she's wrong. It's evening when they arrive in Castel San Gerolamo, and Marieke remembers how it was - until last year - the return after the holidays, Luigi's embrace, the desire to see her friends again, to start school again, to sing "Castel San Gerolamo rocks." Instead, Giovanni drags himself home, upstairs to his room; he touches all his things as if they were foreign as if nothing now belonged to him. He has changed. There is a distance, now, between "before Menton" and "after Menton." Something happened: a gain, a loss: both. The three members of the Ferraro family find themselves in the kitchen standing, awkward, as if they were guests waiting for the landlord to invite them to sit down. Marieke opens the fridge. Luigi did the shopping - eggs, milk, butter, fresh sausages; he prepared a pasta sauce, the one with aubergines he knows she loves. He had bought her a bouquet.

Not a shred of an excuse to argue, Marieke thinks. Not even the flowers are ugly. He even bought fresh croissants for breakfast the next day. Impeccable, reliable, unbearable Luigi.

***

Mother is unbearable.

There is an indescribable mess everywhere, too many bags scattered all over the floor, shoes, magazines. All this stupid stuff. And yes, of course it falls on to me: I am the one that has to bring all of it downstairs and load it into the car. Countless journeys. My arms are sore already. Look – just look at how much stuff. Jesus, what an unbearable bore. I am tired. I am sleepy. I'd like to go to bed and sleep forever and instead we have to close everything down like getting ready for a war, the shutters and the windows and the door and climb down those steps that I have climbed down a hundred times with my heart on fire, the haste of a rabbit in my legs, and now I go up and down like an idiot with these bags, but what the fuck. "What's the matter, honey? Why that face?" my mother repeats over and over, as if I were a child, but you know what? I've had enough: your child has grown, he's a big boy who doesn't need you anymore. Go away. Enough. Leave me alone, leave me alone with the thought of the hands of my Amber, Julie, Amber: her golden golden eyes, her hot mouth, her wet tongue leave me alone, leave me the fuck alone

and I try to slip away, but "Come on, Giovanni. Come on," my mother repeats. "Come on." I can hear it in her voice, there's a knot in her throat, and I know it, because I'm an only child, and I know my mother so well, I do know her melancholy and anguish and her regrets, and I know that she knows, that Marieke has lost me, forever, and for a moment I feel lost, too - but then the hard desire for Julie prevails, it wins, she wins, Amber: you win. I'm all yours. I breathe in – I fill my chest with fresh air, savouring that deep breath, I feel strong and big and dizzy. Amber.

***

He writes five letters – though he sends only two – on that first day without her, with the Walkman playing Pink Floyd at top volume in the futile attempt to cover every noise. He has no appetite for music, but he can't possibly open his mouth to speak. He can't bear to hear the voice of his mother. He pulls out the photograph Julie gave him: a small square, straight out of one of those self-service vending machines used to take pictures for passports. A few centimetres that show her thin face, her hair piled up on her head seemingly at random, and all her features upturned – her eyes, nose, mouth all facing upwards. Another note envelops the photograph as if it were a present, a scrawled hurried note with her address, phone number, book and music titles she loves, that

Giovanni needs to listen to – he must get his hands on them as soon as. Or else.

He alternates different states of mind, he is delirious with happiness and desperate, he knows nothing about her, doesn't know where she lives, doesn't know her friends, her school. He loses his breath.

***

But you've already guessed what will happen, right? Sixteen years of age. His first love. At the seaside. A handful of weeks. A pretty girl. Thousands of kilometres. I'll tell you what happens, inevitably: that summer love fades along with one's tan - but: shh, Giovanni doesn't know it yet. It happens that the distance breaks his legs, his breath, their future - but: shh, don't tell him too soon. Let him still believe a little longer. Poor fool.

It's the Eighties: a time when social media, Instagram, Twitter, texting, don't exist as yet - the distance between Paris and Castel San Gerolamo feels like that from the earth to Mars. Can you remember the letters one wrote, back then? Long and detailed: pages and pages of closely written, sometimes indecipherable handwriting, followed by a walk to the post office, the purchase of stamps, and then the impatient wait for the recipient's reply. Time, time. And then a letter would come. Quick: open the envelope, tear it, read the letter, recompose the envelope, because everything is important, everything, not only the written words: pen, paper, handwriting, envelope, stamp, scent. Giovanni writes to Julie and writes again and again, without waiting to receive a letter from her. Because he knows - he pretends not to know, but he does know that when you're almost seventeen and as pretty as a fresh strawberry, you will not waste your time thinking about the young Italian boy met on holiday, you are not going to squander half an hour with pen and paper and write what you do, what fun you're having. Friends call you, your ex calls you, your own city: Paris! calls you, with its smell, its taste, its fashionable music. Billy Joel and Lionel Richie and *Every Breath You Take*. Julie sings, shrugs. She goes out. The holidays, that fling with the cute curly-haired boy in the summer. So long ago.

While in Castel San Gerolamo, it is still boiling hot. Julie's violent silence. The lack of a reply, his anxiety rising, another letter sent, and silence received, and then: "Enough, enough, I must talk to her." He locks the door, grabs the phone, dials the number slowly: breathe, concentrate, breathe, but there's the answering machine. His voice trembles while he leaves a message. His hand trembles. His heart trembles. "It's Giovanni, call me, will you? I miss you so." You idiot, you fucker. I miss you, I said. Pitiful. Pathetic. But why the fuck did I say that?

(But it's true, it's true, it's true).

***

"I miss you too, Giovanni," Julie says, rounding her nasal '*n*'s in that peculiar French accent that Giovanni adores, that makes him think of her as a delicate, exotic thing, like mango. Giovanni melts, he calms down, but it doesn't last long.

How can I stay away from her? How can I live without her? It is a catastrophe, impossible agony. He calls again: "I forgot to say: please, Julie. Please write."

"Yes. Later."

***

But on that Saturday afternoon her friend Marianne gives her a ring, there is a party to go to, and Julie meets her friend Agnes' cousin, leaning against a door just like Lafcadio in Gide, and kisses him.

***

In Castel San Gerolamo the deafening silence resumes, and despair rises, one centimetre per hour. Giovanni calls Julie again, the following Sunday, but other voices answer the phone, not hers: first her brother and then her mother.

"Could you please ask her to call me back? Yes, it's Giovanni. In Italy. Thank you. Merci," he adds, feeling ashamed.

Silence.

So he phones again and leaves a message on her answering machine. He doesn't even say his name. He says: "Can you call me, Julie? I need to talk to you." And he leaves another message, and another, until Julie with her nutty, nasal voice replies: "Can you please stop calling me. I am here and you are there, I'll see you next July, maybe, but then, Giovanni, really: it was just a kiss, it's not as if we got married, so. OK, see you next year, yes?"

And he says nothing, he has trouble breathing, he locks himself in the bathroom and looks at himself in the mirror, crying.

***

"It's the end of August and December is in my heart," Giovanni writes on a notebook where sometimes he jots down his poetry. It's still scorching hot, the grapes nestled on the vines of the vineyards in the hills surrounding Castel San Gerolamo give off a ripe, sweet aroma. Giovanni is lying on the bed in his underwear, in his room up in the tower. He thinks about Julie all the time, morning, night, always. He hates everything and everyone – his friends, his father, most of all: his mother. He goes out, he walks, he sees Riccardo for an ice cream, he plays football, locks himself up again in his room, the Walkman constantly on, over his ears, to drown the sound of his thoughts. When he can't take it anymore, he picks up the phone and calls her. As soon as he hears her voice, he hangs up. When he hears the impersonal voice of voicemail, he leaves a message.

"Hello."

"It's just me" (why *just*? It's me, me, me, it's *me*).

"I hope you're fine."

"Sorry I called you too many times, I wanted to hear you."

"Talk."

"Remember."

"To remember on one's own is absurd, it feels as if I made it all up."

Sometimes he does not hang up, but breathes in the receiver ("like a pervert. It makes me feel dirty. But I want to hear her voice. Nothing else. Is it too much?") It is too much. One Sunday afternoon, when he returns home after a football game, his mother says:

"There's a message for you on the answering machine," she says, not looking at him in the eye. She is trying not to humiliate him.

Julie's voice is like silk, like velvet, like silk. She says "Giovanni" with one n. "Giovani," she says. And Giovanni clenches his fists and smiles. He smiles, before hearing the rest. "Giovanni. I have another, so. Don't call me again. *Basta.*"

***

Days pass, one without her, two without her, ten without her, fifteen without her, a whole month without her. Memories like flashes in the dark – shattering, violent: her face, her eyes, her hair. Yes, like a punch: again and again, even when he already feels as if he can't get any lower: he tries to pull himself up, but lays down again: right, left. Punch, punch.

The deafening silence of the phone, of the letter-box, his pathetic reading books of poetry in his father's study – he copies verses in a notebook, sniffing. He falls asleep crying, thinking of her. He wakes up tired and thinks about her. He eats and thinks about her. He walks and thinks of her. He sees his friends and thinks of her. He breathes and thinks of her. And it is all a cliché, a fucking cliché, because love is a cliché, to fall in love is a cliché, to have your heart broken is such a cliché.

Giovanni is sixteen, and he wonders: but what is this love which everyone talks and writes and makes films about? What is the nature of falling in love, what is its function, its history? He, Giovanni, is he in love with her, Julie, Amber, yes, with that girl, that person, really, or is he only in love only with an idea that he - he, Giovanni - created? Is it a need? A void wide open in his heart, as big the Grand Canyon, a void she alone, could fill up, fly over, like a helicopter? She came too close. It crashed, like Thelma and Louise on their raucous adventure.

***

Inevitably, jealousy follows. Because it is easier to pick on another rather than on her. To remove the responsibility for lifting him off her shoulders. Off her. It wasn't her fault, maybe. There must be another. There *is* another. Another boy - who kissed her, who touched her, who smelled her sweet sweet scent, that looked into her eyes, those yellow pools that seem gold; or piss.

"Ass piss slut cunt"

"Fuck shit piss cunt."

And I think of her new boyfriend increasingly, he becomes the Other and I even give him a face and a voice and muscles and hair and a dick, and I cover my ears but I can't stop to hear him, he calls her my bitch, my little bitch, and I listen again and again to the tape of the answering machine with her voice on it, one two three times, her nasal accent drives me crazy, makes me shrink with desire and hatred, but what the hell, what a fucking whore, but I listen to your voice once three ten times and I'm sick and I feel like I am exploding, I grab the device and fling it against a wall. The tape gets all tangled - now I don't even have her voice any longer. I can't hear her any more.

***

Marieke watches him like a cat who is about to spring forward, to strike: she looks carefully, aiming at the object of her interest: her hind legs ready to leap, her nails to resheathe, the jaws open wide. No: even better: she's like a lioness - thirsty for justice, ready to fight to save her cub. Her battered puppy, who instead of running over to her and get licked, prefers to turn his back on her and stay all alone. Lonely and alone rather than with her.

I hate you, I hate you, I hate you.

THE HEART OF THE OCTOPUS

Luigi moves around him slowly, with grace, careful not to make any noise, not to be heard. What can Luigi remember of the first disappointment in love, of the first time you get a broken heart? He remembers enough to seek a solution: a hot, true, simple joy. A live being, to hug and to look after. A puppy. He seeks and finds him – a reddish mongrel, a mix of spaniel, cocker, who knows what else, funny, awkward, tremendously cute. Giovanni notices him immediately, returning from school; he's hiding in the doorway, intent on gnawing on a slipper. He falls onto his knees, pressing his lonely lips in the dog's hot fur, smothering him in a tight embrace.

Argos, he calls the pet - platitudes from high school, but Argos is worthy of its name: the dog seems to recognise the need that Giovanni has of him. He's faithful, he always waits for the boy, he follows him everywhere, sleeps on a pillow at the foot of his bed. Argos is the friend that Giovanni has never had, that he will never have: present, affectionate, loyal even when his master is not, even when he leaves, when he treats him badly, when he ignores him, when he even kicks him for revenge. The dog always comes back and sniffs his hands and looks at him as if to say: 'do with me what you want'. Argos is the girl he'd like to have: totally his.

***

Slowly, inevitably, as nature dictates, Giovanni goes through each of the five stages of grief and loss: denial and isolation; anger; negotiation; depression; acceptance - but this last one is slow in coming.

School starts again; if nothing else, it gives a rhythm to his pain - a dull rhythm, always the same, as pale and as stale as yesterday's bread, yet somehow useful: counting the days from one term to the next, time passes. Time passes. Autumn comes, there is the grape harvest, the light fades a little more with each passing day; it gets colder. The first frost. Giovanni can't stand the warmth of home, the lights, the fire crackling; he can't bear his mother; he goes out as much as he can, with the excuse to take the dog out for a walk. He runs with Argos through the lush Piedmontese countryside, leaves rustling under his feet, Argos barking happily at his side. Chestnuts, persimmons, apples, pears. The leaves of the chestnut tree in front of the house turn into red flames, and yellow - yellow as Julie's eyes: they were – are – yellow, hazelnut, and brown, sometimes there was a splash of green.

From his observation post in his bedroom in the tower, Giovanni watches the leaves of the tree turn red and yellow until they dry up, and fall.

***

Leaves fall and die, like my heart.

***

The house on the hill is surrounded by a garden that is almost completely lawn; on the other side of the road is the vineyard, some fruit trees, and Luigi's orchard. On the left side, downhill and slightly hidden, is a garage, a tool shed and a little Wendy house painted orange. It was once Giovanni's den. One Saturday morning, after taking Argos for a walk, Giovanni looks for the keys to the shed, hidden under a stone by the door. He finds them and walks in, and for a while rummages amongst the various boxes of stuff piled up here over the years and end up here and in the attic: lamps that no longer work, a wrought-iron bed, a gold-framed mirror, boxes full of plates and glasses, all the stuff that Marieke does not want to give away. She is a hoarder, perhaps because she lives so far away from her home country and needs to keep things as a museum to the past. Giovanni opens the boxes at random, examines their content: here are two pictures of when he was at nursery, there he is at a basketball game, here he is on a school trip. His brown curls, skinned knees, the laughing green eyes. He can't recognise himself in that carefree child.

Behind the cabin he finds a rake; orderly, calmly, he collects the fallen leaves that have gathered under the chestnut tree; with a stick he beats down the few that are still attached to the branches, and he piles them up into a crunchy stack of bright yellow and red leaves, flashing like flames. Argos barks, runs in a circle, excited. Yellow. Giovanni throws the photographs he has found onto the top. He takes a lighter from his back pocket, and sets the whole thing alight.

***

Winter comes, without snow. Spring comes – and it hurts. It always hurts like mad, Spring, always - that awful tenderness you can't escape from. When you're seventeen, it kills you. Giovanni dies inside, a stab for each leaf that grows. He feels all shredded inside.

He discovers Plath, Neruda, and Yeats. Catullo. He knows that on the 10th May it is Julie's birthday. He sends her a note: *odi et amo*.

***

Giovanni has an argument with Luigi, one day, during lunch. An argument over nothing.

"Fucking hell. You just don't understand!" he shouts and leaves the dining room slamming the door. Then, silence.

Think about it: it's the Eighties: in those days a child, an adolescent, would never raise their voice, with their parents, with an adult. They would not slam doors. Not in houses like this, 'respectable', with old-fashioned parents; not in schools where pupils used to stand up when the teacher entered the classroom; when ipads and mobile phones did not exist to transform every meal into a silent ritual of hands clasped around dark rectangular devices. Thirty years ago, families had their meals together at the dinner table, they did not interrupt one another, people said thank you and please and had discussions about this and that.

Luigi and Marieke remain in their chairs, dazed – you see, people in Castel San Gerolamo might remember 1968 as a great year for Barolo; but the legendary protests of that year didn't have an echo, here; in this village, children never rebel, they are as quiet as sheep. Marieke gets up to follow her son. Luigi places a hand on her arm.

"No. Leave him alone," he says. "I am sure he's more mortified than us."

Giovanni reappears as they are eating their desserts and sits down without saying a word. He takes another apple from the fruit bowl and bites into it. It looks as if he's devouring a chunk of meat.

***

It's a Sunday afternoon. Grand auntie Mimmi, Luigi's mother's sister (a little lady with tight purple curls, all shrunken and hunched), and uncle Stefano (Luigi's twin brother, with whom he shares his accountancy practice), his wife and daughters (Lorella and Graziella, a few years younger than Giovanni) have come over for lunch, today, and stayed until four o'clock. After tidying up, the Ferraros have coffee and chocolates in the living room, and they all sit in front of the television, where they're showing, once again, the old film *Shane*, with Alan Ladd. They have all watched it several times before, but there is nothing else on. Marieke and Giovanni are sitting on the leather sofa, Luigi on his dark green tweed armchair, Argos is crouched in a corner; nobody talks for an hour and a half. When the final poignant music resounds in the house on the hill in the village of Castel San Gerolamo, the living room is full of sighs.

- Giovanni sighs a sigh of love, a feeling he has felt for the first time and that he has lost, also for the first time

- Marieke sighs for her middle age, for her expanding waistline, for her perpetual anxiety, for her life that is passing in front of her eyes like a carousel, without being able to stop it and get on

- Luigi sighs; and he sighs because he is not Shane the rider, and not even a strong, loyal Johnny. He strokes Argo.

***

But no, no, I'm doing this all wrong: I'm showing Giovanni as a pathetic (and therefore normal) teenager facing his first broken heart. But no, no: it is right at this point that the true story of Giovanni's heart begins. It was not a *little* heartache, something trivial and banal, a simple summer tryst. It was an educational experience - or its opposite. Here, now, everything starts; here, now, everything starts to crumble.

From adolescence, we develop and internalise a large autobiographical account of our lives, one that establishes who we are, who we were, and who we could be in the future; the first experiences remain imprinted in our psyche with a vividness and a clarity that does not fade in the same way other more mundane memories do. You never ever forget your first love: when you fall in love for the first time the neuronal circuits that regulate anxiety and fear change. We can't recall our fourth kiss, or the twelfth, but almost certainly we are able to remember many details of the first. What is called "romantic" love is a dopamine surge identical in all cultures. Romantic love is involuntary, difficult to control and in general it doesn't last long; moreover, the first relationship signifies both the first time you fall in love and also the first time you have your heart broken or break a heart. After that fateful first one, you can have many relationships, better or worse, but there will never be one in which you've never been hurt. Our first relationships form our psyche for life. Giovanni has met a young woman and has been touched deeply inside, in an intimate, unknown place, so very deeply in fact, that he has fallen into a kind of trance: he has fallen madly in love. When Amber left him, his brand new identity as a young man has crumbled, like a breadstick. How do you begin to put together the crumbs of a broken breadstick?

***

THE HEART OF THE OCTOPUS

Why yes I do go to church, sometimes, on Sundays, with my great Aunt Mimmi, who believes in those things; at Christmas; sometimes at Easter. I am Italian, and like most Italians, I was baptized and confirmed and did Holy Communion, even if nobody in my family is particularly churchy. Whenever I go to mass, I do so to please my auntie. It's to help her, to display my godliest smile and excellent manners, so that she can show off her lovely nephew to her friends. I go because mother is Protestant and would not enter into a Catholic church even if you paid her, and I respect her for this, I do, but sometimes I am aware I need to represent our family. That's how it's done, here. Although: come on, let me say it out loud and emphatically: no, I don't believe in Jesus and Joseph and the Virgin Mary since I left primary school - come on: it's stuff straight out of a fairy tale, like Santa Claus and the Tooth Fairy. But in a soul: oh yes, I do believe in what we call soul. I do. It's what makes us human, is it not? What distinguishes us from beasts. I'm studying philosophy: according to Plato, the soul was placed between the spinal cord and the cerebellum; Descartes thought it was in the pineal gland. For John Carew Eccles, Nobel Prize for neuro-biology, consciousness lies in pyramidal forms of sensory-motor cortex. For Aquinas, man is body and soul, namely matter and form; it is therefore at the same time spiritual substance (that is, a reasonable being, with intellect) and animal being (with a body informed by a sensitive and vegetative soul). For the doctrine of the Catholic Church, the soul is the vital principle from which every bodily action flows, that of the muscle-skeletal system as much as that of the psyche.

And you, my soul, where are you? Why did you abandon me? I can't find you anywhere. *Animula vagula blandula*: where the fuck did you go?

***

Luigi looks at him with a new tenderness – he remembers how hard it was, to fall in love.

"Can I stay home tomorrow? I have a test, a Greek translation. I'm not ready."

"Of course you can," Luigi says, but Marieke bites back:

"Of course you can't", she replies. "Why didn't you study in the first place? It is your problem. Your responsibility. What do you think that the whole wide world stops for your little heartbreak? Don't be ridiculous. Pull yourself together, wake up, and move on. You can't lose your head for love. For a little bland girl, furthermore ..."

"Julie's not a little bland girl!"

" ... Who has treated you so badly. My son certainly deserves better than that."

Giovanni goes out, slamming the door. It's becoming a habit.

"You're too hard on him," Luigi intervenes.

"But that's the truth. And you know what? He knows it, that's the truth."

"For him the truth is this great big love ..."

"No. Giovanni knows well what is the truth and if you hang him on a tree upside down, truth would fall out of his mouth. Face it. It was a passing thing. A summer fling. He'll get over it."

"Do you think so?"

"Of course. Everything passes. *Tout passe, Tout Lasse, Tout Casse.*"

"And?"

"And: you have to be tough, with young people. Especially when they are stubborn. You must be strict as you would with a puppy that keeps doing his business on the carpet. Argos was already older, and it had been weaned and had learned to go outside, but do you know how you teach a puppy? You hold it by its collar and you stick its face in it. In its own poo."

"Poor Giovanni. You are too tough. He's only young ..."

"Giovanni is young. And foolish."

"He's lost his head ..."

"Young, foolish and headless."

"He's fallen in love…"

"And she left him, and badly. You know what? That's good. That's great. It's much, much better to learn the lesson now, early on: stop having your head in the air and your heart open to adventure. Better to take a whack now than when he's studying for his Baccalaureate. Better to understand that the world is hard and bad, and that it will hurt you. You will get hurt. Shit happens. Better to have shit when you are little, and caviar when you grow up."

***

Giovanni is a good swimmer - Marieke, freestyle champion aged twelve, has taken him to swimming lessons with religious rigour once a week, since he was three years old. Giovanni doesn't have the makings of a champion – he is weak, he tires easily, he suffers from earache, Trino's pool is far away, he doesn't have enough time – nor is he interested in becoming a champion, to win a medal, to have his photograph published in the local newspaper. Undeterred, Marieke continues to take him swimming every Friday night.

It's six o'clock. Giovanni is tired, cold. He tries to protest, but there's no way: Marieke doesn't do excuses.

"Are you exhausted? I tell you what: go to bed early, tonight. Are you cold? Get into the water, you'll warm up in no time. You have a little cold? Well: your nose is a long way from your heart."

And here he is, QED, in the water: up and down, up and down the twenty-five metre pool. Marieke is like an eagle: she does not take her eyes from his back. Sitting on the steps of the area reserved for spectators, right in front row. She observes everything. She keeps tabs: every week he has to do at least thirty lengths; once a month, fifty. Today is that day. Marieke counts.

"Thirteen; fourteen." She looks at him hit the water with his arms, his legs kicking furiously. "Eighteen, nineteen." Giovanni stops by one end, looks at her. "Come on," she whispers. The pool is not that big, there are very few spectators; he hears her perfectly.

"I'm tired."

"Tired of what. Come on," she repeats. "*Kom Op.*"

Giovanni jumps on the spot, moves his neck from side to side, his shoulders up and down, massages his back. Then he dives back in and starts to swim. Marieke starts to count all over again. "Twenty-nine, thirty, thirty-one." The other lanes are empty, except the first, used by a group of children who dive in turn. "Forty-one, Forty-two," Marieke counts. Giovanni stops, puts his hands on the edge, looks at her.

"I'm dead tired," he says. "Really. I can't do it."

"Of course you can," Marieke replies. Giovanni bows his head, remains motionless. Marieke is waiting. She waits a bit longer. And when nothing happens, when it is clear that Giovanni has no intention to move, she takes off her shoes, pulls up the hem of her trousers, climbs over the fence that separates the spectators' gallery from the pool and walks over to her son, who finally raises his head. Marieke – incredibly slowly, so slowly that Giovanni isn't sure whether it is a hallucination, a kind of film in slow motion, or his utter disbelief - lifts one foot, and puts it down over his hand.

"Seven to go. *Kom op.*"

***

Giovanni is in pain.

Giovanni weeps, despairs. Giovanni plays with Argos and hits him, hits him and apologises, hugs him, burrowing his nose in his thick fur. The pet reminds him of his mother's mink coat: as a child, like Lucy in *Lion, The Witch and The Wardrobe*, he liked to sneak into what Marieke used to call the armoire, to sink his face in the fur, which was soft, hot, and smelled of mamma, a softer and warmer mum than Marieke, a true Mother, a SuperMother, a mother-mother, something that Marieke had never been. Argos's hair has a wild scent, doesn't smell of her perfume *Calèche*, but the feeling that it produces (safety, tenderness, abandonment, love) is the same.

One day he loses Julie's photograph and looks everywhere for it – he pulls out all the drawers, looks under the bed, under the cabinet, he even, with great effort, moves the dresser. He turns out the pockets of every pair of trousers that he owns, rummages through the papers on the desk, between the pages of books on the shelves, under the books. Nothing.

(Marieke found it, and hid it. Giovanni will discover it many years later, among her letters, and will weep with rage).

***

Every grief is different. And yet when you try to describe what it feels like, to be grieving, you realise all descriptions sound the same. Pages and pages of literature are devoted to the notion of loss, and whether that loss is due to abandonment, death, or disappearance, it does not matter. Loss is told in such a way to become a stereotype, a cliché. A heavy heart, rivers of tears, weight loss, sleepless nights. The film one plays in one's mind, images of the happy time when one was happy, inevitably followed by the return to reality, resulting in a slip back to anguish. Blood and tears.

Even falling in love, or the joy that comes from falling in love, is equally inexpressible, inexplicable – each time it is a unique and personal experience, and yet it is also universal and generic, and there you go, swimming again into an ocean of clichés. We can't do anything but rinse out our mouth, spit out the dirty contents, and try to find new words, not those that have been licked sucked and sucked to death, like candy.

***

Time passes.

Six months, one year, three years: it doesn't matter. I don't care. Yes, Giovanni studies, he's a good boy, he tries to delete his amber-ish memories with the learning by heart of Cicero and the Greek lyrics (look at him, now: in his room, sitting at his desk, hunched over the vocabulary as if it were Playboy magazine, while actually he's translating Tacitus and Seneca).

***

Lying like a turtle over the surrounding hills, Castel San Gerolamo is a beautiful village made up of well-kept homes, surrounded by meadows and vineyards, compact, and: c*orrugated*, is how Marieke describes it. "Because everything: the houses and streets and trees - everything follows the wave of these soft rolling hills." Soft, ductile, malleable - the opposite of its tough inhabitants, all grumpy, dour.

The village doesn't change much, in all these years. There aren't VIPs and more or less known celebrities to discover the Monferrato region of Piedmont, to buy castles and villas and build pools and spas, to push tourism forwards. Now, in the Nineties, there are only a bar and restaurant where people go on Sundays to eat tongue in *salsa verde* and *carpaccio* and *agnolotti* and the delicious *fritto misto*; and local farmers tend to the vines, theirs and those of those wealthier owners who can afford to live elsewhere. There are very few immigrants, Eastern European and North African migrants haven't yet arrived - the local population ages and decreases, young people leave, only the old and children remain, and it is a shame. "It's a *darnagi*," they say. It is a local expression that means disappointment and compassion and love for the things of the past and the pleasure one feels looking after them properly, and the sin that it is to let them vanish. It's a shame that Castel San Gerolamo is not in Tuscany or in Umbria, where it would receive thousands - hundreds of thousands - of wealthy Americans on pilgrimage, fascinated by local history and the delicious food and wine. Yes, there are churches to visit - but not cathedrals frescoed by Fra Angelico or Giotto. There are beautiful wineries - but not the huge farms of Chiantishire. There are curiosities, interesting local history, but nobody cares enough to make something out of it.

For example, in the Eighteenth century Giovanni Battista Boetti, a Dominican friar, was born in Piazzano, a local village. Under the name of *Al Mansur*, the Victorious, at the head of eighty thousand men, Boetti conquered Armenia, Kurdistan and Georgia and reigned for six years as an absolute monarch; he even managed to seduce Tsarina Catherine II, Empress of Russia. An incredible, legendary story: had it happened in Florence, the council would have erected a magnificent statue in the middle of Piazza della Signoria. But here, there is only a little sign affixed to the front of the house where he was born. Or look at the castle in Camino: it is said that in 1494, the count Scarampo Scarampi, lord of the Marquis of Monferrato, was accused of treason; after a long siege, he was captured and beheaded. Apparently Scarampo still roams around the remains of the castle, holding his own head in his hands ... but once again, we are in the Monferrato, not in California. The story hasn't inspired a blockbuster film, or a novel. The rolling hills are gorgeous, but everyone leaves.

Giovanni can't wait to run away from it all.

***

Everybody had talked of the Baccalaureate as a ritual, a trial, real evidence, the marking of the passage from adolescence into adulthood. I am relaxed, my shyness resembles politeness, good education, composure. When it comes to Latin, I quickly realise I've already translated that passage of Pliny, and I have memorised *Phaedo* by heart. I get top marks.

I am told I have the world in front of me, I simply have to make a choice: and you know what, this story of 'having a choice' seems to me an astonishing rip off. If I choose, and I'm wrong, I can't even blame someone else - only myself. They tell me that this is precisely what it means to grow, to become adults: the understanding that the responsibility is always and only and especially of our own making. What an effort. What a fucking weight. I'm only eighteen.

To choose is a verb that means to pick out (someone or something) the best or most appropriate of two or more alternatives. Me, well: I'd choose to sit still and watch the passing of time, just like a soldier looks at the corpses of his enemies that float in the river, down south.

THE HEART OF THE OCTOPUS

***

After his Baccalaureate, his great aunt gives him an envelope full of money. Instead of spending it travelling with his mates, as suggested by his father (but who is he referring to? wonders Giovanni. Pietro, Riccardo, Lorenzo - whose idea of going for a trip means a visit to nearby Milan, two hours by car?), he decides to follow his mother's advice and to go to Switzerland. Marieke has worked hard at this, requesting brochures from prestigious colleges and leaving them around, ready to be found. Giovanni takes the bait, reads them, makes calls, asks for further information. Eventually, he chooses to spend six weeks at an exclusive summer school in Montreux, Switzerland, to study English and French, to learn horse-riding and windsurfing ("a truly unique place" Marieke calls it, her eyes shining like a diamond ring in the mouth of a crow). The main house was a former luxurious hotel, surrounded by manicured lawns, tennis courts, a colossal swimming pool. He makes friends with Filippo, the boy he shares the room with. He comes from Turin, he's nineteen years old, bold and anxious, like Giovanni, as curious and as intimidated by the place as he is.

On Saturday night, when they are allowed to leave the college, they split the cost of a taxi with a group of friends to go and drink in a bar in Vevey; it is the same place where girls of another exclusive school gather on the same night, and the two groups eye each other, sniff one another until it's almost time to leave; only then they start to talk, to exchange names and the promise to see each other again. The following Saturday they meet again. Giovanni drinks two beers and kisses two girls (Mimi and Orsina); the next he drinks three beers and kisses three girls (Shaila, Margot, Babettli). On the third weekend, he sets eyes on "Leila, a fascinating, taciturn girl from Saudi, a little chubby but with black, glowing eyes and sporting earrings heavy with diamonds and sapphires as big as eggs, probably worth billions.", as he writes home. Leila lets Giovanni explore her mouth, neck, breasts – but: above her bra - and unexpectedly, and with surprising dexterity, opens his zip and shoves her hand in his pants.

On the fourth weekend in Montreaux (Saturday, August 4th 1984, at 10:40PM approximately), Giovanni loses his virginity, on a lawn next to the lake, to Leila.

***

Stars were falling, crickets were crying, while I sank into Leila's butter, her flesh open and hazelnutty and wet, offered to me as if to a god. I took her – that's the correct expression, isn't it? - without telling her it was my first time. Surely it was not the first for her, but I didn't mention it. She smells of incense and I don't like that scent, her legs are covered with dense and thin and soft hair, and it is this softness that surprised me. To have her under me, as hairy and soft as a cat, a pussy cat, yes. Yes. It made me want to crush her with my weight, with the pointy bones of my pelvis, to crush and to hurt her, but she seemed pleased, she was kind of moaning, perhaps she was pretending, but I tried to press my body on her, again and again, squeezing, pressing, compressing, pressing. I understood completely the origin of the expression: to screw. I came all of a sudden, too fast, falling onto her like a soldier shot to death.

***

He throws Leila aside – a bit like discarding the glossy golden wrapper of a chocolate. After her there are the Swedish Pia, the American Serena. In late August, his diary bulging with new addresses, he returns home.

***

Now, don't think that Giovanni has forgotten Julie, even if it has been exactly two years from the end - and the beginning - of their short story. He *always* thinks about her; every day. No: several times a day. When he gets up and when he falls asleep, when he's studying and when he isn't studying, when he's reading and eating and breathing and even - or especially when there is the warm body of another girl in his arms. That sense of recognition, that abandonment. That discovery.

But it's autumn, he must enrol at university, find a place to stay. After many hesitations, discussions, quarrels, he chooses to study Law in Turin. Marieke wanted him to be an engineer, his father kept telling him to follow his heart and study literature.

"And then?"

"What?"

"What would he do? What career would he follow? Would he become – what: a teacher? A professor? *Hou je bek*," Marieke says. "It isn't the Fifties. We have to have your eyes open to the future, choose a solid profession."

"He could become a journalist. Or a writer. He could work for a publishing house," Luigi tries to argue. "The point is that Giovanni has to choose what he likes, what he will be. Not us."

"But I'm only eighteen! I don't know what I want to do, what I want to be. It's too early. I want to study something that gives me several options - lawyer, judge, notary, who knows."

"Perhaps an international career," Marieke sighs.

"Mamma dreams of you in De Hague ..."

His aunt Piera, Luigi's sister, lives in Turin. Through her formidable network of bridge players, she helps him find an apartment near the university: 365,000 lire a month for two bedrooms, a lounge with a kitchenette and a bathroom. Giovanni goes to inspect it with Marieke. She opens every door, checks the windows, the locks. The following week he returns with Lorenzo, a boy from Cantavenna, the son of one of Luigi's clients, with whom he'll share the rent. Lorenzo is studying Medicine, he spends all his time studying in the library. Perfect.

THE HEART OF THE OCTOPUS

***

"I open and close the kitchen cabinets. I look at my plates, and they are solid in my hands, cream coloured. There are four wine and four water glasses. Two large mugs, and two small cups with matching saucers. Three pots, a colander. And in the wardrobe in our bedroom, sheets, blankets, pillows. All new, all mine. My life starts now."

***

Back home in Castel San Gerolamo, Argos lies down, as always, on the threshold of Giovanni's room, which has remained intact - a museum to Giovanni and to his childhood. The red train he loved so much carefully arranged on the windowsill, his collection of airplanes on the top shelf of the bookcase, above his many books: the Encyclopaedia at the top, modern classics - Pavese, Fenoglio, Dickens – on the lower shelves. In the wardrobe, his clothes seem to him dated, passé, musty, as if they were those of someone else, not his own. Those white sneakers. Those tight jeans. That t-shirt, too short for him. They don't belong to him - not this room, not these clothes, not this house. Argos gnaws a shoe long abandoned. Giovanni is elsewhere - and yet, and yet, even his new bedroom, in the apartment next to Porta Nuova he shares with Lorenzo, is not "home." He feels a new feeling, strange, confused. At Montreaux he had learned an English verb that he had never heard before, and that now he looks for it in the dictionary.

To long for: to want something very much especially if it does not seem likely to happen soon. Synonym: to yearn. There you are: to feel an intense desire for something. *To long for* implies an almost physical yearning, and this is what he is experiencing: the feeling of not being well, not quite, not completely; to have an irresistible *longing for* something different, more, less, something that is elsewhere, not here. As if in Giovanni were on tiptoes, elongating his thin long body in search of something. Longing for: something, someone, somewhere.

***

We leave Giovanni today, on this sunny October day, in his two-room apartment in Turin.

He's satisfied, content, pleased. "Warm, inside," is how he puts it. He is happy to be away from his small, short-sighted village, away from his mother who always breathes over him sighs of dissatisfaction, smothering him, full as she is of anxieties, of expectations. Giovanni wants to dream his own dreams. He's a pleasant young man, provincial, a little timid. He attends his lessons; he studies with pleasure. He gets along with his flatmate, who's not home much. His only entertainment, on a Friday afternoon, consists in meeting his friend Riccardo in town, to drink hot chocolate in a posh café. They chat, they discuss the news, their studies. Sometimes they go and see an exhibition; sometimes they go to the cinema, to a gig, a dinner party.

In Castel San Gerolamo the big house at the top of the hill is desolate without him; that Marieke agonises and is consumed by his absence, alternates pride and despair, that old desire for reflected glory; that Luigi continues to work in his office with his brother. He comes home for lunch and dinner but his real passion is to grow stuff in his orchard - his soul is in his little garden. Argos misses his owner even if Luigi takes him regularly for a walk. They pine together for Giovanni: son and master.

A few kilometres away, Giovanni feels reborn, renewed: there is so much to explore, the streets and squares of Turin, the Po river, churches and museums, his university. He goes home every two Fridays. At twenty past six, waiting for him at the bus stop is his mother, ready to swallow him whole. During those visits Giovanni can't wait for it to be Sunday evening again, when he can return to Turin. But let's leave him, now. Let's leave Giovanni in the autumn of 1984.

The rest is another story.

PART II

At long last, Giovanni graduates with a thesis entitled "The false procurator and his apparent representative." Mr Guarnieri, a solicitor with an established practice and a friend of his Aunt Piera, offers him a job dealing with administrative and tax law. Only once he has passed the interview and signed the official employment contract, Giovanni tells his parents (who knew already, as Aunt Piera can't keep secrets). Marieke rushes to Turin, check-book in hand; they seek and find a new flat for him: a studio in via Mazzini, in an elegant building with a porter and marble stairs, not too far from his office and the Po river. Marieke takes her son shopping, buys him two new suits, a briefcase. In the evening, Luigi joins them, reserving a table at "Cambio," one of the best restaurants in Turin. Giovanni walks in in his squeaky new shoes and they are already there waiting for him, his family, seated at a round table, intimidated, embarrassed, unspeakably proud: Luigi, Marieke and his Aunt with a champagne flute in her shaky old hand.

"*Salute*," Luigi says.

"Cheers," Giovanni says.

"Cheers. Bravo, Giovanni," Marieke says, beaming.

"Thank you."

"It's only the beginning," Luigi says. "You'll see."

"We'll see."

We use the future tense when we discuss events that are somewhat uncertain; or when the event is at a considerable distance of time in the future. Finally, his future is here. Giovanni feels excited and impatient. He sings an old song by Luigi Tenco: *Vedrai*. You'll see you'll see that change, maybe not tomorrow, but one day, everything will change. You'll see.

***

Mr Guarnieri is old-fashioned, his office is out of date and out of style, with a thick carpet that muffles one's steps, leather armchairs, antiquated lampshades - furniture his many wealthy clients approve of. Guarnieri & Co. counts five associates, three trainees and two secretaries, a blonde and a brunette. The solicitor sports old school manners, he has a peculiar way of teaching the juniors, he is fussy and slow - but it doesn't matter. Everything is fine for Giovanni, who fits the study like a leather shoe made to measure fits a problematic foot: he's diligent, not at all haughty, composed. Humble. Self-conscious, shy, introverted, but with bright flashes and a loud laughter, out of tune, like a cascade that comes out of his open mouth, his fingers lightly tapping on his knees. He's polite, respectful, modest. The perfect example of a Piedmontese boy from a good family. Colleagues and clients and secretaries - everyone in a friendly chorus, in unison - welcome him with total, paternal acceptance.

He likes the office, the relationships between the various partners – the ones that get on and the ones that don't, those that in fact detest each other; who is respected and who isn't, who is idle and who works hard. He likes to get in early, when it is still dark – he lives only five minutes away – and quickly attend to what needs his attention, sipping coffee prepared by Cinzia, the brunette. He likes to see approval in Guarnieri's shining, myopic eyes, he likes the sense of belonging that a steady job has bestowed upon him. He's "part of the team, of the squad," as Mr Guarnieri repeats, whose passion for football, and Juventus in particular, permeates all his sentences. Giovanni pretends to cheer over Baggio's exploits, Giovanni nods, Giovanni readily agrees, while inside, he's bursting with anxiety - there's a whole world to learn, to memorise: names and items and situations completely different from the abstractness of university.

He is in the office twelve hours straight, from seven in the morning until seven in the evening, sometimes even on Saturdays. He doesn't go out much, at night – he's never been a disco type. He decides to attend a sommelier course, with the dual purpose of learning something new and of meeting new people, but neither is successful. He enrols at a gym, but doesn't feel at ease, and ends up never going. On Sundays, he is often invited to lunch by his aunt; he takes long walks along the Po. He is alone most of the time, and wish he could bring Argos over to his flat, see him wag his tail madly when he comes home in the evening, feel his weight at the foot of the bed when he wakes up; but it would be cruel to leave the dog alone all day, and he's accustomed to the countryside, the city would kill him. He sees him when he can, when he returns to Castel San Gerolamo, and the dog runs to meet him with his mouth open, drooling, crazy with happiness, to see his boss, his lord, the one for whom he would happily die. Giovanni runs alongside him, slower but equally happy, drunk with life and hope.

***

I am as lonely and as satisfied as a Benedictine monk: work and home, home and work alternate in a regular manner, a secular, capitalist *ora et labora*. In the office, after the first few weeks, I have settled down, I feel recognised: with time, associates and clients have come to know me, remember my name. And also because slowly my own work feels approved of: I work methodically, I work well.

"Bravo, Giovanni. Well done," Guarnieri said last Tuesday, and I blushed with pleasure like a spinster. Talking about spinsters: I'm definitely turning into one: at the end of each day I walk out of the office, I stop to do some shopping – a pound of *prosciutto crudo*, a bit of *fontina* cheese, some fruit – I walk up the stairs, open the door, close it again behind me, and here it is, My Little World. I sit on the couch and look around with lustful eyes: my lair, my shell. It is the first time that I've lived on my own: truly alone, not with a roommate. Nobody comes here, no one knows whether I open the windows to get some fresh air, if I change the sheets, plump up the cushions, whether I leave wet towels on the floor (I don't; I don't; I don't). Sometimes I remain in my pyjamas from Saturday afternoon to Monday morning, without going out - what a relief, this liberation from the world. Nobody knows if and when I get up, at what time I go to sleep, if I watch TV for hours or read or wank. If I eat, and what, when, how (mostly pasta with pesto in a bowl decorated with little flowers, whilst watching television). Am I sad? Not one bit.

I'm truly a Bachelor. Nobody moves what I touch. The empty glass remains exactly where I left it the night before, on the bedside table. In the sink, the pan I did not feel like washing last night is caked over with dry pesto, as hard as concrete. On the floor there's yesterday's paper or the one from the day before yesterday, and my slippers. This mess in my studio – my cell – is kind of subdued, it's very Piedmontese, *sotto voce*: the sofa-bed still unmade, the light bulb that I have not changed, the empty fridge, cabinets full of spaghetti and tinned tomatoes. It makes me smile: I have made this mess. I lie in it. I like it. I discovered the virtues of the bath tub, and every night I soak for a while, before going to bed; I lie in the water with a book and a glass of wine. I feel exactly like that water: fresh, firm, fluid.

***

Giovanni buys a plant - a small palm tree - and a goldfish that he names Mario. Both die within a few weeks. Too much water, too much food, too much attention. He learns another lesson: less is more. Care less.

***

Giovanni looks after his flat properly, not as a student – he cleans it thoroughly once a week; he dusts and hoovers and mops, using bleach liberally; he puts on loads of washing separating white and dark items, puts the laundry out to dry on the narrow balcony; he discovers he rather likes to iron, and is fastidious about his collars, his cuffs. And he enjoys cooking, not for himself, but for his few friends. He calls them over regularly for dinner. This weekend he's invited the boy he met in Montreux, and Gianpiero, a former college friend. He prepares mushroom risotto, a salad, a big bowl of tiramisu. They have a glass of Prosecco to start with, then drink a whole bottle of Dolcetto, they laugh, they smoke, they listen to music, they try some Irish whisky. When his friends leave, at half-past one, full of good intentions (yes, they'll go running together on Sunday mornings, they'll reserve a table for their

Carnival dinner at the Rotary club, of which Gianpiero's parents are members, they'll go on the pull, next Saturday night, at a new club) the little studio is full of smoke. Giovanni opens the window, looks out, his elbows resting on the windowsill.

"Wine makes me see hundreds of stars, thousands, billions, trillions! All there to wink at me, to twinkininkle (Is that even a word? But it's perfect, it really is) in the sky as black as the bible. They make you feel so small, these stars so far away; I can't begin to imagine planets and our Universe, or other galaxies beyond ours: I get dizzy. I am here, a little human being on Earth, surrounded by stars – they are so vivid and so close that one could almost mistake them for fireflies and lock them up inside a jar. They are diamonds on a velvet cushion, drops of fairy dust, god's tears, flashes of fire, and I admire them high above the city, while I sit in my flat all alone, but I am not alone, not now, not in this city full of stars, this cold night full of stars. I feel alive, like never before. A few weeks ago I said to myself: is this what it is, life? This? And now I say: "Yes, yes, yes," breathlessly. "Yes. Yes. Yes."

***

In mid-December there's a Christmas party in the office, with panettone and champagne, funny anecdotes about clients, several toasts to the coming year. Cinzia giggles, Mr Rossi's eyes linger on Mariarosa's neckline, lively like wasps. Mr Guarnieri gives Giovanni a fountain pen (which he puts in his desk drawer, along with the other three pens he already owns), he shakes his hand vigorously.

"Merry Christmas!"

"Happy Christmas to you, sir," Giovanni replies. The office is half empty. Cinzia stays back as it is her duty to close up for the holidays. Giovanni offers to help: together they lower the blinds, close the curtains, water the plants, lock the doors. There is a strange intimacy, in the darkness, in the hushed atmosphere of the silent office. No hope for romance, he thinks, looking at her plump lips while she's applying fresh lipstick before leaving: Cinzia is in her fifties, is happily married. He's not even sure he needs romance. He quite enjoys being single; not forever, no; but he's not ready, or hasn't met the right girl yet. He likes to spend time on his own as much as he likes the nights out with his mates. He's had a couple of one-night stands, in the last few months, and has enjoyed them – the frisson of the first kiss, the thrill of those new hands on his body, the mutual understanding that there wasn't to be a sequitur.

Giovanni returns to Castel San Gerolamo for a week. The ritual is always the same: on Christmas Eve there is dinner with his grandparents. The Ferraros host Christmas lunch, with his uncle and aunt and cousins. Marieke puts out their best dinner service and crystal cut glasses: three each, for water and white wine and red wine. In a corner, the large fake Christmas tree is hidden by tens of baubles, and glittering tea lights, snow globes, hanging stars, Santa Claus figurines, a huge angel on top of the tree; she always goes over the top with the decorations, always – and they stay up until mid-January. Giovanni is this year's focus of attention.

"Hello stranger," his Great Aunt says, holding him tight.

"A real man of the world," his uncle says, and Giovanni sees pride sparkle in his parents' eyes.

"Well, not really…" Giovanni says.

"Do you have a girlfriend?"

"No, he doesn't," Marieke replies. After Julie, they've never discussed girls. "He has to work hard. He can't let anything distract him," she adds. Giovanni winks to his uncle as if to suggest that he *is*, really, a man of the world, with girls falling at his feet, but: well, his parents don't know. His uncle winks back. Let them believe what they want to believe.

"How many parties have you been invited to for New Year's Eve?"

In truth, Giovanni has no plans; the prospect of spending the last night of the year by himself actually appeals to him. He imagines lying on the sofa, drinking a whole bottle of Prosecco, watching a mediocre TV show with people pretending to enjoy themselves. He gets a last minute invitation to a party near Superga, where he eats and drinks and flirts, and comes home late, tired, happy: there he is: sitting in the back seat of a taxi, admiring the city lights in front of his drunken eyes, the taste of alcohol that goes up and down along his oesophagus like a wave of the sea. He didn't drink enough to be sick - sure, he will have a headache tomorrow, but nothing more. On the other hand, he feels cheerful, lucky to be exactly where he finds himself right now, in this darkest pre-dawn. Look at him, at 3:13 am on January 1st:

"Sitting in a Mercedes as black as the Mafia, with the driver who has a pseudo-leather jacket as black as the Mafia, and they are matchy-matchy like my mum's bedspread and curtains, and he doesn't speak and doesn't ask and doesn't as much as glance at me in the back mirror; who knows what he thinks, who knows why he doesn't celebrate this night with someone: he's like me, we are men, alone, but not lonely. I feel not just my eyes but the whole of my being suddenly open: no: wide open; there is a whole massive world out there, but out there is out here, I am in it, I am a part of it, Christ it *is* there, I can almost touch it, yes indeed I can hold it with both hands. I feel like Gordon Gekko in *Wall Street*, cocaine, money and money and the lights of the city, Turin isn't Manhattan but god god god how beautiful it is, with its French boulevards, its impressive palaces, elegant squares, majestic and subdued at the same time. And all these shining lights. I wish I could see Julie now, my Amber, now, right now, while sitting in the back of this black Mercedes, zooming through the city in this black night. I want her to see that I am not a needy little boy. I am a man. You know like when Olivia Newton-John comes out at the end of *Grease*, wearing a tight black leather suit, with high heels and whore-curly hair, and sings *You're the One*

That I Want and John Travolta stares at her, his mouth open like a trout? That's precisely the reaction I'd like Julie to have when she sees me. No more provincial baby, but a man who comes out at night, and goes home when it's almost morning. The bars are all closed: what a shame. I'd like to tell the driver: 'Here, let me out here, please', and see him fly out to open my door like I'm Queen Elizabeth, and walk into a five-star hotel and order an English breakfast with eggs and bacon and buttered hot toast. But no, there is no stylish hotel around here, I can buy some bacon tomorrow, never mind, but it will be a good year, yeah, I know it, I know it. RIP my eggs and bacon, my Queen Elizabeth – I feel like a king all the same. And you know what? Julie, look at me, Julie, look at me look at me straight in the eye: Julie: Fuck you."

***

Giovanni is busy. There are deadlines he can't miss, a couple of parties he wants to go to, a ten km run he has planned with his friends. He enjoys his own company, the busy days followed by quiet nights in, the contentedness of his suppers, the DVDs he rents on Friday nights, with a takeaway pizza, and the joy of porn, which he has re-discovered after twenty years from the first dirty magazine. One summer, when he was still at primary school, Marieke and Luigi had gone for a trip to the US – the journey of a lifetime, they kept repeating. Giovanni had been sent to his maternal grandparents at Egmond Aan Zee, in northern

Holland. He had spent weeks there, mostly with the children of their neighbours. They took long rides with their bicycles, dived into the cold sea, played among the high sand dunes; in the evening he returned home to his grandmother, an unsentimental woman who took care of him in a distant but practical, quick, accurate way.

"Go and have a bath, now. Dinner is ready in half an hour," she would say, and he obeyed instantly, not like at home with his mother, who had to beg to get him to do anything - get changed, brush his teeth, turn off the light and go to sleep. "Please. *Alsjeblieft*."

Grandma was tall and thin and had a voice you couldn't say no to, and big, bony hands that she did not fail to use; Giovanni remembers a slap on the right cheek that had turned him almost deaf - and only because he'd said he wasn't very hungry. Lesson learned immediately; from then on, his plate was spotlessly clean, after every meal. He didn't have his favourite toys, during that summer at Egmond, he didn't have his favourite food, nor his best friends; but Giovanni enjoyed the freedom to do what he wanted for hours, without control, without an adult checking on him, telling him that this was forbidden, that was dangerous, that it was too early or too late or to put on another jumper or to take it off; he left his grandparents' house at eight in the morning and came back at seven in the evening, dirty, tired; no one asked him what he did all day.

THE HEART OF THE OCTOPUS

He and his new friends explored all around, on foot, by bicycle, in the water, in the sand, in the neighbouring villages; they were looking for treasures, like pirates: they found crabs, little fishes, flowers, shells, pieces of cloth, cardboard, glass. They collected everything as if they were precious objects, jewels that he hid in a box under the bed. They competed all the time, for everything: who arrived first at the beach, at the square, at the street lamp at the top of the road; who could drink a whole bottle of lemonade; who had the courage to dive off from the bridge. His friends were Annie and Matt and Jonas, also parked by their grandparents all summer long; Jonas was the oldest, a real teenager (he was almost fourteen) the one whose approval they tried to gain, bringing him presents, offering him bottles of Coca Cola, buying ice cream, candy. Jonas was cool, he was three years older, he wore red tennis shoes and a denim jacket and sometimes a bandanna on his head, which everyone had tried to emulate, even though no one could muster the same coolness. One day he had brought a dirty magazine – nothing sophisticated, certainly not *Playboy*, Giovanni thinks trying to recall the details, remembering the sense of misunderstanding, of sudden excitement, of a tingling between his legs as he turned the pages and saw a bottom – no: an arse, for the first time. An arse, I repeat, not buttocks: firm and tanned, belonging to a naked blonde girl who was lying on her stomach on the sand, on a tropical beach. An arse the likes of which he had never seen, magnified and offered to the viewer (not unlike the way certain plates were photographed in the cookery magazines his mother used to buy, with dishes that looked succulent, dripping butter, ready to be devoured by the eyes of the hungry readers). Giovanni didn't know that the correct name was pornography. Giovanni was ten years old, he was a child interested in everything. He had looked at the magazine with curiosity; he did not expect his grandmother to get mad with all of them, and with a rage he never seen before. She had insisted on burning the magazine in a bonfire in the garden.

"That's how they burned witches," Jonas had said. Giovanni had said nothing, he had taken a slap, hard; had gone to bed without dinner, in the face of Dutch liberality. Almost twenty years ago, Giovanni thinks. When I was pure and innocent, like the first apple. I had not yet understood that everything in the world, even the most perfect, was damaged. Everything could rot, like fruit. How wrong was I.

***

It's Marieke's birthday – she is turning fifty. On Saturday night of January 21st, the Ferraros' living room is decorated like an American yard at Christmas, or at Halloween, with a riot of fairy lights hung around windows, doors, and flowers and candles and balloons everywhere. Marieke invited twenty people. Someone sent her flowers; others a bottle of champagne; still others arrive with boxes of chocolates, books, CDs. All guests wear fashionable clothes and high heels; Marieke is in a velvet blue dress; she has had her hair styled that afternoon, with curls that fall loose on her shoulders: a Botticellian Venus of a certain age, whom Luigi proclaims beautiful, and to whom, before the guests arrive, he gives a ring with a small rhomboid diamond in a white gold setting (which she wears immediately, even if she prefers yellow gold – if it's gold, she says, you need to be able to see it).

Giovanni has designated himself DJ for the evening with the help of the stereo that someone has lent for the occasion. Standing behind a table upon which the equipment is resting, he observes the various groups of adults chat and dance to the rhythm of the hottest songs of the year. The men stand on one side, drinking whiskey and talking about work. The women prefer white wine, and pull each other onto the centre of the room turned dance-floor. Daniela, Grazia, and Donatella dance together, laughing; Donatella's boobs swing like her name, under the blue silk shirt - Giovanni continues to look at them and look away, but those elongated, hard-boiled tits attract him like a magnet; he imagines the shape of her nipples and their taste, guesses how heavy they would be, resting on the palms of his hands. Marieke follows his gaze and observes her friend's breasts and her son's Adam's apple which rises and falls when he swallows.

"Gravity. Thank God it applies to everything and everyone," she thinks. She's overwhelmed by a disturbing mixture of physical revulsion and at the same time of unexplainable pride for that male son of hers who looks enchanted by Donatella's body, free and warm under the blouse, while incredibly her husband doesn't pay any attention to her, taken as he is by a discussion on the merits of Nebbiolo, on this year's tax return, on a new restaurant in Moncalvo, on Nebbiolo (again; his conversations are always circular).

Marieke drinks another glass of wine. In Castel San Gerolamo the revolutions of the Sixties and Seventies did not take root – of course, there has been the contraceptive pill since 1971; divorce was introduced in 1974 and abortion in 1978. But here there is only a confused echo of feminism, of the progress made by women: you can clearly see it tonight at this party, where men smoke and drink and make jokes that become scurrilous as the night goes on; they laugh too hard, make rude comments; Silvio even slaps Donatella's backside. And she, not at all annoyed, turns around with a spicy, flattered smile that the four haughty men reflect, pointing it out with grins and elbows. Donatella looks at her friends with an expression that says: "Here, girls, do as I do. I can still turn heads, you see? despite everything, despite my age, my wrinkles, the force of gravity." She bends over slightly and wags her bum. Marieke empties her glass, observes her husband, observes her friends, wonders casually who is unfaithful to whom, whether Luigi would ever betray her, but all of it light-heartedly, as if it didn't really concern her, as if it wasn't about her, but someone else. Right then Luigi smiles at her with a tenderness that she knows she doesn't deserve.

On the other side of the garden, Giovanni too observes everything: he does like Donatella but finds the whole scene rather tasteless. These people, he thinks, are in their fifties; they are old, they must be as old as his parents, and yet here they are, *still* slobbering and shaking and rubbing, thinking about and actually having sex. At fifty! That flabby flesh. All that swaying. How revolting. He sees his father approach his mother, take her by the hand, wrap her in what might be a dance step, or a hug; he looks quickly away. When he turns again, a few seconds later, they are still embraced. Giovanni feels an itch – but this time it's different; it's an itch of shame. He looks away again, concentrates on a CD, hears Marieke's laughter; now the tingling sensation spreads all over his body, crawling over his skin, as if he were allergic to something.

"I'm allergic to my mother," he thinks, deciding to get back to Turin as soon as possible. After that night, finding excuse after excuse, he doesn't return to Castel San Gerolamo for a whole month.

***

It's the beginning of February. Luigi has to go for his check-up in Alessandria; he and his brother plan a day out, with an excursion to visit some of the best wine cellars of the Langhe region. He comes to pick him up early, and brings him back in the evening. He finds the lights off, no food in the kitchen: on the counter there are still this morning's breakfast cups to wash, the box of cookies, the carton of milk. Luigi calls his wife, worried.

"Maria?" Silence. He puts the milk in the fridge, the cups in the sink. He doesn't wash them: he stands and looks at them for a few seconds, for a minute, then he shakes himself awake. "Maria!" he shouts, climbing the stairs two steps at a time, expecting to find her lying on the floor - a broken leg? A heart attack? She is in the bedroom, hidden under the blankets, her eyes red, swollen. Wet tissues are scattered on the floor.

"Giovanni," she murmurs. Luigi takes her in his arms, and Marieke lets herself be hugged. It is so rare for his wife to show any sign of vulnerability, of weakness – in fact, he can't remember ever having seen her like this. She's been busy, in these last few months; there was the harvest in October, coinciding with a rare visit from her mother from Holland; and a sofa needed reupholstering, Giovanni's room had to be re-painted, and then there was Christmas, then New Year's, the preparations for her birthday. Then – suddenly - the absence of her son hit her like a bullet: a sharp and unexpected pain. It feels like a hole in her chest, blood flowing out of an open wound.

Her friends tell her that it has happened to them too, that it is normal, so normal in fact, that it even has a name to describe it: empty nest syndrome. She needs to be distracted: she must find a new hobby, enrol in a yoga class, rediscover the relationship with her husband. She should cut her hair, or let it grow longer, colour it; lose weight; plan a holiday. A safari in Africa, a cruise in the Caribbean. Marieke has no intention of spending two weeks in a prison on the sea surrounded by strangers, or of watching exotic animals from a sports car.

"I don't care about anything. I want to do like Argos, and wait in front of his bedroom door."

"He will come back," Luigi says. "He comes back whenever he can."

"Not for ages."

"Darling, you have to accept that he has his own life. But also: it's not as if this was new. Him being away. He's not lived here for years now, since he started Uni."

"That was different. *Godverdomme*. He was a boy. He was studying, returning home every weekend. He was still a bit mine. Not now."

"He's still your son. Our son. You'll see. Giovanni is not the type who forgets his parents and moves to Australia."

"That's the weird thing: that I would want him to. I do want him to go away, far away, as far as possible from here, and yet…"

"And yet?"

"And yet I want him to remain. Here. With me."

At this point in our story, she doesn't know how she'll regret this wish. Marieke has gone through motherhood in her own way, with a good dose of boredom and a larger one of regret: for what might have happened, for what she could have become, anything but a typical provincial madam. Stubborn and ignorant Marieke, stubborn and tenacious Marieke, stubborn and needy Marieke, Marieke wife, Marieke lost in the role of mother for so many years - and now: what is she? If Giovanni goes away, what is left of her?

She knew this day would come – all women know it, from the day they give birth. The day when our former baby (who's learned to walk and talk, who started nursery and then school, who's built a circle of friends with whom he does things independently from us, who has ideas and thoughts he doesn't share, that has secrets) ignores us. We, who conceived them and kept them well fed and warm in our soft uterus; we who read fairy tales and the same books *ad nauseam*, we who repeated and made them memorise prayers, times tables, logical and grammatical analysis, we who taught them to do *everything*, we have to sit on the side-lines and allow them to be themselves, to be independent. Yes: leave them alone. As they say, with a trite expression: we have to give them wings to fly. And yet, of course we must continue to be there for them, should they need us, should they fall off their wings, à la Icarus. But if they don't want to see us: disappear. If they decide not to talk to us: keep quiet. Once upon a time there was a mother at the centre of the world - like the system that placed the Earth at the centre of the Universe, while every other celestial body fluttered around it. And no, I'm sorry, *het spijt me*, it's not you but the Sun-your son that is in the middle of our solar system. Not you. You are peripheral. You stand aside, quiet and good and shush.

The transition from one system to another costs tears and fatigue. Willpower. And a long time: it does not happen from one day to the next, but with a slow, continuous advance that should prepare a parent for the definitive detachment. Marieke thought she was getting used to the idea; that when it finally came, she'd be ready. Actually she finds it's more like a tear: crash, and the fabric of her family is broken, a gash and the pieces from one have become two, one here and one there. She has witnessed Giovanni grow up and become a child and a boy and now a man; but sometimes when she looks at him she can still see the baby he was: it's in his eyes, in his gestures, in the way he behaves. She is his mother, and recognises aspects of her son that nobody else does: she sees it all, what no one else can, even what she hopes not to see: his lack of ambition, his poetic, pathetic delicate nature.

And that anger, so well hidden you forget it's there. But it is.

***

Time passes. It passes as it always does, it passes that you don't even realise it, and when you do: it's already gone. Time is smoke. Giovanni is good at adapting, and he quickly gets accustomed to office life - his clients are all different, their needs disparate, but his pace is always the same: alarm, breakfast, a short walk, office all day, lunch consumed at a café, a long and laborious afternoon. Every week is different and yet the same, every month is different and yet the same. Days and weeks pass by, entire seasons merge into each other inducing in him a kind of numbness, a relaxation, a weakening of the soul. Boredom slips smooth and sensual into his veins, like a snake.

The noun boredom means weariness, ennui, lack of enthusiasm, lack of interest, lack of concern, apathy. Giovanni reads Thomas Mann: "Emptiness and monotony may stretch a moment or even an hour and make it 'boring', but they can likewise abbreviate and dissolve large, indeed the largest units of time, until they seem nothing at all." He doesn't have much time for reading, only in the evening, before bed: he begins *The Magic Mountain in* January and finishes it in July. "Rich and interesting events are capable of filling time, until hours, even days, are shortened and speed past on wings; what people call boredom is an abnormal compression of time caused by monotony." Giovanni is not bored, not *really*, but he *is* tired, exhausted. The heat of the summer dulls his thoughts. "We know full well that the insertion of new habits to the changing of old ones is the only way to preserve life, to renew our sense of time – and thereby renew our sense of life itself. That is the reason for every change of scenery and air, for a trip to the shore: the experience of a variety of refreshing episodes."

Giovanni closes the book, sighs. He needs a vacation. The next day, he books a two-week holiday in Greece with his friend Filippo.

***

THE HEART OF THE OCTOPUS

I spent five years in secondary school, drinking Homer up as if it were milk for breakfast: I translated Plato, Aeschylus. I visited the Parthenon on a school trip, I read the *Odyssey* and the *Iliad* in original language, I can recognise the face of gods and heroes. I thought I was prepared. I expected blue sea and white square bungalows and windmills - and to govern over it all, presiding over the island as the goddess Athena: a serene calm, with old men sitting in tavernas playing cards and drinking ouzo and shuffling rosary beads in their calloused hands.

Yeah, right.

Instead, we arrived, Filippo and I, with our trolleys bearing our name tag, fresh faced as scholars, flaunting not muscles but a sort of pathetic thinness, our t-shirts so white, so well ironed; and you know, Mykonos from a distance does take your breath away, so blue and so white and: here white is not simply white but: WWWhite! Dazzling and sunshine-on-snow kind of glowing, so bright it makes you squint. We arrived at the hotel and looked around – there was nobody apart from waiters and waitresses and the hotel personnel, even though it was late morning, and I expected to find the beach dreadfully crowded. We checked in, went upstairs to our room and got changed, dropping our immaculate shorts for swimming trunks and flip flops; we draped a towel over our shoulders, and with a book and a bottle of Evian and our body greasy with the safest sunscreen we descended down to the still deserted beach. And we read and swam and read a bit more, and slept a little under the umbrella, and I swear every ray of sunshine was like a drop of bliss. To be in heaven must be like this, I thought, the idiot, the dickhead. How short lived it was, my tiny slice of paradise, my celestial first hour, before turning into one of Dante's circles: at 4PM Northern European boys with piercings and tattoos, Scandinavian girls, topless, all offering their barely covered flesh to the sun-god descend onto the village. Oh Christ, how un-erotic to see all this meat: red and burnt and swollen, like a Sunday roast in the hot August sun, the tan marking today's bikini shape on their body. I don't understand why the human race loves the sun so much, all this exposed flesh makes me feel sick. I regret leaving Mann for the rapper Jovanotti, whose music I hum ceaselessly because his songs are so true, about these girls that fly over here looking for an exciting experience, the freedom and the thrill of the new, for a Mediterranean adventure just like - presumably – my mother did thirty years ago when she came to the Monferrato.

The days are calm and bright and serene; but then by late afternoon the atmosphere of the whole island is transformed. The Greek population disappears and the Barbarians descend, with succinct clothes, heavy make-up, high heels and short skirts, plunging necklines, deafening music. And in the morning we witness the wreckage before it is cleaned up: discarded bottles and food wrapping and pools of vomit in the streets. But there is nobody around apart from us, because everyone goes to bed at dawn, as Jovanotti sings:

"And the girls of the night are all beautiful

And sometimes you fancy one at night in a club

But when you see her again in the morning, she looks like a witch,

The night plays its game and serves

To make everything a little bit nicer."

***

Giovanni and Filippo strive to swim against the current, snubbing the lifestyle of their peers; they go to bed at midnight when the others come out to party; they get up when the others go to sleep. The two groups are barely aware of each other's existence, taking turns in and out of the hotel as if through revolving doors, entering and exiting in turn. But one evening, while they are sipping an ouzo before dinner, two blonde girls wink at them. Giovanni looks at his friend.

"Do you think they are talking to me? To us?"

"Yes. You two."

They quickly consult each other, decide to stop resisting. "Let's make a deal, here, right now: promise to me that we'll never tell anyone, e-v-e-r. What we'll do tonight will stay here, in this room, on this island, between us," Filippo begs. "I've had enough of being a monk. Let's get completely drunk, let's get stoned, let's drink red bull and vodka, let's smoke grass, let's shag any girl we want. But: shh. Cross your heart and hope to die."

Giovanni raises his right hand, kisses his crossed fingers, places them over his heart. He keeps nodding with relief, like a plastic Chinese doll.

What follows is a shameful, shameless, unforgettable night. Now, let's be clear. Filippo does not concern us; we don't care about him. We want to focus on Giovanni, minute by minute. Look carefully: there he is, Giovanni, in front of us. Can you see him? His friend has gone to dance with blonde number two; Giovanni is sitting on the low bench, thigh against thigh with blonde number one, who is Scottish and is called Kate, and is not really blonde but:

"Strawberry blonde, actually," she says. Giovanni says that rather than strawberries her hair reminds him of red beer, of ale, and this girl, this voluptuous Kate, whose shoulders are as round as wine barrels, Kate giggles and whispers something that Giovanni doesn't hear, or doesn't quite understand, her Scottish accent thicker than cream, and quite without warning she straddles him and kisses him and he remains passive. She moves on top of him while he remains resolutely still; but then suddenly he overturns her, his tongue starts digging into her mouth. She tastes of beer and salt, he puts his hands under her shirt, touches her, caresses her with his fingertips, touches her, touches her, touch me, touch me, until she tells him panting:

"Let's go to my room, it's not far away," **a**nd off they go into the night

THE HEART OF THE OCTOPUS

***

    and in her bedroom she undresses quickly, and she is quickly naked and kind of raw with these soft pink legs that certain English girls have, although she keeps saying she is Scottish, and she has very blue eyes and her tits are so fucking full and her hair below is so sparse and fair that she looks nine years old and almost deflates me but I force my tongue back in her mouth and place my hands on her arse and she pushes me towards her with a perfect pace and she turns into a Houdini and her hand sneaks inside my pants and she touches me and I get it up like a good little soldier and I swear this lasts three minutes three

    She wastes no time, this blonde, this little red devil

    There is no time to think

    To ask

    To wonder

    I throw her on the bed and take off my clothes, quickly, quickly, there is no time, quickly her shirt on the floor and my trousers on the floor and our underwear on the floor and she looks at me whilst lying there, looking at me whilst touching herself whispering something that I do not understand and I fly onto the bed, too, and we start kissing again and I suck her face her lips her tongue her brown nipples

    She touches me

    I touch her

And she opens her eyes and looks at me and whispers something but I can't hear what she says - the blood in my ears like a thunder like swarms of mosquitoes

"What?"

"I said: do you have a condom?"

And I say: "No."

"Oh," she says, and stops moving. Just like that.

Her breath that three seconds ago was laboured and hoarse returns to normal - immediately, I swear - and she casually plays with a strand of her hair and even covers her tits with the sheet like they do in American movies, where they never ever let you see an actress's naked body, there is always a blanket, a bra, something. And I stare at her and say nothing and she looks at me and brushes her hair back, red-faced

And I am panting so badly I feel like fucking Argos

And she tells me: *verbatim*: she says, scowling: "Well if you want, you can go down on me," and I burst out laughing because it's the funniest thing I have ever heard. And she looks at me and doesn't understand: "What's so funny?" she asks.

And I laugh and laugh and I raise my right hand and I give her an open-handed slap, so hard that not only her face but her whole head turns onto one side and if she hadn't been already half-lying she would have fallen and she covers her reddening cheek and looks at me but doesn't say anything, she looks at me with her pink puffy mouth slightly open and I give her another slap on the other side and don't wait for her to recompose herself, but turn her onto her stomach and hold her down and fuck her from behind.

***

At dawn, he's back at the hotel. Sober, cold, horrified.

Filippo is still awake, sitting on the bed in his underwear, drinking large gulps of water from a plastic bottle. He smiles at him, but then he sees the scratches on his face and neck:

"Jesus, Giovanni. What happened? What did you do?"

"What happens in Mykonos stays in Mykonos. I don't want to talk about it," Giovanni responds, his voice cold. "We made a deal. Now shut up and go to sleep."

***

Are we going to talk about it?
No.

***

Within a week from their return, Giovanni falls ill - a banal but brutal cold, with sneezes, swollen red eyes and a streaming nose at first, which turns into bronchitis with the most persistent cough – he coughs so much he can't even speak. Mr Guarnieri sneaks into his office, tells him to go home.

"If you carry on like this and don't look after yourself properly, you'll end up in hospital," he says. Giovanni had pneumonia, ten years before. The memory of that awful time stayed with him. "Go and see a doctor," Guarnieri says. "I'll get cross if you are back in the office before next week."

Giovanni goes home as ordered; he looks into his medicine cabinet, finds an old bottle of cough mixture; he is shivering. He tries his temperature: 39.5C degrees. He goes to bed. Luigi calls him, but Giovanni can't talk, he's coughing too hard, so hard he is sick. He cleans up. He switches on the telly, switches it off again; he can't read, can't concentrate on anything. He can't even sleep – he stays in bed, wide awake, his eyes open, his body shaken by cough and shivers.

The next day, from under the covers, he hears the sound of keys turning in the lock.

"Who is it?" He whispers, while Marieke walks into the overheated studio like a breath of air: the lioness is back. She hugs and kisses him, relieved. "Mamma? It's you," Giovanni murmurs, exhausted, lies back on the pillow. She brought a cake, the one with apples and pine nuts he loves; a radio, a hot water bottle, a few books; she makes leek and potato soup, prepares a pot of tea. Giovanni feels painfully, disproportionately grateful.

"Thank you, mamma. I mean it."

"Don't even mention it. It's awful to be sick and not to have anyone around to help you."

"Yes."

"I'm here now. I know it when you need me."

"Yes."

"Nobody looks after you as well as I do."

"Yes," Giovanni manages to say, lying on the bed wrapped in a blanket knitted by his Great Auntie, while he looks at her rushing around like a whirlwind; Marieke changes the sheets and remakes the bed; she wipes the floor, cleans the bathroom, scrubs the bathtub till it sparkles. She goes out and comes back twenty minutes later with two shopping bags to fill the empty fridge.

"All done," she announces at six o'clock. "I'm going back to see your dad now, otherwise he starts worrying."

"Thank you, thank you, mamma," Giovanni repeats, thinking it had been years since he had said anything so sincere. Since he had truly meant it.

Marieke smiles, says goodbye, leaves. Later, alone in her car, the radio on, she feels the love for her son spread in patches on her chest, like sunburn. She feels hot, clammy, her heart pounds in her chest, tears prick her eyes, pour over her cheeks.

***

Winter unfolds along its pale days; my enthusiasm for the new year decreases and ladders through, like a pair of tights. Routine sharpens its teeth: every day is the same as the one before - work, home; home, work. Cinema. Shopping. Dinner out, a walk. During his rare visits to Castel San Gerolamo, the smell of another place and another time clings on to him like a protective film, making him want to leave as soon as he's arrived, and his departure is invariably followed by the return to the solitude of the city. And then it starts snowing one day in mid-February - all night, all day, all night - and the city becomes paralysed for forty-eight silent hours. "Turin is just enchanting, quiet and whitened like an old lady. Magic, like a Frank Capra movie. I almost expect that an angel, as white as snow, would appear suddenly from behind a corner and offer me a new, glittering life. Or a pair of wings. I expect a miracle."

***

Mr Biagi, one of the founders of the practice, goes into retirement. Guarnieri employs two new junior lawyers: Marco Ferrari (tall and blond; he comes to work on his gigantic motorbike - an excuse to be able to wear black leather trousers that are a bit too tight over his compact muscles) and Carmela Montaperto, a Sicilian young woman with black hair, as tall and thin as a birch.

Mr Guarnieri organises a welcome dinner; a lively evening, almost festive. Giovanni arrives late and finds himself caught between Mr Bianchi and Dr Zaffalon, and observes with envy the other end of the table, dominated by the younger members of the team. They laugh, they drink, they make jokes, with Marco holding forth as if he'd been in the office for decades; one can't but detest certain types, so self-assured, so assertive. As if they were born to conquer, to seduce. It's in their nature; their self-confidence is palpable. Look, now, at the women at this table: a solicitor, a trainee, two secretaries: educated, mature, emancipated women: look at them, trying to get Marco's attention for a second, flickering their eyelids and touching their hair like teenagers, all a sigh, a languor, an abandonment. The men, too, stare at him like chimpanzees watching a gorilla, a lion cub its father: all staring, admiring Marco's perfect teeth, his hair too long, but only just, his impeccable suit over his bulging arms.

Giovanni tries to pick up the thread of the long, garbled speech Bianchi is making; he has definitely drunk too much, and he has no idea of what he's talking about - a technicality on taxes imposed on the artistic heritage. Giovanni nods, but he can't help it, he keeps turning over to the right of the table like one's tongue is attracted to a painful tooth, like a magnet is to iron. He feels the way he felt when he watched his high school classmates: small. Invisible. "I'm just going to finish my coffee and leave," he decides. But it's Guarnieri who leaves first, followed by Bianchi on unsteady legs, and Zaffalon and slowly, everyone else. At the end, it's only the three of them at the empty table. "Marco will certainly want to be alone with Carmela, and I'm going to be in his way." But no: all three leave together to have one more drink at another bar, and incredibly it's Giovanni's turn to hold court. He tells his new mates of his first months in the office, he makes fun of the secretaries and the other partners, of the office décor, of some idiosyncratic client. Marco and Carmela laugh, offer him another drink, they beg him to tell more.

***

It happens quickly: at first he's alone and a bit lonely – yes, yes he's satisfied, I have told you already, happy professionally, he likes his flat, he's content with himself and his newly acquired independence. But when Carmela bursts into his life, the rest loses colour, loses sparkle. Carmela is like a 150-watt light bulb: bright, shiny, sparkling, dazzling, brilliant, luminous, iridescent.

Carmela is intelligent and sharp and has flair and knows what she wants and she always gets it. As an archer in a forest, among ferns and trees, who spots her prey: she points her arrow, holds the bow in the direction of the target, tends the string, lets the arrow fly in the air, kills the prey.

Giovanni falls at her feet.

***

It happens like this: they get closer and closer. They chat. They discuss a common case, then talk about something more personal; they go and drink coffee together; the following week they have lunch together, and then one evening a cocktail together. And when Marco shoves his elbow into Giovanni's stomach and asks:

"Can you tell me why don't you try to score, with Carmela?"

"Me? Isn't she interested in you?"

Marco bursts out laughing:

"She likes you, you fool!"

Oh how he laughs, because Giovanni is a really a bit slow, and you have to scream in his face. And this is precisely Carmela's task, whose ideas are like flames, like flags, and loves to hoist and wave them.

"Of course he's not interested in me. Marco is gay."

"Oh. Is he?"

"Giovanni, sometimes you seem a man born in the wrong century," she tells him one night as they are having dinner in a restaurant behind Piazza San Carlo.

"Not that that's a bad thing," she adds. "I'm sure you've always been regarded as a good son. A good boy; a good student; someone who never got into trouble. I bet your parents are proud of you."

"Yes, I don't know. Maybe," Giovanni says, thinking of his benevolent father, his suffocating mother. "Now it's my turn to ask. No, actually, look: *I* shall tell you something about yourself," Giovanni says. "I can see your family has an illustrious past," he says, bending over her hand to admire her family ring, but in the meantime checking out her hand and her beautiful thin wrists and long fingers, with nails painted pale ink. He turns her hand to inspect her palm, all intersected with illegible lines; he runs his forefinger along them, as if he were consulting a map.

"Well then: can you read into my future?" Carmela asks.

"Sure," he responds immediately. "I see a meteoric career, a brilliant future. Your private life, however ..." Her hand burns in his.

"Yes? My private life what?"

"I see you've had your heart broken, and more than once."

"You see that, do you?"

"Yes. I see a succession of flings, which haven't left a single mark."

"And what about the future?"

"Now I see a young man – hold on, what did you say: a good man, yes: a good young man, who is poring over your palm, and he takes your face into his hands, and kisses you."

"What are you waiting for?"

***

Carmela is like the trill of her name

Carmela is tall and willowy like an exclamation mark

Carmela has these long thick Medusa-like curls

And emerald eyes, as green as an apple, oh Carmela, these eyes so clever and straight and pointy like nipples, eyes that prick, like pins, ouch Giovanni do be careful, don't get hurt, but it's late too late as his blood runs runs runs like crazy in his veins, as warm as coffee, which Carmela loves only if it's black and strong and hot with no sugar, Carmela has black eyelashes as thick as mink fur, Carmela has a narrow waist that makes her look like a lady from the eighteenth century, Carmela has hairy armpits, with hair that is black and thick and curly, and with a pungent odour that makes his head spin, Carmela has tiny feet, nails painted pink - a delicate colour that does not suit her, because Carmela has the power of the sea, of oranges and almonds, of Sicily: a place he never had any intention to visit but he'd go and live there tomorrow. No: immediately. Now.

Giovanni feels like he's been born again; indeed: just born, because it is as if he's never lived before. Carmela teaches him how to breathe his first breath, the very first, the one that a newborn exhales coming out of the vaginal canal, stained with blood and mucus. It's a miracle, to fall in love: to really fall in love, from deep inside: bowels on fire, heart on fire, cock on fire. His breath smells of fire. Sparks, flames, ashes: the stages of love. Giovanni is a torch.

Carmela Montaperto is twenty-six. She has a brother, an older father and a young-ish mother, a degree in Law and a Master's in business studies; she speaks perfect English (she's lived in San Francisco for a year), French (she went to school in Switzerland, paradoxically, not far from the college where Giovanni was, near Montreaux), Spanish (her nanny was Ecuadorian). Carmela is educated, studious, a bad cook and expert lover, has few girl-friends and many boy-friends, has travelled far and wide throughout the United States and Southeast Asia, knows how to play tennis as a pro (not to mention skiing and horse-riding). Carmela, in a few words, has that *savoir faire* that one can't buy, but that is imprinted on one by the family, as a legacy. Carmela is perfect. Plus – icing on the cake – she comes from a noble family of Norman origins.

"I'm telling you: it's true. My father has a family tree that goes as far back as the eleventh century," Carmela says. There is no trace of self-conceit, in her explanation, perhaps a touch of irony. "Bollocks, of course. But: isn't my ring beautiful?"

She wears a gold ring bearing the family's coat of arms - a horseman galloping, brandishing a sword at shoulder height, ready to strike.

***

It is evident: for Giovanni, eroticism goes hand in hand with the exotic – think of it: his mother, Julie, Leila (we're never going to mention Kate). Carmela is the most Italian of them all and yet somehow the most exotic. Agrigento is a thousand kilometres away from Monferrato, Sicily is not only an island, it is a world apart, alien, strange - like monkeys, like avocados, like sushi. Had he been born in another family, or in another era, Giovanni would certainly have followed the trail of a scent from elsewhere and left for the South Seas or the North Pole; he would have migrated, away, as far away as he could, hunting for alien landscapes and creatures. Here, now, he just needs to smell the scent of lemons in Carmela's clothes, hear her 'r's pronounced hard against the palate; see her move a curl behind her ear - a perfect ear, round like a cherry, pink as her lips - and tremble with desire. He closes his eyes, his flared nostrils quiver.

"My Piedmontese stallion," Carmela calls him, without subtlety. That's another thing he loves about her: the utter lack of tricks, of feigned innocence, of make-up of any sort.

"I can't pretend; you see me as I am. That's me; yours truly," she says. Yes: one thousand kilometres from the courteous falsehoods that reign in Piedmont. Carmela walks around the flat stark naked, she even has breakfast completely naked; not for vanity, but for convenience, for honesty. For love.

***

Giovanni and Carmela keep their relationship hidden from their colleagues at the office, for discretion, for convenience, out of habit, and because - according to her – to love each other and work together is the perfect recipe to make sure that their story will not last. Presumably, everyone knows that there is something between them. But what, and when, and how, nobody knows for sure.

They leave the office at different times, never together.

"I have to do my things," Carmela says. "See you later," and reappears in the doorway of his studio after a few hours. She stays over at his three or four nights a week; he rarely goes to hers, as she shares an apartment with a cousin that Giovanni has never met. For the first six months of their relationship, they go out to dinner or to the cinema or theatre, but not with anyone else – they want to be together, alone, to tell and understand each other and to get to know each other, to touch each other and make love.

Julie had been his first love: the chaste love, innocent, young, pure, virtuous, simple, frank, virginal; Carmela is anything but *innocent*. If I check the opposite of 'innocent' in the dictionary of synonyms, I find: pervert, evil, malicious, wanton, libertine, libidinous, lustful, wicked, vicious, cunning, immoral, shameless, lewd, obscene, and I get puzzled and alarmed and upset - that is not what I mean, when I try to explain Giovanni's second love. I'll tell you what it *isn't*: a childish love, consummated simply by holding hands, staring into each other's eyes. It *is* flesh, desire, desire, inspiration, almost pain: like when he's about to have an orgasm, he can feel an almost painful sensation before he reaches climax and ejaculation. Giovanni's love for Carmela feels like that, at the beginning: a state of feverish and involuntary excitement, so intense as to make him sick.

Furthermore, Giovanni doesn't know how to handle a relationship. He finds it hard to learn the mechanisms of how it works, how to maintain it and cherish it – all stuff he can't possibly grasp and assimilate in a few days. As if he had taken up a new sport or a new hobby, he has to learn its basic rules. Imagine an athlete who decides to train for, say, the high jump: he must absorb the correct technique - the four phases of approach, take off, flight and landing. In addition to the rules and techniques for winning, one must also learn how not to get hurt, how to fall and get up again. He trains hard, every day; when the day comes, he runs, but as he is running, he feels a throbbing pain: he's broken his knee ligaments (or an arm, or whatever). At that very moment, as he falls over, or as he is failing that jump, he knows that the medal, the tournament, the gold of the Olympic Games has gone. We know that in order to win an athlete also needs to know how to lose, and when you lose you should not cry but continue training, even longer and more intensely than before. Giovanni, in his new role as a boyfriend, as the other half in a couple, must learn how to do it well: how to fight, how to make peace, how to behave the day after, the week after, the month after. It's a new world, confusing and tiring and for the first three months he feels constantly on alert, sure he's going to make a mistake, terrified of losing Carmela.

Look at today: Friday, March 10th, the day before his birthday, three weeks since they have become lovers. Giovanni left the office at six-thirty, anguished: Carmela hasn't talked to him all day, she's ignored him, so taken as she was by her duties of efficient lawyer (on the contrary, Giovanni's productivity is at historic lows); they haven't discussed the weekend, what to do, where to go: will she go to his place? Will he to hers? Will they spend together the next forty-eight hours, as they did last week? Giovanni doesn't know, and not knowing induces a state of great anxiety in him. Should he tidy up or leave the studio as it is? Should he go grocery shopping or hope that the jar of pesto already opened a few days ago is not mouldy yet? Should he buy croissants for tomorrow morning? In the end, he does some shopping in the local deli, climbs the stairs to his flat, opens the door and sits on the sofa, leaving the shopping bags on the floor - two bottles of wine, bread, ham and cheese, fresh pasta, two cakes with lemon cream. He just sits there, and waits. He waits with his coat and shoes and tie still on; he can't bring himself to get up, pour a little wine into a glass, pretend he's not waiting for her. He sits in the room, alone, still; it becomes increasingly dark. And at eight o'clock the phone rings:

"Hi, it's me. Have you already bought something to eat?" she asks, just like that, with a disarming naturalness, as if it were obvious. And perhaps it is. Giovanni – exhilarated, exhausted - springs up and tidies frantically, splashes water under his armpits wet with perspiration, changes his shirt, sets the table with care, with cotton napkins, with candles. Then he sits back down again (on the same spot on the sofa, still warm from earlier), his throbbing head in his hands, and waits.

Carmela arrives twenty minutes later, distracted, breathless from running; but natural, normal, as if they had spent every Friday night together in the last ten years.

***

The first dinners together with the inevitable candle and eating one-handedly – the other grabbing Carmela's hand as if she were about to fall, as if he needed a foothold.

Hold me tight.

Look into my eyes.

***

The first weekends together are spent almost exclusively in bed – they chat, they read, eat, make love, they get up to get a glass of water, a cup of coffee, have a shower and dress to go downstairs to buy something to eat, but then they run back upstairs, let their clothes fall onto the floor and go back to bed. On Monday morning, they go to the office languid with sleep and love.

One Sunday, Giovanni lowers the newspaper he is reading, leans on one elbow, looks at Carmela.

"Listen."

"Yup?"

"I am falling."

"What?"

"I'm falling."

"What do you mean?"

"I am falling in love. I have fallen. Please, don't hurt me."

Carmela walks over to him.

"Never, ever."

"I love you."

"Me too. I love you too."

There: they said it: they are a couple.

***

Giovanni can't concentrate on anything - everything takes second place on the podium of his thoughts. He thinks of Carmela all the time; he looks at her, dreams of her, breathes her in, all day, all night. He works badly, can't even follow the news. He sleeps badly when Carmela isn't in his bed and sleeps badly when she is, because he can't not touch her, and if he touches her, he can't stop.

Carmela is soft and sweet and transparent.

Like glass. It makes me think of high school and of Professor Cerruti, who taught chemistry. He'd explained that glass is a liquid with high viscosity, which solidifies on cooling. I remember he had asked me about the difference between glass and crystal, which if I don't remember incorrectly is that crystal needs to have oxide lead content in excess of 24 percent. Glass has similar properties to diamonds, which are crystalline in nature. The secret of diamonds? Refraction, total internal reflection and dispersion. Light is refracted in a more decisive manner than with normal glass, making the diamond really shiny. There: Carmela is made not of glass but of diamonds, Carmela so bright, Carmela full of light, like clean water, pure and clear and without blemishes. Carmela when she washes, Carmela when she gets dressed, Carmela with her little round belly that reminds me of the hills around Castel San Gerolamo, her legs toned and straight, her compact boobs, warm like milk, Carmela makes me want to be nursed by her, ah, Carmela, Carmela who loves me, Carmela, Carmela whose breath smells of hay and grass, my queen, my fairy-tale princess, where are your wings, your magic wand, fairy, angel, angel.

Treasure.

***

It takes months before they establish a routine - Carmela is unpredictable, inconsistent, random, dis-ordered, moody: she never does the same thing every day, she's always full of energy, with a burning desire to *do*: Giovanni feels lazy, apathetic, in comparison, and if on the one hand he's stimulated to do more, on the other he suffers in silence. In the weekend, he would like to sit at home and watch some bad television, to potter about with no plan, no agenda; Carmela always has a project, something to learn, to play, to bring to fruition. This Saturday afternoon, for example, she tells him he must be patient, as she has to finish some chores, which are scrawled on a sheet of paper. To do:

- Research exemptions from taxation, including government bonds that have been subject to donation, and that those subject to inheritance;
- Call her friend Silvia, who lives in New York;

- Write a letter to her mother, who insists on receiving a written missive fortnightly;
- Listen to *Le Nozze di Figaro* at least twice before next weekend - she has tickets to go to La Scala for the show conducted by Muti and directed by Strehler;
- Do forty minutes yoga;
- Prepare pasta with sardines ...

All of this, while Giovanni reads a magazine sitting on the sofa, feigning imperturbable calm. Pretending, because in truth he is incredibly agitated, listens to every word Carmela says on the phone, spies on her movements, reads from behind the notes on inheritance taxes, hums *Non Andrai Più Farfallone Amoroso*. He gets up and sits down and gets up and drinks a glass of water and looks out the window and lowers the volume of Mozart and folds her abandoned socks and places them on a chair. He sighs, and remembers all those long gone afternoons filled with sighs in Castel San Gerolamo, and finally says: "Enough," and throws himself on Carmela's body, which is lying on the floor in the *Chaturanga Dandasana* position.

***

Don't think of Carmela as of a passive creature, indifferent or blasé: she too has fallen head over heels for this unusual man with green eyes and a sad, pensive face, hollow cheeks and full lips. Giovanni is odd, displays an old-fashioned courtesy and easily disarms even a disillusioned woman like her. Carmela comes from a world full of privileges, which she has always enjoyed without even acknowledging them, and which she has left behind as a form of rebellion. Her parents wanted her to return to Sicily after her graduation, but she dug her heels in the ground, deciding to remain up north. She's found a flat, a job,

"I live on my own. No one sees me, no one can say no, that's not good, that's not the way it's done, that you can't even think about certain things."

"And your parents? How did they take it?"

"Badly, of course: however, I am the youngest child, their little girl, the second, the female, the spoiled; and I know how to smile cutely and plead with my big eyes like an abandoned puppy, and eventually I get what I want."

Giovanni quickly learns the rules of the game: how to argue and how to make peace, which buttons to press and which not to, ever; what to talk about and what to avoid in Carmela's golden world. Her father is sacred, untouchable, as are her sporting abilities, of which she is extremely proud, and whose tangible laurels (three gold and two silver medals for skiing, swimming, riding) are well showcased in her room (the only ornaments she does dust). Giovanni can scoff at and tease her lack of home-making attitude, her culinary dis-ability, the fact that she and her cousin have hired a maid once a week trying to tame the disorder of the tiny apartment. Carmela is not even able to prepare tea: I mean, everyone can succeed. But no: she can't wait for the water to boil (she gets bored, looking at it while the kettle warms up, becomes impatient, turns it off too quickly, before it actually starts boiling), pours water on the bag which she proceeds to extract far too soon, and serves a warm and beige broth. She cooks seldom and not well, but when she does it is to prepare exotic dishes - Thai curry, Vietnamese soups, Hungarian goulash; she finds a recipe, purchases mysterious ingredients, fragrant herbs which quickly become mouldy in the refrigerator, jars that end up at the back of the pantry.

She is not interested in having her obvious charm celebrated, her attractiveness valued, her grace and elegance appreciated - presumably she's always heard her appearance praised, the beauty of her eyes and hair and heart-shaped mouth, but never! dare touch her erudition, the culture she continues to accumulate as Scrooge his gold coins. Carmela is schoolteacher-y, has opinions on any and every subject – on literature, on art, on theatre, even abstruse subjects like Forties Chinese cinema or US propaganda in the fifties, or Korean modern art. She has been to a Jeff Buckley concert in Dublin, she drank at Hirst's Pharmacy in Notting Hill, seen the Biennial at the Whitney Museum of American Art; on her bedside table there is Tolstoy but also Kureishi and Philip Roth and some commercial fiction. She has been everywhere, has read and seen everything there is to see and read. She is curious. She likes to see, travel, displays a particular receptiveness for external reality, she shows qualities of high sociability - in short, she is your typical Jungian extrovert, who favours the knowledge of the outside rather than concentrating on the inside; she will start seeing a therapist only at thirty-five.

"And she gives me a lecture, a proper lecture - standing with her finger pointed as if she were at a desk and I was the little pupil at her feet. She explains the origin, life death and miracles of any author, opera, painting, the socioeconomic background of la la la di da ... and she doesn't even realise she is doing it; and if I remark upon it she gets cross, she asks me whether perhaps I'm envious: it's not her fault if she's visited so many European and North American museums, if when she was eight years old her parents were already dragging her to watch a ballet, to listen to operas…... and I say: Oh no my love, educate me, how could I resent it? Not only do I love you, but I'm learning so much ... and she gets her smile back and I say: note to self: never criticise her immense, prodigious, legendary culture. Never."

***

Giovanni keeps tabs. They have been together for:
- Thirteen days
- Two Weeks and four days
- Four Weeks tomorrow
- Two months

After three months, he stops counting the days: yes, it is true: he does have a girlfriend. He is in a relationship. An official relationship. It is official, it is proper, it is steady and yet is the most natural thing in the world, like brushing one's teeth (her toothbrush in his bathroom) or put on a load of washing (her nightdress among his sheets). And doing trivial things: even taking a bus feels different; with her, it's an adventure.

Together, we enjoy the *little* things of life. I buy sweets and the dark chocolate she likes, and she puts her arms around my neck; she knows that I'm crazy about almond paste, and calls her mother, who sends a package: straight away, straight away. We like to go to a sad little bar near Porta Susa - one of those slightly seedy cafes, a little dirty, with the inevitable drunks slumped on a chair in a corner, stale crisps on the counter, soft peanuts with grains of salt congealed on the surface, that have been in that bowl for who knows how long. We ask for two glasses of *Barbera* (now we don't even need to ask for them, the man at the bar pours them as soon as we enter, leaves them on the counter for us to pick up) and we're there for an hour, some nights, before dinner. We sit down, we drink, we read a magazine, browse the newspaper. We almost don't say a word – we have been together all day, we had lunch together, we worked side by side for an hour to study a common case. We don't really need words. And yet other times we're about to leave and start discussing a topic we both feel passionately about and can't stop chatting, standing there on the front door with our coat on, like two idiots. We *need* to talk and talk and talk about something that can't be delayed. It needs to be addressed *now*.

Filippo goes out with a new girl called Anna who is a little bland but nice, and yesterday he called me and asked me if *we* were free Saturday night.

"We who?" I asked.

"Who do you think? You two: you, and Carmela."

We. Us. Wonderful pronouns - letters as sweet as Sicilian *Marturana*.

Last night I dreamed of her father, despite never having met him. I dreamed that I was waiting on the doorstep and he appeared, dressed all in black, with a stick in his hand. I was afraid he might hit me, I wanted to escape, but Carmela took me by the hand and brought me to him. Her father lifted his baton, who at this point had become a sword, and placed it on my right shoulder, and as he did so I knelt in front of him, like a knight. Charlemagne.

It was his full acceptance.

I woke up singing.

***

One morning he's in Carmela's flat, waiting for her to get ready – he making himself a coffee, sipping it slowly standing by the window. He looks out, leans over to look at someone who's passing by, a car that is parking, a pigeon flapping its wings. She is still not ready. He closes the window, goes into the kitchen to wash his cup, walks over to the shelves that occupy an entire wall of the room, reads the titles of the books carefully arranged, divided by genre (history, psychology, poetry, fiction). He picks a book out, reads the blurb, puts it back in place, takes up another: a leather-bound hardback - WH Auden: *Collected Poems* and opens it, and there on the first page there is a dedication, written in black ink by a nervous hand:

"Carmela: Carmela, I plagiarise Auden but not too badly:

I'll love you, dear, I'll love you

Till England and Sicily meet

And Scottish sheep drink Sicilian almond milk

And the salmon sings in the street.

I love you, I love you, I love you. Andrew. London, November 1993."

He closes the book and puts it back where he found it, on the bottom shelf. He holds his breath. He sits on the couch. He goes into the kitchen, then quickly back into the living room, he sits down, gets up, approaches the shelf, looks at the book, back, sits down, gets up, comes back, opens the book to the first page, he reads it again, puts it back in place. From the bedroom, the noise of the hairdryer and Carmela humming a song, unaware. He reads once more the dedication, of a man to his woman: and his heart is filled with bile, as bitter as cocoa, as green as his eyes. Carmela leaves the bathroom, finally ready, clean as the spring that is trying to get in through the closed windows:

"Who is Andrew?"

"Excuse me?"

"I found a book. Andrew gave it to you. Who is he?"

"Oh. Andrew."

"Yes: Andrew."

"Yes. Giovanni, Andrew. It's an old story."

"I asked: who is he."

"It's someone I knew, years ago."

"A lover."

"A friend of mine."

"Yes, right. A friend who tells you he loves you, who gives you a book of love poems," Giovanni hisses, his face red.

"A friend. With whom I had something. Something happened. A long time ago, Giovanni. Years ago. I don't even know where he is, now," Carmela says, honesty softening her face.

Giovanni doesn't listen, his ears are buzzing, he's panting as if he'd been running, anguish trapped in his throat. "I'm jealous. Who would have thought I'd be able of such a feeling? Of course I knew that Carmela was not a virgin; she'd obviously had someone else before me: but I had never asked. To be honest, it had never really occurred to me. Now I do want to know, and *everything*: who was the first, the second, the sixth, the last one before me; I need to have a list of names, surnames, places and situations. I need to know who was the worst and who the best."

When he goes home, Giovanni takes eight glasses from the kitchen. He stacks them up, balancing them under his chin. He opens the door to the terrace, and throws them onto the street, one by one.

THE HEART OF THE OCTOPUS

***

"See, violence runs the family, like the Montaperto family crest suggests."

There you are: nothing is perfect if it lacks a defect: Carmela's teeth have sharp canines like Argos's. Carmela growls when she gets angry, or hisses like a snake, her eyes narrowing to a slit, like the windows of a tower that you have to conquer. He throws himself against the door of the tower, trying to break it open. Carmela is not a woman *sotto voce*. Carmela gestures wildly and yells and screams, leaving Giovanni stunned at first, his eyes open wide like those of a child whose snack has been taken away, and then less and less. He learns to respond, at first arguing vehemently, he learns to shout back. A shout for a shout. They fight, my good god, how they fight!, and with what strength, with what incredible violence. And how they love to make up after an epic fight.

No, don't be confused: Giovanni knows what rage is. He has always known it, and felt it in short bursts: a snap rather than an explosion; anger glowing like fire but somehow controlled, manageable, which mostly remained boiling inside him, in his chest and liver and heart, like autumn must before it matures. Have you ever seen the eruption of a geyser? Exactly in this way, all the unexpressed anger bottled down in Giovanni's belly learns to find release. See: Carmela comes from a loving family that fundamentally she trusts, and that trusts her; she's a self-confident woman, able to recognise in others signals of reliability and interest and love. That's why fighting doesn't scare her - she sees it as a form of communication, a kind of heated dialogue. For Giovanni, who hasn't experienced the same loving tender care from his parents, and who basically doesn't feel worthy of being loved for who he is, fighting is difficult; a fight seems an irremediable catastrophe, an end, a kind of death: the first few times, he remains passive and astonished in front of Carmela's outbursts; petrified when she raises his voice, when she slams the door and returns to her flat (only to call him back ten minutes later, apologising profusely, whispering words of love that he is almost incapable of hearing), when she throws an object at him (a shoe, a newspaper). It takes him time to accept that one can discuss and solve, scream and make peace; it takes him months, in the safe and private shelter of their relationship, before realising that he, too, can externalise his emotions. As if Carmela had said: "Honey, let it out for good: to keep it all inside will resolve in you getting gastritis, colitis. You'll get it. Just let it out." And as if he were granted a special permit, Giovanni finally can scream and scream until he is hoarse, until he can sense his neck swell up, stretched by veins about to explode, and a hot face, shaky hands. That's how far he goes: he thrusts forwards his face, which becomes red and swollen like that of a turkey - she screams too, mind you, she is equally congested and livid, here: yes: livid - and she's as tall as he, what a surprise, to have eyes in line with the green lawn of Carmela, Carmela, who puts her hands on his shoulders and pushes him, not too hard, a little push, and he lets himself be pushed and falls, and she also falls over him and eventually they kiss and make peace and

***

We'd planned it for the longest time, the right month the right day every smallest detail of this stupid weekend, and it's too late to back out, too late to escape, even if I would like to, and I hold her hand too tight and she thinks it is for her and smiles a two hundred carats smile.

She smiles to give herself some courage, to give me courage, and I hold on to those teeth and I ride them like a surfer and I say - too loudly because that's how the brave talk: "You'll like my parents. You will. They are like the wine that my father makes from the grapes that grow in our vineyard: free-range, lively, genuine. We are like that, we: the people from the Monferrato. We seem open, extroverted people, but we were born and raised in the land that grows *Barbera* on these hills: we share the same carbonated surface, that in fact hides murky bottom. Bubbles conceal the thick crust of dregs. I can vouch for this: we are as honest as this wine, as genuine and frank as our *Grignolino*."

Year, right; yeah, right. I can guarantee that she won't like my parents at all, but Carmela is as polite as a nun and won't dare tell me, she will seek excuses for not setting foot in Castel San Gerolamo ever again. Amen. In any case: what a hideous journey, the two of us travelling by coach to the countryside as if it was a school trip – and my poor hills, thin and meagre as it's early Spring. Everything looks cheap: the pale houses surrounded by their pathetic little garden, the housewives on the balconies putting out their wash, the wide empty roads with no pavement. Carmela expects to see a lovely country cottage with fireplace – the type of little cute building one would find in the English countryside – and inside, nineteenth-century paintings and vases filled with geraniums, collections of dried up, crucified butterflies inside glass cases, leather-bound volumes, worn carpets: a sort of faded nobility, not exactly tired, but: exhausted. Instead at my parents' she'll see damp patches on the walls because of the humidity; and shiny furniture the wrong shade of mahogany; and a horrid oilcloth on the kitchen table in what my father keeps calling 'our nook'. And my parents wearing slippers - Christ, yes: slippers.

We get off the coach and there he is, my father, waiting, smoking a cigarette; he throws it away as soon as he sees us, and in that gesture there's all there is to say, all I don't want to be, and yet despite it all, I feel a wave of overwhelming affection for this man who loves me more than anyone else in the world, who quietly worships me as if I were one of his heroes: Churchill, JFK, Einstein. I hug him and he looks at Carmela with undisguised admiration and shakes her hand and holds it in his a fraction too long. You know what? It doesn't matter. In the car there is Argos, who gets into convulsions when he sees me, and howls and almost cries with joy.

Carmela pats him behind the ears, distracted but loving, Christ but how does she always get it right? She pats the dog and in the meantime she is all chirpy and chatty with my father throughout the eternal eighteen minutes that it takes to get home; she doesn't make any comments, she doesn't snigger sideways to suggest something - disappointment, horror. Not even a chuckle, a raised eyebrow, a wink; nothing. And here is the hill and here is our house at the top of the hill, surrounded by vineyards, flanked by cypress trees. It looks almost cute. We enter the courtyard and my mother runs out flapping her slippers and I blush: with her hair freshly blow-dried and the smell of hair spray lingering around her, her white blouse and skirt a bit too tight, her hands sliding over her body to hold it down. She keeps rubbing her red hands, adorned with golden rings that are too small for her fingers, and make them red and angry and fat. And her accent is more Dutch and guttural than ever, but who knows, maybe the fact of being foreign is a plus. I don't know.

"Carmela, Carmela, finally!" And Carmela smiles and they smile at each other and we walk indoors where a smell of cooked vegetables and wet walls and dog hair lingers, but it doesn't matter, because Carmela squeezes my hand and I am proud and sad and proud and ashamed of my shame, and it's a sensation I have all weekend, despite everyone's efforts, and I am proud of all except myself. My perfect Carmela manages never to say what she really thinks, ever, swallows her views so as not to offend anyone, swallows the heavy food and the heavy wine and never complains, in fact even asks for the recipes, even writes them on a slip of paper that I know she'll lose right away, and swallows and smiles and thanks and wonders and admires and praises and thanks again, her cheeks a painful rictus, Carmela accepts everything and smiles and keeps thanking my mother. Who suddenly starts mentioning the Mafia and Sicily and I'd love to punch her in the face but Carmela smiles and is silent and smiles and swallows. And my mother says: 'You who are a Southerner, a *terrona*', and Carmela swallows and smiles.

Carmela Carmela my perfect Carmela, oh god but I want to marry you, I want to be yours forever, my rose, my goddess, my queen, my Arabia Felix.

***

The table is set with a finely embroidered linen tablecloth, golden rimmed plates, silver cutlery. Giovanni would have preferred a simple supper, but is grateful to his mother for having made such an effort. Marieke has prepared a special dinner, a mix of Piedmont and Dutch classics: *bitterballen* (a kind of meatballs), roast peppers with *bagna cauda*, followed by ravioli with butter, sage and parmesan, and - after a pause, and served with coffee – *Boterkoek*, a cake made with almonds, which is like a buttery biscuit, served with sweet *Moscato*.

"This tastes a bit like the desserts of my hometown!" Carmela says, continuing in her dogged ostentation of enthusiasm.

She and Luigi have held court all evening, chatting casually about this and that - Turin and the Piedmontese countryside, Argos and the German shepherd she had when she was little, Palermo and the Greek temples in Sicily, the Guarnieri practice, the price of rentals, the new Prodi government, the film *The Postman* which has just won an Oscar, and Luigi jokingly likens Carmela to the actress Cucinotta.

"But come on, Dad. Please," Giovanni says.

"You are flattering me, Dr Ferraro."

"It's the truth," Luigi says.

"No, it isn't. That's not flattery, my dear. She might be beautiful, but she's so vulgar..." Marieke intervenes. She has said little throughout dinner, but has continued to touch Giovanni's arm, to take his hand. Now, getting up get their coffee, she strokes his hair, brushing up against his ear, and Giovanni recoils, as if stung by a wasp.

"Come on, Carmela. I'll take you upstairs to settle down," he says, and takes her away, quickly. The light is fading, the smell of mint perfumes the warm air, cicadas sing, the sky outside is purple. The first floor is divided into two areas by the staircase; to the right, a short hallway leads to his parents' bedroom, their bathroom and a small study. To the left, the guest bedroom and a steep spiral staircase that leads to the tower. Giovanni brings her bag into her room – the vaulted ceiling is frescoed with flowers against a blue backdrop; there is a large wooden bed, two trunks embroidered petit point.

"You see," Giovanni mutters, embarrassed. "It's that my parents are a bit old-fashioned; they would rather we didn't sleep in the same room. Ridiculous, I know. But I don't know what to say, how to make them understand. They'd say it's a matter of respect. Is that all right?"

"Of course it is. It's absolutely fine," Carmela says. Argos slips into the room and settles in a dark corner – he isn't going to take its eyes off his master, even for a second.

Later, in darkness and in silence, in pyjamas and no slippers, with his heart in his throat – 'I'm not even sure why' - Giovanni walks down to the first floor.

"Shh, Argos, shh, be quiet," he whispers. Argos pricks up his ears but remains in his corner. Giovanni lowers the door handle, he opens it quietly, sneaks inside. Carmela doesn't seem surprised to see him slip into her bed.

"Shh," they murmur at the same time, laughing under the covers – duvets have not yet made their appearance, in Castel San Gerolamo, it's all a complicated system of sheets and blankets and heavy quilts.

"Your mother put a hot water bottle in my bed."

"Let me feel it," Giovanni says diving inside the bed, touching her feet, tickling her. She opens her legs. Carmela grits her teeth, stifling a gasp of surprise and pleasure.

***

Remember that at the beginning of the book I showed you a scene as if it were a movie? To look at something is not like reading: to watch a movie is to do it through the eyes of another, whereas when you read you are free to imagine a scene as you prefer it. And although the author accurately describes the physical characteristics of a character, the reader uses his own imagination - individual, specific. At the cinema you watch a story in which the external and exterior details have been created specifically for the viewer who can lazily sit in front of the screen and cease to imagine a world. He sees it. It's there. There is no need to make unnecessary efforts: the director has already done it all; he opens a curtain and takes you into his realm. Now that's what I am trying to do with you. Behold, there is a certain sense of adventure, with me taking hold of your hand and leading you - at my pace, now fast, now slow, and watch out because I am not going to wait for you.

Castel San Gerolamo. Exterior night, the dark night of the countryside. Scene 1: the barking of a dog, the sound of restless animals (chickens, foxes, a cat in heat). It's May, but it's cold - watch: I'll show you how the dew gets entangled in the branches of trees, I'll show you the shivering of flowers, the grass flattened by frost. All the different scents and aromas – well, I can't make you smell those, but if I show you the small mint plants, the apple trees and flowering pear tree, you can imagine the smell of the rhododendron that expands into the cold air, in the dark. The camera follows the curve of the road, lingers on the vineyard, enters the backyard of the Ferraros'. All the lights are off, the shutters closed. Even the house seems numb, closed in on itself. We enter through the front door, have a peep in the kitchen - empty, clean; in the dining room there is only the tablecloth, abandoned on a chair like a ghost.

We go back, walk up the stairs, along the corridor. We open a door, slowly, slowly: not even a squeak. We enter a dark room, and as you get used to it, it progressively appears less dark, shadowy. We get closer to the bed. Wait. Careful: Marieke is asleep on one side, her arm resting on her eyes, her earplugs on, her nightgown open on her full breasts. Luigi is sleeping belly up, snoring powerfully. We get out of their room, walk back along the corridor towards the left. Here too, all is quiet. No: wait: a rustle. Soft, the carpeted thud of a step. And, there: the door handle is lowering. And Giovanni - naked, skinny, white - leaves Carmela's bedroom under the curious gaze of Argos and walks up the spiral staircase to his room, where he almost falls upon his childish, single bed. He hugs the pillow and falls asleep right away.

***

In June, Giovanni buys a used Fiat Uno: dark blue, three years old, fifteen thousand km: perfect. He drives it only on weekends, sometimes in the evening. He leaves the office, goes back home to get changed, and by eight o'clock he is outside the studio Guarnieri, parked in second row: two gentle taps of the horn and Carmela appears at the window, waving with a grin as wide as her palm. She runs downstairs breathless, flushed, opens the door and jumps right in and kisses him while he's already in first gear – the two of them laughing, running away like Bonnie and Clyde.

It's a car, nothing more, but Giovanni feels liberated from the restrictions of public transport, free go to and from Castel San Gerolamo when he wants to, to explore the villages around Turin, from either side of the Po river, and to push on, towards Lombardy, the lakes. Novara and Pavia, Lecco and Arona, Milan. He is not alone on these excursions; Carmela is always at his side: his girlfriend, his companion (a word that comes from *cum + pane* = "with bread." A companion is someone you eat with, one you break bread with, one you share a table, a meal, a bed with).

They decide - taking turns - a destination, study the road map, read the advice written in the travel guides, book a room in a modest pension, dine in local restaurants, stroll along the streets of the new city, stopping for a coffee, a glass of wine, an ice cream. They enjoy the *little* things, they keep repeating, continually delighted by the discovery of the pleasure that each of them draws from small gestures made together. Carmela is the driving force in their couple: Giovanni is lost in the choice of a restaurant for the evening, she focuses on the cultural activities of the area. Giovanni would spend the whole afternoon sitting at a bar watching the world go by; Carmela after a short while quivers with anxiety: there is so little time, there is so much to see and do. Quick, quick, let's go, let's go.

THE HEART OF THE OCTOPUS

In July, they decide to travel to Andalusia for their first real holiday. Giovanni buys new linen shirts, shorts, swimming trunks; he packs his suitcase carefully. On the day of departure, he feels a knot in his chest he can't ignore nor loosen up, which suffocates him. He picks Carmela up; she comes downstairs sporting a wide-brimmed straw hat and sandals with vertiginous heels; Giovanni's hot restlessness raises by one degree: a whole week, twenty-four hours a day: twenty-four times seven, times eight days – one thousand three hundred and forty-four hours together. Round it up to one thousand five hundred. Are they too many? Will they get bored with each other?

Giovanni drives to Caselle airport, sweating, silent, restless. Carmela seems not to notice anything, continues unabated to make small talk, to tell old anecdotes about the Sicilian holidays of her childhood. Suddenly a plane flies over the Fiat Uno, so low that it seems to touch the roof. They both yell: "Look!" The knot in Giovanni's chest melts, he takes her hand, brings it to his lips, kisses it - a characteristic gesture that he repeats every time he trembles with fear before facing a new experience, before jumping into the future with his eyes closed.

"God, I love you."

"Me too," she says, her eyes glistening.

The flight to Seville is short and exciting – it's only his third time in the air, and Giovanni is astounded and delighted by everything: the flight announcements in Spanish, the hostess with an orange vest and ponytail who winks at him, the shopping cart full of snacks and soft drinks. He orders a Prosecco and olives and peanuts and crisps – it is easy to feel rich on a budget airline. In Seville they take a taxi to the hotel, leave their suitcases and go out quickly into the streets of the city full of flowers, full of a contagious cheerfulness. They follow whatever their guide book recommends, methodically, day after day: they eat tapas, visit the cathedral and the Giralda, the Alcazar, the Museum of Fine Arts, the aquarium; they take a carriage drawn by a white horse, a touristy double-decker bus, a slow boat on the Guadalquivir. They attend a flamenco show. They walk for hours under the hot sun, hand in hand, mesmerized by everything, even by the most squalid neighbourhoods - including the area where their three-star hotel is located, where whores stand on the sidewalks, drunks keep them awake at night. They fall asleep in each other's arms and they are still in the same position when they awake. In the bathroom there are two sinks: they brush their teeth next to each other, looking in the mirror. They dress and undress, wash and comb their hair and pee facing each other, without inhibition or exhibitionism: simply together. A real couple.

***

On the third day they take the train to Cordova, only forty minutes away. Like almost all men, departures disturb Giovanni; he's tense and monosyllabic and solemn until they get there. They reach their destination at noon.

"This is called the Mezquita, a mosque that became a church, isn't that amazing? Its construction began in 780 and ended in 987," Carmela reads her guidebook. "It is undoubtedly a work of a Muslim maestro. Observe first the Orange Tree Courtyard, with fountains and the well dating back to the tenth century. Did you see? Really? OK. Let's move on. On entering," Carmela continues motioning to walk into the building, "one feels as if immersed in a real forest of columns and arches in which the colour and shadows play an important role. Once you have gone through the high wall through the main entrance, called the Puerta del Perdon (1377), you enter a courtyard full of decorative orange trees (do not eat the oranges: they are bad!)."

Giovanni isn't listening any more, he moves a few paces away from Carmela, who continues to read. Giovanni looks around in the shadows.

"Keep going. You enter the building - here, we entered, here, here -... building consisting of 856 columns supporting arches painted white and red, according to the Saracean taste. The darkness, stained a dark shade of red, makes the atmosphere even more suggestive and the continuous repetition of the many spaces, so similar to each other, can make you lose your orientation ... But: are you listening?"

"No," Giovanni replies.

"Oh come on. Listen. You have to."

"No."

"Listen."

"No," Giovanni repeats, walking along the hall. Carmela runs after him.

"Listen. Why don't we visit it, and *after* we read the book? We ain't in any hurry."

"Please, don't say we ain't."

"We aren't in any hurry. Why bother to read everything straight away? Can't we just look around?"

"Because it's important to understand what we are looking at. Contextualize it."

Giovanni's eyes go to the ceiling and Carmela sees him and glows with anger - her eyes two fissures of a dazzling white in the darkness.

"All right. OK. Fine. If you don't want to read and know, be my guest. I continue my tour with the guide. See you at the exit."

Giovanni, of course, takes a step back and hurries to the side of his girlfriend. They walk along in silence, Carmela pretending to be immersed in reading, Giovanni avoiding her eyes.

"Sorry," Giovanni gives in at the end. "It *is* an amazing place. Really. And of course I want to know everything - I've never been in a church such as this one. In a mosque. But I also want to absorb the atmosphere, I want to wander around and get lost among the columns, maybe sit down somewhere and watch who comes and who goes."

"I'm not forcing you to stay with me. But I can't enjoy the visit if I don't know what I'm watching."

"Oh come on," Giovanni says, taking her elbow and pulling her along. "Come on," he repeats in her hair that smells like the oranges on the orange trees in the courtyard outside. Carmela surrenders. Isn't it amazing, isn't it *refreshing*, this alternation of strength and weakness, without being afraid, without having to win at all costs? A couple therapist would definitely say that arguing is healthy, wholesome – that is, *if* the couple is really intimate, complicit, only if and when one is certain that he is being understood, only if one understands the other completely. According to Jung, a woman who is at ease with her femininity is able to express - without fear and indeed naturally - masculine traits such as strength, tenacity, courage. If, however, that woman expresses too much with her Animus, the man does not react well: he gets agitated, loses patience, he feels threatened. He rejects her. There are similar problems when it is the man to show too much of his soul, when he rejects a typically male role, when he appears weak, unable to take a position, by refusing its responsibilities. Often, Jung suggests, the worst quarrels occur when the woman shows her masculine side and the man his feminine side; she becomes imperious and hard, he petulant, hysterical, and they get on each other's nerves. This is the case of Giovanni and Carmela, she strong and he weak, she overbearing and domineering, he passive and accommodating. But not always. That's the beauty of their union: neither is too proud to go back, to admit defeat. And: basically: the one who wins never speaks of his victory, and never of the other's defeat.

THE HEART OF THE OCTOPUS

***

At the end of the week they return home, and their routine changes – now they spend all their free time together. When, on the Wednesday, Carmela has planned to have dinner with her friends and after sleeping in her own apartment, Giovanni foretastes his night alone, a bachelor evening like he hasn't had for ages – yes, he's going to go home early, watch a movie, read a book whilst soaking in the bathtub with a glass of wine, and he'll go to bed early, for once. Rather than what he'd planned, he spends a terrible night. He can't sleep, alone, he turns around and gets up and drinks a glass of milk and eats a cookie and returns to bed but sleep eludes him, flies out the window like Peter Pan. At three AM he is still awake, and at five o'clock he is awake once more.

The solution is only one, and Giovanni immediately acts upon it, proposing to Carmela to live together; for a lucky coincidence, both of them can give notice on their flats in September; they have a few weeks to find a new apartment.

"After all, we are always together. I sleep at yours six nights a week, you have half of your wardrobe in my closet, but: two toothbrushes, two sets of make-up, not to mention the shoes. We simplify everything."

"And what are we going to tell my parents? And yours? "

"We are adults, Carmela. We have a job, a salary. We can do whatever we want. Do you want to?"

THE HEART OF THE OCTOPUS

"Fuck, Giovanni. Of course I want to!"

***

Carmela is nice. It is a fact, such as: spring follows winter. Or: we all die. Yes, she is a bit schoolteacher-y, she must continually give lectures on what she knows (and she knows a lot, so the lectures take place daily). Yes, she is petulant, but God she makes me laugh. She's witty, she is cheerful. She is a fantastic mimic, she gets other people's facial expressions and replicates them to perfection - but without offending, without humiliating - and always finds the right joke at the right time, making everyone laugh. Yes, of course: she is a narcissist, she really likes herself, and could easily, I guess, go into politics, one day (because in the end all politicians are clever mythomaniacs, crafty exhibitionists). But she has gravitas, nous. Intelligence. Culture, but also humour. And lightness. Carmela wears life with lightness, as if it were a silk dress, crisp and delicate.

I like Carmela – I *really* like her: I like her wild hair, her slightly stocky, mobile neck, her hands whose nails are too short and with cuticles all bitten up. I love her laughter and I like how easily she cries, she gets moved over nothing (like Giovanni, for that matter). I like her smell, I like her loud, not very noble way of sneezing. I describe her like this, in bits and pieces, because she is an important character; but in some way secondary. A duchess; a countess; at most, a princess: never, ever a queen. I could write a whole novel only about her: she has so much to say, to teach, to tell. But I have already made my decision, and that is to follow Giovanni, *his* story. See, I know it already: you don't, but now I want to tell you, before you start liking her too much too, skipping months as an athlete who wants to beat the world record for the long jump: here's the run-up, here is the revelation. Carmela will not stay on these pages much longer. Her relationship with Giovanni will end badly. With a crash. And you will not like her that much. "And then?" you ask. After the end of their relationship, she'll move to Rome, where she'll keep working as the brilliant lawyer she already is. At forty, she'll fall in love with an English historian, professor at Yale, she'll move with him to the United States. They will have a daughter. And twelve years later, on holiday in Greece with her family, she'll die in a car accident.

***

They find an apartment they both like; Giovanni even does a bit of DIY, redecorating their bedroom; they buy a double bed. He carries Carmela in his arms, that first day, through the doorstep. And I tell you that the smile she gives him –homely yet sensual, provocative and strong, ecstatic and real – that, he'll remember for a lifetime. They make love three times a day, they eat too much or forget to cook, they often open another bottle of wine at dinner, they fight over the housework, because of Carmela's untidiness, they decide to find someone who will clean and iron – and they are very, very happy.

In late September, Carmela goes to Sicily for a couple of weeks - Giovanni misses her to death; he can't sleep, he becomes melancholic, pathetic - he slips into bed wearing her dressing gown, smelling it like a dog that has lost his master, an old bruised dog, whose only relief comes through his nose. After four days, Carmela's aunt Caterina dies, suddenly, and Giovanni decides to go to the funeral. After all, they live as husband and wife: it is his duty to be near her, offering his condolences to the family, whom he knows is as traditional as compact. The first available flight is in the evening. He lands in Palermo at eight. He hugs Carmela, who is beautiful and sensual in her tight black dress, her eyes filled with tears, and takes the back seat of the silver Jaguar driven by Mr. Montaperto's chaffeur, who keeps looking at him in the rear-view mirror for the duration of the trip. When they arrive - Giovanni tired, red with sleep - he almost bursts out laughing. Because of nerves, of disbelief, of wonder: what stands before him looks like a scene from *The Leopard*: the eighteenth-century villa is truly impressive, well-lit in the dark night, located in the middle of an enclosed park with terraces and balustrades, preceded by a large square formed by two semi-circular areas and with a striking façade in the middle of which is the imposing staircase.

Giovanni walks up the stairs, following Carmela. Her father opens the door and takes his hand into his.

THE HEART OF THE OCTOPUS

***

From the Christian lexicon where charism was a special gift given by God to a person to allow him/her to spread the Word and to do good, the meaning of the word *charisma* changed to indicate a kind of magnetic influence, the own innate gift of some personality capable of having an incredible, powerful influence on the masses – which should inspire goodness.

Carmela's father - Domenico Montaperto - takes Giovanni's hand into his and Giovanni feels surrounded by a golden halo; he feels wanted, loved, chosen: like God chose Israel; like Sleeping Beauty, awakened by the Prince, who asks her to dance with him. Domenico possesses that gift that few have: a gift that one can analyse and try to imitate, usually with poor results. His deep blue eyes stare at him, continuously, as if Giovanni were saying particularly important, incredibly interesting things; when he finally stops shaking his hand (a tenacious, dry, persistent crunch) he touches his elbow, continuing physical contact. Most people, even when they seem to stare at the other person, actually give their attention through listening; it is difficult to talk and stare at the same time, you get distracted, lose your train of thought. A person who has charisma - Clinton, JFK - can speak *and* stare, at the same time, with an insistence that could be excessive, but somehow isn't. Dr. Montaperto has good taste; he is a well-respected man; he used to be a solicitor, too, but is now retired, living a life of ease but not excess. He's sporty, he plays tennis and golf, he loves to travel, to eat and drink and read, he loves the theatre and the opera; he even goes to the gigs of his boyhood idols, the Rolling Stones and Rod Stewart and Billy Joel. Short but not stocky, slender, he has a rather big nose, thick eyebrows and wild grey hair which is slightly too long and back combed, and is undoubtedly a handsome man, more beautiful than his daughter, than his son. In his presence, Giovanni feels awkward and small, inadequate - yet mysteriously at ease, because Domenico soothes, relaxes, inspires. Yes: he does inspire. And inspiration always has at its core a kernel of seduction. Giovanni is blatantly seduced by Domenico Montaperto and his family, by their taste and their wealth, which is evident as not exhibited; by their grace, as Luigi would call it.

Giovanni falls into Domenico's eyes like a fly into a spider's web.

***

The night: a silence.

We climb the (marble) stairs, me clinging on to the railing (made out of a type of wood as blonde and smooth as oil, without a scratch) as if I were afraid of falling.

"Your room," Carmela whispers in my ear, opening the door and I cast a glance on a cavernous space that seems to me as immense as a gym, a church, a museum - our whole apartment would fit in here - and I turn around and she touches my lips with a butterfly kiss, which means: "My darling, forget the night tour." Amen, I sigh, and I tell her that I love her. The bed - huge - with 100% Egyptian cotton sheets, super-smooth and super-silky, with a tiny cinnamon stripe, and a cinnamon blanket, and many, many scattered cushions, so many I am not sure where to put them: on the floor? On a chair? It looks like a hotel room, neutral, all taupe-y, all in good taste but a bit generic, characterless; heavy curtains of a darker brown, still-life paintings that might be worth billions but are as mute as fishes; I take off my shoes and my swollen feet sink into the thickness of the super-thick taupe carpet; I discard my clothes and go into the bathroom to take a shower, and voilà! the taupe theme continues with marble everywhere: and modern taps that look like fountains, and you push a button to release water at the ideal temperature, and a quantity of bottles and soaps and lotions and tiny shampoo bottles like those of a hotel but made of crystal rather than plastic, *ça va sans dire*, with intricate tops, clearly all terribly delicate and valuable. A blonde wood desk and blonde leather chair as soft as a baby's bottom, and at the sides of the bed identical bedside tables with identical lamps and two bottles: one of Evian and one of San Pellegrino; two packets of tissues, fragrant and not; magazines (L'Espresso; the American edition of Vanity Fair); a few books (Simenon, Tabucchi, Chekov). I sleep very badly in the very comfortable bed.

The next day, I expect to hear some noise before I get up, but when I go downstairs everyone is already there at the table, sitting quietly in front of the remains of their breakfast, which they had clearly eaten long before me. I have a huge appetite, I devour the slice of toast with orange marmalade but I do not ask for another one; I would happily bite my fingers, but I say thank you, that's fine thank you, I drink the bitterest black coffee with enthusiasm, three cups, and I shake for an hour. It's so hot it feels like August and I sweat in my dark grey suit and I walk up to the family chapel (!) located at the bottom of the park (!!). Women dressed in black, a couple even with a hat, sober men. No one cries - so much for the clichés on the south of Italy, dear mother. And there's a refreshment in a room that looks like a ballroom, with a colossal crystal chandelier reflected on the shiny parquet floor, antique still lives and even more antique carpets and tapestries depicting Moses saved from the waters, portraits of noblemen and noblewomen, and I don't dare do anything, say nothing in case it's all wrong. I want them to like me. The Montapertos are kind and caring as a mother, better than my mamma. I feel like Cinderella.

Carmela tries to divide and share her attention among all - parents and uncles and aunts and various relatives, whatever, I can't remember a single name. I attach myself to a cousin or something that I discover later be her aunt Maria Vittoria who lives on the Lake Orta, and when I say I attach myself I mean it, something like superglue, until Dr. Montaperto ("Giovanni, please: call me Domenico") approaches and takes my arm and we walk like idiots the length and breadth of the room that it takes a quarter of an hour to walk around it, and he grills me but respectably, pretending not to, and I might be an idiot, yes, but not an imbecile and I'm game and try to play the role of the young man who is humble but ambitious, intelligent but quiet, one that does not brag, who does not pray, who does not bend. A man. He nods, twists his body so as not to stop looking into my eyes.

Across the hall, Carmela smiles at me and melts my heart. I gulp down champagne like it was orange juice, which is what Domenico is drinking.

Of course all this alcohol goes to my head and in the afternoon I go "to have a little rest," as suggested with sublime tact by Mrs. Montaperto, who does *not* ask me to call her by name. I pass out immediately and sleep the unconscious sleep of the dead, and wake up three hours later to the sound of china cups tinkling; tea here is served at five o'clock on the dot, as if we were at Buckingham Palace. We talk some more, we walk some more, we have another tremendously enjoyable evening, and I do find it shocking: it upsets me to be so enamoured of this family, to love it more than I love my own. It's not the money itself – it's all that is behind it: the estate, the park and the boulevards lined by ancient olive trees, and this house - god, this villa, I can't even use exclamation marks as they would be so out of place here, in this calmness, this way of life. I feel part of it; behold, I feel a sense (ridiculous, baseless, unreasonable) of belonging. As if all this: things and people – the Nero d'Avola of one of the family estates drunk at dinner in crystal glasses as fine as a feather, the pink Bukhara rug, the huge cream-colored linen napkins embroidered with the initials of the great-grandmother and Carmela's elderly great-aunt Wilhelmina, the fountain that hints at Versailles and their cat Orlando, and record collections and paintings and the vast library where we go and have a cigar – *all of this*, and in saying this I make a sweeping gesture with my arms to indicate the lot: as if *all of this*, as I said, was destined to belong to me. Family included, of course: not only my beautiful girlfriend but also and especially her parents, her uncles and cousins and grandparents.

Domenico hugs me on the doorstep.

"I'm so glad to have finally met you, Giovanni," he says. "I'm delighted my daughter has finally met a man of honour. A decent man. Really decent, in the true meaning of the word."

I give him a hug, probably too tight. When we get home - together, for the first time after a trip - Carmela opens the mail, and I the dictionary:

Decent: Adjective [from the Latin *decentem* 'becoming, fitting, proper']. 1. Conforming with generally accepted standards of respectable or moral behaviour; appropriate; fitting; not likely to shock or embarrass others; 2. of an acceptable standard; satisfactory; good; kind, obliging, or generous.

Yes, I am decent. Qualifying adjective. I'm sure I have been called many names, in front or behind, but nothing had ever made so proud.

***

THE HEART OF THE OCTOPUS

Giovanni is sitting on the aeroplane, on the way back to Turin, towards home. Giovanni is in love – with Carmela, sure, but no longer with Carmela the enterprising, exotic, intelligent woman I have described; he's now in love with her in a broader sense. Imagine a present packaged in the most incredible wrapping paper - a Christmas box like those that are prepared in luxury stores, where the paper is opaque and rigid, and the bow flat, all in a silent and elegant combination of colours. Carmela is the actual present; the paper and the ribbon and the card are her family, her origin, her house with the gardens and the tennis courts and the swimming pool. Carmela-package, crisp and brilliant, even more perfect than before, certainly more complete than before. Giovanni works harder than ever, to forget about the sense of inadequacy he felt; now, he wants to have what she has; he wants to *be her*, with those parents and that estate. And since one can't be transformed into something else as if by magic, he magnifies the love he feels for her. He makes her the centre of everything.

"That's exactly it: I am Carmelacentric. Carmela my sun, and I her planet, her moon, she stands still and I move around her, I move, turning and spinning, doing anything for her, anything to accommodate her needs, her moods, her pleasure. I have become her shadow. Her moon. Her star. Carmela my universe, my reason for living, the light, the air I breathe, the water I drink. I oxygen: she hydrogen. I cloud, she: sky. I grain of sand, she: desert. I drop of blood, she: heart. My heart."

THE HEART OF THE OCTOPUS

***

In Italy, a Law graduate has to pass an exam arranged yearly by the Ministry of Justice to become a *Procuratore Legale*. The exam is notoriously hard, and it takes months before one gets to know the results. When they are published, six months after taking the test, it turns out that Carmela passed it, not me. There's no other easier way to say it: I failed. Oh, it doesn't matter, my darling, I say with a sweetness that I don't feel. Of course I am not upset, you deserve it, you did study so much more than me, you were better prepared, it doesn't matter, indeed: it's such a good result, honey, darling, my love. Please do come home early tonight, so that we can open a bottle of wine, celebrate.

"We must have champagne," I cry and I rush out to buy it, that's the thing to do, the least I can do, what her father would do, and I run downstairs and run to the store and run until I have no breath and tears fill my eyes and I want to punch the wall as they do in movies, and my good jesus I wanted to pass, I wanted it so badly, and yes, you know what? Yes: I wanted her to fail, she and her airs, she and her intelligence, and I feel like I lost an important game; a final. You know when at the end of a match, the players from both sides shake hands in a very sporty, very fair kind of way, but the truth that everyone knows is that one of the teams has won and the other has lost, and the winners take their shirt off and give it to the losers and vice versa, they exchange their muddy T-shirts wet with sweat, but even wearing the winning shirt, those who have lost have a sad face and are all hunched up and disconsolate, and I feel that way, as if I had lost the game, the match the final; I have the slouching shoulders of the loser, the downcast eyes of the loser, the bitter smile of the loser.

And I buy the bottle of champagne and go back home a loser, and I pop the cork, and I'd love it to make it fly straight into her merry eyes, into her wide mouth full of white teeth, jesus yes, what I'd give to wipe away that fucking winning smile.

***

"I need a holiday, Giovanni," Carmela says. "I need time to see my parents and my friends and celebrate the exam results and make a plan. I feel I am in limbo."

Carmela is restless, fidgety. She feels unsettled. She's bored with the slow Turinese pace, with the Guarnieri practice, tired of her little routine, of Giovanni's insistent breath that burns on her neck. When she feels hounded, she starts running away like a wild fox chased by beagles, a fox that tries to hide in burrows, that slips away from under your nose and you try to sniff her out but she's gone already.

She tenders her resignation; now that she is a Procuratore, she needs more challenges. She needs to take on more responsibility, work in a bigger practice.

"It will be better to find a job elsewhere. For both of us. I need to recharge my batteries," she tells Giovanni. She flies to Sicily for three weeks, and returns with a shorter haircut, a suitcase full of new clothes, and unexpected developments regarding her career. In Palermo she met Rosa Maria Pinelli, a solicitor that deals with family law. They talked about the type of work she does, to protect the human rights of women and children, and of her project to open a new office in Milan. Only later on, Carmela realised that the meeting was nothing more than an interview; three hours later she had received a job offer; she had accepted it. She'd start working in Milan from mid-October.

"No, it's better that way, really," Giovanni reassures Marieke on the phone, his voice choked by panic. "Actually in this way we avoid spending twenty-four hours a day together, which would be unhealthy."

"Are you sure?"

"Yes, yes: of course we are sure. Commuting to Milan isn't such a drama. She'll be at home from Thursday to Monday morning, and I can spend one night in Milan during the week. Carmela needs stimulation. Better a different job than a new boyfriend!"

When something is about to escape, you hold it forcefully: look at the hands of a child whose balloon has slipped away, his knuckles white from the effort to hold it. To keep it.

***

THE HEART OF THE OCTOPUS

To Keep: the list of the verb's synonyms reads: retain, hold on to, keep for oneself, retain possession of, keep possession of, retain in one's possession, keep hold of, not part with, hold fast to, hold back; save, store; hang on to, stash away. They are useful to describe what Giovanni tries to do as soon as he realizes that Carmela is running away – in her own way, but she is definitely running away, slipping through his hands like a snake, a fish, an eel, a thing that darts here and there between your fingers, slipping through your hands and eventually managing to escape, no matter how hard you hold it.

They have known each other for eighteen months. They live together. They are comfortable in each other's company; they love each other. But watch them more closely. Giovanni looks sideways at Carmela, constantly asks her about her well-being, on her exact level of contentment: is he looking after her properly? Too much, too little? Does he offer her the kindness that she expects, or should he be more careful, more present, closer? And in bed, is she satisfied with their sex life? Should they do more, less, in a different way, more exciting, less monotonous? Time has not given Giovanni the lazy serenity that often characterises new couples. Giovanni is and continues to be an anxious young man, apprehensive: instead of relaxing, enjoying the relationship, he basks in anguished thoughts, spies on Carmela's moods trying to predict them, in order to be even more accommodating, to ensure that she loves him more, better. In short, he's developing a form of emotional dependence for which the search for love becomes almost the only reason for his existence. Sure, Giovanni "works," in the sense that he goes out to the office and interacts with colleagues and clients. Inside, however, he behaves as if he had the role of love-donor, one-way only: his way; as if whatever Carmela does - whether she's cheerful or sad or tired or busy – had a direct correlation and was explained by what he does or doesn't do. This continuous search for love shares certain characteristics with addiction to substances like alcohol or drugs. Carmela is his heroin. Carmela who sends him into ecstasy when she is with him, when he sees her, touches her, when she's controlled and controllable, safe with him. She is indispensable to him. He couldn't live, without her. When she isn't there, he has real withdrawal symptoms, which throw him in a shocking state of panic.

When something tries to escape, we strive to catch it. When we are afraid that our pet might run away, we lock it in a cage; and if we take it out for a walk, we keep it on a tight leash.

On a Saturday night - Carmela at a yoga class with her cousin – he lights all the candles they have: he counts them: twenty-two. He puts a bottle of champagne in the fridge. He sits on the couch waiting, holding a velvet box containing the engagement ring on which he spent a fortune, at the pre-eminent jeweller in Turin. When Carmela opens the door, her rosy face softened by the light of candles, Giovanni asks her to sit down. He kneels down, slips the ring on her finger.

"Will you marry me, Carmela?"

THE HEART OF THE OCTOPUS

"Of course I'll marry you," she says quietly.

***

We make phone calls – first to Castel San Gerolamo (where my parents' response is opposite: Marieke is as quiet as Luigi is tearful) and then to Sicily - Domenico is playing tennis, when he answers he's out of breath; we tell him, and he throws his racket in the air that falls on his foot, he swears and shouts a triumphant cry of love for his daughter and I hang up quickly, before he has time to talk to me of honour, of decency. Before he gets to the dreaded conversation "from man to man." It sounds like a threat.

I return the diamond ring to the jeweller's to be resized, and it is as if the lack of that golden circle invalidated the promise we made to each other: no ring, no wedding.

"We're engaged," I tell anyone who happens to be around: my co-workers, our neighbours, my most distant relatives. The newsagent where I buy *La Stampa* every morning, the waiter where we go for a glass of wine in the evening.

"But what do you mean you haven't told her. You saw her last night and you didn't mention it!" I cry in disbelief when I find out that Carmela has not passed on the announcement of their wedding to her cousin. "Why ever not?"

"I don't know. She seemed depressed, and it is not news that may cheer her."

"When will you tell her?"

"I'll see her next Tuesday for a drink - so I can also show her the ring, too."

I find it hard to sleep, the mind a volcano in constant eruption lists all the things we need to sort out: the ceremony, refreshments, and the flowers, the clothes... Carmela sleeping beside me is snoring softly ... and I think of all what we have not yet said, we have not discussed or decided ... I thought every girl on the planet was eager to get married: yes, that the idea of the fairy-tale prince who asks for the hand of a maiden would sting the soul of even the most progressive feminist in town. But my distracted girlfriend thinks of everything else but: she thinks about the party next weekend; she wonders where to spend Christmas; she studies all the minutiae about the case she is dealing with - whether the co-heirs share a responsibility to pay certain debts - and that seems to worry her far too much. And she had to look for a flat in Milan, and finally found it - a studio that when I walked in I time-travelled back ten years –tiny, but in the fashionable neighbourhood of Brera, not far from the office, with good links to the train station. I don't like to think about her there. There, alone in her studio, she feels like a single girl: one of the women of *Sex and the City*, a show she is watches with such discernible fun and that I find frankly gross. These girls claim they want a relationship and they go around fucking right and left, anyone, anywhere. But I'm here! I want to scream. You do have a relationship! We are a couple - stop pretending that it isn't so.

It is as if the marriage, with a capital M, was a goal to be achieved; a destination.

And here we are, I tell myself, I delude myself, we are metaphorically ready; we have our suitcases in the trunk, a bag with sandwiches and drinks on the seat beside us, the road map, and our favourite CDs. We are in different cars, but: similar. The race official waves the flag, and with a foot on the accelerator, we are off: and I burst out of the ranks and accelerate and change gear quickly, too quickly maybe, from second to fourth and into fifth, while Carmela still limps, lingering on, still in second gear... I check in the mirror, she's a dot on the road behind me. Just don't go into reverse, I tell myself, and somehow we will reach our destination.

Let's just get there.

***

Carmela flourishes in Milan, as they say widows do. Commuter life suits her, she says. She likes to get on the train and read for a couple of hours, to work undisturbed, headphones over her ears to cancel external noises, to help her concentrate. She leaves full of enthusiasm and comes back excited, spreading around a strange smell, of paper and dust and of the train's stale air. She loses weight.

"Like all brides," Marieke says, but Giovanni knows that Carmela isn't thinking about their marriage at all. She hasn't gone shopping yet, or even to try dresses on; or a veil; or a hat. She hasn't yet bothered to call the priest, nor the Council - they have not even discussed whether the rite will be religious or secular.

"If it were for me," Giovanni confides to Filippo, whom he's begun to see every Tuesday, his 'bachelor' evening. "Me, well: I would have already organised everything. Instead, it's as if she were happy to be my eternal fiancée. And me, here, waiting like a dick."

"Maybe she's simply scared, deep down?" his friend suggests.

"Scared of what?"

"Of losing her freedom. Her youth. Of making mistakes. Of eating more than she can chew. Don't we all have it, deep down, a certain fear of growing up?"

"And what am I to do – stand here and wait till she's ready? Just: wait?"

"Precisely. You can't do anything else."

And Giovanni waits, and time passes, and his waiting increases: indeed: magnifies. And he is afraid. He no longer mentions marriage. They no longer talk about their future. When by chance he makes a hint, Carmela says she's tired, she wants to enjoy the weekend, her boyfriend, they'll discuss the wedding another time. Giovanni, frozen, throws away the magazine he had bought for her, that showcased spectacular wedding dresses; he stores in a drawer details of hotels that specialise in wedding parties; he carefully folds back in their envelope copies of his certificate of baptism and confirmation that Marieke has mailed him; he throws into the rubbish bin the list of people who should be invited, the brochures for exotic vacations for their honeymoon.

***

They decide to spend Christmas each with their own family.

"It will be the last time," Giovanni says.

"The last time?"

"Yes: the last Christmas we won't spend together. You don't really intend spending it without me, next year, Ms. Ferraro?"

"As they say here when one has a Master's degree, like me. Call me Doctor," Carmela corrects him.

"Doctor Ferraro, then."

"Of course," she responds.

They celebrate their 'little' Christmas, as Carmela calls it, on the 23rd of December. Homemade *ravioli* with truffles, fried pumpkin and olives, broccoli braised in red wine and black olives. Carmela prepares a traditional Sicilian donut, the "*buccellato*," with a rich filling of dried figs, dark chocolate pieces, jam and dried fruit; they drink sweet *Passito* from the island of Pantelleria. They exchange gifts under their two foot-tall, under-decorated tree: a pair of earrings for her, with a diamond teardrop, and for

Giovanni a beautiful dark brown leather briefcase, marked with his initials.

"It looks like a doctor's bag! I like it very much."

They go to bed and make love for the last time this year.

"To next year," Giovanni toasts with a glass of sparkling wine.

"Yes," Carmela responds.

"It will be quite a year."

"Yes."

"Our wedding."

"Yes."

"And then a nice trip somewhere. We need to decide where."

"Yes, yes. Come here, now," Carmela says, taking him in her arms, between her legs.

"Promise that when we return home after Christmas we begin to make plans."

"Yes, yes. Now come here," she repeats, and Giovanni obeys, finally silent.

***

In Castel San Gerolamo, Giovanni is besieged with questions from relatives and family friends - all want to know a date, a place, the details of the wedding party. Giovanni sidesteps, dodges, avoids. He escapes. He does not know what to say - no, actually they have not yet set anything. They will see. Decide. Of course he's happy. Of course he wants to wed Carmela as soon as possible. Of course: when they'll make some decisions, they'll let everyone know.

Then he keeps quiet.

Carmela keeps very quiet too; since she's gone to Sicily, she's rarely called him. Giovanni calls her, and often she is not home. She's gone out. She is in town with her father. She is playing golf. Tennis. She is riding her favourite horse. She's gone shopping with her mother - but as soon as I hear from her, I'll let her know you called.

"Is there anything wrong?" he manages to ask her, one evening.

"No, Giovanni. But of course my parents spoil me, take me everywhere, like a prodigal daughter."

"I can't wait for you to come home, honey. To our home."

"Yes," Carmela says with a sigh. "And what's up with you?" she asks, but doesn't even wait for him to answer. "Sorry, darling, but I really have to go now, call me tomorrow, goodbye, goodbye," she says, and then there is just the awkward silence of interrupted communication. Giovanni stands with the receiver in his hand.

Like years ago with Julie: he feels like a complete fool.

***

In February, Carmela does not come back to Turin for ten consecutive days, as she's busy with a trial. Giovanni drives to Milan, and finds himself short of breath as he opens the door of the studio, like a thief, a spy, a scoundrel. He starts to go through her drawers, her sweaters and socks and underpants, to see what she brought into *this* flat, her flat: here, without him. He opens an envelope, it's a bill, he puts it back in its place. He unscrews the top of her perfume, checks the cabinet in the bathroom, walks to the bed to smell the sheets. He tidies up, fills her empty refrigerator ("I never eat at home, it makes me sad"), he sits on the bed, sighing. Later, he surprises her when she comes out of the office with a large bunch of flowers.

"What a cute little lover," Carmela's boss Mrs Pinelli says as she walks past them on the threshold, and that diminutive "little" sticks in his throat. "Have you been standing here long? How could I blame you? You should stay as long as necessary. Your girlfriend is just charming," she adds. "Worth the wait. Charming," she repeats, and that adjective buzzes in his ears. Yes: charming. A charming woman.

Absolutely, Giovanni would like to tell Ms Pinelli, who got on her bike and disappeared from view: ab-so-lu-te-ly: Carmela is charm personified. He looks at her, now and later on, while they take an apéritif and again during dinner, and he sees that she doesn't eat anything, and drinks too much, and laughs making ringlets with a strand of hair around her fingers, and he can see that men stare at her; all these fucking Milanese men, these insolent vain bragging Milanese men, he can see how they gape at his Sicilian girl, his girl, his woman, and he knows that if they could they would touch her, but hey do they know that she is his, his woman, and he's going to marry her and make her even more his, his own, forever his own, like a thing, an object, a piece of land, a vineyard. And Carmela, this charming woman, she also sees them, these men with eyes as long as hands and their cock pressing inside their tight pants and she knows who would happily oh so happily slip in between her taut firm thighs and yet she smiles, the bitch, his wife, his Madonna, his whore, and she smiles and he'd like to punch her angelic face and he suddenly pulls her close to him and holds her tight he squeezes her too tight and they end up quarrelling because she feels out of breath and in Milan she's finally learnt to breathe again, she tells him, finally, after all this time, she can breathe, let me breathe, and he takes her by the wrists and holds them but she is not intimidated, she is smart, what a clever fucking slut she is, because she doesn't cry, she doesn't pathetically meow like the others, she isn't a shy weak little girl: she holds her head high, she screams as loud as he does, beating the ground with her foot, she even gives him a shove, and he hugs her, and she lets herself be hugged because she's tired and has been drinking too much and wants to go to bed, and they grab a taxi and they hold hands all the way back to her studio flat, and they collapse on the bed that Giovanni has made all fresh earlier and he's about to fall asleep when he hears her voice whisper: "Don't you ever do that again."

THE HEART OF THE OCTOPUS

***

It's Sunday evening. Giovanni has gone to Castel San Gerolamo for the weekend - there was the confirmation of a distant cousin whom he had met only twice in his life, but it's one of those things you have to do. He hates standing in church, among his parents, as if he were a child. He hates the ceremony, too long, and then, later, he hates having to drink low-quality wine, to eat too much food. He hates the smiles, the hand-shaking, the heavy make-up of the ladies, their perfume, the ridiculous ties, the garish tablecloths, the flowers. He hates having to smile to relatives who comment on the absence of his fiancé, he hates having to go back to sleep in his old room in his grandfather's tower, all alone.

He drives back to Turin with the radio blaring. He parks the car and looks up to the windows of their apartment, sees them open, and his heart skips a beat. He lingers for a few minutes in the car – he'd like to run upstairs, lift Carmela up and bring her into their bedroom and love her with all the strength and energy and anger that he has inside and has not been able to express, that he does not know he feels; instead, he sits listening to the patter of rain on the roof, a tic-tic-tic that becomes a roar, and he still waits a bit longer, because the rain might stop, and he does nothing: he sits and waits. Which is exactly what he's been doing all these last few months, waiting for things to return to normal, for Carmela to be the way she was.

Giovanni sits in his Fiat for an hour, until the phone rings and the guttural voice of his mother echoes into the wet car.

"Are you back?"

"Yes, I stopped for a coffee, I've only just arrived."

"And how's Carmela"?

"I haven't seen her yet."

"Say hello on my behalf."

"I shall."

"Giovanni: are you all right?"

"Yes."

"Are you sure?"

"Yes."

"You have a funny voice."

"What do you mean: funny? I'm tired. I'm going to go, now."

"Let's talk again tomorrow, Giovanni. Call me."

"Yes," Giovanni says and finally picks up his bag and opens the front door.

***

Giovanni's dreams are commonplace, easy to decipher: he dreams of walking in a hall whose floor is covered with egg shells, like those sheets of bubble wrap used for fragile items. But these are real eggs, chicken eggs or quail eggs, thousands of them, hundreds of thousands of them. Giovanni enters the room; no one else is there; he knows he has to cross the huge room all the way to the other side – metres and metres covered with thin shells of eggs, crispy, ready to explode. He walks with little uncertain steps, faltering, stalling, expecting to hear a crunch and a crush every time he moves.

Everything is about to break down.

***

It is a day in late winter, almost spring. The calendar says that there are still two weeks to go before its official start; but you can smell it, sweet and warm, like a breath.

Giovanni is happy, this spring morning. He looks at himself in the mirror, his cheeks slightly tanned, his eyes merry; he smiles. The day before yesterday he's come back from a short break in Spain; the excuse was a conference of international law, but he didn't feel like attending the convention. He sauntered through the streets of Barcelona, ate tapas and drank Cava, walked for hours under the Spanish sun, admiring palaces and churches - rich, heavy with Catholic faith; he liked to sit in outdoor cafes and drink glasses of cold beer, trying to see himself with the eyes of a passer-by: still a young man, slender, on vacation. He returned to Turin on Sunday evening: Carmela went to pick him up at Caselle airport, holding an ironic sign that read: *Giovanni* with a black marker at the exit from the terminal.

THE HEART OF THE OCTOPUS

Today he wakes up early. He hears Carmela in the kitchen; she's making coffee; he gets up, takes a shower. He chews his biscuits slowly, trying to delay the start of the day. He kisses her on the front door, goes downstairs, she is at the window waving her hand like a child, like a queen. It's sunny. It's March. His heart sings in his chest. On Thursday they are invited to dinner to her cousin's; only three nights without her.

The day passes like every Monday – it passes. Carmela sends a short message when she arrives in Milan, with two XX; he replies with three XXX. At lunch, he eats a sandwich at the bar downstairs, the one he likes most, and has veal chop a là Milanese, warm inside a cold ciabatta bread, freshly made. He reads the newspaper. Back in the office, he works all afternoon, and when he finally finishes and goes outside, he is convinced that it's lighter than yesterday – only just. He walks home, stopping at a deli to buy half a roast chicken, some salad. When he gets home, he stores the food in the fridge, opens a bottle of beer, pours a glass and drinks it all, standing at the kitchen counter. He pours more. He hates their empty apartment.

In the bedroom there is a modern desk, made of clear glass, with a new laptop, which both of them use; they check their e-mails, the news, they work a bit. They say it's not healthy, to keep electronic gizmos in the bedroom, but there is no other place. And they're always careful to switch it off, at night. Not during the day: during the day the computer stays on, ready to be activated. Giovanni finishes his beer, pulls the chicken out of the fridge, out of its bag, puts it on a plate, nibbles at it, distracted. He removes the cap of a second beer. He looks out the window, he sits, turns on the television, plays with the remote control, so many channels but – like an old song by Bruce Springsteen: 57 channels and nothing on. Well. He's going to have a bath: yes, a warm, relaxing bath, a beer and a new book by an Israeli writer at hand. He takes off his clothes, hangs his trousers and jacket in the wardrobe, puts the shirt in the laundry basket, in a corner. The basket bangs against the desk, the computer screen comes to life, grey, then brighter, suddenly full of colour and life; he realises that it is still open on Carmela's Yahoo account homepage. He'll often think about this very moment, later: the precise moment when his right hand gets hold of the mouse to take a peek. I'll just have a look, he thinks, he swears. A harmless peek. Giovanni stands in his underwear in front of the computer in the bedroom, intrigued, curious. In good faith. Faith, loyalty. Faithfulness.

Giovanni sits down and reads.

***

Dear Carmela, the letter begins - there is no doubt it is a letter.

Dear Carmela,

It's Sunday evening and here I am, sitting at my desk, facing the window - it's a clear night, the moon is not full but incredibly bright, the top of the trees sways in the breeze. All is silence - in this room, in the building, in the street. All is silent, and the moon is shining and it's late - I do not know how late, but in the last hour I have witnessed the slow phenomenon of people who go to bed - the lights in the windows of other houses across the street that are put out, one by one - one here, the other there. One by one, slowly, all the windows have become dark rectangles, almost invisible. My light has stayed on - I can't go to bed; I tried, and I stayed there for an hour or so, under the duvet, completely immobile; I got up, and here I am, again, at my desk, in the middle of the night. No, I cannot sleep - since I met you I can't sleep.

Carmela, Carmela, Carmela - your name makes me feel like I'm skating on ice, the letters of your name dangerous, cold as fire, Carmela, I repeat, and I am so alone - this is the worst loneliness, lonely lonely loneliness, to fall in love with a woman, a person with a slick name, and to want her so painfully here, now, and know that I can't, it will take a long time before I can have you, here, now. This isn't a familiar sensation, you know, I did not know that the process of falling in love could be so damned painful, memory is short and tonight my blood flows in my veins flows swims fast, fast, fearless and hot, and in my blood is mixed this night - tonight, tonight - with this moon and the memory of your face - a face like no other, never before, never after, impossible to see any other face after yours, Carmela. Your face, which is not a face, face is too mild a word, too familiar, almost fake, lower case; a face is something that knows beauty salons and facials, creams and foundation and all those things that you do not

THE HEART OF THE OCTOPUS

care about, your face is a Face, flesh and thick and full and mine. I want to kiss your eyelids as I did last Wednesday - only a few days ago, and it feels like a year ago - your huge eyes, ravenous, so deep, and your body new and strange and easy and hungry, your legs around mine, your back in my hands, thin and new and strange, your hands playing with my body like no one has ever done, ever, my sudden seed between your swollen breasts, gleaming like ice. Carmela.

***

It isn't a scream. It's a roar.

PART III

Giovanni undoes the laces of his right shoe. He slips it off. The heel drops heavily on the floor and the dull *toc* it produces bounces off the bathroom tiles, echoes in the hallway and then drops down from step to step up all the way to the floor below. Giovanni stays very still, pricking his ears up like Argos, who is downstairs and repeats the gesture. Argos, who has returned home with him, his true master. Finally. Giovanni stops breathing.

"But this is my house," he thinks. He can make all the noise he wants; he won't disturb anyone. Only his wife.

"My wife!"

He takes off his other shoe and starts to undress, folding his clothes with care, item by item; he washes his face - the water is warm, but it manages to dissolve the veil of lethargy that has covered him like dew - too many words, too long a day, too much laughter, too many emotions. His heart beats faster. He passes a wet hand over his eyes, stands naked in front of the window watching the enormous rising yellow moon. He can hear the crickets. If it wasn't for the crickets, it would be so quiet.

He sits on a stool, washes his face again. Slowly, he puts on his pyjamas. First the top, made of thick cotton, with the initial G embroidered with blue thread on the breast pocket, then the trousers, which are too long for him. He walks along the dark corridor barefoot - he left his slippers at home.

"At home! But this one here is *mine*. Home."

A house, a wife, a dog. What else could he possibly ask for?

Along the corridor, one step at a time. He hesitates just outside the door. He knocks briefly and enters without waiting for an answer. They call it the red room. The mirror over the fireplace reflects the spacious bedroom, the red-clay walls, no paintings, no carpets to cover the parquet floor, it's furnished with the necessary: a wooden wardrobe, a chest of drawers, a desk, a bed.

"Bianca?" The room is lit by the moon. The mirror reflects a void, an absence. Giovanni loses his breath yet again. Once again the beating of his heart doubles. "Darling? Where are you?."

He walks with caution. As he approaches the untouched bed he perceives a noise behind him. A shadow that becomes a sinuous body runs towards him. Her long hair loose on her shoulders, hot and dark as chocolate, her chunky legs, the delicate waist, the ribs visible under the surprisingly round and heavy breasts, naked and screaming Bianca laughs and runs towards him and jumps on him, laughs and shakes and then falls onto the bed, she laughs and hugs and laughs and pulls at his trousers, laughs and sits down beside him. Giovanni kisses her palm, the inside of her wrists. They're both naked. Bianca looks at him without embarrassment, she says:

"My man."

"My woman."

"Mine."

"Mine."

***

In the room lit by the moon, the mirror above the dresser reflects the naked body of Bianca straddling Giovanni's, who is lying on his back.

Giovanni strokes her face with the tip of his fingers, strokes her forehead, nose, mouth. Bianca's lazy body tenses above him, her hair pats his chest like a weeping willow's leaves brush the water of the river below. Her lips reach Giovanni's. His tongue licks her nose, mouth, her teeth, sucking her salty lips. They taste of blood.

Her perfume.

Her flavour.

Bianca sighs, almost a groan. She lies down beside him. Giovanni kisses her again, keeping his eyes open, looking at her closed eyelids. He slowly moves from her lips to her neck, from her neck to her breasts, down her body, always watching her – he looks at her while he kisses her armpits, he observes her shiver with surprise and pleasure when he lingers on her breasts and on her red nipples, as fresh as strawberries, and Bianca groans again, he watches her while he moves down onto her belly button, on her round belly, on her thighs smooth like butter, he looks into her watery eyes while he moves inside her, above her. Bianca: warm as the earth. Warm as his blood, warmer than his blood, solid as a rock. He watches her as her moans become a cry. Her cry of pleasure is like a cry of pain.

They fall asleep, curled up like two commas, his back against her belly. Bianca keeps her hand wrapped around Giovanni's warm sex, curling his coarse hair around her fingers. Her fingers seem like a shell sticky with egg white.

Her hand: a nest.

***

The letter? Do you want to know what happens after he read the letter?

Suffice to say, Giovanni makes his discovery on Monday night. He yelps like a dog, just like Argos if you hurt him. He reads and rereads the letter, again and again and again, alternating roars and tears, anger and grief and a sense of helplessness and loss. It was so obvious, and yet he didn't see it, you idiot, you bitch, and now, what now. He doesn't know what to do, he feels lonely and desperate and alone and what a bitch, oh yeah right she had a new job, yeah right: away from him, in Milan, fucking Milan, fuck you. And: he: he: he: Davide, Davide, one who writes these things, and to her, to her who is mine, who *was* mine, my woman, my Carmela, Carmela my apple. Another man's had her, Davide. Davide saw her, wanted her, and he tried and he succeeded, Davide – somehow, somewhere, he's touched her and kissed her and fucked her, my Carmela, who is no longer mine. His. Giovanni's eyes burn, his heart burns, his cheeks burn, the pride of a male betrayed, cuckolded, with the cock of another, I bet she liked it more, Davide's cock, you bitch, Carmela. And all the images he would not want to see and that are projected onto his mind as if onto a screen, he can't forget them, he can't delete them, he remembers Carmela's mouth and Carmela's eyes, her smooth neck and her hoarse voice and her tongue, her face when she comes, she closes her eyes and shudders and lets out a soft moan and then smiles – now Davide has seen that face, too, has heard her moan and seen that smile. Just as it happens in some movies where the main actor suffers a shock, a revelation, Giovanni feels sick. He covers his mouth with one hand and runs to the bathroom to vomit. As if he needed to expurgate Carmela not only from his heart but from his guts, his bowels, like spoiled food. Something bad that he needs to get out of his system.

Emissions. Expulsion. Purge.

He undresses and throws his clothes on one side and remains under the hot spray of the shower for a long time. Then he puts on a pair of jeans and a black shirt and a black jacket and he moves so swiftly that he looks like a cat, a black cat, and black are also his dark tired eyes and his hair and he slams the door without locking it and he goes down the steps two at a time, quickly, quickly, and gets in his car and engages the first gear and then he's off – he crosses the city at night, and he does not even know what time it is now and in the ears there is a buzz that stuns all other sounds, he can't hear the radio, he can't hear the music, he hears only the loud thud of his heart.

***

He leaves Turin, takes the motorway A4 to Milan. He slams his foot on the accelerator and speeds up. His Fiat runs on the road, the other vehicles step aside as soon as they see him, hunched over the steering wheel, the high-beam headlights signalling to make room for him, he's coming, he's in a hurry, he can't slow down, move out of the way.

It's just after nine o'clock of a spring evening, it will be light for a while still. Giovanni drives along in the fast lane; he hasn't turned the radio on, hasn't heard the news, and doesn't know that two lorries, for reasons yet to be ascertained, have clashed near the exit of Santhià, towards Milan. One of the two lorries is reversed between the emergency and the service lane, while the other truck is across the other two lanes and its load has poured onto the road, completely blocking the traffic and starting a queue of over 11 km. On-site ambulances have arrived to treat the drivers, while the traffic Police has intervened with four patrols. Traffic intensifies. A lane is closed. Giovanni is forced to slow down and then to stop.

To punch the steering wheel doesn't help much, but he does it all the same; to cry doesn't help, but he does it all the same; to swear and howl and bang his head against the window does not help, but he does it all the same, until a sharp pain in his left ear makes him desist. He is stuck in his car for over two hours. When the motorway reopens, Giovanni takes the first exit and heads back to Turin.

At one o'clock in the morning, he's home again. He sits at his desk and reads all of Carmela emails, incoming and outgoing messages, deleted messages. He researches Davide, finds out who he is, what he does, where he lives. Then he opens the drawers, rummages through her papers, carefully examining mobile phone bills, their home phone bill; he checks and compares dates in his diary. The phone calls made early in the morning, or late at night. The date and the length of each conversation. He sits down at the computer once more, rereads certain messages, cross references certain dates. Crying, biting the inside of the cheeks until they bleed. Her flesh and his, their blood, their warm breath.

He goes to bed at five o'clock when dawn begins to dye Turin pink. A few hours later, he calls his secretary. He says he's in bed with the flu; he won't come in, today or tomorrow. With an overexcited tone of voice, he tells Carmela he's spent the evening with a group of friends he hadn't seen for years, he'd drunk too much and slept too little. He feverishly talks over her voice, he can't bear to hear her speak, Carmela-snake, Carmela the viper, Carmela Medusa, he doesn't want to listen to her lies, he does not want to hear her say she loves him, because it is not true.

Who gets betrayed reacts in very different ways; some hide in a dark room; some pretend nothing's happened, shrug their shoulders, and – at least when they're in public – overcome the pain as if it was nothing much. There are those who expose their wounds, and those who hide them. Giovanni weeps, Giovanni cries, and then Giovanni thinks: I must hit where it hurts the most; where it burns the most. Giovanni wonders: what's Carmela's most delicate, most fragile spot? What is her weakness? What is Carmela's Achilles' heel? Daddy. Of course. Not me, not her job, not her Mummy. But: Holy Saint Dominic, always ready to run for his baby as soon as she falls over and scrapes her precious little knee. Did you know, Domenico, that your daughter is a slut? Yes: your sweet, your little saint: Carmela.

According to the traditions of the Carmelite order, the Virgin Mary (in company of many bright angels and the Child Jesus) appeared on July 16, 1251 to an English priest, Simon Stock, Prior General of the Carmelite Order. I look up: Saint Carmela. I find many:

Blessed Carmela Garcia Moyon, martyred during the Spanish Civil War;

Blessed Carmelites of Compiegne, martyr during the French Revolution;

Blessed Carmen Sales y Barangueras, founder of the Conceptionist Mission Sisters of Education;

Blessed Maria Carmen Moreno Benitez, martyr in Barcelona;

Blessed Maria Carmela Viel Ferrando, virgin and martyr.

And you? No, you aren't a virgin, you aren't a martyr. You, Carmela Montaperto: what can I do *to* you?

***

He comes up with a plan; he has a week to prepare it. Preparing for it gives him an undefinable, terrible sense of satisfaction - more than once he finds himself rubbing his hands, grinning. He's slow, precise.

"Do you know how you climb Mount Everest?" Marieke used to ask him. "Step by step. One step at a time. One foot after the other." Right, left, right, left.

First, he installs a program that allows the ability to monitor the computer's activity, including passwords. Then he buys a digital camera - a Kodak DC210 Plus, paying 1,068,000 lire. It is not difficult to learn how to use it, and he tries it every day - in the morning before going to the office, during his lunch break, in the evening; it has a CompactFlash 8MB as standard equipment, which can take no more than thirty photographs at a time before it needs a memory clear-out. He photographs himself in the mirror, their apartment, the streets around the office. He buys a printer, and matte and glossy paper, to see which one works best.

On Wednesday evening, he leaves the office early, runs home to get his car and by 6PM he's already in Settimo – he's seen so many times the sign marking the Taboo Sex Shop, shortly before taking the motorway. It's just as he expected it to be – a badly lit shop with a musty, dusty, dirty smell. They sell VHS cassettes, the first DVDs, books and posters. In the second room, darker than the first, there is a glass case that reminds him a little of that of his Uncle Monteverdi; rather than containing precious notebooks, valuable Dictionaries, it exhibits a series of sex toys that make him blush with pleasure and disgust. He buys three.

He travels further south, towards Castel San Gerolamo. He turns the radio on and opens the window, he feels all revved up, the bag with vibrators hidden under the front seat. He surprises his parents while they are having dinner.

"Ah-ha – perfect. I'm just in time for dessert," Giovanni says, laughing. He feels sorry for them, tenderness and anger, all together. Marieke, slightly plumper, ruddy, looks dazed, while Luigi jumps up and clings to his neck. "No reason. I just wanted to see you," Giovanni says to explain his unexpected appearance. He refuses dinner but accepts a glass of Barbera and then a second, and a slice of cake and a second, and the offer to stay the night and leave early the following morning.

"You know what – whilst I'm here I think I should go and say hello to Uncle and Aunt – I haven't seen them for ages," he says. "Just a quick hello," he says, and buries his face red with shame, in Argos' fur. No, he can't wait a second, he has to go, immediately, right now: the plan can't wait. Driving along the dark country roads, he gets to the busy junction at forty miles per hour, enters the gate, rings the bell. The door opens, and he walks in and embraces his uncle Stefano, who is surprised to see him, and drinks two glasses of home-made lemonade, then excuses himself and runs upstairs to the family bathroom. He knows where to search. In the cabinet under the basin; here is the shelf full of medicines. Here it is: a box of Rohypnol, which had been prescribed to his aunt when her mother had died. He remembers they had discussed it openly – did she really need such a powerful sleeping pill? "Even an ogre would sleep with one of these!" Giovanni takes the whole box. He leaves for Turin at dawn, the Rohypnol inside one of his pockets, the camera in the other, the sex toys in the booth.

***

I give her a beautiful weekend. I'm full of attention but not suffocating, in fact I even pretend I'm invited for a drink with a friend on Friday night, to leave her alone for a couple of hours - I want to see if she writes any emails. I buy her a pair of earrings; I take her to dinner at the horrid Indian restaurant that she loves, where she has to thank the waiters thirty-five times to show how liberal, anti-colonialist, not elitist she is. We go to the cinema to see *American Beauty*, and I try not to fall asleep. On Saturday, I suggest we invite her cousin with her new boyfriend to dinner, and I help prepare and cook, I set the table. I buy three bottles of wine: *Prosecco* to start, *Laguna* for the entrée and a wonderful, silky Merlot for risotto; and a bottle of *Limoncello*. For later.

Later, after the successful dinner party, when our guests have finally gone and I can stop smiling, I tell her to close her eyes and put in her hands the package with the earrings. She claps her hands; she looks like a little girl. She has red cheeks, bright eyes, wet with wine; her teeth are stained with a red patina from the Merlot. I kiss her, tell her that she deserves my gifts, that I love her to death. Does a shadow appear like a warning flash on her face, or do I want to see it? She wobbles slightly. I kiss her again whilst I offer her a glass of Limoncello; she declines, but I insist.

"I bought it especially for you," I say, not lying. I sneak into the kitchen, mix the liquor with the tablets I crushed earlier. "Cheers!"

"Salute," she says, gulping down the drink in one go. I help her to bed. She falls asleep before I finish brushing my teeth.

At work!

Just like Napoleon is reported to have said: "My Lord, please give strength to my enemy, so that he can live long enough to witness my triumph."

***

No: I'm not going to give you the details. I reassure you and tell you that Carmela doesn't feel too awful, the next day. She wakes up at five o'clock in the morning with a bad headache, and vomits; Giovanni rushes at her side like a nurse on call, with a glass of Alka-Seltzer and a wet flannel. He brushes her hair away from her sweaty forehead, gathers it up; he helps her to get changed; he cleans up the mess in the bathroom. Carmela goes back to bed and sleeps until noon. When she gets up, she doesn't remember anything.

***

In the end, the four usable photographs, those in which Giovanni does not appear, nor the apartment – he's even had the foresight to change the pillowcases, choosing some made out of a shocking pink cotton - could have been taken anywhere. The four images in which Carmela *seems* awake, and engrossed, which are also the most spectacularly erotic, are carefully inserted into manila envelopes, with the addresses typed and printed and glued on and a note that mentions Davide. He sends them to Domenico; to the solicitor Pinelli; and to a recording studio of hard core videos in Rome, with a request for information on how to become a porn star. The last: icing on the cake: to himself.

Then he just sits, and waits.

***

THE HEART OF THE OCTOPUS

The photos arrive on Thursday. He sees it right away, the envelope in the mail box, and even if nobody's looking he likes to pretend not to know what it is. He turns it over in his hands, stacks it with other mail, goes up the stairs. He can hear the landline ringing, then his mobile phone. It's Carmela. He doesn't answer. After five minutes, the phone rings again.

"Hello?"

"Hi. It's me."

"Hello, darling. Is everything all right?"

"It's that. Something is going on. I don't quite understand."

"What?"

"I'll tell you tomorrow when I get there. Please, Giovanni: just don't open the mail, please."

"What mail?"

"Letters."

"Why?" he says, half laughing.

"I'll tell you tomorrow. Please." She's crying.

Carmela arrives the following day. She opens the door, says his name.

"Giovanni?" Her voice, already in the past. "Giovanni?"

When she sees him - seated with his legs crossed and arms folded, with the open envelope on the sofa next to him, the photos scattered artfully around, his eyes closed as if he didn't want to look at her – she doesn't say a word. She kneels beside him, touching his hand. He recoils.

"Giovanni. Honestly, I don't know how it happened. I don't know who took those photographs."

"What about Davide: who is he?" Giovanni opens his eyes, looks at her: that face all white and delicate, like a crumbling wedding cake.

***

Carmela is not that upset by the photographs. She's surprised, of course. Shocked. She can't quite recognise the *mise en scène*: those underpants, that bra, those cushions. How and when it may have happened, she has no idea. Who could it have been. She suspects someone has been able to manipulate some images, superimposing her head over the body of another (and yet how do you explain the moles on her tummy and on her right leg, the bracelets on her wrist?). But Carmela is great, in every sense, and although I am not quite implying that the whole episode slides off her shoulders like rain; not quite, not exactly, but: almost. What do you think she makes of some rubber cocks, after all, in the big scheme of things? What do you think she makes of this mini-scandal, of this mysterious violation (of her body, her privacy, her intimate relations)? What do you think she makes of Giovanni? What do you think she actually makes of this relationship - in truth, it is from the beginning of the cohabitation that doubts have grown on her and have not ceased to exist but have proliferated, inside her: about Giovanni, about the nature and the purpose of monogamy, about that anguished, suffocating love of his. Giovanni's love was like a plastic bag on the head: you put it over your hair just for fun, and then it slides down over your eyes and nose and mouth, and the more it goes down the less you are able to breathe. Yes, she loved him; yes, she let herself be loved. She enjoyed playing with new rules, learning them, deciphering them, seeing where they were going. But no, come on: seriously: Carmela would never have married Giovanni, at the end.

She has left her job (but she immediately found another: even better than the previous), she has quarrelled with her father (but they are reconciled, and they are closer than ever), she has dis-entangled, dis-engaged (literally, returning her engagement ring); she's lost both the boyfriend and the lover; well, so what: she wasn't that serious about it all, nothing is irremediable. In her world, which is so different from that of Giovanni's, things happen, take a certain turn, but they don't have to continue ad infinitum. Things are done, things get rid of, nothing stands still; τὰ πάντα ῥεῖ καὶ οὐδὲν μένει: everything flows, nothing stands still. And in that change there is a great beauty.

***

As a child, Giovanni imagined that avalanches originated from snowballs. A tiny ball started to fall, and rolling down the mountain it would become bigger and bigger until it'd be huge, and powerful enough to overwhelm everything - trees, cars, people

- in its path. His photographs are like that original snowball: the avalanche, all that is left behind. Giovanni follows the consequences of the emails sent in real time through Carmela's electronic mail (which he reads obsessively) by all the characters of this obscene story.

In Carmela's Inbox, he finds:

-A message from Davide who, being accused of having been the offender, leaves her;

-Many from Domenico, who tries to explain how he has been: almost ashamed for the dis-honour that his daughter's behaviour had caused him; he begs for her forgiveness, which she immediately and obviously concedes. Father and daughter reconcile in an even stronger, deeper bond;

-A peremptory one from the lawyer Pinelli, who asks for an urgent meeting.

-A thrilled one from Extasi (sic), hard core video agency, that offers her an audition right away, all expenses paid.

Giovanni also reads the exchange of messages between Carmela and the rest of the world, the incredulous friends to whom she's told everything, and those in whom she didn't confide. He keeps quiet. He does not say a word to anyone. Marieke and Luigi can't understand what happened, call Carmela, from whom they receive implausible and unsatisfactory explanations, but do not dare ask him direct questions, because they are polite and they come from Piedmont, and exhibit a stiff upper lip worthy of Prince Charles.

THE HEART OF THE OCTOPUS

If Carmela shrugs her shoulders and moves on (she resigns, moves to Rome, changes job), for Giovanni it is a much more complex state of affairs. The horror at the discovery of Carmela's infidelity has been tempered by the pleasure of hurting her; and the two feelings alternate in a kind of manic fashion inside him, with the added shame of having committed such depraved acts; and with the sense of shame there is even a sweet taste in having succeeded, with no one noticing or suspecting anything. Just like in the movie *Rope* by Hitchcock, where the only reason for murder is the challenge: Brandon and Philip are young snobs who consider themselves Nietzschean supermen, whose overwhelming intellectual superiority makes them believe to be exempt from the laws and conventions that govern the rest of humanity. They kill for the sheer fun of it, and get away with it. "The good and bad, what is right and what is wrong were invented solely for the ordinary average man, the lower man," Brandon, the mind of the murder, says. To kill a man just to feed their intellectual vanity is comparable to using the sensual body of his girlfriend for revenge. A small, pathetic act of vengeance.

***

This is my business – my own fucking business (literally); no-one else's but mine. And yet everyone seems entitled to stick their nose into it. My mother has that sad downward look straight from Diana at the Taj Mahal: she the poor victim. She! And my father: super-embarrassed, all quiet and sotto voce, as if somebody had died next door. He whispers another of his Latin proverbs, *Decipit frons first multos,* and then keeps silent. Oh, his almost-daughter-in-law has hurt my poor little boy. But she seemed such a respectable young lady, she came from such a good family. She was impeccable, courteous, so well-behaved. They peer at me sideways ("Perhaps he's done something to deserve it," they think) and I behave like the proverbial Sicilian mummy: I can't see, I can't hear, I can't talk. And no one knows what to say but they all treat me lovingly, with affection, understanding. With sympathy, literally (it means to suffer together). As if Carmela was dead: the poor widower. As if I were a fragile porcelain statuette, one of those precious Limoges pieces, made of clay, or kaolin, that comes from the Chinese and means "stone of the hills": a material that is difficult to extract, that is found in rare deposits, and that is extremely delicate. If it only feels a vibration, a crack is formed on its surface. Right: cracking. Something inside me is broken. I am broken. Look at me: a fragment here and one there.

***

What saves him is his father's stroke.

Two weeks have passed since Carmela has left. Eighteen days since he sent the photographs. Giovanni has lost seven pounds, has grey circles under his eyes, doesn't sleep. One night he even tried to take half a tablet of Rohypnol, but not even the sleeping pill, however powerful, worked: instead of sleeping, he felt confused, foggy, disoriented. His head and body felt heavy, his tongue thick and thirsty. And playing vivid in his mind, again and again, the images of the staging he prepared; Davide's email; Carmela's face, shaken by tears. There is no remedy to his despair. He has lost the woman he loved. He's lost everything.

It's Friday, it's a little after eleven o'clock at night. Giovanni is just about to get up and go and spy on Carmela's electronic mail, again, when the phone rings. He hesitates, then answers, hears the voice of Marieke who yelps like a dog. Luigi has had a stroke, was rushed into hospital. Giovanni drives immediately over to Castel san Gerolamo.

Luigi had had a long soak in the bath, like every week. On leaving the tub he had felt his head spin, he had slipped and called his wife, who rushed in; Luigi tried to explain what happened, but found he couldn't speak. In fact, he could no longer move his right arm, he murmured words that were not words, but a tangle of guttural sounds, out of breath, meaningless. Marieke had called an ambulance, called Giovanni in Turin, called her brother-in-law, prepared a bag with pyjamas and two pairs of underwear and socks and a toothbrush, forgetting his robe and his slippers. The ambulance had taken them to the hospital in the nearby town of Alessandria.

Luigi is sixty-two years old

(But: "I'm not that old")

He is not fat, but is five or six kilos overweight

(But: "Have you seen my brother, who has a huge belly?")

He smokes since he was a boy

(But: "Just ten cigarettes per day")

He lives a predominantly sedentary life

(But: "And my vegetable garden? Do you know how much physical activity I do when I work with my spade, turn over the soil, when I sow, when I water all that ground?")

It happens. What do you expect? Well, at least for Maria to take the situation in hand - home, business, finances – to help him on the road to recovery, with time and patience. Maria: so strong; Maria: so tough; Maria: a lioness, a spectacular pain in the ass, a woman of steel, a know-it-all, who is capable of assembling and disassembling, that you can never teach her anything because she knows it already or she gets offended. She is a Monteverrrdi, she can do anything.

    Oh Almighty Maria

    Maria Admirable

    Oh Maria

    Maria most Prudent

    Maria most Venerable

    Maria most Renowned

    Maria most Powerful

    Maria most Merciful

    Maria most Faithful

    Mirror of Justice

THE HEART OF THE OCTOPUS

Oh Holy Maria

Seat of Wisdom

Cause of Our Joy

Mystical Rose

Pray for Us

Morning Star

Pray for Us

Health of the Sick

Refuge of Sinners

Comforter of the Afflicted

Queen of Angels

Yeah, right: health of the sick. Pray for us.

Marieke stalls, Marieke hesitates, Marieke falters, Marieke melts; Marieke deflates, Marieke flounders, blunders, fumbles. Marieke Mystical Rose. Marieke, Star of the Morning, Ora pro Nobis. Marieke takes refuge in her foreignness, her Dutchness as if she needed to belong somewhere else; Marieke sits on the armchair in the living room and stares at the wall for two hours straight; Marieke without Luigi doesn't know what to do, where to go, who to be. Who would have thought that? That she'd turn into the walking, breathing cliché of the little lost woman who can't achieve anything without her man: et voilà! And now, wait: wait for the arrival of the prodigal son who runs home like Zorro, to save his mother.

***

To save himself.

***

Luigi recovers, leaves the hospital after a few weeks, but he's certainly not able to continue the life he led before. He needs time, care, weekly visits to a speech therapist, an occupational therapist. Marieke also needs attention. They need him. So, Giovanni spends the summer un-making his own life, piece by piece: he leaves the apartment; he resigns; he says goodbye to his life in Turin and moves back into his parents' house in Castel San Gerolamo. His bedroom in the tower is full of boxes containing his former life; he repaints it – enough of the nautical theme; he throws everything out and fills the wardrobe with his clothes, the shelves with his books; he meets with his uncle, and together they take the reins of the family accountancy firm. All around him is an approving chorus: oooh, what a good son he is. What an absolute star.

It seems impossible that only a few weeks before he and Carmela were organising their wedding, their honeymoon, debating whether to go to Sardinia or to Provence. Now he finds himself where he was born, in the bosom of his family, but with the roles reversed: he the adult, the young and strong man solving everyday problems, while his parents - old, inert, passive - watch him do. Paradoxically, to look after them is good for him, too; it makes him feel useful, great, alive. Fuck Carmela, fuck Torino, fuck everything.

He is having a new door name plate made: it's official: "Mr. Luigi Ferraro and partners" becomes: "Giovanni Ferraro and partners."

***

Months go by. A year passes. The memory of his other life fades. Two years, two and half, three. Giovanni works, has a new group of friends - other lawyers, two architects, sons of his father's colleagues. He takes Argos for long walks. He works. He plays golf. He works. He plays tennis. He takes Argos for long walks in the countryside. He's good at his job, his father's old clients not only don't leave the practice but invite others to join. He earns well and spends little; he buys a red Audi TT coupe, skis in Cervinia at Christmas and goes to Sardinia in August. He wears impeccable suits and a short haircut which perhaps befits a man older than him; he reads the *Corriere della Sera*, he roots for Juventus football club; he regularly goes out with one of the secretaries, but he doesn't consider her to be his girlfriend (and she knows it); he lives with mamma and papà, sleeping in his old room in the tower, now with a double bed. In short: he's a predictable, affable young man, more at ease in the sixties that in the new millennium. He repeats the way of behaving he has seen all his life: his dad's, his grandfather's, his uncle's. He wakes up and goes to work in the morning and comes home in the evening expecting to find the table set and the food ready, his shirts washed and ironed and folded in his wardrobe. He doesn't tidy up, he doesn't cook, he doesn't do any domestic chore; what had become a habit, in his years in Turin on his own and then with Carmela, has come to an end. He doesn't have time, he says. It doesn't interest him. He doesn't read – he doesn't have the time, he says. Carmela isn't there any longer, to force him to read a stimulating book, an intriguing article – she used to force him to attend art exhibitions, showed him documentaries, booked the best seats at the theatre, was interested in everything. Now at most he reads a thriller on holiday, forgetting its plot as soon as 'the end' appears on the last page; he reads the newspaper every day, but is not particularly interested in politics – neither Italian nor international. His new friends are disengaged, too; they follow the news, but don't participate: these are the years of the second Intifada, of the G8 in Genoa, the end of the Troubles in Northern Ireland. Castel San Gerolamo is impermeable to foreign news. At most, they share a joke about Clinton – *that cigar*, that dress– but that's all.

Luigi has retired from business and takes care of the vineyard and of his vegetable garden. One by one, he is reading all the books he has purchased over the years and that had remained stacked in a corner of his study. Marieke is the one who suffers – of course she's happy to have Giovanni back; she needs him. Yet a part of her also wishes he were away, far away, to do something new and exciting on his own, to discover unknown places, different people, obscure professions. He's *'verkwist'* here, she says. Wasted. Squandered. Like the offshoot of a rare flower destined for an exotic country, which gets mysteriously planted in the middle of a rice paddy, and drowns in too high waters. He is already under water, submerged to the shoulders. Only his head is sticking out. Soon it will be covered, too. And he is not even realising it.

***

Bianca is sitting with her sister Luisa at the café Vietti, in Trino Monferrato.

She is nineteen. She's wearing her favourite dress, a sky-blue cotton dress with little roses embroidered around the collar line. She is petite, with a fine bone structure, a slender build; she's wearing her dark hair tied in a knot on the back of her neck – it is so tight that the mere sight of it makes your own temples hurt, it pulls hard at the skin on her forehead, elongating her black, shiny eyebrows, under which her white-blue eyes stare at the world around her. Bianca's eyes are her most singular, disturbing feature. They are an incredibly light shade of blue – as light as her pearly skin, they are almost white, so clear that the pupils lose themselves, as if they were swimming inside the iris. They make her appear vulnerable, helpless, which is far from the truth. The condition of being born second and last, of being the baby of the family, has not granted her any privilege; motherless since birth, she's been taken under the wing of her older sister Luisa - twelve years older than her – who has practically raised her. She has made her study, pushing her to attend an early years foundation stage course, from which she has just graduated; Luisa is a skilled seamstress (all the ladies come to her to have their clothes made, their jackets and coats repaired), she has taught her sister to iron, sew, embroider, crochet ("I raised her all on my own, to make her perfect. I have been a strict teacher. Now my mission is finished. She is ready for life"). Bianca's aspiration is to become a nursery teacher.

One end of the satin ribbon that is used to gather her hair up slips into the ice cream bowl and laughing she lifts it – covered in chocolate – to show it to Luisa. She raises her eyes. They seem even lighter, brighter, pierced by the sun. Pure and transparent like the finest diamonds. Fresh and clear as water, a colour that reminds him of when fog rises from the vineyard, in the autumn dawns. Giovanni, standing in front of the counter, his hand waving a couple of notes under the nose of the waiter to pay for this coffee, sees her for the very first time. His sudden sigh turns into a sob, he brings his hands to his mouth, blushes, trembles, sways, hits a waiter, apologises, shakes his head, staggers, stumbles on the shoes of his friend. When Riccardo - who comes from Rocca Delle Donne, like Bianca - offers to introduce them, Giovanni has already decided: it must be her. If she won't lower her eyelids, if she'll allow him to get lost and float sleepwalking in those extraordinary eyes, it'll be her. The palms of his hands are sweaty.

He can smell her perfume. Please. Let it be her. If she'll look at me directly, when I shake her hands. If she'll be kind.

Bianca raises her white eyes, smiles. She smiles. To him.

Yes: yes: it's her.

***

Giovanni falls in love. He starts suffering from insomnia, he loses his appetite, can't concentrate at work, he loses three games at tennis. He works little and badly. He feels as if he's not breathing properly. In the office, he's distracted; he goes home early, runs with Argos in the fields, never stands still. He manages to meet Bianca a few times – not on proper dates, but studying a course of action with his friend, move by move, as if it were chess. Bianca enchants him.

"She's so different from us," he tries to explain to his mother. "Her manners are just exquisite, she's polite, but her education doesn't hinder her; she acts naturally, she's got this strange trilling laugh. I don't know how to explain it – there: she's free."

After Amber, a Bianca, which means white, pure: how ironic. But Bianca really is whiter than white. Not like Carmela. Carmela was (is) grey: kind of dirty. And in some way, red: presumptuous, superb, fully aware of her value. Bianca is reserved, humble, simple. Modest.

Giovanni doesn't quite know how to behave: to play the part of the provincial squire feels terribly out of place, with this girl.

"She's a bit too young," Marieke says.

"Exactly. She's perfect."

"At nineteen years of age?"

"Exactly. She's perfect."

"She knows nothing of life."

"Exactly. She's perfect."

What is one to do with such a simple country girl, probably a virgin? How does one conquer her love? Step by step, one foot after another, right, left, right, left: that's how you get to the summit of Everest.

Giovanni feels as if he were playing. As if he were going back to a distant and magical and pure time, where girls are not malicious, at a time when they don't know (yet) they are as good as men, that they can be better than men. When all they want is to take care of someone. Of him.

He calls her often, and then every day; he invites her out for coffee; and then for an apéritif; then for dinner at a fancy restaurant; to the movies, and again for dinner, this time at Castel San Gerolamo, to meet his parents. At first Bianca speaks little, she is intimidated, a little embarrassed; she answers questions slowly, in an undertone, but then she slowly melts, and talks too much, loudly. She helps to clear the table; she strokes the dog; she is eager to please. Later that evening, when they are about to leave, she doesn't know whether to give a hug to the Ferraros, or shake their hands; she decides for a generic "bye-bye" just like a child who doesn't know whether to address her friends' parents formally or not. There are more dinners, walks in the woods. One Sunday, Giovanni invites her to visit with him the Po River Park, a protected area, established with the intent to promote the river ecosystem. They rent two bikes and ride all day, up and down the hills, among woods and vineyards, gardens, orchards. They cross the river between Fontanetto Po and Gabiano, taking the small ferry. It is on the ferry that Giovanni kisses Bianca for the first time. While kissing, he opens his eyes and looks at her: Bianca's eyes are shut tight, her arms straight; she's breathing hard. Giovanni detaches himself and smiles, takes her hands and rearranges them: one around his neck, one on his back.

"Like this," he says.

"Oh. Ok," she says, as pliable as clay. He kisses her again.

"Yes. That's better."

The following week, Bianca invites Giovanni to Rocca Delle Donne to introduce him to her father, who runs a newsagent's in the main square. The apartment in which they live, above the shop, is exactly as he imagined: too clean, too shiny, not a single book in sight; paintings with coarse colours, crocheted doilies under flowerpots. The village is one of the most beautiful places in the entire Monferrato, nestled on a rocky ridge overlooking the Po, and the house - small, dark - opens up unexpectedly: tall French doors in the kitchen open up onto a terrace with spectacular views: the lazy river that winds up, the rolling countryside, so alive, the mountains all around. Further down, one can see all the way to the monastery of nuns, built in 1167 and closed in 1492 with a papal bull that accused of "disorderly conduct" abbess and nuns, who in time became true *dominae* of the area.

The meeting is a success. "I liked her father. Umberto is a simple man, affable. And forgiving - after lunch we played draughts, and I won. Well: he let me win."

Luisa, Bianca's sister, shakes his hand, crushing it with hers. With dark hair pulled up and small round glasses, she looks like Heidi's Fraulein Rottenmeier: and with Miss Rottenmeier's she shares a pensive look, cold manners, tricky questions. His Bianca, he thinks, is Heidi: naïve, younger than her already young years, inexperienced, so sincere he'd cry. Her large white eyes look at the world believing it is all as good as she is; as good as bread. Ms Rottenmeier-Rottweiler is ready to devour anyone who'd hurt her: just like Marieke with Giovanni, she is the guardian, guard, jailer. Her father Umberto – he's good too, and he's also naïve, trusting and ignorant, a very decent man, one Domenico Montaperto would certainly approve of. He shakes Giovanni's hand with both of his, moist with emotion. He proudly takes him downstairs, to the newsagents'; Giovanni hovers in the shop praising each stand, each shelf, postcards, a basket full of special offers, from old calendars to carnival masks. He says all the right things; Umberto likes him: he is invited again, and after a few weeks he returns. And again, and again. Marieke and Luigi reciprocate by inviting Bianca back. One afternoon after lunch, Giovanni kisses her in the vineyard, in front of everyone. Six months later, he leaves for Rocca Delle Donne with the symbol of their future in his pocket - the most banal, most romantic and innocent representation of the future of a couple: an engagement ring. A round diamond, with a simple platinum setting. He places it on her ring finger.

"They say there is a vein that leads directly from this finger into one's heart. Will you marry me, Bianca?"

"Yes," Bianca says. "Yes. Yes. Yes."

***

Giovanni could not handle the humiliation he'd suffered. He believed the only way he could overcome that sense of mortification would be a relentless need for revenge for the offense received. From resentment to revenge it's just a short step. And then? Well: it depends on how you interpret the situation. According to the cognitive theory of emotions, the way you feel is directly proportional to the way you think. As Hamlet said: "Nothing is really good or bad in itself – it's all what a person thinks about it." Could one possibly see a positive side to being humiliated? I am an optimist, I see everything in pink and gold, but if someone treats me badly, and I realise they are doing it intentionally, well, it becomes difficult even to smile at them, let alone forgive them, or passing over. I know that one should redefine the situation by re-sizing the effect of the episode and try to break the link with one's sense of self-worth; I remember I had been taught a great lesson by my Latin tutor Ms Torello, a long time ago: when something goes wrong, pretend to go up an imaginary ladder, and look downwards. From high up, it feels as if one could face and confront anything. Learn to put things in perspective. Evaluate them, belittle the bad. Never pretend that they did not happen; never ignore them.

Carmela was fire, flame, hot oil: she burned him. If the type of pain she inflicted upon him were visible, you'd be able to see it on Giovanni's face: it is as if Carmela had taken a layer off his skin, pulling and peeling it off slowly until she'd taken his entire face off. And after that, his whole body, like the martyr St. Bartholomew. Just like when one burns himself: not all lesions become scars. The shallower wounds, such as the delicate abrasions or superficial burns, do not leave any mark. But after serious burns, it is imperative to cool the skin; one has to apply ointments, massaging for a long time, until cream penetrates deeply. Bandage it all up. Wait a while. Repeat the procedure. There are several therapeutic approaches against scars; it is especially important not let it do what it wants, but try to shape it with proper tools. These tools are both medical (massages, creams, patches, any micro-infiltrations of drugs) and surgical (scalpels, lasers). Giovanni has been scalded; what has been affected isn't just the most superficial skin layer, but also the underlying layer.

These burns cause intense skin inflammation, swelling and the formation of vesicles filled with liquid (blisters); they are very painful and the healing is slow. Giovanni has not even gone to A & E. He just put his skin under the cold tap for a few minutes, he's applied a plaster, and has tried to move on. In truth, the skin under the patch has never ceased to burn; it feels raw; it continues to hurt.

Carmela's betrayal damaged him deeply – even before she was unfaithful, even beyond the matter of her unfaithfulness. She opened his eyes onto the possibility of Another Life; to be someone else, to want something else. She made him understand and appreciate it – and then she took it all away. Giovanni both knows and doesn't know the extent of the damage. His ploy? To avoid similar situations at all costs. To avoid women. To avoid love. To avoid those he isn't able to control. What he doesn't know is that the addition of Carmela + Julie = helped him have an image of women that shares little with reality. He doesn't understand this completely; he doesn't know himself that well. Enough to stay away not from girls, but from a relationship. A quick fuck, yes; girlfriends, no.

Now he's met Bianca. He asked her a few questions. Actually, no: let's say it as it is: he interrogated her; he wanted to know exactly who, when, where, how. Exactly *what*. And she - submissive, trusting creature, not unlike a docile cow, all wide eyes and with those lashes that cover them like curtains, like tents – she's confessed everything. At seven years old, her cousin Marco took her by the hand and led her into the bathroom, where he asked her to pull up her dress and show *it* to him; at eleven, by accident, she discovered masturbation; at thirteen she had her first period; at fifteen, she kissed a neighbour, sans tongue; at sixteen, a boy three years older, avec tongue. And then there was the phase of birthday parties held in dark rooms, where she kissed - with tongue - three classmates. One touched her breast. Today, aged nineteen and three months, Bianca is a virgin; she has never seen a naked man, she has never seen or touched a flaccid, or an erect penis. With Bianca, he doesn't need to be afraid of anything. Bianca is young, Bianca is as pure as sugar, as salt, she has no stains just like her name. She has no one with whom to make comparisons. Giovanni is the only one: the one and only, like God.

***

Luisa doesn't help at all in the wedding organisations. Her work – to prepare Bianca for life - is finished. She is happy to leave the reins to Marieke, and to return to her sewing machine. Marieke brings the necessary documents to the Town Hall, chooses what flowers should decorate the church (and what kind of bouquet the bride should be carrying), contacts the three best local restaurants for the buffet, insists on the presents for the witnesses, "refined, all silver-plated, of course," she goes with Bianca to try on wedding dresses.

Bianca agrees on everything. Details are just details, nothing more.

"It doesn't matter. What is important isn't that one, single day, not the wedding day, not those twenty-four hours. But: our marriage," Bianca says. The house interests her far more. There are few, for sale locally; they see them all. Eventually they find one in Castel San Gerolamo, at the other end of the village from the Ferraros'. It is an old farmhouse, painted yellow, on top of another hill, called *The Willow* from an old weeping willow planted near the stream that runs at the end of the garden. It has thick, cold walls, vaulted ceilings. There is a large entrance hall with a stone staircase; on its left the living room, followed by a long and narrow room, which will be a library; on the right, the dining room and the kitchen. Upstairs, there are three bedrooms (each with a balcony) and two bathrooms (that need redoing). Each room is painted a different colour; in each, there is the original fireplace, a parquet floor, huge windows. It is airy, bright, strangely modern. Outside the land is almost entirely laid to lawn with some fruit trees and a large chestnut tree, a vegetable garden and a small vineyard, with vines that produce just a few hundred bottles a year.

"Do you like it?" Giovanni asks her.

"Oh, yes."

"It needs work. And the garden is bigger than I wanted. And the orchard ..."

"I can look after that. I'm used to looking after ours."

"With Luisa's help," Marieke intervenes.

"No, actually; not with her. I do it all on my own."

"Really?"

"Sure. By myself. I do everything in the garden."

"Ah, well then. I'm not going to say anything else, then," Marieke says, motioning as if she's closing a zipper on her mouth.

"Look, Giovanni: here I could grow potatoes, carrots, green beans, and: there: an apple tree, a pear tree, a peach tree. And in that corner we can keep a couple of chickens."

"My father will surely help me with the vineyard."

"You: a winemaker?" Marieke interrupts again.

"Why not? Wine flows in my veins, after all." Giovanni places an arm on Bianca's shoulder, pulls her closer. He laughs, and a sense of relief and well-being floods through his body like water. He wanted to escape, from Castel San Gerolamo; now he's back. It's so easy to be happy, when waiting is over. Waiting is definitely over.

***

You start to like Bianca, don't you? She feels like a breath of fresh air in stuffy Castel San Gerolamo: yes, just like opening a window at the beginning of April. A draft of warm air, but a fresh warmth, which makes no sense, but you understand me, right? Because it is undeniable: this story is oppressive, claustrophobic. That's how I felt when I used to go to the countryside with my grandparents, when I was a child: I did it because I couldn't not (children have no choice), but also because my grandfather loved the place to death, the countryside, and I was his favourite, and how could I not make him happy.

He was like Luigi in this novel: a good physician, well-read, well-spoken, wise; but apart from medicine he loved his vineyard. Not that he cultivated it himself. But he liked going there on weekends, walking, talking to the farmers. He liked *fritto misto* and *carpaccio* (specialties of the area), and to tear fruit from the trees – plums, peaches - and eat them when they weren't ripe, which gave him gout (I recall his swollen fingers), but my grandfather did not care a fig about gout. I found everything simply horrendous - the humid air, the dust, the huge spiders, the frantic ticking of a clock in the bedroom; the rough sheets; the aforementioned raw meat, which I imagined worms would come out of; the Piedmontese dialect, which I did not understand; and the smallness of the place, which choked me. All of this, I'm trying to make you feel, right on your skin: because of course this is a novel, but I recognise the place; that stagnant air, and the sensation that nothing, ever, has changed or can change. Old ladies will always wear their hair short and curly, and you'll always find them in the kitchen or in the garden, where they cultivate their horrible dahlias, their ugly carnations; and their husbands, who are fortunate enough to work outside, come home for lunch and dinner and speak little. Curiosity is what's missing: to know- and to want to know – what exists out there, beyond their orchard and their well-kept garden. What's beyond the river, the sea, the columns of Hercules. Because my problem is not necessarily with those who remain; it is with those who do not look around. There are things and beautiful people to see, interesting to discover, in the Monferrato region. But you have to open your eyes, ask yourself questions, ask, answer, search, run away from your predetermined destiny, find your own way, even if it is around the corner, in a house in the same village, but on another hill. Instead in this Castel San Gerolamo everyone, everyone, everyone, accepts his and her destiny, glued to a fixed point. This is the horror of the countryside I remember. The horror from which I escaped, and I seem to have by the skin of my teeth.

Instead, Giovanni, dickhead, goes back there running.

***

It is October 4th. Giovanni collapses on a chair. The canvas bends under his weight like a sail in the wind. It is the happiest day of his life: the day when the young woman he loves has become his wife. He looks at Bianca who's conversing with her sister, animated, flushed yet fresh in her long white dress. He listens to her thin voice, as thin as autumn rain, thinner than the skin of grapes, as sweet as Moscato. His little Bianca - she barely reaches his shoulder's height – with her chubby hands that she throws up in the air like flowers, his Bianca with her immature and solemn face - a Madonna by Henry Moore - so beautiful she makes him shake. And she's never been so beautiful as she is today, Giovanni thinks, watching his wife on that wedding day. She has never seemed purer, in dress and manner, more real and more solid than anyone he's ever known. And she's his. His Bianca, slender, and white, and shining, like God.

"Well, well: look yonder. Isn't this just wonderful," his father says, sitting beside him. He takes off his grey jacket moaning softly. It is an exceptionally warm, humid autumn. In the nearby vineyard, the grapes are tense and swollen - like the breasts of his wife, thinks Giovanni, sweating. "We won't forget this year. A son who is getting married and a vintage year for wine, too. Two wonders of the world."

They sit side by side, father and son, watching the rows of vines that stretch over the hill. Behind them, the party continues, the murmur of chatter spreads from one crowd of people to another. Everyone has come: uncle Stefano and his family; Giulio with Rosetta Mombello, Filippo and auntie Mimmi, even old Virgilio from Cantavenna. Bianca's best friend Carlotta, with a new boyfriend. From the Netherlands, three pairs of blonde cousins, joyous, wearing high heels. Marieke, squat and rotund in a blue dress that is a bit too tight, with a hat she designed herself, whose feathers cling on her sweaty forehead. But she is happy, Marieke, relieved. She laughs.

Even more than laughter and chatter, it's the aroma of the rich *fritto misto* that spreads through the air –the couple have chosen an unusual menu as their wedding dinner: not elegant, not refined.

"But it represents exactly who we are," Giovanni explains. "We're hungry country folk, both in our heart and in our tummy. Genuine. It would be stupid to get married in Monferrato and eat Norwegian salmon. We're doing what Kate Winslet did in her pre-Hollywood era, celebrating her first marriage in a pub, with sausages and mashed potatoes."

It's a royal fry-up: starting from vegetables with onions and zucchini and eggplant, different types of meat - liver, brain, veal, beef in delicate crumbs made out of breadsticks, sausage, sweetbreads, strands, ribs - and sweet semolina, macaroons, apples, pears. Barbera flows like a river. It is a strong Barbera, as sparkling as Prosecco.

"Its alcoholic content is over thirteen percent, this year," Luigi says, full of pride.

Mist rises from the warm earth in clumps and condenses in the October air. Giovanni surrounds his father's shoulders with a long, thin arm; he's very tall and very thin, almost effeminate in his composed grace. His voice is low, he has a strangely high-pitched laugh, but there is such abandon, in his laughter – his mouth wide open on the dazzling white teeth, his hands imparting a kind of rhythmic tapping on his knees. His face is interrupted by the horizontal line of his eyebrows over his sage-green eyes. His full-lipped mouth, inherited from his mother, is the most attractive part of his body, together with his feet and hands. They resemble the hands and feet of Christ, with pale, bony fingers, full of knots. Giovanni looks down at his shoes. It is hot. He adjusts his tie. He shakes his wrist to let his watch slide down from the sleeve of his jacket. He looks at the time.

"It is still early. I bet you want tonight to arrive quickly, Giovanni."

"Oh, yes."

"There are a few more hours before sunset. Stop thinking about it. *Carpe diem. Carpe diem, hic et nunc*: enjoy this moment, here, now. Enjoy your day. This magnificent afternoon. See around you, everyone's so happy. Look at your uncle Stefano, blind drunk. How he's looking at his wife. And your wife, all shiny with love. Really: she seems to glitter. Or are you scared?"

"Of course I'm not. No reason to be afraid," Giovanni says, and his heart trembles like that night in Montreaux, so many years ago. He's going to make love to the girl he loves, with whom he wants to spend the rest of his life, next to whom he wants to grow old; with a virgin. Bianca is so young. She is so charming, so whole and intact, pure as water, as her name. Giovanni has never had sex with a virgin.

"Well: I have never been a modern girl, like all the others. Not me. It isn't a matter of being religious. It's because I want my first man to be also the last. I want this thing they call sex to only make sense if it's done with my husband. Yes, Giovanni, I'm old fashioned," Bianca had explained. He's afraid of hurting her. The verb "to pierce" comes to mind. Bianca takes leave from the group of friends with whom she was talking, hugs Carlotta. She approaches him right then when he's think of a gash. Sweating.

"Dance with me, Giovanni, my groom." She stretches out her arms towards him, she takes his hand into hers to help him get up. On her ring finger, her wedding band shines. Sweat pours down into Giovanni's eyes. Yes, his bride shines.

***

When it's finally night time, and all the guests have left, even the Dutch cousins who didn't seem to understand it was time to go. Now they are alone for one night, before going on honeymoon.

"Can you lock everything up?" Bianca asks him. "I'll start to head on upstairs."

Giovanni looks at her while she's climbing up, her white dress like a firefly in the dark. He closes the shutters, both external and internal, then the curtains. He locks the door, from the inside, for the first time. He turns off the lights. He makes sure the gas is switched off. He takes off his shoes before going upstairs to take a shower. His pyjamas are neatly folded on the edge of the bathtub. He brushes his teeth twice. He's ready. He walks down the hall, stops in front of their new bedroom. Should he knock? Yes, he should. He knocks.

"Yes?" He hears her say. He doesn't answer, opens the door. Their first night. Giovanni walks in on tiptoe. "Bianca?" He can't hear any noise - just the thud of his heart. "Darling? But where are you hiding? Come on. Get out of your hiding place." Suddenly he perceives a movement, and a shadow slips out of the darkness and pounces on him, it's his wife, Bianca, her long hair loose on her shoulders, hot and dark as chocolate, with her stocky legs, a delicate waist, her ribs visible under the surprisingly round and heavy breasts, Bianca who does not try to cover herself up - the ivory silk nightgown abandoned on the floor, forgotten, unnecessary – Bianca naked and shining and even brighter in this new nudity, Bianca laughs and jumps on him, laughs and makes him fall on the bed, laughs and kisses him furiously, laughs and tells him to take off his pj, and helps him to take it off, the funny trousers, laughs and sits on the bed kneeling next to him, she looks at him, looks at his body without embarrassment. Giovanni kisses her palm, the inside of her wrists. Bianca looks at him.

"My man."

"My woman."

"Mine."

"Mine."

***

Later, his face next to hers, on the same embroidered pillow, they talk. They laugh. Giovanni can't believe one could laugh so much. He thinks of Marieke's whining voice counterbalanced with his father's silence. He wonders if it's normal, to have so much to say, if it is normal to giggle about trifles, every day more loudly – nobody can hear them. He's never seen a couple like them. They are different. They are special; and they have found each other. It could easily not have happened; they might never have met; if only that day, he had not hesitated a little longer, at that café; if Luisa had dragged her sister away, rather than encourage her to stay, to have another ice cream; if only Riccardo had not been with him to guarantee him that first, fateful introduction. If Carmela had not betrayed him; if they had gotten married: what would that be like. The infinite possibilities of a different life. He thinks back at himself a couple of years ago, the state he was in. The wounds on his back. Now he's almost healed.

"I'm a real man, now." A man who has a woman waiting for him at home every day. A man with responsibilities, with a full, rich future.

"Do you want to have children?"

"And you?"

"Of course."

"Can have three? Or five? I want a big noisy family. Adventurous, free. As happy as you are."

***

It's autumn, the Mediterranean sea is cold, Giovanni and Bianca are bourgeois young people with money to spend, they want (but fear) the Exotic. They decide to spend their honeymoon at the Maldives. Obviously. The *idea* of paradise: sea, sun, sand, Italian clubs that guarantee good quality food, water bungalows, massages with scented oils, flowers on the pillow, colourful fish to admire, flip flops and bathing suits, long days that give a sense of an exotic yet domesticated holiday, with little trips to nearby atolls, to take pictures of the local fauna in the markets (what amazing colours, what incredible aromas!).

You rest, you relax, you get bored gently, in the Maldives. This isn't, however, a plain and simple holiday. It's their honeymoon: a tradition dating back to the Babylonians, where the first month spent in the company of one's spouse is the sweetest of their conjugal life. How sweet are the Maldivian tropical nights. Giovanni and Bianca swim, read, chat, sleep, make love. Giovanni is surprised at just how young his wife is: like Tolstoy when he married Sophia Andreyevna - she was eighteen and he thirty-four. A man, with a little girl. Bianca still has a certain girly, playful demeanour, a clumsy running style: she seems reticent, almost shy, but then slowly her confidence builds up, she lets herself go. And then she gallops over and into the ocean, diving in head first and then re-emerging with a colossal spray of water. She jumps, giggles, twirls, she never stands still, she doesn't shut up, she takes off her shoes under the restaurant table, she fiddles with the cutlery, laughs out loudly, with her cheerful, mischievous, selfish voice - she only cares about herself and Giovanni. She opens her eyes wide with surprise and delight, just like the tour guide Mr Silvera, in that novel by Fruttero & Lucentini, who keeps hearing: look, look! Look, Mr Silvera! She does the same: look, Giovanni! Look at the moon, the amazing presentation of the food, the music, the other tourists, the flowers the sea, look! Look, Giovanni! Look at the room the wine the menu, the sand, the shells, the bed, the bathroom, the taps, the sheets, the pillows, the sea view, everything. Just look! Look! Look, look!

Giovanni is indulgent, Giovanni is enchanted.

They land at Malpensa airport ten days later. Luisa comes to pick them up. Luisa is a practical woman, sour, disillusioned, worried about her little sister: she sees the couple walk out hand in hand – Bianca slightly behind Giovanni who is almost pulling her. Smiling, happiness stuck to their faces like their tan.

***

A new routine takes shape day after day, week after week.

The radio wakes them up before seven, and after it goes off they stay in bed for another half an hour, in the warmth of the bed which is slightly too small for a couple. Then they get up, Bianca goes downstairs to make coffee, Giovanni has a shower and gets dressed and then goes downstairs also; they have breakfast together; at eight fifteen Giovanni kisses her on the doorstep. Three days a week, Luigi drives Bianca to Trino to attend a teaching training course. When she doesn't need to attend, there is the house that needs looking after, and she likes to do everything herself - she paints the dining room a bright yellow, she cuts and sews curtains for every room, she makes cushions, tablecloths, a multi-coloured blanket for their bed. Every three Sundays, they are invited for dinner at Luigi and Marieke's; sometimes they visit Umberto; they invite friends to dinner, showing off their sophisticated, adult way of life.

Giovanni returns home for lunch whenever he can, when he is not too busy - he likes to improvise and pay unannounced visits, sneak inside while Bianca is busy doing something - bent over the sewing machine, or with a brush in her hands, her hair pulled up, a fiercely concentrated look. Startling her from behind, he puts his hands over her eyes. She shakes with excitement.

"Guess who is it."

"You're here!" She screams. Often, after lunch, they run upstairs to make love before he has to return to the office for the afternoon.

"Well. I'm the boss, after all," Giovanni says, shoulders straight. "Are you happy?" he asks.

"I couldn't ask for more," she replies, purring.

In the evening, Giovanni sometimes stops the car on the main road before climbing up the hill; from down here, their home seems a hut, with windows all lit up. A Christmas nativity; a crib. Only snow is lacking.

And when he comes in, he can smell whatever Bianca is cooking - nothing fancy, she's not a great cook, she isn't Carmela, who liked to experiment with exotic recipes, though the results were often disappointing; Bianca prepares pasta, soup, apple pie, roast chicken, but the aroma is the right one: of home. Of family. The heat, the fat scent of melted butter, of rosemary and sage, of the wood burning in the fireplace. The smile of his wife. He doesn't need anything else.

***

It sounds like a Raymond Carver story but without a bad ending. Here we are: me in front of her, she in front of me, sitting at the ugly Ikea table. My old Argos lies in his bed in the corner, and nothing happens. She asks me questions. I reply. I ask her a question. She responds. She's made a frittata with herbs and onions, this evening, served with a salad and sautéed potatoes. I could smell the onions when I was still outside; tomorrow my clothes will reek, and my hair will stink and my breath too, but who cares, the frittata is warm and good and the potatoes as well. And my wife is here next to me, and here is my home, sticky with reality, a different reality; everything feels new, everything moves me and you know what? maybe I drank too much Barbera tonight – last year's wine that has over fourteen percent alcohol content, and it floored me.

The banality of life.

Bianca has a bit of salad stuck on her left tooth but I'm not telling her; she is perfect right now, unaware of her green tooth, beautiful and ugly, imperfect, perfect Bianca. My friends had told me marriage is not that great a thing, after all; and you know what? They were wrong, or lying: marriage completely fulfils me, it infuses in me a sense of total possession: I have her whenever I want; whenever I feel like, I can touch her, kiss her, or ignore her; I can talk or not, it doesn't matter, whatever: she is *mine* - my Bianca, I tell her, and she smiles with a tenderness that I don't deserve, she is MINE, she with teeth full of salad and a smile like a Madonna, she looks like a child but she's my woman, and I pull her onto my knees as if she were my daughter; and we have another evening in which nothing happens; we eat the frittata, the potatoes, an apple, a cookie; then we go into the living room, light a fire, sit next to one another, leaning against the ugly pillows that Bianca sewed with the usual childish enthusiasm, under the ugly blanket; we watch a movie on TV; I open the door so Argos can go out and piss; he goes out, pisses, comes back in; I'm distracted, I read, I add wood to the fire, close the curtains; I sit, I look at her profile, her big nose, those pale lips, her hands busy playing with her hair which is tied into a pony tail; I take the elastic band out, I run my fingers through it; at eleven o'clock she yawns. I yawn too.

"Come on," she says. "Let's go to bed."

"I'll follow you," I say. "I'll be up in a minute," I say. I close up, have a sip of wine, walk upstairs. I sneak into our bed, which is already warmed up by her body; I'm not going to make love to her tonight, I'm tired. It doesn't matter: I don't have to prove anything, I don't need to show her I am always hard. I'm hard when I want to be hard. Whenever I fancy.

We fall asleep holding hands like Hansel and Gretel.

***

THE HEART OF THE OCTOPUS

One of the key issues that influence the choice of a partner rather than another is the realisation that childhood experiences are at the root of any loving relationship. John Bowlby was a British psychoanalyst who in 1988 formulated the so-called 'attachment theory', which describes the affective and emotional bond that is to be established between mother and child, and from this the dynamics within a couple. In fact, the way in which we bind ourselves emotionally to another person reflects the model of the mother-child relationship, because it is on this very early relationship that mental representations of ourselves are based. If one wasn't loved as a child, in fact if one had to beg the love that was not coming spontaneously, one will not be able to understand it, to modulate and implement it during future experiences of being in a couple.

To marry someone means to enter into a contract: it is an act of faith, with an underlying promise of fidelity and mutual obligation. This can be truly and fully assumed when it is consciously wanted and internalised, that is when the partners are dedicated to the relationship, when they formulate a common project of life and a commitment to make it happen. There is another condition that needs to be met, and this is the so-called "secret deal" that represents the psychological and emotional motivations underlying mutual choice. What attracts us to another person is a cocktail of fears, needs, and desires related to our private history, our family models. The secret pact is successful when partners meet and satisfy each other's emotional needs.

Giovanni and Bianca, for various reasons, have never felt loved as children. Bianca, raised by her father and her sister, lacked maternal love which is the basis of a healthy sense of personal safety. Giovanni has always felt loved by Marieke, but in the wrong way; not for who he really is, but for who he could have been - not him for better or for worse, but: if only he had changed a little; if only he had been more like her. The disastrous subsequent relationships have made him even more suspicious, even more insecure - enough to make him believe that, well, perhaps he doesn't deserve to be loved.

Finally they have found someone to love, and to be loved by. Watching them is like having *hanami*, the Japanese tradition of cherry blossom viewing: the personality of Giovanni and Bianca bloom and flourish like Sakura, cherry trees in April, in Japan: secure of each other, secure of the love for each other and of the strength of their relationship, confident about the future, for the first time, they can let go; they can drop barriers, fears and be themselves with the total conviction that they will be accepted as they really are.

***

Marieke has a copy of the keys to the *Willow* - three keys strung together in a silver ring with a tiny pendant that depicts a green enamel tree. Here she is: it's ten o'clock on a late-November morning (cold, fog, the air so thick with moisture that your face feels wet). Marieke, wrapped in a beige scarf that looks like a blanket, is on the doorstep, keys in hand. Should she ring the bell? Of course she should, but she doesn't. Should she knock? Of course she should. But she doesn't. She pulls out the keys from her handbag and opens the door.

Bianca, who is in the bathroom, doesn't hear anything. Marieke goes into the kitchen, prepares the coffee machine, puts it on the gas, extracts two cups from the cabinet, smells them, pulls a face, washes and dries them and places them on a round pewter tray, adds a jug of milk and the sugar bowl, and brings the tray into the living room. She sits down onto the velvet chair on the right side of the fireplace, and waits for her daughter-in-law. Who, when she finally comes downstairs and finds her mother-in-law, doesn't seem surprised; she isn't perturbed, distressed; she is ready for anything. Bianca drinks her lukewarm coffee, and she talks: about the weather, the pillowcases that she's sewing, about the blue wool sweater she's knitting for Giovanni, about what to cook next Saturday night, as they have invited two colleagues of Giovanni's with their wives, and yes maybe she'll make a risotto and a roast, and then she asks after Luigi, and after various relatives, and she smiles, she talks, she finishes her coffee. Marieke offers advice: she should change colour for the cushions (red would be better), she should prepare a pumpkin soup and of course she is going to give her the best recipe. She should wear the dress that they gave her as a gift for her birthday and that fits her like a glove, and she will send her trustworthy old housekeeper Viola to do a deep clean for the autumn; maybe Bianca has little time and hasn't really noticed how dusty it is. And it's the first house she has: one must learn to manage it. Bianca accepts every word - compliment or criticism that is - with a gentle smile.

Marieke can't stand her. Christ, this girl: good she's good, she's humble and not stupid, she's not learned, not privileged. She isn't Carmela, who was everything and more. And yet much as Marieke disliked Carmela, it was nothing compared to her aversion to Bianca; Carmela, yes, Carmela made her feel inadequate, clumsy, ignorant. Lower, in every possible sense. The conflict with Bianca, however, is born out of pure control of her territory. She feels invaded, like Crimea by Russia. She can't and does not want to share with this unknown young woman the son she has raised and cared for, for more than thirty years. The apple of her eyes, the beating of her heart, the ultimate purpose of her life. Carmela was temporary, that was always obvious: like a pretty bud in a vase, that blooms and then it's gone, that has no roots; Bianca is not going anywhere. Bianca is forever, like the olive tree of Luras in Sardinia, which has a circumference of twelve meters and an age between 3500 and 4000 years. An olive tree so strong that there is nothing that will bring it down. Christ, how unbearable.

***

Luigi? Ah, Luigi. Naïve, harmless, near-sighted Luigi, who reads in his study all day, who accumulates books and knowledge although he has nobody with whom to discuss it. As he likes to repeat: *Bene vixit qui bene latuit*, which means that, all things considered, a life spent hidden away was a life that was worth it (which is a sentence derived from *bene latuit qui bene vixit* written by Ovid in the *Tristia*. The affinity with the Epicurean λάθε βιώσας 'live hiddenly', which was also the motto printed on the noble emblem of Descartes, is evident). Let's put it this way: Luigi is happy. No: Luigi is content. He isn't a complicated man – that's why I had said he was simple. The relationships he forms with others – family, colleagues, clients - are simple. He loves his son with a spontaneous, normal love. He wants to make sure Giovanni is okay. He wants him to be happy. He sees that Giovanni is comfortable with his wife; what else could you ask for? What else should be expected?

Luigi got married for love to a young Dutch girl. He knew little of her. He knew little of everything. Right now – this very minute – he is at home, sitting on one of the dining chairs. The door between this room and the kitchen is half-open. He hears his wife bustle around, clanging pots and pans; if he closes her eyes, he can see her perfectly: her every single movement: the opening of the doors, the trouble she has when she bends over, the little grimace that trembles on her cheek when she makes an effort, that gesture of pulling down the hem of her skirt even when she doesn't need to. The left hand curling a strand of hair behind her ear – he's loved that gesture of hers for thirty years, like many others he's not even noticing, now. When she smells her hands. When she scratches the back of her head. When she puts on her shoes, first the left and then the right, always in that order, and when she slips them off, in the opposite order. The way she holds a fork, a pen, the steering wheel. Marieke is far from perfect, nor is their marriage - as he likes to say, *Non bene, si tollas proelia, durat amor.* Luigi knows that his wife regrets – not always, but at times - spending her life in Castel San Gerolamo; what other extraordinary things she would have done... *if.* If only. For him, regret is a feeling that doesn't really make sense - remember: first of all, he is a practical man, who has been dealing with laws and decrees every day, for years. He doesn't often use the word: 'if' followed by a subjunctive; he uses the indicative: certainty, what we have here now.

Who does Giovanni resemble the most? Each and both of his parents, like all children. Giovanni has always done what he wants, in the end; and what Luigi wants, as his father, is to see his son able to walk on his legs and have a roof over his head. Clichés, clichés: Luigi knows their strength and rightness. He knows that life is not a painting by Caravaggio, it's not theatre, where shadow is dramatically juxtaposed to light. In life, light and shadow coexist harmoniously, in hundreds of shades. His son knows the light, but he knows that there is also shadow.

Luigi hears moving about in the kitchen, he imagines Giovanni in his new home, just six hundred meters from here, on the other side of the village, sitting in the living room while Bianca prepares dinner – the soft sound of the tablecloth laid on the table like a sail in the wind, the clatter of dishes, the clunking sound of cutlery, the dingdingdinging of glasses. The knock of a wooden spoon that stirs a sauce in a pot. The steps silenced by felted slippers. The housewifish noises of each and every house.

***

Not during the week, no. I'm too distracted by office problems - the recent simplification and rationalisation of the rules relating to money laundering, Dr. Miglietti with his perennial fiscal problems; Giulia, one of the secretaries, who is pregnant and goes on maternity leave in three months and must be replaced, and the new trainee who will start next Tuesday – when I finally reach home I'm tired, with the brain full, fried. I am deaf to everything: everything, apart from knowing how lucky I am to have a wife who works better than a butler, better than a maid, better than a personal assistant. I find my dinner ready, my shirts are washed and ironed, in the bathroom there is a new jar of relaxing bath salts, there is plenty of food in the pantry. She is also the one that calls the plumber or the electrician if something doesn't work properly; she is the one that books an appointment for the annual visit to the dentist, to the optician. Who calls in at my parents' to ask if they need anything, to accompany them to the doctor's, to collect their prescriptions. Now that Argos is not well, it is she who notices it first, who rings the vet. We never have to fight over who does what as was the case with Carmela; neither do I have to take care of it, in addition to my day job.

"I'll do it," she says. I forget it instantly, and I find, a little later, that everything has been resolved without my intervention. What a relief.

In the weekend we go foraging for mushrooms in the woods; to Alessandria or Asti to do some shopping; at a new restaurant in Moncalvo to eat truffles; to visit her intolerable friend Carlotta or her father and her sister; and she always follows me, docile, cheerful, as if she didn't have any other plan or wish to do something else; in fact, as if what she really wanted to do was to please me, to do what I do, what I like. She leaves me reluctantly when I visit my father on my own to ask his advice on the vineyard – she follows me with her candid blind eyes, and I know that she misses me already.

I don't know exactly how she spends her days, from morning until evening. Twelve hours alone. For example, I know little of the course she's taking: she doesn't tell me much of her companions, the teachers, the practical work she has to do with the children. When I ask her, she responds matter-of-factly, without detail, without examples, without passion. Her passion, she says, it's me. And I see that: she kind of switches on, with me. Of course this attitude derives from the discovery of sex, but it's not just sex: it's me.

THE HEART OF THE OCTOPUS

"Giovanni, you are my life," she told me more than once. Suddenly I am taller and stronger, like a child after hearing his mother's compliments (which I never received, from mine). I feel even more handsome. "You complete me," she tells me: a sentence I had heard only once, uttered by one of Filippo's girlfriends, and that at the time had made me shudder with horror – what a far-fetched idea, I thought. How repulsive to imagine that one would be incomplete without another. As if, alone, one was missing a part of the brain, or of the body, or of the heart. And yet now I understand it. Now it makes perfect sense: love is the glue that binds together, the nail that unites two disunited parts.

Two, one.

***

One Saturday morning, Giovanni goes downstairs to prepare breakfast. Argos doesn't run to him anxious to be let out; he lies motionless in his bed, with no energy. Giovanni walks over, kneels down beside him, strokes his head. Argos looks at him with eyes full of tears, leans his cheek on the palm of his hand, and dies.

Giovanni buries him in the garden: his dog, his friend, the creature that had helped him overcome his grief for the loss of Julie. He feels sad, but this time it's a healthy, natural feeling, like losing a ninety-nine-year-old great-grandfather who has been ill for a long time. He'll miss him, he thinks holding in his arms the heavy body wrapped in a white sheet, smiling at Bianca who is

THE HEART OF THE OCTOPUS

watching him from the window upstairs because she finds it "a bit creepy." Digging the soil is hard work, sweat sticks to his back, he takes off his jumper, rolls up the sleeves of his shirt, he whistles - and then he stops, no, you can't do that, Argos is dead, his dog, how can one whistle in such a sad day, but it is also normal, life begins again, and people die but life continues, and then who knows, perhaps we can buy another dog, maybe a puppy, a puppy like my wife, and he looks up to the first floor where she is standing by the window, as Romeo looked to Juliet.

He keeps digging until the hole is big enough. He kneels on the ground, takes Argos's rigid body in his arms, slips it down the bottom of the hole; he adds his blanket, the pillow crocheted by his mother many years before, his favourite toys, his ball. Then he starts covering the hole with soil.

"It's his heart, he just can't take it anymore," the vet had explained two weeks earlier. "You see, dogs often suffer from heart disease, usually of genetic origin. Here the problem is due to the heart valves, who have lost the ability to close properly. It would take the heart of an octopus to solve this problem. Did you know they have three hearts?" he'd said. As soon as Giovanni got home, he looked up "Octopus" in his encyclopaedia.

"The word *octopus* originates from the Greek πωλύπους (polypous), from πολύς (polys) "many" and πούς, (Pous), "foot." It is a cephalopod mollusc very common in shallow water, as it prefers rugged substrates, rocks, rich because of cracks and caves to hide. [...] It is considered one of the most intelligent invertebrates; for example, it has been demonstrated that the common octopus has the ability to learn if subjected to tests of learning by association and by observation of others of its kind, capacity that had been demonstrated only in few mammals. [...]Their tentacles have autonomous "minds": two-thirds of the octopus' neurons reside in their tentacles and not in the head. It may therefore happen that a tentacle is able to solve a task as opening a shell while its owner is busy with other matters, such as the exploration of a crevice in the coral barrier [...] The octopus has three hearts with a closed circulatory system, with two atria and one ventricle, which pumps blood throughout the body. When the octopus swims, this third heart stops beating, because it prefers crawling on the seabed rather than swimming, an activity that leaves him exhausted."

Giovanni thinks of the heart of the octopus while covering Argos's body with soil. Three hearts, he thinks. The three parts of a single organ, he thinks while lifting the earth with a spade, dropping it into the hole.

"Three hearts, like me: Julie, Carmela, Bianca." When he's finished, he kneels, pats the little hill with his hands. "There you are, Argos," he whispers. It's almost invisible. Tomorrow he can plant some flowers over it. He wipes the palms of his hands on his trousers. He sniffles. And now, what?, he thinks. What do you actually do, on the grave of a dog - pray? "Thanks, Argos," he whispers. He throws down his spade. He comes home dirty, sweaty, tired. Bianca is standing on the doorway, waiting for him: Bianca: his third heart.

***

They never fight. Bianca's mood doesn't go up and down, it's as constant and straight as the line on the horizon, like a road, like the ECG of a dead man. A horizontal line, yes, but high: always lively, positive, cheerful, free from humoral or hormonal changes; she wakes up smiling and falls asleep smiling. Giovanni, who over the years has become angrier, calms down instantly, with her. He returns home from the office pissed off with the world, with that idiot of his secretary, with his incompetent colleague, with the shitty traffic; he walks in and sees her – just her back, as she's in the kitchen, peeling potatoes. He calms down immediately. Here she is, his wife, the man-whisperer, who can quieten the rabid, the irascible. Who tames them, like a circus trainer with a wild animal, a lion, a tiger. Bianca belongs to a universe far away, to a different galaxy, to a slow and placid world full of benevolent, contagious serenity. She's like a little girl, eight or nine years old, who always wants to know the reason of things, who asks "why?" of everything. She loves to write letters to her sister, to read sentimental novels and gossip magazines her mother-in-law gives her. She likes to play cards, or board games with simple rules, Monopoly and Scrabble; and she's competitive, she does want to win, but not at all costs; she never cheats. She's affectionate, helpful, outgoing, curious. She likes the teaching course she is attending although Giovanni thinks she prefers to chat with the other girls at the nursery than to work with the children in their care. The various friends / colleagues have very specific roles: Laura is the group's leader, the one that seems to make all the decisions, to which the others conform; Paola is the diplomat, the one who mediates the situations between trainees and their boss and parents of the children, between the trainees themselves; Bianca is the observer, she looks but doesn't propose, doesn't decide, doesn't participate fully, and often becomes the group's scapegoat. Sometimes they fight; who'd seemed the new best friend – "new rising star," Giovanni says, teasing her - becomes the enemy, and vice versa. She's learning; every experience becomes an opportunity that matures her, that forces her to take account of several factors, not just of how she feels at any given time. She's known her best friend, Carlotta, since they were in the same class, in primary school; Carlotta now lives in Casale, teaches maths, they see each other less often, and each one is jealous of the other: they quarrel, they make peace, they talk endlessly on the phone, and when they are together they are unbearable, they revert to being teenagers who become hysterical with laughter for no apparent reason; they speak a jargon that excludes him, they swap clothes, makeup, perfume. Giovanni gets irritated; he tries to make Bianca understand that he doesn't care about Carlotta; actually, he can't tolerate the idea that the two of them might share confidences, that Carlotta might know something of their intimate life. He hates to think that Bianca has secrets she only confesses to her best friend. He hates the idea that Bianca has a private life, which excludes him.

"I don't understand why you want to do this teaching course. Why don't you stay home and look after the house, after me?" **h**e asked her one day. Bianca's reply was to laugh.

***

The term fetish indicates the inanimate object which is attributed a magical or spiritual power, by virtue of a semantic shift that transforms it in its common value and invests it with a symbolic meaning. Freud describes the phenomenon as the result of sexual impressions experienced during early childhood; in the fetishist's unconscious fantasy, the fetish is a substitute for a woman's penis. Consequently, the woman's genital organs lose their erogenous quality, in the eyes of the fetishist, and erogeneity is transferred to the fetish which becomes the source of excitement, an idealized object capable of providing sexual pleasure. In this way, fetishism provides a means of displacement and, indirectly, the validation of the child's fantasy, which is fixed on an object closely linked to the female body.

Bianca's body has parts that, just by looking at them – only thinking of them – make Giovanni's heart speed up, accelerating until his pulse reaches over a hundred beats per minute, two hundred. He gasps for air, he feels weak, his heart palpitates, he starts sweating. When he's alone, he thinks about her and masturbates. If he's with her, if he happens to stare at her *there*, he can't help but put his hands on her, raise the hem of her skirt, unfasten the buttons of her blouse.

• Bianca's *hands* are pink, plump; there is a dimple at the base of each finger. She doesn't bite her nails, which she keeps short, oval, without polish. She wears only two rings, always: the engagement ring, and the plain wedding band, which she never takes off, not even at night. She doesn't write much by hand; her writer's bump callus is almost inexistent. The lines that intersect her palm are neat: a long life line; a very straight fortune line; the love line crossed by ditches and ruts and islands. A palm reader once told her she will have three daughters. But what they don't tell you just by looking at them, these hands, is just how warm, how soft they are. They are as warm and soft as your favourite pet: as an Angora rabbit, a chinchilla, a new-born owl, a fox cub. They also have the mobility of a little animal– they don't stand still for a moment - and an unusual heat. Sometimes she places them on my tummy, and what I get is an instant erection.

• Bianca's *nose* is as straight as a ruler, as a stretch of road which then curves downwards forming a little hollow with the mouth. The philtrum (from the Greek: φίλτρουphiltron = love potion - ancient Greeks considered the philtrum to be one of the most erogenous spots on the human body) is a vertical groove in the midline portion of the upper lip bordered by two lateral ridges or pillars. The lower end of the groove and the ridges form the central portion of the Cupid's bow of the vermilion. In Jewish tradition, the sub-nasal groove is the mark left by the Angel of Forgetfulness on an infant's upper lip before birth, to silence the infant from telling all the secrets in the universe to humanity; the infant then forgets the Torah he has been taught. Bianca's philtrum is very pronounced; her upper lip looks swollen, moving upwards excessively, not allowing her to close her mouth completely: it is always disclosed in an eternal sigh, with slightly bared teeth. Can you remember the actress Carole André, who played the part of the Pearl of Labuan in the television series *Sandokan*, in the Seventies? Exactly like that. The result is a pout, a curl of the mouth, something that drives me crazy, that makes me want to bite it, to tear it with my teeth. I want to kiss her there, just there, not touching her tongue or her lower lip, not going even close to her teeth and palate and gums. I just want the upper lip, her philtrum, nothing else.

- Bianca's *thighs* are stocky. It's strange, because she is petite and lean in the rest of the body, but her legs are chubby, with accumulations of fat around the buttocks and the top of her legs - the so-called "culottes des cheval." They are swollen with cellulite, although she is an active girl who exercises regularly. Her thighs rub against each other when she walks, causing widespread redness (a colour such as ham when it is sliced thinly, and is neither red nor pink, but a shade in-between), a rash that's not particularly painful, but annoying. That's why she prefers to wear trousers instead of dresses, jeans and leggings instead of skirts - and that's why I love to see her in a dress, preferably short, preferably without tights. The mere idea of her firm, thick, bulky, sweaty thighs drives me crazy, I imagine them rub, rub, rub against each other, I think Bianca must feel a sensation of burning just there, and the more she moves the more it burns until it actually is painful, she lifts her dress, her skirt, lowers her tights and looks between her red legs, and there they are, hundreds of tiny dots, like pimples, like a spider bite. I love kissing these red angry pimples, like a game of join-the-dots, with the tip of my tongue – I'm in ecstasy when I make her legs wet with saliva until they glisten.

• Bianca's *neck* is the opposite to her legs: if those are thick, this is incredibly thin and delicate, and long like the most famous ones - Mrs. Agnelli's, Audrey Hepburn's, of the women painted by Amedeo Modigliani, or the Parmigianino's Madonna. It's elegant, slender, crossed only by a line in the middle - the so-called ring of Venus - and a mole the size and shape and colour of a hazelnut on her right side. Bianca rarely wears necklaces, and when she does, it annoys me: when we go out in the evening, she likes to wear a long pearl necklace, which she coils around her magnificent neck – one, two, three four times. She looks great with it, of course: but I want to see that neck naked, vulnerable: sometimes I put my hands around it, around that swan-like neck, and squeeze a little: no, not too much, not enough to scare her; I certainly don't want to strangle her: I just want to apply a slight pressure, just to feel her pulsating life under my fingers. It looks like a blade of grass, the stem of a flower – you'd just need a little pressure to break it.

I love Bianca's body. I revere it. The curve of her breasts. The dimple in her lower back. Her – how did Henry Miller put it? Yes: her sweet, sweet cunt: one in a million. But not only that: all of her body. I stroke it, dwelling on every hair, every pore, every wrinkle. Its imperfections, its imperceptible flaws are what excites me the most: the moles, the seborrheic keratosis under her breast, the rosacea spreading on her cheeks, a few pimples, a café au lait spot on her back, her tiny wrinkles - god, she will drive me crazy, when she's sixty. Bianca smiles indulgently at what she calls my "obsession," and her smile forms a tiny cobweb around her eyes. My desire is kindled like a fire in the woods, in the month of August.

***

On the day of the feast of the Immaculate conception, Giovanni goes out early in the morning for a mysterious mission; he returns with a Christmas tree – he has managed to fit it into his car, between the seats, with the tip protruding from a window. A real tree: Bianca didn't know one could buy them. It fills the air with the fresh, lively scent of the woods, and the young couple has fun decorating it with ornaments in part inherited from their families and in part bought and chosen by them: a cute robin, a white rocking horse, two silver bells, tied with a green ribbon. At the top, an angel with its wings open wide and a fluffy white feather dress.

"It looks more like a swan than an angel," Giovanni says.

"Oh come on. It's gorgeous," Bianca says.

It is a Bank holiday.

"Surprise. Let's go somewhere new. Let's spend some money. Come on, get ready," Giovanni says, and they drive to Milan. They don't go there often - since he's returned to Castel San Gerolamo, Giovanni hates the city, its crowds, the smog, the traffic - but he's certain that Bianca will love the Christmas decorations, and in fact there she is, looking up, mouth open admiring the lights, every sign, every banner, every drape.

"Look!"

They walk for hours along Corso Vittorio Emanuele, and in Piazza Duomo, where there is a flea market; they drink hot chocolate at Cova's in via Montenapoleone; they buy delicacies from Peck's; at the largest store in town, the Rinascente, Giovanni buys her a perfume, a lingerie set with black panties and bra, a silk nightgown, a red hat she decides to put on at once: with her red nose and bright eyes, Bianca looks like a gnome of the woods.

"Come on: no more shopping; it's time for a cocktail. Let's go to Brera. Come on, come on," Giovanni says, pushing her into a taxi. He's a new man - talkative, open, spontaneous; so different from the husband she has known for a year, the intense, reliable, conscientious, authoritative, responsible man: this Giovanni, this one here tonight, seems to be twenty-one. It's all too exciting. Perhaps it's the two Martinis drank quickly and without any food, perhaps it's the Christmas lights, maybe it's the memory of a different Milan, one that frightens and attracts him, or the danger of running into someone he knows from when he was with Carmela, or into Carmela herself. Maybe it's because Bianca knows how to laugh with him, knows how to play the game; whatever the reasons: Giovanni takes off his gloves and puts his hand between her legs in the taxi that takes them from Brera to a new location on the canals. Perhaps it's an metallic whiff of sex that lingers on his fingers, or the music that overwhelms them like a tsunami, the darkness and the lights and the lights and the lights and the crazy speed of the taxi; whatever the reason: tonight, he wants to be someone else. Another.

"Let's check into a hotel," he says. He doesn't ask a question; he has already made a decision. He does not bother asking Bianca what she wants, what would she like, what she'd rather do. He treats her like a child. His little girl. He's decided they'll spend the night in a hotel, like a clandestine couple, and they'll drain the bottles from the minibar and make love at least three times. In an exciting bed, because it's new. Like another honeymoon, he says. Bianca nods. Of course she nods; she does nothing else. He is the one who chooses; and he chooses a four-star hotel on Viale Certosa, which perhaps is not quite romantic, he says, seeing disappointment veil her eyes, but come on, it doesn't matter. We are elsewhere: is it not enough?

"Of course it is," Bianca says. She is now tired – it's two in the morning - dazed by music and alcohol. Of course. Sure. She lets him undress her, and obeys the order to try on the outfit he's bought for her, and she stands with her new underwear and the new bra and then the new nightgown, and then she lets him strip her off, again. Finally, she lies down on the bed, closes her eyes. Giovanni climbs on top of her; she keeps her eyes closed - for tiredness, for pleasure - and then suddenly she feels a dry, cold slap on the cheek – she hears first the noise and then feels the pain, a few seconds later - and opens her eyes and there's Giovanni, her husband, who looks deadly serious, his eyes filled with desire and challenge. Bianca closes her eyes again, pretending it isn't happening.

***

"It's just a game, all right?"

She looks at me with those wide white eyes, like a frightened rabbit in the headlights.

"Come on," I say. "It's a little game. An erotic game."

"Oh."

"Yes. Sorry. I didn't mean to offend you. Some women like it, actually." I see a flicker of jealousy, of anger, of shame, of incomprehension. A hint of excitement. "A game, I told you. But I won't do it anymore if you don't like it."

She doesn't know what to do, I see it in her clear eyes; they are so bright, even now, in this dark room.

I smile and then I become serious again and then I smile again and she acts like a mirror, and I lose patience and slap her once again. A backhanded slap, like those my mother used to give me when I was little.

She closes her eyes. I kiss her quietly, slowly, totally chastely. I lie down beside her and stroke her face with the tip of my fingers, as you do with something infinitesimally tiny, or fragile.

"I am inexperienced," she finally says. "I don't know what to expect."

"Shh, my love. It doesn't matter."

"You have always been so sweet," she says. Sweet: an unbearable adjective.

"Yes, but sometimes a hint of spice is a good thing.

"As you like it."

"What did you say? I didn't quite hear."

"As you like it."

"Only if you want to, too."

"As you like it."

***

Giovanni wakes up. He rolls onto the other side of the bed and finds it empty though still warm. He's in a good mood, light-headed; in his mouth lingers the weary taste of winter Sunday afternoons: there were too many roasted chestnuts and too much grappa, at lunch. He went upstairs to lie down for a nap, "twenty minutes at most," and suddenly it's four o'clock. He sits on the edge of the bed until the ceiling stops spinning, he rises cautiously, pulls back the curtains on the grey day, on the light that is about to disappear. From downstairs there are muffled sounds of dishes being moved about, of glasses and pots. Giovanni rubs his warm hands against each other. They are preparing dinner. It's Christmas Eve.

He puts on his trousers, a shirt rigid with starch, formal grey suspenders, and he goes downstairs into the kitchen which is invaded by cooking smells, and steam. Three polished faces greet him, all lined up in front of the big oak table: Bianca, Luisa and Marieke are working together to make the ravioli: Bianca rolls the dough into a thin sheet; Luisa, standing next to her, forms small meat balls with the mixture (prepared the day before) of three roasts, ham, sausage, eggs and grated Parmesan cheese; Marieke, finally, folds the dough around the meat and seals every parcel with a little water.

"The *ravioli* for tomorrow."

"What about a quick coffee?"

"Oh come on. Go for a walk into the village, which will do you good. Enjoy the fresh air. Go and join your father and don't come back for a couple of hours. Dinner is at seven-thirty."

THE HEART OF THE OCTOPUS

At Pier Vittorio's bar, he has an espresso, followed by some alcoholic drinks, to stimulate appetite. The men – dressed to the nines – laugh and drink, in the cold air, full of the strong smell of wine. They play cards. When the church bells ring nineteen times, the bar is besieged by those returning from mass; they exchange the latest gossip and the last good wishes. When he closes his shop, Umberto joins them too, and they all return together.

"We're here! We're hungry!"

The three women are putting a series of dishes on the table. Beginning with tiny pizzas the size of a hundred lira coins, vol-au-vent with fondue, followed by spinach *cappelletti* in a broth, boiled trout – horribly dry - that they all drown in mayonnaise to make it edible.

"A special applause to Bianca and Luisa, the real stars of the night," Luigi says. The sisters kick each other under the table. Marieke scowls, jealous of the obvious intimacy between her son and her daughter-in-law, jealous of the closeness between the sisters, jealous of their youth.

"What on earth have you done to these unfortunate chestnuts, Bianca, I wonder?" Marieke asks, spitting out a boiled chestnut.

"Nothing really. I just cooked them with cloves and fennel seeds."

"They're so hard. It feels as if I'm chewing wood."

"Why don't you cook them, then," Luigi says looking up at the ceiling.

"What are you of all people talking about? You, you never eat anything! Look at him therrre, thin as a blade of grass," she says, rolling her eyes, looking like a crazy horse.

"It's time," Luigi says.

"Time for what?" Luisa asks.

"It's time of the ritual, isn't it?" It's the moment Luigi calls "the savage ritual": the exchange of gifts. Scattered on the floor in the blue living room, the beautiful one, there are piles of parcels, that the members of the family - one by one - collect and distribute. Luisa receives a pink blouse; Marieke the same, but white, of course; Umberto and Luigi, a pair of leather gloves. Bianca gives Giovanni a gold pen.

"It was my grandfather's."

"I will use it always, my darling," Giovanni says, kissing her on the cheek. Marieke's are covered in red patches. Clumsy, inadequate, she abruptly interrupts them.

"It's my turn, now," she says, placing a small parcel in Giovanni's greedy hands. The coloured paper rustles between his fingers, it falls onto the floor, revealing a round brass compass, with the red arrow pointing to the north. "My gift comes from afar. Far in the sense of time, I mean. This was uncle Monteverrrdi's. Nobody has ever used it, after him, and it's unfortunate. He always had it with him, during his journeys, to find his way home; Now you have a real home, your own home. Well: it's yours, Giovanni."

"Thank you. Thank you. I have never seen anything so beautiful," Giovanni says, admiring the compass, rubbing the golden box as if it were a magic lamp. He turns it over and wipes it with the cuff of his shirt until it's shiny. Bianca lowers her eyes, lifts her chin in defence. She manages to seem severe even if (or precisely because) she's shy; her raised chin is a sign of both her weakness and her strength. Giovanni realises her embarrassment, puts away the compass, gives her his gift. He gives her small package for her. He's chosen carefully: it's a white gold necklace, with a pendant depicting the symbol of infinity: ∞. He doesn't know whether Bianca knows what it is.

"You see, this symbol that looks a bit like an eight on its side; can you see it? Well: these two circles represent two universes which follow one another without ever ending. An English mathematician named Giovanni Wallis invented it, in 1655. You're my world, my universe."

They clink glasses. Giovanni drinks, his eyes fixed on Bianca who is trying to connect the hook and the eye of the clasp. Her arms are raised behind her head, her dress has short sleeves. Giovanni sees her armpits that haven't been shaved for a few days, with the black hair that is growing back. He swallows, whilst his erection unfolds like a flower in his crotch.

***

"Giovanni!" Bianca calls. She opens a window and a gust of cold air rushes in. "It snowed last night, look: it's all white."

"Close up, quick! You'll catch a cold."

"Yes, yes: it's all covered in white. It looks like all's been erased. As if the world was new; we have to get downstairs, leave our footprints in the snow."

"We could build a snowman, when I get back. And you can make hot chocolate."

"Yes. Later. Now, come here."

"I have to go, it's late."

"Just a moment. Come here."

"Where?

"Here."

Later, Giovanni goes upstairs to comb his hair and get his bag. Bianca is waiting for him downstairs, sipping her coffee. She accompanies him to the door.

"Don't get cold, darling," Giovanni says. Bianca doesn't wear shoes or socks. Never, when she's at home.

"It's a matter of being cautious, you know. Prudent. One's ends should always be warm. As the old saying goes: if your feet are warm, your heart is warm," he says, hoping not to blush. The word "foot" somehow embarrasses him – it makes him think of the exquisitely sexy Madame de Récamier as painted by Jacques-Louis David and Francois Gerard in the early 1800s – virginal and erotic at the same time.

"I can't stand having warm feet. And I have a warm heart. Boiling. It's so, so hot."

Giovanni pulls a strand of hair away from her face; his fingers linger on her neck, he traces the outline of her lips. But where have I found a girl like this, he wonders. A girl that looks at me and it's as if she is seeing baby Jesus on Christmas day, with the same enthusiasm, with the same sense of amazement, the same blindness. He looks into her white eyes, in the white light of the morning, on the doorstep; yes, his heart is warm, too. He wants to tell her but is ashamed, so he puts on his your hat and opens the door and turns to kiss her, like every morning; and when he's just about to leave, and knows that she can't look at him in the face and see his discomfort, he says:

"Keep it warm until tonight, that heart of yours. For me."

***

Giorgio Lupini, one of Giovanni's partners, is arrested for a corporate criminal offence in a case related to tax evasion. Giovanni hadn't noticed a thing. For six years the man, through a whirlwind of false invoices issued in the name of a company he held, had helped his clients to avoid paying taxes, moving their money into their Swiss accounts. The mechanism he used – through inactive companies, constituted on purpose – helped pass the money from Italy to the Confederation without anyone knowing anything: the accountant was the only one to manage the records, with a commission that ranged between 20 and 30 percent.

Neither Giovanni nor the other partners knew what he was doing; one day the *Guardia di Finanza* appeared in the office, acting as if they were FBI agents, paralysing all activity, forcing the staff to open all documents, to review closed files.

The damage is severe – some of his oldest, most loyal customers immediately leave the firm. With a managerial countenance he never knew he had, Giovanni and Stefano Ferraro decide the best course of action is a clean break with their past which has been fatally compromised: they dismiss the other two partners, change the name of the firm, take on two new trainees and three secretaries, start again from scratch. For a few months Giovanni works like a dog, leaving early and coming home late, sifting through various documents into the night, even on weekends, but soon things settle down again. The office merges with another, to become one of the most important in the whole Monferrato area. This means an increase in his shares, more responsibility but also, in a sense, less work. He learns to delegate more, to manage better; he takes on two more employees. He likes it, because he likes to give orders, to be in control.

Bianca continues to attend her teaching course. Her (vague) ambition is to open, one day, her own nursery in Castel San Gerolamo; she would like to become a small entrepreneur, employ other girls, be around kids all day. She likes the word: educator.

January becomes February, February becomes March. They go and watch two films at the cinema, they go three times to eat out, they host a couple of dinners with friends - Carlotta, who comes over for a weekend, and Riccardo, who has separated. At Easter, which is unusually late, in mid-April, Giovanni surprises Bianca with a trip to Paris; they visit the Louvre and the Pompidou centre, Notre Dame and the Musee d'Orsay, Montmartre and the Eiffel Tower. They walk along the Champs-Élysées holding hands. The penultimate evening, back at the hotel late after the de rigueur dinner on a boat on the Seine, they find a note from Luisa, asking them to call her back as soon as possible. Umberto had a heart attack. Despite treatment, despite the speed of the ambulance that has transported him to the hospital in Casale Monferrato, where there is a new Cardiology department, Umberto's weary old heart didn't make it.

They return home with the first flight, the following morning. It's so sad to see the shop locked up. It's sad to see Luisa with a black dress that drains all colour from her cheeks, a hard stare in her eyes. There are many practical matters to attend to - the announcement in the local paper, and then the priest, the church, the funeral, the cemetery. Within a few weeks, everything returns to normal. If it wasn't for the fact that a decision about the fate of the shop needs to be taken, nobody would even mention Umberto's name any more: you could call it survival spirit, self-preservation, or the mere passage of time, that makes us so used to the continuous cycle of life and death. People come, people go: that's life.

Luigi has another mini-stroke, from which he recovers quickly; Marieke stumbles on a step and breaks an arm. Finally, like icing on the cake, Luisa announces her decision to sell everything and move to Turin with Gabriella, to attend a high fashion institute and become a professional dressmaker. For her, her father's death is a liberation: she can finally do what she wants, be who she really is, live with the woman she loves, publicly. Everyone is stunned; pleased and happy for her, of course, but who could have ever expected this, Miss Rottenmeier? The one who is worst off is Bianca; she feels as if she were losing the last person in her family. She needs to be comforted. She needs her husband to be the life preserver he's shown he can be. And you know what: he actually *is*: present tense, most present. Giovanni, solid like concrete, is always at her side to support her, to offer help (crucially, *before* being asked) to organise this and call that, to procure tickets, flowers, handkerchiefs; to prepare dinner; to give her a massage on her tense shoulders; to fill the bath tub with scented salts. Rather than snogging her, he gives her a cuddle; and every day, he buys little things for her: a book, a magazine, a CD, a cream, a candle, a soap, a notebook - nothing of value, but each object says: I think of you. I am here. Count on me.

One day in late spring, Bianca calls him at the office to tell him to come back soon, she has a surprise. Giovanni drives up to the house, all excited; he slows down; the car slips noiselessly into the courtyard. Bianca is on the threshold - silhouetted against the light, he can sense her more than really see her. He can distinguish her outline, not the details. He hears laughter and exhales a sigh of relief. It's a good evening. She raises her arm to show him something, but Giovanni still does not understand, is too busy to get out of the car; with his right hand he pulls his jacket and bag from the back seat, with his left hand he holds two bags; the car keys are dangling from his mouth. He closes the door with a kick. He approaches, curious, cautious. And now he is in front of her, he can see her shake something with her hand, a long and hairy thing; he looks at her: yes, he can see her now. And he hugs her, his Bianca, short-haired as a boy, and god she looks ugly but he's never going to tell her, he kisses his wife who raises her hair in triumph - the ponytail of the long hair she's had amputated; here it is, yes, the scalp has the value of a limb. To cut one's hair is a powerful symbol of change, rebirth – what matters if this new hairstyle makes her face look too big compared with her slender neck, what matters if her white eyes appear huge, if this short hair feels thick and frizzy like fur?

"I love you," he whispers.

***

At the end of June Bianca finishes her teaching course and becomes an educator for children. The nursery where she did the internship offers to hire her from the following autumn, and she eagerly accepts. It is her first real job, underpaid but still paid; having some financial independence makes her feel really adult for the first time; more than being married, which seems to be playing a game, to be playing family.

It's been a busy year; Giovanni had to work harder, and in a different way. Some clients pay late or not at all, his job seems to become harder and harder - tax obligations and deadlines that the state imposes on taxpayers continue to rise. The law is constantly changing and requires updating. He is buried under a hill of paper. They need a vacation. They decide to take a road trip - to start off with a goal in mind (England, Scotland) and get there slowly, trying to enjoy the motion itself, the "motion towards." Giovanni buys a new car, a Mercedes.

"Like an old, rich accountant," Bianca says.

"No: like a family man," Giovanni replies.

At night, for weeks, they plan their trip. They both like to bend down over the map and decide what road to take; where to stop where to sleep. Shall we go through Switzerland? Should we cross over to France, or stay in Germany? They do book some hotels but not all of them, leaving a few things to chance, so they can change their minds, should they decide to stay longer in one city and leaving out another altogether. The day of their departure, the trunk of the Mercedes almost doesn't close: they have clothes, sun creams, road maps, wine and water and instant coffee and powdered milk, blankets and pillows, a quantity of CDs and guide books.

They have a wonderful trip. Of course, things do not work quite as they had planned; it rains and rains and rains, a couple of the hotels they booked are shabby, dirty; Bianca gets a bad cold, Giovanni diarrhoea. But they are together, make decisions by mutual agreement, often are surprised to want to do the same thing: to stay a few days in Reims; get away quickly from Dover; stop in Oxford; start immediately from Sheffield. Away, away, farther and farther north. They are enchanted by the Scottish pubs, by the green meadows that look like velvet, by the roads that wind through the hills dotted with white sheep, with friendly people, almost Mediterranean in their warmth. They get drunk on reddish, warm beer, eat soggy fish and chips, unlikely pink candy covered with thick icing sugar; they dance, they sing their hearts out. They return home to the *Willow,* three weeks later, fatter but hungry for sun and pasta *al dente*; they have the weekend to arrange a few things before they restart their normal life. On Saturday, Bianca goes to Turin to visit her sister, leaving Giovanni to his papers; and when she returns, she finds him quiet and grumpy, perhaps offended that he's been all day alone, perhaps with the kind of depression one feels at the return from the holidays. She pours wine into a glass.

"Summer is ending, another year has gone," She hums, stirring a sauce. "Ready for the new year?" she asks.

"It's not as if it's January," Giovanni says.

"It feels as if it was. As if we were still in school - everything starts afresh, in September. And then we are together;

do not long for faraway places: we are here, together, you and I. Think of all the things we will do, this year. Stop with this melancholy."

Giovanni looks at his wife, who surprises him with her kindness, with her young wisdom; he takes her in his arms, strokes her short hair, kisses her gently behind the ears.

***

October marks their first wedding anniversary. It's called paper anniversary, the celebration of the first three hundred sixty-five days, and tradition wants something made out of that material.

Giovanni has booked the best table at the Corona Reale restaurant in Moncalvo. They have a glass of champagne before dinner, then tagliolini with egg yolk and white truffle, hazelnut cake. They hold hands. After the meal they exchange gifts: Giovanni has had a book printed, with all the most beautiful love poems he could find; it took him weeks to prepare, with Luigi's help: there are Sappho and Yeats, Keats, and Emily Dickinson, Saba and Neruda, Quasimodo and Cavafy.

"I'll keep it on my bedside table, I'll read one poem every night," Bianca says. She gives him a leather diary, engraved with his initials.

"Thanks, honey. Perfect. I'll start it on the 1st of January."

"So you can write down all your deepest thoughts."

Giovanni smells it – it has a fresh leather scent - turns it in his hands, finds a little key.

"Look, you can also lock it up."

"Yes, indeed. It really is a secret journal."

"And you promise you'll never read it?"

"I'm not Bluebeard's wife! I don't want to know your most secret secrets."

"Only after I die, OK?"

"It's a deal," she says, shaking his hand.

***

I remember thinking, with Carmela: we like the same things. No, not exactly: we enjoy the same *small* things: our short trips by coach, sitting right at the front to enjoy the panorama; our usual drink at the local bar, ordering the same wine, every night; our afternoons spent lying on the sofa, reading the Sunday newspapers, listening to music; our excitement when those parcels arrived from Sicily, our ecstatic joy when we'd find our favourite treats; the pleasure in inviting our friends for dinner, going to the theatre, reading the same book in bed at night, side by side. How happy we were with our *small* life, our *little* routine, while outside the big uncaring world kept turning over and over. What holds together Bianca and me are not the *little* things, the stuff one does every day, that one doesn't even notice any longer. It's the *big* ones, the important, fundamental ones: we are a family, the two of us, we are together for better or for worse, for richer, for poorer, in sickness and all that. We are not interested in aperitifs, in society gossip, the mundane. We don't just chat; we talk. We talk about life and death, of legacy, of the meaning of life, what we'll leave behind when we'll be no more. The things that truly matter. Fuck art. Fuck the opera, theatre, literature, fuck everything: except us.

***

The grape harvest is in mid-October. Luisa comes to help; she seems like another person, since her father's death, more fluid, lighter – all traces of Miss Rottenmeier have disappeared. Could it have been Umberto who forced her to be a village spinster? Giovanni wonders. Not really, Luisa tries to explain that evening, sitting with her sister on the sofa by the fireplace. Umberto had turned into a tyrant after the death of his wife - maybe it was his only way to bring up two daughters alone. He was old-fashioned, stern, grumpy, vaguely depressed. He imposed lifestyles better suited to the nineteenth century that to the present day. He was fiercely opposed to modern clothing or hairstyles, to make-up of any kind, to nights out with friends. Luisa had always expressed talent in cutting and sewing, and interest in the course she is now attending; Umberto had always denied his approval. He wanted Luisa to become a teacher, or a nun.

"Maybe he drove me to be gay!"

"But don't you think one is born gay?"

"Well. He certainly wanted me to be different from what I was and am."

"I know. It's the same, in a way, with my mother. She would have liked me to be President of the Republic. An MP, an architectural genius, an explorer, I don't know, something amazing: certainly not a provincial lawyer. No, I don't fit the dreams she had for me."

"Well, on the one hand it is inevitable that a parent places in their child a series of expectations, of ideals - in general, what they themselves did not become. But sometimes the situation gets out of hand."

"Look at your mother, Giovanni," Bianca intervenes. "A classic case of manipulative mother, who forced you to meet her emotional needs, so that she'd get some compensation for her misery."

"You're probably right."

"Do you know what they're called, the children of manipulative parents?" Bianca asks; she likes to show off knowledge of the psychology lessons she's attended recently.

"No," Giovanni says, amazed at how much the sisters must have talked about him. He is vaguely flattered.

"Emotional puppets; innocent victims of emotional blackmail."

"But I am not a victim."

"That's just because you found me, darling" Bianca says. "Thank your guardian angel. Because whoever gets manipulated in this way, sooner or later becomes really angry, rebels, decides that the responsibility they gave him is unacceptable, and cuts all ties with his family".

"Luckily I found you," Giovanni says. "You saved me."

***

November goes by. Then December. It's the first Christmas without Umberto, without Luisa.

"It doesn't matter," Bianca tells Giovanni. "You're here with me. That's what is important."

But she's distracted. Maybe it's because she is tired, maybe it's because of the work load. Maybe it's the winter blues, or the fact that she still misses her sister. Giovanni buys again a natural Christmas tree, even bigger than the one they had the previous year, and new, glittering decorations. Bianca declines the invitation to go to Milan or Turin to purchase gifts; she's worn out, she keeps saying. Dog-tired. Depleted.

"I can't wait to have a few days off."

The work in a nursery includes activities for children ranging from three months to three years (nappy changes, meals, assistance of any kind). By law, there should be an educator every five children. But who is expected to respect this rule? Who controls? Bianca finds she is looking after seven, eight toddlers at any one time. They are adorable, of course, but exhausting. And then, all the books on psychology and pedagogy that she's had to read, the thesis that she's had to write: and for what? All that just for changing nappies, cleaning shit? Other teachers exploit her willingness, her young strength, her enthusiasm. For them, it seems, it's a bit like working in a parking lot. The child-machine is parked, washed, pumped up with food-oil, and when it's done, it stands until the legitimate owner returns to get it.

"When I have my own nursery," Bianca sighs, "You'll see. It will be completely different," she dreams.

Giovanni is busy too, trying to cover the holes opened by his fraudulent colleague. He remains in the office until late. On Christmas Eve, they are but a shadow of what they were in late August: they have lost weight, they are utterly worn out. Luckily they will be guests at Marieke and Luigi's, from Christmas Eve to Boxing Day.

"And then I want to sleep until the 6th of January."

It is a more modest dinner that the one they had the year before; the gifts they exchange, too, are more practical, less extravagant - an Angora blanket; slippers; a tablecloth. Bianca bought for him a document holder. Giovanni gives her a parcel wrapped in silver paper; he regrets having bought something obvious, such a banal present: a dress. It is too late to change it.

Bianca opens the package, unfolds the dress, blushes.

"It's a lovely shade of blue," she says. She gets up and walks over to Giovanni, blushes a little more. "It's such a shame that this year, however, I won't be able to wear it," she says.

Giovanni asks a question with his eyes.

"It'll be tight on me in the next couple of months."

"To a baby boy!" Marieke says, raising her glass for a toast. The living room is overwhelmed by a chorus of "Oh."

"Call Violetta, too; tell her to bring the other glasses, and one for herself, Luigi says. "*Edamus, Bibamus, Gaudeamus!* I'll be a grandfather!"

Marieke's eyes moisten. Glasses clink. Giovanni drinks, his eyes fixed on Bianca. He is looking forward to when his parents will leave, when he'll be able to take his wife into his arms. His heart clings in his throat. Sometimes he can't breathe, so great is his joy.

PART IV

1st January

It's the gift Bianca bought for me for our paper wedding anniversary; I put it away because I wanted to begin it on the very first day of the new year. I've never kept a journal, not even as an adolescent. Frankly, it seems rather self-indulgent, childish. A downright regression: will pimples start to flourish on my cheeks, next? And anyway, how does one start? With: "Dear Diary?" Dear Diary,

It's your first page, white, untouched, virgin - like Bianca when I married her. Like the snow that has settled on the countryside last night: what perfection, to wake up on January 1st with a clean slate. As if a miracle had happened, something from a science fiction movie, a bit like a 'purple cloud' new year. We are a new human race, which has to start from scratch. Reinvent ourselves. And you know the funny thing? A little of it is true, it's not science fiction. I am to become a father. Bianca will have our baby. There can't be a more perfect beginning.

Of course it feels strange. What the hell, you're my diary, my conscience: I can make a full confession: I am scared shitless. The responsibility is terrifying. The fear of making a mistake, because mind you, *everyone* makes mistakes, with their children, *everyone*, even those with the best intentions, perhaps *precisely* because their intentions are so good. You give them too much, too little, you are too severe, too little, you hold him too much, you give him the wrong stuff to eat, you should have put him to bed at a different time, enrolled him at another school. It's an obstacle course. You should have insisted for him to take Mandarin rather than German. Piano lessons, not guitar. You didn't read Shakespeare to him, you didn't take him to Kung Fu lessons, well then: what else did you expect from him? Or: from her? Because they might become drug addicts, or whores.

Every so often I forget that Bianca is pregnant. She strokes her belly, which is still flat. She opens up the last button of her trousers because she says she feels swollen even if I assure her she isn't. Could we be paranoid as a result of a test which might even be wrong? No, it can't be a mistake: under my instructions, Bianca repeated the test three times, to be absolutely sure; the line has showed up a positive symbol every time. Pregnant, she is pregnant. Yet I occasionally forget, then I feel guilty because I'm not thinking of this tiny creature, this embryo floating oblivious in her womb. At night, I never fail to remember. The creature has taken away my sleep. I worry about everything. I worry about my wife, who is exhausted and sleeps all the time; I worry about work, yes, I will have to work harder, to earn more money, but at the same time I want to spend less time in the office, I want to stay home with them, with my wife and my child - Christ, my child. And I think of all we have to do in these nine months: prepare the nursery, buy the crib, the pushchair, a little swinging chair, baby bottles, baby food. I don't even know what a child needs.

"A child only needs looove, please don't worry," Marieke says, rrrolling away. "This baby will have a roof over his head, two parents; and two grandparents who will love him to distraction: he'll lack nothing. Stop worrying." Yeah, right.

Happy New Year, dear diary. I go to bed worrying, worried sick. Bianca is already asleep.

***

The snow fall is spectacular - schools and offices close down, the TV talks about a natural disaster. At Castel San Gerolamo traffic does not circulate; roads have been blocked since the day before yesterday. Everything is white, fresh, muffled.

At the *Willow*, Bianca is in the kitchen, facing the window, bent over the sink – she's washing her hands – she's wearing a knitted jumper, baby-blue like the very light blue of her eyes. She wipes her hands on her jeans, whose top button is left open, takes out all the ingredients from the refrigerator and the pantry and places them on the table, along with a couple of bowls, two spoons, a little pot, the mould. She follows a recipe that she's copied down on a notebook. The butter has softened on the stove - a yellow butter that smells of hay that Violetta buys from some relatives in Piazzano; she melts it over a low heat, with chocolate and milk, stirring slowly. She chops the hazelnuts; adds sugar. She whisks the egg whites with the sugar until they are light and foamy, adds the melted chocolate and stirs. She measures the flour and the baking powder, mixes and blends with great concentration. When satisfied with the creaminess of the mixture, she pours it into the greased and floured mould and bakes it in the oven. The cake is ready after forty minutes. She sprinkles powdered sugar over the top; she garnishes it with hazelnuts.

The oven has been on for a while, and in the living room the fire is on. It feels hot. Bianca takes off her jersey, and remains in short sleeves, she washes her face with cold water so that her skin cools down.

"It's stopped snowing." Giovanni shouts from the living room. "It's raining!"

Bianca raises her eyes - her face still dripping with water - towards the window. The sky is grey, but not as grey as lead as it was until a few minutes ago. It is now a light, airy grey; the first drops of water seem wet snow flakes, but slowly they become real, heavy drops. They do not need to talk, Giovanni and Bianca. If you sneaked into their home now, it would seem as if you were joining the set of a feel-good advertising, false as Judas: the usual dance of a happy family that gorges on biscuits in a delirium of happiness. But it's true: sitting on the floor, listening to the music of the rain against the windows, they eat the cake, and now and then they get up to observe the thawing which is repainting the countryside green, clearing away all that whiteness. They have nothing to say; they don't say anything.

***

After the long break due to Christmas and then the snow, Bianca continues to work at the nursery, but gets tired very easily and is told off a few times by the headmistress, who is not aware that she is pregnant. Bianca is sitting down in a corner, stupefied with afternoon lethargy, instead of playing actively with children who have been allocated to her; they start drawing with crayons and, unsupervised, end up writing on the walls. Bianca is not even aware of it, and gets reprimanded. Another time, the children who are having an afternoon nap are sleeping on mattresses on the floor. Bianca sneaks into the room and falls asleep next to them – she is awoken by an angry colleague and receives a second warning. The third time, it's the end of the day. Bianca is standing by the door, so absorbed in her thoughts that she does not notice that a small group of parents is trying to get her attention and have the gate opened. They are all tired, hot, eager to leave with their children before they run on, and start shouting at her. This time the headmistress calls Bianca into her office.

Bianca - emotional, prey to sudden mood swings - starts crying uncontrollably. She calls Giovanni, who rushes into Trino. He opens the office door, sees his pale Bianca, her eyes red and swollen, asks for an explanation, raises his voice. Protector, guardian, paladin, he unsheathes his words like a sword; woe betide anyone who mistreats his wife. Headmistress and Giovanni discuss the situation – her pregnancy – as if Bianca weren't present; they come up with a solution – to reduce the hours to a manageable part-time for the coming months and review the schedule in the spring.

They leave hand in hand, Bianca and Giovanni; they don't seem like a couple but father and daughter. Bianca looks at him as if he were a hero, her hero. No one had ever taken her side, before; no one had rushed to her aid; no one had made her feel the way she feels right now: cared for, protected. Don't forget that she's an orphan – she's never had a mother to look after her. Luisa had been, until now, the one who'd taken care of her, but in a different way: as a big sister, not as her champion. It is as if in her eyes Giovanni, suddenly, had become a Man. A husband, ready to be the father of her child.

***

After nine weeks of pregnancy, Bianca suffers a miscarriage.

***

February 5th

Dear Diary,

I'm sorry to begin February with a sorrowful note, but one has to write those, too; perhaps especially those. Bianca lost our baby, last Thursday. It was eight o'clock in the morning and I had just left when she started to bleed; she called me immediately. Fortunately, I wasn't too far away. I took her to the hospital where she had an ultrasound. The gynaecologist looked at us with an expression suited to the occasion and told us that the Bianca was suffering a miscarriage; this is how you describe the loss of the fetus that is not caused by external intervention before the 22nd week of gestation. He told us that the causes are unknown; that for the most part they are due to chromosomal abnormalities. Most often, this means that the egg or sperm was containing the wrong number of chromosomes, and the fertilised egg could not develop normally.

"It was a very sick baby," he said. He did not say it, not really, but he implied it: it's better this way; you've been almost lucky; it could have been worse. He smiled. "Bastard," I feel like hissing, because I am angry, I'd love to punch someone. I smiled, too. He advised us to go home, to return in a week to see if the entire foetal tissue present in the uterus gets expelled. Bianca is young and healthy, and will recover quickly, and there is no reason why the next pregnancy should have the same result. It happens. It happens to many women; in fact, new research reveals that a variable percentage from 10 to 25 percent of pregnancies end in miscarriage. Then he turned to me, told me to support her in the coming days and weeks. Of course.

A week has gone by. We returned for the check-up; the gynaecologist reassured us that everything is as it should be, that the miscarriage has been complete, all the pregnancy tissue has left the uterus. He lowered his voice – because of embarrassment, or shame, or respect – and whispered:

"You can try again for another baby as soon as you're ready," he said, smiling his priestly smile, and discharged us.

Physically Bianca's fine - but psychologically she has taken it very badly. She is twenty; one doesn't expect to suffer a miscarriage, at twenty. I've never seen her so upset. Not knowing how to react, what to say, how to comfort her, I asked my mother for advice. Tearfully, she told me that she had had two miscarriages, one before and one after I was born; and putting aside for a moment the fact that she has to be the prima donna, always, even when it isn't about her – still, this revelation troubled me; and I cried. I don't know what upset me the most: the thought of my mother as a girl, twenty years old, active, desirable; of her precious youth, of her beauty that I have never even glimpsed, yet I know that it has been there, at some point; the loss of brothers or sisters; the pain it must have caused. I would have liked not to be an only child: it would have removed a bit of attention from me, it would have balanced our relationship. When one gets to know such a thing, it seems one is meeting parallel lives - what would have happened *if*.

And what if my, if our baby, had he lived? Does it even make sense to speak of it as of a real baby, or was it just an *idea* of child, a thought, a dream, a meatball made of bones and blood, but without a soul? Am I really that sad, to have lost a meatball? Bianca haunts the house aimlessly, she goes upstairs and then comes down, enters the kitchen, the bathroom, the bedroom, with steps so light I almost can't hear her; she startles me. She looks at me and I smile, but don't know what to say. We always discussed what was happening to us. There were so many first times: the first dinner and the first lunch and the first walk, and the first time we made love, the first laugh and the first cry, the first argument; the death of Umberto, the departure of her sister. How many significant events, and all in just over a year. She told me that I can't understand: that this is something that is just hers, because the body is hers, not mine. I am not part of it.

I say this to you only, dear diary: it bothers me, not to be part of it. I feel excluded.

I tried to work harder, this week - more, and better. I did it to return home later, to leave Bianca to face the grief for her loss alone, and to have some time to myself to readjust, to take back control of my life. Last night after dinner, in bed, I took her in my arms. My intention was to make love, tenderly, affectionately, but when my skin made contact with hers we both burst into tears.

It takes time. It takes time. We have time.

***

February 20th

I want her so badly; she excludes me. I can't enter her body, I can't enter her head. I remain an outsider, outdoors, with my face pressed against the window, like Andersen's *Little Match Girl*. Bianca, I tell her, I implore her, I shake her: I am here, right in front of you. Can you see me? Can you see that I wanted this baby, too? Can you see that I want you? I want to go back.

"Give her time," my mother said, starting to repeat wisdom sayings:

"Time heals all wounds."

"Yesterday is gone: tomorrow has not yet come."

"We have only today."

"Sadness flies away on the wings of time."

"In the garden of time flowers consolation."

"Time is a sort of river of passing events, and strong is its current."

"Time flies over us, but leaves its shadow behind."

"As we speak cruel time is fleeing. Seize the day, believing as little as possible in the morrow."

"Give her time," Marieke tells me over and over. And I can only say: "Of course."

"Give her time, time, and time," my mother continues, her voice sounding like a litany.

***

February 27th

Dear Diary,

How angry I am when I have to admit it: mamma, you were right. Bloody hell, mamma, you *were* right.

"As always," she would tell me if I told her; fortunately, she doesn't know.

A week has gone by and everything is different. Bianca is back. She's returned. And I laugh at my melodramatic tone, before and now: I spoke of how I felt excluded, as if she were a members-only club; and now I am speaking of her "return" as if she were resurrected, Jesus-style, at Easter. But she's always been here, my Bianca: precious, sweet, tender, immature, young, tired Bianca. Serene, positive, optimistic.

She decided (with a nudge from me) to resign from the nursery. She needs to bounce back, to take care of herself and me and us. And then she wants to try to get pregnant again. The headmistress accepted her resignation, with immediate effect. She's come home unemployed; magnificent, strong, formidable Bianca.

When I walked in, she was sitting on the sofa and offered me a brave little smile that made my heart melt. We lay on the floor, next to each other, looking at each other, smiling. I stroked her face, cheeks and forehead, her chin and her nose and her mouth and her eyes, those eyes that can't lie, those eyes purer than water, and I saw everything inside them: the pain and the pleasure, the past and the future, death and life. I told you, didn't I?, that the things that unite us are not small, but big. Now we have one more: a private and personal grief. Ours. No one else's. One more thing that unites us, that brings us together.

***

March 12th

Dear Diary,

Yesterday I celebrated my birthday: I turned thirty-five.

Bianca woke up first – I saw her, lying still half-asleep: a naked body moving sensuously, like a cat, with soft steps; she's like a cat in the evening, too – when she is tired, she curls up into her chair or crouches down next to me to let me scratch her head and throat. She sneaked downstairs to prepare breakfast, and she brought it up to me to bed on a silver platter; coffee, orange juice and a slice of apple pie she had made yesterday (she even put it in the oven to warm it up). And a pink flower in a glass of water. In one corner of the tray, a package wrapped in blue paper; I opened it straight away: a pair of gold cufflinks in the shape of elephants. I had never seen anything like them; she told me that she found them in a shop in Turin; they come from India. They are beautiful, and strange, and I really like them (I'm sure my mother will detest them). I put them on right away, with the best white shirt I own.

We went out in the evening - Bianca had booked a table at a new place near Serravalle – far away, yes, but new, different. You have to celebrate, right? Bianca wore the dress I gave her at Christmas. She had her hair pulled up with a shiny satin ribbon that fell over her shoulder; she was wearing high-heeled shoes, which made walking difficult, but also gave her a soft, wavy kind of pace. It was as if I didn't know her. What I don't know turns me on. She knows me, she knew that.

It took almost an hour to get there, stopping at one point to kiss - one of those kisses full of saliva that made me feel sixteen again. I would have taken her there and then, at the side of the road – but I restrained. Delayed gratification, delayed enjoyment, is even better. We got hold of ourselves; I opened the door for her; we entered the room - everybody looked at us. No: they all looked at my wife. We chose the tasting menu, including a magnificent seared tuna glazed with balsamic vinegar, panzanella with prawns, and then a plate of scialatielli which reminded me of Carmela - but just for a millisecond, I swear.

I looked at the menu.

"Don't order dessert. I baked a cake for you!" Bianca whispered in my ear. We returned home later than I thought: "we have to celebrate, right?" is what we kept repeating throughout the evening. There was a scent of spring in the air, sweet with grass and leaves. Violetta, the cleaning lady sent over by my mother on a regular basis, had made a fire earlier, and now it was almost dead, but not quite – I just needed to revive its embers. I was tired; I started to yawn. But Bianca had prepared the cake, with candles. She told me to make a wish, and while I blew the candles off, and the room got darker, she started to strip off slowly, in front of the fire. She lay on the floor. I took off my clothes too, lying next to her. She pushed my head down between her legs. When I heard her scream I reached up for air. I kissed her, and she straddled me, with a kind of bold freedom she had never displayed before. We went to bed, fell asleep at once, and when I woke up in the middle of the night, we were still embraced. I had her once more, half-asleep - you have to celebrate, right?

I am thirty-five years old: I'm a man. I thought that at this stage life would become monotonous, repetitive. I never thought that you could be so absolutely satisfied. When I was a child, the mere sight of my great-great-great uncle's notebook, in which pages and pages were covered with drawings of exotic trees, tropical flowers, maps with details mountains and rivers and lakes, moved me to tears. I've never wanted, as my mother would have liked, to have an amazing career. The dream of my childhood was to find, somewhere, someday, the homeland of my soul. I recall a recurring dream I used to have before I met my wife; I was walking in the desert, among golden sand dunes. The air was dry and hot, the blinding sun was high the sky. I was tremendously thirsty, I was sweaty, and tired, my mouth was dry; I continued to walk in vain, increasingly desperate for a bit of water. I've never had that dream again, since I got married - and this morning, on second thought, I realised why: I have found water. Bianca is my water.

***

After a snowy winter, spring begins with a flood.

Bianca has braved the rain - that lasts for weeks - and has gone out. "Just doing a bit of gardening," she said to Luisa, who was here visiting for the weekend.

"Again? But it's raining!"

"It doesn't matter. It doesn't bother me."

"But you've been gardening all of yesterday."

"And I'll do it again tomorrow, and the day after. I don't have to go anywhere, now that I'm officially unemployed."

"Oh come on, stay here with me. I'll make us a coffee."

"No, I want to be outdoors. It does me good, even if it's cold, even if it rains. I like to get my hands in the soil - I never realised it was so alive, like a creature, a pet. It kind of breathes, moves, it's full of life, of worms and insects."

"That's disgusting."

"No, it isn't. It's life: a bit of flesh, a bit of blood, a bit of dirt that hides a heartbeat."

"I'd rather look after plants. Or flowers."

"Me too. And grass. Grass is such a humble thing; so ordinary that we don't even properly observe it."

"Well, there is nothing to see. Not much."

"You're wrong. it's beautiful, really. Sharp but delicate, fragile but tenacious. It has the best perfume in the world. The amazing thing is just how fast it grows. Like hair. It seems a form of rage: that constant unstoppable growth."

Bianca closes the door behind her, pulls on her gloves. In the past weeks she has found and fenced off a small plot in a sheltered corner of the garden. She's going to grow a vegetable patch with potatoes, and tomatoes, and celery, leek, cauliflower, zucchini, onions. She kneels down. She dips her hands into the wet soil, listening to the regular patter of the rain on her hat.

***

April 6th

Dear Diary,

It's Easter Sunday. We had lunch with my parents. There were my aunt and uncle as well, and my cousins (aged, fat). We ate roast lamb, potatoes with rosemary, gravy so good and thick I ate it all up with bread, a large salad of bitter chicory, and the Dutch cake my mother makes. After lunch we sat down for a game of cards; we had just started when Bianca got up abruptly, pale: indeed: grey, and ran outside to vomit. I thought she had eaten too much. My mother looked up from her cards and said:

"Ah-ha. I thought as much."

And I, ignorant, dumb, stupid idiot: "Thought so what?"

"A woman has eyes to see. I saw. I knew right away: from how she was breathing. And you two wimps, you didn't notice anything!"

I walked outside. My wife was crying. I tried to reassure her, to comfort her. I told her that I was happy. That this time everything would be fine. I am certain it will be: and we'll have a wonderful, intelligent, funny, lively child ... She stopped crying, she surrounded my waist with her arms and held me so tight my ribs hurt. I told her, to hold me a little less tight. She started to laugh (I never tire of hearing the sound of her laughter, a series of throat notes, clinging to each other like a bunch of grapes). She loosened her grip. "I just want him to be healthy. And maybe a little less delicate than his father," she said.

We went back inside. Dad opened a bottle of his favourite Grignolino. Mamma said that we should wait before celebrating because "you never know." Bianca didn't hear (she was outside, being sick again); I looked at her with the angriest face I could muster. We returned home walking slowly. She went immediately to bed as suggested by my mother.

"At least for the first two months," she prescribed, I don't know with what authority, but we listened to her as if she was a famous obstetrician. I moved into the guest room, where I'll sleep in the coming weeks, so as not to disturb her. I'm writing, now, in this room; it's dark, narrow, humid; Violetta has made up the (single) bed, put a glass of water on the bedside table. I asked for an extra blanket. It's after one o'clock. I can't sleep. I got up, I sneaked into the bedroom - our bedroom. Bianca was asleep, turned on her side, her lips slightly parted. I looked at her for a while, to see if she'd wake up and let me sleep with her in our bed. She kept sleeping. I didn't dare wake her, I returned to my little room. I did not sleep.

***

May 6th

My mother rang the bell last night and came in with a parcel. I was about to take it, but she gave it to Bianca. "You open it, but it's for both of you, really." Come on, come on, open it up, discard the paper, with the ardour of a birthday. It's a book: thick, hardback, colourful. Bianca exhales a hysterical kind of giggle, I rush to discover what it is, and am disappointed as a child receiving a tie for Christmas. The book is a guide to a "serene pregnancy, to accompany the expectant mother." It meticulously tells the extraordinary progress of the child in utero, week after week, from conception to birth; it gives advice from how to stay healthy to how to choose the right type of birth, how to relieve pain during labour, and then it discusses complications and medical emergencies. Of course there needs to be a chapter – or two – on medical emergencies. In short, this gift is the perfect way to agonise, to feel deficient - because we will be found lacking, for sure - to dream the undreamable, to bite off more than we can chew, and so on. But of course I read it, a bit on the sly. I read what happens during the tenth week: at this time, the embryo becomes a fetus, I read, and this both interests me and drives me mad.

So one feels less guilty if one has an abortion within ten weeks; or in the case of an embryo used for research purposes. What miserable pettiness comes out of science, sometimes; how pathetic that it needs to distance itself from ethical issues, changing – literally – the terms of the dispute.

I accompanied Bianca for the first visit to a gynaecologist, in Alessandria; Bianca had blood and urine tests, an ultrasound. This is one of the most memorable moments in a pregnancy, our book tells us; first of all, it confirms that the pregnancy does exist: the first ultrasound is also the first picture of our child. The first photograph.

How exciting to see what at first looks like a shapeless mass, to listen to his or her heartbeat, which seems absurdly loud and fast like the wings of a hummingbird, and to think - to realise, finally: that it *is* there. It's here, yes, it's here: my baby. Our baby.

Who, unaware, continues its unstoppable growth, showing more detail in each and every ultrasound. Frankly, I find these black and white photographs slightly embarrassing: they show a tiny, uncoordinated seahorse that clumsily wags its tail. As it was said when I was a child, obscenely: like a spastic. Of course I'm afraid of something happening, of course I'm scared it might be less than perfect. It's all that bloody book's fault. All these examinations offer nothing but anxiety; I would like to fall asleep and wake up after Christmas when our child is born, when we have a son or a daughter, and all's well that ends well. However, we need to wait for another six months.

"The second and third trimester!" Our bloody book chirps. "The most exciting months!"

***

At twenty weeks, Bianca returns to the hospital to perform a morphology ultrasound, whose fundamental objective is to verify the size of the fetus and its organs, which are analysed in a well-defined sequence. The evaluation of the fetal face includes an attempt to visualise the upper lip for possible cleft lip anomaly; then it looks in detail at the baby's bones, heart, brain, spinal cord, face, kidneys and abdomen. It also determines the amount of amniotic fluid and the placenta, and its localisation. Finally, the news that every parent looks forward to receiving:

"What is it, doctor?"

"A boy," the gynaecologist says. Giovanni squeezes Bianca's hand, hard, full of pride and emotion. A boy: what he'd secretly hoped for: a son. An heir. Blood of their blood, flesh of their flesh. It's real, alive, his.

***

The law of diminishing returns, formulated by the English economist David Ricardo assumes that if one input in the production of a commodity is increased while all other inputs are held fixed, a point will eventually be reached at which additions of the input yield progressively diminishing increases in output.

So: we imagine that it's Friday, the last working day of the week. We deserve a break - from work in the office, from home jobs, from everyday life. We decide to go for a pizza; yes, we think: we really feel like pizza, beer and ice cream: and from five in the afternoon we think about that pizza. We think about which one to choose from the extensive menu; perhaps with ham and mushrooms, or with olives, capers and anchovies, or with spicy salami. And the very idea of pizza - piping hot, juicy, with a charred crust, melted mozzarella that creates long threads of melted cheese - makes us want it even more. The afternoon is eternal, but in the end it's time to leave, to go home. We change: we take off that work attire - dress, jacket, tie; we comb our hair, we renew our make-up - all of this contributes to the sense of expectation, of waiting. We arrive at the pizzeria hungry, excited;

we enjoy the idea of the weekend, we think of the plans we have for the two days of freedom, which open wide before us like a horizon. We order a beer that arrives straight away. We drink a sip, and it is so good, fresh and crisp, bitter yet sweet, perfect to prepare the taste buds for what is coming. We order; we casually snack on a breadstick; we drink another sip of beer; we wait. When the dish finally arrives, we smile at the waiter, knife in hand, ready to cut into pizza; and what fragrance, what an extraordinary aroma! We take the first bite and it seems the best food we have ever tasted; the first slice: exquisite; the second slice: sublime; the third slice: mm-mm, good. We demolish the first quarter, then half; our hunger diminishes, then it ends; after three quarters, we are satiated; we find it hard to swallow the last slice. We can say that not only we didn't really enjoy those last three slices, but that actually they have caused some discomfort – a swollen belly, tight pants, a burp discreetly hidden in the fist of one's hand. If we also ordered an ice cream, the same thing happens, but even more quickly: the first spoonful is delicious - it washes away the taste of anchovies, salami, capers - the second and the third also, and then – well, you know what? We simply have had too much, we feel sick. We are so full of food that whatever we put in our mouth has a negative impact on our metabolism.

I know it will seem blasphemous, but I want to apply the law according to which each additional unit of a specific factor, without prejudice to all other factors, produces progressively fewer returns – yes, I'm going to apply it to Bianca's pregnancy. A test;

another test; blood and urine tests; the first and the second ultrasound; and then one every two months. In short, this child is monitored and visited constantly. And if the first tests, the first ultrasound - especially that of the fateful twenty weeks - are thrilling, exciting, impressive, tearful, touching; well: after four or six or eight times, Giovanni's eyes stop welling up; in fact, they dry up like prunes. Of course one wants to be reassured that everything is proceeding as it should; but the sheer thrill of the first time has gone. There is impatience with the inevitable delays taking place at the hospital, the slowness of the midwives, for that obscene rummaging, rummaging with latex gloves inside his wife's vagina during gynaecological examinations.

The forty weeks of a pregnancy are too long - it is unthinkable to sustain a feverish excitement for such a prolonged period of time. Goethe wrote that anyone would stop looking at a rainbow if it lasted fifteen minutes. There are days when Giovanni doesn't think at all, about the baby. Obviously, for Bianca it's different: how can she possibly forget it, she, who has it inside her, and feels it moving, turning, kicking? She can see her belly grow and become a round ball that makes movements slow, tricky. But for Giovanni, out of sight is out of mind.

***

Summer of 2003 represents a true planetary climatic anomaly because of the longer and more intense heat wave (lasting over four months) affecting almost all the European nations. In Italy the temperatures remain above the average of the period with values close to 40°C in many cities. Castel San Gerolamo is no exception, in fact: it feels as if one is breathing soup, so warm is the air, so dense and heavy. The sky is pearl grey, beads of sweat form on one's face, back, neck, between the legs, on the nape. Shutters are closed during the day, open wide at night, trying to catch a breath of wind, as elusive as Fidel Castro with the CIA: you never capture it.

People talk of nothing else - among friends, neighbours, on television, on the radio: the heat, the mugginess, the humidity, the swelter, the closeness. Forty degrees, forty-one, thirty-eight. Sales of air conditioning units and fans exceed all expectations – all stores have run out. Ah, if only we had a good old fashioned storm to freshen up this stale air! Oh, I can't wait for rain! Between the stifling heat, work, and pregnancy, to go for a long journey might be imprudent; Giovanni and Bianca decide, nonetheless, to flee to the mountains for a couple of weeks, to enjoy a cooler climate. They choose Cervinia. Actually, it is Marieke who chooses on their behalf.

"Cervinia: Of course. It is in the mountains, yes, but it's also glamorous," she says. "And of course you have to stay at the Hermitage, the only five-star hotel," she says.

But how on earth does she know these things, Giovanni wonders. Marieke is not an educated woman, and yet she's somehow always well informed; she reads gossipy magazines, watches television, stores away curious and occasionally useful information. She manages to convince them; they make a reservation, and at the end of July, they escape from the scorching heat of the Monferrato. As soon as the car begins to ascend, they feel better. They get to Cervinia in the evening. The sky is blue; stars shine, as do the tall mountains: it looks like a postcard. Built nearly forty years before the Neyorz family, the Hermitage is an elegant, wooden, intimate chalet, at 2000 meters above sea level, right at the foot of the Matterhorn. The rooms are comfortable and well furnished, with lots of wood but never with that sensation of being in a Swedish sauna. From here several direct paths lead to various shelters. I'll show you a picture of the holiday: here it is: this photograph shows Giovanni and Bianca, in shorts and hiking boots with red laces, during one of their daily excursions. Bianca, whose belly is clearly visible under the tight, taut shirt that looks like a sail, held by the leather straps of her backpack; Giovanni is next to her; his curls fly in the air as blue as the sea; he's holding up a pathetic half-litre of wine. Not exactly what we'd call a triumph, a mini-bottle; more the *idea* of pleasure.

They return to the hotel in the afternoon, take a nap; they try a different restaurant every night; they go to bed early. They walk holding hands. Bianca rests her head on Giovanni's shoulder. They kiss. They make love. Giovanni feels liberated - they stopped talking about the baby two hundred times a day: what will we call him, will he have your hair and my eyes, what will he do when he grows up; which limb might he be growing, right now. Here they haven't brought the horrible book, which talks about "sweet season," as if instead of a child a woman had a chocolate cake in her belly. It offers advice on what to eat, what to wear, how to live. And then there are gigantic blow-ups of hands and feet and "little'uns" galore, and illustrations and graphics, and scans of the fetus and microbiology pictures.

"Jesus: what a nightmare."

"I really don't understand why you hate that book," Bianca says.

"You see: a child is a miracle. I don't want to see it under a microscope; I don't want it dissected. I don't want to know *everything*."

"It's the twenty-first century. It's science. What do you want to do: go back? To the parcel carried by storks in their beaks?"

"You know me well enough, Bianca: don't accuse me of being something I'm not. You know, I remember a book I read as a teenager - a dreadful novel my father had given to me: *Belle du Seigneur,* by Cohen. Bullshit, of course, but with a nugget of truth. The two main characters fall in love and continue to love each other until there is a bit of secrecy or ambiguity between them. For example, when they start to live together, they have two bathrooms, so they do not see that the other person has bodily functions and needs, like everyone else."

"What? That they both wee and poo?" Bianca laughs.

"Exactly. A mystery."

"Do you want a mysterious child?"

"What can I say: sorry, but yes. I do."

"And when I'll go into labour, and you'll hear me moan and scream and watch me bleed, what will you do?"

"I don't know. I'll be with you. In good times and bad, in sickness and in health."

***

At the end of the holiday, Giovanni must return to Castel San Gerolamo, but he insists that Bianca remains in Cervinia.

"There is no reason to come back home. Not in this heat."

"But I want to be with you."

"You'll be with me forever."

They talk to the manager; they call Luisa and Carlotta - the two girls will take turns to join Bianca. Giovanni drives back home.

Even his parents are away on holiday in the Dolomites. Giovanni is all alone - it feels like a blast from the past. He has lots of work to catch up on; if he had still been in Turin, he thinks, he might go to the cinema, he'd probably eat at a nice restaurant, or have a drink in a new trendy bar. Here, there isn't much choice; Bianca is not with him; he'd rather and stay home with a DVD, a book to read. Porn on the computer, and a glass of chilled white wine.

Heat surrounds him, it encloses, it encircles him; only in the office, or at the supermarket, with air conditioning at full speed, he can breathe. Even the house on the hill, despite the thick walls and the closed shutters, feels hot. Giovanni takes off his shoes and socks, soaks his feet in a bowl full of cold water; he adds some ice cubes – they melt instantly. He feels intoxicated by the weight of the incandescent light, dizzy because of the low and heavy air, he's bothered by the incessant buzzing of the flies by day, and by that of mosquitoes at night. He can't sleep; he has a cold shower several times a day, doesn't use a towel to dry up, tips the fan right onto the bed, at night, leaving the windows wide open; he falls naked, over the sheets. He finally falls asleep late at night; he wakes up drenched in sweat.

He feels lonely. He misses Bianca more than he could imagine; he misses her body next to his, in bed, in the car, on the sofa. He misses her excited, boring, monotonous chatter; he misses her scent. He calls her often, but when he hears her cheerful voice – she's clearly enjoying her time with her sister and her best friend - he gets annoyed, can't find anything to say, hangs up quickly. Yes, we're having fun, she admits, feeling guilty. She hasn't laughed so much in years, away from the daily chores, from routine.

"And away from me," Giovanni whispers, and she doesn't hear him, or pretends not to hear.

When he goes to pick her up in Cervinia, two weeks later, and finds her fatter, tanned, relaxed, he makes her pay for it. He makes up a story – he drove to Turin to visit Riccardo; and they spent a silly night together.

"Ah, honestly: what a night."

"What did you do?"

"Things bachelors do. You don't want to know."

"À la Marilyn Monroe? Like in *The Seven-Year Itch?*"

"Exactly. We went out for dinner and then into some bar. Just forget it." He wants her insecure, suspicious, tormented. Bianca isn't a jealous type. She has no reason to be, she thinks. She trusts him. The place is messy; the bed needs to be done up; the fridge is empty. She slowly tidies up, empties the suitcase, loads the washing machine, prepares a salad with the produce of her vegetable garden, of which she's proud: fragrant tomatoes, lettuce, cucumbers, peppers as yellow as a beak. They sit down to dinner next to one another, vaguely inhibited. She puts a hand on his arm.

"I missed you," she whispers.

"Me too."

After dinner, they sit side by side on the sofa; Giovanni's fingers linger on Bianca's swollen belly – and he suddenly realises he hasn't asked her anything about her pregnancy.

***

"Did I want him? No. But now, well, now he's here, and I can't ask you to take him away. But really: you should have told me, Giovanni."

Silence.

"I'll have to look after him. I'll be the one that cleans after him, that feeds him, who takes him for a walk."

"I'll do it, too."

"But you work!"

"Well. Over the weekend." A pause. Whispering.

"Sorry."

"Oh."

"Sorry, Bianca. It's that. Well. I wanted to surprise you. And I thought that you might be a bit lonely, at home, now that you no longer go to work. I thought he would keep you company."

Silence.

"We should have talked about it. We should have discussed it. We should have made a decision to-ge-the-r. He's not a plant."

"Sorry," Giovanni repeats.

"Well. Listen. Bring him inside, now; he's ruining my flowers. There, he's digging a hole in the hydrangeas," she says, and Giovanni goes out immediately.

Pablo is a Labradoodle puppy, a cross between a Labrador and a Poodle – a valuable bastard, combining the gentle nature of the first with the intelligence of the second. Marco Salvini, one of his partners, offered him to Giovanni, and he (missing Argos), took the chance. It's a beautiful little dog, with long, curly, chocolate brown hair, he looks like a stuffed animal. And like all puppies he's curious, affectionate, enthusiastic; he runs and jumps and plays and nibbles and digs. Within half a day he ruins all the flowers that Bianca has grown.

"Luckily, it's October," Bianca sighs. "If we were in May, I would have strangled it. I would have strangled you."

"Let's give it a try. If you really don't want him, I'll take him back."

"A week. We'll talk about it in a week."

Bianca doesn't like dogs; she's never had, nor wanted one. Now that she doesn't work, she'd decided to devote herself to the running of their home, to the preparations for the baby's arrival. She makes herself busy; she enjoys her time alone. For Giovanni, on the other hand, a dog is a friend, a companion, a necessity: just like Argos had been all those years ago, to help him get out of the depression for Julie's loss; perhaps it was the only reason that made him return to Castel San Gerolamo from Turin every weekend, when he was at Uni. Pablo is not Argos. Not yet. To decide to adopt a dog now, three months before the delivery, is not a random choice: it is as if to say: you'll look after the baby; I'll take care of the puppy. And he is adorable: a goofy, soft, slow, destructive puppy. And of course, he ends up staying.

***

September goes by, October goes by, November goes by. Bianca gets bigger and bigger. She is quiet, passive - as if her growing belly ate away at her strength.

THE HEART OF THE OCTOPUS

She never wants to do anything: Giovanni proposes walks, outings to restaurants, to Turin, to go for a walk in the woods with Pablo: Bianca never feels like it. Giovanni stops asking. It is not that she's depressed; she's focussed entirely upon herself. The nine months of pregnancy involve gradual changes in the body and mind of a woman. This time needed for the baby's growth is also essential to the maturation of parenting skills that are the basis of the mother-child bond. The first description of a specific emotional investment towards a woman's fetus was studied by Donald Winnicott in the Fifties: he called it "primary maternal preoccupation" and it is the particular involvement that the mother develops during the last trimester of her pregnancy. Winnicott observed that primary maternal preoccupation develops gradually during pregnancy; it's as if the woman focussed her whole attention, thoughts and fantasies only on the fetus that is developing inside her, to the exclusion of everything else. Bianca is totally in tune with her body, its needs and requirements. She behaves like a new-age mum: she eats when she's hungry, only what she fancies; she sleeps when she is sleepy, in bed or on the couch or in the car; sometimes, she sleeps for hours. Sometimes Giovanni comes home in the evening, and Bianca is still in bed; Pablo has peed in a corner of the living room; the place is a mess; dinner is not ready, the fridge is empty.

"Sorry, darling. I was so tired," she says then. "This baby just needed to sleep," she says, stroking her belly. Giovanni smiles, tense, tired, annoyed.

"And what about me?" he's about to ask. But he doesn't. He cleans up Pablo's pee, he sets the table, he puts the kettle on to boil some water for quick pasta.

"It will pass," his mother told him the other day.

It will pass.

***

November 22nd

Dear Diary,

A diary is written to confess one's secrets.

I've just returned home after taking Pablo out. I'm tired. My wife is far more tired than me. She sits on an armchair in the dining room, with knitting needles and a ball of yarn – she's making a hat for the baby - or she reads, her fingers crossed on her belly, which continues to grow. She talks little, so little in fact that I am a bit embarrassed. We spend whole evenings in silence. I read the newspaper, Bianca knits. She embroiders bed linens, towels, blankets, preparing a kind of trousseau for the baby, as if she were a nineteenth century dame. She roams around like a ghost, like a maid who lifts every ornament that needs to be wiped; and I feel like another thing, an object that she pays brief attention to; her way of rubbing dust off *me* is to offer a few kind words; and then as quickly, she puts me back in my place, on a shelf. Job done. There are some nights when silence clings to the air, like a spider, hanging on invisible threads. A silence that breathes quietly like my wife when she sleeps, her tired face abandoned to sleep, totally vulnerable. Sometimes under her eyelids I can glimpse the flicker of her eyes moving in the middle of a dream. Her legs move with violent jerks under the sheets. Who knows what's going on in her dream.

She has changed so much, in recent months; there is a huge distance between us. Enclosed within the core of concentration that revolves around her belly, it's as if she's been emptied of muscles and nerves to become an inert mass of flesh without content: like a teddy, a stuffed animal. A creature immobile and absent: a goddess. It's a strange sensation, difficult to explain. Before pregnancy, I felt as if she'd become a kind of extension of my body; she seemed to have acquired the ability to mould herself on me, to anticipate and satisfy all my desires. On the rare occasions when she visited her sister in Turin, or Carlotta, I missed her in the way an amputee experiences a phantom limb, even though his cognitive and empirical experience tells him it is not there: she was a piece of me. I returned full and complete only on her return. She wanted me, I wanted her, with such desire, such hunger. I wrote a poem, during one of these absences - I never dared show it to her. I wrote that our bodies looked like the sweaty wood of a jigsaw puzzle, an interlocking game for children: one's skin completed the other's, each of us the inside and the outside, in turn. We exchanged humours, secretions, fluids, all with different density and colour and smell – they were swallowed or absorbed, confused, until there were no more certain boundaries, it was not possible to determine where I began and where she ended. There was no end, no beginning, just the pleasure of being one. Between us there was no border. Now there is, it separates us as a river divides sand dunes: it's a border that has acquired its own form, every day more complex and more cumbersome. A real no-man's-land.

Bianca cut herself off from me. Her flesh has become fleshier, her skin has a spongy texture; even her breath and her own peculiar smell have changed; they remain alien to me. And her body, Christ, her body looks like a mythological creature of enormous proportions; her belly that invades the whole torso which is a continuum with her giant breasts, white as the milk of which they are full. I find her - forgive me - revolting. She's swollen and hard and bouncing like a ball; her skin as white as her name, but with swollen surface veins, with brown stripes like streaks that run through her thighs. God, how I loved those chunky thighs, that body. Now, it's all too much. There are two people in there, I think. It gives me the creeps, it makes me shudder. I find it repulsive. A monster. A miracle. A monstrous miracle. A miraculous monster.

***

"I think about the baby. All the time," Bianca says (Me, too, I think. A complete stranger).

"I try to imagine him: a mixture of the two of us, maybe my hair, Giovanni's eyes, my height, his grace," Bianca says.

"Yours – you are far more graceful than me," I say (lying). "My Bianca, full of Grace."

She smiles like a Raffaello.

"Gorgeous. You are so gorgeous," my father adds (because you don't see her naked, I add to myself).

"Can he hear me?" Bianca asks. "Do you think he can hear my heart beating?" Bianca asks again.

"I don't know. I think so," my father replies.

"Well then, Giovanni. Come on: look it up, quickly. What does the book say?" She demands. Bloody book. I am asked and I do it: straight away. I obey orders.

"The voice of the mother is especially strong because it can travel through her body tissue, rather than through the air… Startling sounds have been shown to increase a fetus' heart rate and, conversely, soothing sounds can slow it down… Many pregnant women report increased fetal movement in response to loud noises… There is strong evidence that listening begins as early as the sixteenth week of fetal development. The voice and intonations of the mother, to which the fetus is exposed during gestation, will be recognised early by the newborn baby, and will foster the acquisition of verbal language… Intrauterine exposure to sound is crucial, because the maternal voice can encourage the baby's attachment to the person who is his main carer… For this reason, it is usually recommended that parents talk to the fetus; the use of a simple and affectionate language, of singing and music, encourages the development of hearing and speech, and increases his sense of and security."

"Then we must talk to him, always. And listen to music," Bianca says. Pablo barks.

"Take him out," Bianca says.

"All this noise can't be good, for him."

"For whom?" I ask.

"Who do you think? The baby," she says.

"You always call him: the baby. What about a name? Have you decided on a name yet?" my father asks.

This is yet another point of contention: my mother has, *obviously*, bought a Dictionary of names: "From Aaron to Zachary: a practical guide to discover the etymology, the meaning and the origin of each name." We have spent months, trying to pick one that would appeal to both of us; in the end, we've decided: his name will be Massimiliano.

Of Latin origin (*magnus- maior - maximus*= big – bigger - biggest), the name arose as a blending of Maximus (greatest) and Aemiliānus by the Emperor Frederich III, who bestowed it upon his first-born son, Maximilian I (1459 - 1519), in honour of two famous Roman generals.

Meaning: High, supreme. Originally, it meant the older of two brothers.

Name day: March 12 (St. Maximilian of Africa, martyr).

Curiosity on the name: The name comes from 'Maximillus' ie the diminutive of Maximus, but it can also be considered patronymic (Maximus' son). Throughout history, various sovereigns and German and Austrian emperors have had the name.

Massimiliano. My son. Will he be lively or melancholic? With a talent for music, or for medicine?

"I hope he'll be a nice kid, our little Maxi," my wife wonders. For now, no, I don't like him. And please: let's not start using diminutives. Because he's all but small: he is big and bulky and bossy, he always comes between us. He's managed to put me aside. I hope he's going to be born quickly, this baby, and I hope everything will go back to normal. To what it was like *before*. I can't bear it any longer.

***

On the afternoon of the twenty-third of December, Bianca goes into labour. Giovanni is in the office, busy with a client; his mother, overexcited, calls him, rolling her 'r's even more than usual.

"Bianca's waters broke, the first contractions started. But they are not frequent. It will take hours. These things last forever," she says, stressing "things," a hint of disgust in her voice – Marieke is not a sentimental woman.

"Don't rush. We are here."

Giovanni rushes over, drives fast along the narrow country lanes, up the hill. He runs to the door; Luigi is standing in the doorstep, smiling. He takes Giovanni by the elbow and accompanies him in the kitchen.

"Drink this," he tells Giovanni, his voice a whisper. The coffee seems sweet and as thick as blood. His father pours another cup. Giovanni drinks it up. It is even denser.

He races to the upper floor; Marieke is standing in the corridor next to their bedroom; his father gives Giovanni a hug and beckons his wife to leave the couple alone. Giovanni enters their room, in which there is a strange scent, sweet as the coffee he has just drunk. He holds his wife's soft hand, he kisses her on her wet cheek. Bianca breaths rapidly. From time to time she breaks into a syncopated shriek. Giovanni asks his mother to leave for a minute; he kneels beside the bed.

"You're doing so well. You are so brave."

The room is hot; Giovanni opens the shutters and the cold fingers of the winter evening sneak into the overheated room, crawl up the red walls. There is a slender crescent moon, the first stars. Bianca is weeping.

"Enough of this," Giovanni says, when Bianca screams. "It's time to go, now. We've waited long enough."

He helps Bianca stand up. She holds her belly with both hands, refuses her coat, her shoes; they don't speak. Bianca grinds her teeth, squeezes his hand. When they arrive at the hospital, she is already eight centimetres dilated. A nurse takes her away in a wheel chair, Giovanni gallops behind - the suitcase that keeps hitting the back of his legs. He doesn't pay attention to where they are going, he just follows the chair, he follows it like a dog chases a stick, mindlessly, like Pablo – he suddenly thinks of Pablo, they left him behind, he thinks of home, the *Willow* in the darkness, Pablo all alone, but they are suddenly in the delivery room, they transfer Bianca onto a bed, the lights are blinding, Bianca is screaming, the midwife chats to a colleague as if nothing was going on, then a doctor comes in, then another midwife, there is a constant coming-and-going, as if this was the most normal thing in the world. Giovanni remains close to Bianca: to her head; he refuses to see what is happening at the other end of the bed, between his wife's legs, where the medics are standing, looking, prodding, touching. He buries his face in Bianca's hair, he whispers rambling loving words, anything: anything not to see. Shh.

"One more push," he hears, and then a silence, and a whimper. He looks at his wife, who is crying, her pupils glistening like golden dots in the misty blue of her irises, drowned in salt water. The knot that encrusted his throat for hours finally melts, the smell of salt inflames his nostrils, the salt of saliva and of their tears, the salt of blood, of tears mixed with sweat.

He is echoed by his son. Slimy, still dirty, he is crying in the midwife's arms; she places his small body on Bianca's belly. Giovanni, in tears, is pushed to one side. Into a corner, again.

***

December 31ˢᵗ

Dear Diary,

Here I am: proud and exhausted.

• Proud: not to have fainted; to have been of some help to my wife; and something else, that I can't quite express: proud of *us*, to have overcome this obstacle, won the test, reached the milestone of being fully grown up. Nothing makes you feel more like a real adult than having a child.

• Exhausted: I swear I have never been so tired in my life, as if I had run a marathon, and not just with my legs but also with my arms and my head, not to mention my stomach. It is a gut weariness - my insides keep twisting every time I think about it.

I'm a father. *Papà*!

Such a long, strange, significant year ends today; I already miss it, and not just because I'm a romantic, sentimental man, for whom the past often seems more important than the future. Even, or especially, because I know that nothing will be the way it was before. Dostoevsky wrote that a man is a being who gets used to everything - I'll get used to us, to Massimiliano, to being a father, to see our trio as a family. My family. For now, it's just an incredible effort.

If I am honest – and I am, here – the baby makes me feel slightly sick (his dry, wrinkled skin, his eyes rolling upwards, his swollen, red sex), I find him boring (his continued mewing, the invariant loop: milk-sleep-poop-milk that keeps repeating and repeating and repeating), he pervades me with a constant sense of fear (the idea that he needs Bianca so, his utter dependency on her). On the first week he basically slept *on* her, sucking all the time. I managed to convince her to put him in his crib, which is right next to her side of the bed, so that she can pick him up every time he has to suckle (Christ, what a horrible word) without turning her into a human dummy. But, see: it's not Massimiliano: it's my wife who doesn't want to detach from him. She has insisted that he must sleep in the room with us - with her, I stand corrected. I tried to sleep with them the first few days, then I had to give up; I was going crazy; he wakes up every two hours; and he makes these awful noises: a tremendous strangled yelp, deadly moans, hellish cries.

"It doesn't work," I said to her, as gently as I could. "Darling, we do need to get some sleep," I said, stressing the "we." "It's a simple choice, and it needs to be yours: either I sleep here next to you, or he does." She smiled the sweetest, the most terrible of smiles, and chose him. "Of course," I said, clenching my teeth like a bulldog. "C*a* va sans dire."

"Yes, of course I mean it."

"Don't even mention it."

"Are you kidding? Please."

"He needs you. More than me."

"But yes, I am sure. Of course."

Of course my arse. What about me, I want to shout? Me, me, me. I am confined in the room with the single bed. I sleep alone.

"It will pass," my mother says.

"It will pass. *Tempus omnia medetur*," my father says.

"It will pass," Violetta says, patting me on the shoulders.

"It will pass," I finished the chorus, my throat as tight as a knot.

I'm waiting.

***

20th January

I can't do anything but wait. Wait for things to change and return as they were - God, I can't wait. I wait and I can't wait.

I started the usual routine again: home-office-home. When I return after a long day at the office, she is never alone to meet me. Never, ever: in the very first days, there was a procession of visitors: Luisa and Carlotta and Riccardo, and my relatives who came to worship the creature just like the Three Kings, *dona ferentes*: everyone wants to take him in their arms for a moment, everyone tickles his chin to make him smile involuntarily, stupidly, everyone cooes with oooh and aaah as doves, as if they were retarded. Uncle Stefano and my Aunt and even my colleagues.

Pathetic. Even now that the procession is over, we are still surrounded by people: there is Violetta, who now comes every day, and my father, and especially my mother, who seems to spend more time at the *Willow* than in her own house. She takes Massimiliano from Bianca's arms as often as she can; she brings something every day – a new toy, a new cute outfit, and then biscuits, cakes, mini-breadsticks, ice-cream. And Bianca, my little, delicious Bianca, now as swollen as her breasts that are soft as a blanc mange, holds the baby closer to her chest, and he sucks as if the milk valve could close up any second, as if there was no tomorrow; and she – my little, my beautiful Bianca: she stuffs her face, eating not for one, not for two, but for three or four people. I can't use a kinder turn of phrase: she is fat, full stop. Every time she eats yet another chocolate, another slice of salami, another cracker, I would like to give her a little slap on her hand, only with the tip of my fingers, and tell her: "Honey. My sweet Love. Put that down. You've had enough. You can't still be hungry."

I restrain myself. I refrain from doing so many things that I'll blow up, one of these days, with an explosion worthy of Mount Vesuvius. I sit on one side. I stare at my wife who does not stop chewing, who offers her magnificent breasts to my son. Massimiliano closes his eyes, swallows her nipples, and sucks away contentedly, his eyes turned up in an ecstasy worthy of Bernini's Santa Teresa. My mother supervises, her own mouth open, greedy.

All this hunger, this insatiable appetite. It will pass.

THE HEART OF THE OCTOPUS

***

February 4th

Dear Diary,

It's Sunday morning. I woke up early, between darkness and dawn - the curtains were pushed aside, from the bed I could see a speck of a pale blue sky: I witnessed the light rise miraculously, the world get up slowly from the Saturday night, which always seems shorter than the others. From under the sheets I could smell a sticky aroma, sweet as a memory. As a beginning. I fell back asleep. Waking up again, a couple of hours later, I found Bianca's head rest in the nook of my shoulder, her soft curves superimposed onto my bony body. She comes to visit me - in my single bed - in the middle of the night, or very early in the morning, as if we were lovers who mustn't get caught by their parents. I put her hand around my cock, which is always hard. She strokes it. When I fall asleep, she slips away again, so I always wake up alone, in my cold narrow bed.

Bianca was sleeping. In the silence I could hear her breathing – I could even hear the beating of my heart. For a few minutes I could pretend that everything was as before. The silence, the still, quiet room still, my wife's legs between mine, her hands on my sex, her breath on my neck. My wife was lying next to me, too close, her eyelids lowered over her alabaster eyes. I gawped at the deformed shape of her body under the wrinkled sheet. It seemed impossible to believe that this un-made body was the same that once I'd held in my arms so ardently, with a sort of delirious passion. It was mine. The slim waist that I could circle completely with my hands. Her thick legs, strong and sturdy under her round ass. Her pot belly, smooth as a fish, her firm breasts, tailor-made for my hands and my mouth, my tongue. I wished that her body would stop being so damn motherly, I wished she returned to have that acerbic youth I liked so much, that so excited me. I wanted my wife back; I wanted her to mould herself upon me like a cast.

I fell asleep, and when I woke up she was gone.

***

At the Willow, it is as if twenty-first century Western civilization had gone out of the window. After childbirth, Bianca seems to have lost the common sense of decency and modesty. And it is interesting that this fact, which fills her husband with horror, is instead enthusiastically embraced by her mother-in-law. Bianca and Marieke are united in the abandonment - no: the *gusto* - with which they talk about bodily functions; of pooing and burping, of milk flowing copiously from Bianca's breasts, of mastitis, of nipple fissures; of haemorrhoids that have plagued Bianca's anus during pregnancy; and of how that pain was but a trifle, compared to the delivery, the perineal tear, the episiotomy she suffered. His wife and his mother discuss the colour, texture and smell of Massimiliano's evacuations with a liberating and embarrassing abandonment ("How yellow it is, look: it looks like mustard," "Can you smell that, like wheat") of his penis with diminutive and ridiculous names ("What a gorgeous little bean, what a beautiful fish, what a handsome pea! Let grandma see it, come on – oh my goodness, what a big big boy!"). Giovanni feels besieged by tangible evidence of these bodily functions: granny underwear, bras for breastfeeding, vaginal pessaries, suppositories, creams - a huge variety of gizmos and detergents. Finally, in an intensification of the offensive: nappies rolled up like a maxi crêpe, overalls full of shit ("Can you believe that, it's travelled all over his back, isn't that amazing"), soaking nursing pads, bloody tampons simply abandoned and forgotten on a chair, on the floor.

Giovanni, who almost burnt the roof of his mouth, one day, rather than spit on his plate a mouthful of hot mashed potatoes, Giovanni whose sneezes seem cat puffs, Giovanni who can't defecate if someone is standing in an adjoining room, who opens the tap when he urinates, who has an iron grip on his sphincter; how could Giovanni possibly maintain that condition of ethereal and romantic love he's cultivated for Bianca until now?

***

February 20th

During the week, I behave like a robot: the alarm goes off at six; I get ready, say a quick hello "that I'm late already," a kiss on the forehead, on the cheek. I push Pablo out to do his business, wait for him to come back and then I run out to the car, reaching it with a Bolt-like sprint, before she stops me, before she tells me to do something, before she has the time to ask me how I am.

Over the weekend, it's different. On Saturdays and Sundays, the alarm doesn't go off; it's me: I have my eyes glued to the clock; I watch Bianca's body asleep beside me. She is still, apart from her bare shoulders that go up and down, slowly, in unison with her breath. Her hair spread on the pillow like a fan. Light comes in from the windows and mixes with the red of the walls. I listen to the silence - on the floor below, I can hear Pablo's nails tick on the parquet, impatient like me. I'm waiting. I listen and listen to the silence of the deaf and dumb house, which is *his* silence. It is an expectation filled with anguish. Because when he wakes up then Horror begins - the hysterical crying, which I can't console and comfort: only she can, and she does, she rushes to him, and then: the pink little mouth attached to her large nipples, as dark as blackberries - those turgid, swollen breasts, that body so fat and so sweet like the sweet fat milk that bathes her swollen breasts - that animalistic look that floods her eyes - Massimiliano attached to her like a calf – I can't stand it.

The air is warm and pink, this morning, in the dim light. We are alone. Not for long. I can't stop stretch my ears. The air is fresh, pink. We are alone. The shutters are still closed. I turn over in bed, tired. I hear a rustling in the corridor.

I prick up my ears like a dog when it smells its prey.

Like the prey when it is discovered.

***

To tell the truth, he is a lovely, placid child. Cheerful. A round baby, almost bald, who always wants to be in the arms of someone, no matter whose; and whose main concern is to have a full tummy, an uninterrupted sleep, and a dry bum; when these three demands are met, he does not cause any problem. He sits in his rocking chair and watches the toys that are hanging over his cot with a hypnotic smile that one generally displays when visiting the Sistine Chapel.

Bianca likes to dip her face in the folds of his neck and breathe in his scent through her nose, noisily. Yes, it's his neck the part of his body on which Bianca dwells: she touches it with her hands, nose, mouth. Front and side, and in particular the back, the nape, where the hair is thinning, and the folds become thicker and harder, where there is a strawberry mark that looks like a drop of blood. Giovanni wonders if Bianca has ever kissed him, on the neck. He remembers her hands through his hair, yes, and behind the neck, but she's never done that specific gesture, with him. To him. Giovanni picks up his son, tickles him, scratches him on his tummy. Massimiliano smiles his toothless smile, rolls up his hand around his dad's index finger, shakes it, slobbers over the lapel of his jacket, vomits a sort of white yogurt on his shoulder. Giovanni puts him back in his chair, fastening his seat belts, as if he were a pilot. But we are not in the Sixties: now every gesture and movement is weighed and sterilized, woe to take a risk. You have to wash your hands with antibacterial gel before picking him up, there are belts everywhere, and chains that keep the dummy in its place, and the monitor is always on, even when he's fast asleep in the room next to them, and you can hear everything anyway.

***

It's March, a morning full of feathers and promises.

Giovanni is in the bathroom, shaving. He moves his face to be closer to the mirror; he almost touches it with his forehead, noticing a pimple on his right temple. It's dark, it's raining, the sky has the colour of dirty water. A flash illuminates the oval mirror, behind his reflected face. Maybe he could, after all, have stayed in bed a bit longer. It's Saturday. He rarely works on Saturdays, but occasionally he does; he likes to enter the studio with the shutters closed and the sharp smell of disinfectant mixed with wood polish. He never stays long: long enough to go through his papers, tidy them up, study new regulations when necessary. Sometimes, he reads his newspaper, using the office as a refuge – he needs a bit of time to himself. He justifies his behaviour thinking that other men play golf, or tennis, for hours; he just needs a couple of hours.

When he goes back to the *Willow*, he takes Massimiliano for a walk in his pushchair; they get back in time for lunch; sometimes Luisa comes over from Turin, other times they invite his parents, a few friends, his uncle. Bianca prepares a roast, potatoes, a fresh salad, cake. In the afternoon, Giovanni takes the baby once more for a walk; they go to the village for an ice-cream, or walk in the vineyard, up and down the rows of vines. Later in the evening, after the baby is finally put to bed, they have dinner, watch a DVD. When Bianca goes to bed too, he finishes off the bottle of wine.

On Sundays the same routine takes place; and then again a week later, and the weekend after that. Their life implodes, their world acquires narrow borders. Home, office, the vineyard, which he's looking after more and more - there's nothing else to do. After pruning, he begins to replace poles and damaged canes, he prepares another row to plant new cuttings, he waters, watches the plants grow, slowly; he straightens them up, looks after them with care. Massimiliano looks at him from his pushchair. Pablo rolls over and over in the white soil.

Weeks go by; month follows month, huddled against each other, they pile up, they writhe. Seasons come and go, come back. The hottest season precedes the colder, the coldest follows the hottest. Time is marked by the vine, by his work in the vineyard. Months have the smell of wine. Time is lost in the life cycle of hundreds of days and nights, time fades along with his skin, greying along the root of his sideburns. A sense of ennui begins to creep in.

THE HEART OF THE OCTOPUS

Can you remember those lumps of tar we used to find on the beach, in summer? Coal tar is a black, viscous substance, obtained by cooling the gas that is formed during the destructive distillation of coal to ambient temperature. It is composed of a complex mixture of condensed-ring aromatic hydrocarbons; it may contain phenolic compounds, aromatic nitrogen bases and their alkyl derivatives, paraffinic and olefinic hydrocarbons. It was a rather common sight, when we were young, at the seaside: blobs of tar would get stuck to the soles of your feet and it was very hard to remove because it was very sticky. You had to scratch it off with sand, and then at home using a pumice stone; it left black streaks that disappeared only after many days. The sense of ennui Giovanni feels is similar to the tar of yesteryear: almost solid, slimy, durable – it anchors him to the ground, he can't shake it off.

At first, it is a slight boredom, which falls like dust over his heart, covering it with an impalpable, white and even veil, like sugar powder. It crawls over him slowly, slowly. As fine as silk, transparent like gauze, boredom wraps itself tightly around Giovanni's life. It is twisted in an inextricable knot around his domestic happiness. Now it presses on his face, suffocating him. He is exceedingly, immensely bored; his life seems like an endless repetition, an infinite loop; look, perhaps if he had never known anything different, it wouldn't matter quite so much. If he could forget what excitement is, just how thrilling love can be; like Jim Carrey in the *Eternal Sunshine of the Spotless Mind*: if he could simply press a button and delete from his brain the memory of feeling exhilarated, of Julie, of Carmela, of the first few months with Bianca: well, then he could accept it. But he can't.

***

Massimiliano grows quickly; he's cute, he's cheerful. He fills the house with his garrulous little voice, competing with Pablo for the attention of adults. He loves to play with water; in order to entertain him, Giovanni has the old fountain demolished and a new one built – a larger, deeper one, with low edges, accessed via three steps. On the highest, he installs the statue of an angel with big open wings. It is made out of white marble, has a round face, short and wavy hair, sensual lips, eyes half closed. Whilst they are at it, they renovate the garden, too, buying new plants and new garden furniture – a round table with six chairs and an umbrella, and two metal chaise longue, which look straight out of a Victorian house. They like to sit there, just in front of the fountain, Giovanni and Bianca. They read, they sip a glass of wine, they look at Massimiliano, who plays nearby.

It is a mild afternoon. They are sitting on the bench – it feels warm and as golden as the air around then, as warm as Bianca's hand that has crept into Giovanni's. Pablo's barking, eager to play; Giovanni takes the opportunity to break free from the clingy grip of his wife, throws a ball into the grass. Bianca pulls Massimiliano up and tries to hold him on her knees, but he can't stay still, he keeps wriggling, he wants his father, who lifts him up and sits him on his lap. The child stares at him with his serious eyes. Giovanni looks away first. He feels uncomfortable.

"When he's older, we can use the fountain as a swimming pool. It's so deep."

"It isn't large enough to be able to swim in it, though."

"Not swimming, no. But he'll be able to sit in it and play," Bianca says. Massimiliano wriggles, he wants to get off his knees, then tries to climb up again.

"Enough, now. You either sit nicely or get off me." Massimiliano stares at him. His son makes him uncomfortable. He's the spit image of Bianca; when Giovanni sees them together it feels like he's watching a science fiction movie. It troubles him, to see their faces mirrored in each other, it disconcerts him to see Bianca's face and Bianca's hands replicated in miniature: small and, chubby, yes, and yet unequivocally identical to hers – every feature, multiplied by two. Massimiliano's eyes are almost as white as Bianca's, and he has her powdery skin, fragrant as a biscuit, and his hair has the same dull colour of the grapes when they are still attached to the vine, splattered with soil and rain. His son interests him so little, he thinks, shivering. He's not even a boy, he thinks, not really; still a formless baby. It is a mystery to him that his wife talks about him as if he were a real person. Everyone in the family is scrambling around him like headless flies - his wife, his parents, Luisa. Giovanni feels left out; nobody cares about him. Every other afternoon Marieke comes over, but not for her son; she is not popping in for an espresso, a biscuit, the latest gossip. She barely says hello to him; she puts the leash on Pablo, holds Massimiliano's hand and takes boy and dog for a walk in the vineyard, up and down, row after row. They come back after a couple of hours. She insists to be the one who bathes him; she loves to feed him; she and Bianca seem to compete to be the one who makes Massimiliano laugh the loudest – the boy commands them like a little king. He's taken Giovanni's place. He's replaced him.

***

In the evening, by the fire, Luigi tells the story of Scarampo Scarampi, Marquis of Camino, who in 1499 suffered a siege and surrendered only for hunger. Once captured, he was beheaded and – says Matteo Bandello: "Mrs Camilla Scarampa, hearing that her husband's head had been cut off, immediately died."

"If you're very careful you will see him, too; you'll see Scarampo, strolling on the tower of the castle with his head in his hands," Luigi says, singing an old ballad: "His head made a jerk, and in the room went off, his head made a jerk and in the room went off." Luigi looks for his son's eyes. Giovanni is sitting on the side-lines. "Do you remember this old song, Giovanni? We used to sing it all the time when you were a boy. You loved it." Giovanni lowers his eyes, doesn't respond. "You don't remember?"

"No, I don't. I'm too tired," Giovanni says.

"It's hard, not to sleep. You lose all concentration."

'Yes, it's hard. It's not easy to become a father, is it?" Luigi says. Giovanni looks at the fire, his cheeks burning. "See, you have to understand that this tiredness will pass. The hard bits will get easier."

"When?"

"Soon enough. But it's worth it."

"Is it?"

"Of course it is. Without children, we are nothing. There is no future. Without children, we are and remain dust. You must have a lot of patience, with Massimiliano and Bianca. It's not easy. I know. But think about it. Children are the future. Nothing makes sense without them."

Giovanni looks at the fire. He should confide in his father. Luigi is a no-nonsense man; he is discreet, lucid, wise – and he is married to a difficult woman. He has seen it all. But his discretion makes him elusive, his sense of privacy makes him appear unavailable, distant. For Giovanni, he represents a figure of authority, not a confidant and he feels unable to open up with him – for fear, for shame. There is a well-known saying: "*Piemontesi, falsi e cortesi,*" meaning people from *Piedmont* are "*false and polite*"; maybe he's too polite. Maybe they both are.

Giovanni looks at the fire and does not say a word.

***

THE HEART OF THE OCTOPUS

Giovanni loses weight, loses sleep. He loses the simple pleasure of things - those little things that made every morning different, pleasant. Nothing interests him, everything bores him, an ennui that that rusts his heart. His own child bores him, Bianca bores him, the dog bores him, the *Willow* feels like a cage. He feels trapped: even the most mundane objects, the commonest - the wardrobe full of clothes, jackets and trousers, well ironed shirts, the fruit plate, the bread basket, the oil cruet - they clinch him in their fists. They make him feel like a prisoner, making him gulp, searching for air.

"I'm suffocating!" He wants to scream. "Help, someone help!"

When he lies down, at night, he thinks with relief that another day is over. A day like any other, after any other. He waits for evening to come and then he waits for morning to come and then again for evening to return. Like an old man in a nursing home, waiting to die.

It's evening. Giovanni goes into the bathroom, undresses, folds his clothes neatly, laying them on a stool, he puts on his pyjamas. He walks down the hall barefoot, into their bedroom; Bianca is already in bed, facing the wall. Giovanni raises a corner of the sheets, slips into his side of the bed, trying not to make any noise. It is a rule tacitly established between them - no contact. It's been weeks since their bodies have touched each other. The last time they made love was a fast, quick affair, free of passion, of emotion; muscles and sweat and the frantic rubbing of skin against skin and a joy as brief as a sob.

Time passes by with unbearable slowness. The passage of time creates an intolerable fatigue in his bones. Fatigue becomes boredom. Boredom generates boredom, discomfort generates horror. Horror spreads over the *Willow*; it completely covers it.

Boredom continues to fall softly, like snow.

***

June 5th

I go to bed exhausted
The next morning I wake up even more tired.

***

They choose to spend two weeks at the seaside. Giovanni needs a rest. Bianca has spent hours looking at brochures of hotels around the Mediterranean, to compare costs, rooms, beaches. Eventually, they book a hotel in Paraggi, near Portofino, one of the most famous Ligurian villages. They lock up their house, trust Pablo to Marieke's care, who takes him grudgingly. They start off, the trunk fully loaded – there are their cases and the pushchair, games and toys and bucket and spade and bottles and the sterilizer, and two inflatable swimming rings: excessive but essential paraphernalia, according to Bianca, for Massimiliano's wellbeing. The hotel is wonderful, the sand is golden, the sea is flat, emerald-coloured, but the holiday is a disaster. On the second day, Massimiliano falls from a chair and cuts his ear; they visit the emergency department of the local hospital: it's not a serious injury, but the wound is in a difficult position to medicate - the only remedy is to wrap the whole head with bandages. On the third day, he swallows a piece of Lego – they visit the A & E again; on the fourth day, he gets a fever. No, nothing serious, no hospital is needed: it's just a bad cold; it's better not to bathe in the sea for a couple of days. They take walks in the surrounding area: there is a path up the hill that leads up to the famous square in the harbour of Portofino, the ancient Portus Delphini, the fishing village mentioned by Pliny the Elder; it is often talked about in the press, for frequent visits of fashionable people. They take an apéritif. Massimiliano manages to get his hands on the bowl of peanuts, he puts a handful in his mouth, chokes.

The next day it starts to rain.

Giovanni has had enough. They have paid for two weeks, Massimiliano's cold is better, the weather forecast indicates it will be sunny in a day or two. But Giovanni's had enough. He empties the wardrobe and the chest of drawers, puts all their clothes back in their suitcases, packs their paraphernalia in the trunk of the car, and they leave to go back to Castel San Gerolamo.

***

THE HEART OF THE OCTOPUS

July 10th

Dear Diary,

My hands are shaking. They have not stopped, in the last twenty-four hours.

It was nearly eleven last night when I got back. Mr. Anderi could only see me at eight-thirty and I had to stay at the office until well after nine o'clock. We finished dinner late; the baby was asleep; we read for a while, each of us sitting in our little corner. The windows were open; a puff of warm air was coming in and a vaguely salty perfume of geraniums on the windowsills to keep away the mosquitoes. Bianca yawned. She said that she was sleepy, prepared a cup of milk. I drank it all alone downstairs while my wife prepared for the night. A good night, I thought, looking out at the darkness. There was a thin crescent moon, which made me want to go out and pee on the lawn. I've seen it done so many times by my father; never, before last night, I realised what pleasure I would get from pissing outdoors, on the grass that has just stopped sweating.

So beautiful, I thought. So peaceful. So *nice*. Yes, exactly: how nice it all is. A kind of joy I hadn't felt for ages. I buttoned up my fly, I came back in and I locked the door. I prepared two cups on the table for breakfast tomorrow morning. I went upstairs and stripped down and walked into our bedroom and found Bianca still awake, her eyes so lively. They seem like wild animals, sometimes, with a life of their own. She was looking at me, and I felt shy; almost embarrassed. I stood there beside the bed in my pyjamas. I took off my watch and laid it on the nightstand next to the glass of water. I noticed there was dust on the bedside table where the glass stood. I wiped it off with my finger. I took off my slippers and lined them up under the bed and then I sat down.

She spoke with a tone of voice that made me think she was joking - there were grains of laughter in her voice, I'm sure.

***

Bianca looks at Giovanni in the dim light. She's in bed, the sheets rolled around her body like a French film from the Fifties. Only her shoulders emerge - white, round, shiny with sweat.

"Giovanni?"

"Yes?"

"Giovanni: listen."

"Yes?"

"What would you say if we were to make another one," she says, her voice a whisper.

Giovanni - who is closing the curtains - turns towards her. He appears lost in thought. Maybe he did not hear properly. "What?"

"I said: what do you think if we made another."

"Another what?" Giovanni asks, walking towards the bed, kicking his slippers off, distracted.

"What do you mean: what? Another baby, of course." Bianca says. "Maybe twins, this time. Or a little girl," she says, hope in her voice.

***

She took my breath away as if she'd elbowed me right in the stomach. I felt as if I were falling: the same sensation you get in some dreams when you fall into a bottomless hole, a sort of well that stretches for miles and miles and ends at the other end of the earth, in Australia or in New Zealand. My heart contracted in my chest: I distinctly felt it: a narrowing and widening and a shrinking - painful brutal sudden. I had to turn over to the other side for fear she would be able to see that I was upset.

Dear Diary,

I'm so scared. The idea of looking once more at her body bloated like an obscene flower. I owe her so much. She gave me her virginity, her purity. She used to be such a sensual girl, uninhibited; she used to enjoy her own body so much; and mine. She had awakened every muscle and every nerve, she had learned every bit of it and taught me every bit of hers. And then my body had to forget itself, slip back into oblivion, try to go back to sleep, get accustomed to the narrow confines and to my hand. Orgasm is no different if the hand that moves between your legs is yours or another's, but pleasure is another thing altogether - it always starts inside your head, and then branches out along one's limbs as a sapling, as a spider's web. The longer the branches, the thicker the web, the more intense the pleasure.

***

My father was beaming, this morning.

"What a day! If this hot sun lasts all through the summer until September, we'll have the most magnificent wine harvest."

I raised an eyebrow: all this excitement, just for a sunny day?

"You know what?" he asked with a satisfied sigh (he sighs ever so loudly – perhaps he's becoming deaf, but every sound he makes feels *fortissimo*). "You know what? Very few things give me more pleasure than a sunny day."

It was my turn to sigh (*sotto voce*). Nothing gives me pleasure. I am indifferent to the weather. To people. To make conversation doesn't give me any pleasure at all - we are very quiet: we listen to Max. We listen to Violetta who sucks her gums, who goes up and down the stairs to tidy up. We listen to Pablo who barks; we listen to the crickets in the grass, to the sound of cars passing down the street, to the rustling of the pages I turn over when I read: we don't talk.

"What's new?" she asks me every day, when I get back home, with an emphasis on *new*, which I think, in her vocabulary, means exciting, as opposite to old and boring. What news could there be? I analyse family situations and devise elaborate appropriate tax planning aimed at reducing my clients' tax burden and protect their inheritance – does she want me to tell her all of this? Mr Rizzo, complains about taxes; Mrs Mosca wants to sell her business to her daughter; Mr Davoli's son came and we'll have to work hard to tidy his business up. Are these the news she wants to hear?

"Pleasure," for me, meant coming back home in the middle of the afternoon to surprise her, and to race upstairs, biting the inside of the cheeks because I wanted her so badly. I swear I tried, to want her again. When she stopped breastfeeding, I was hoping she would go back and be how she used to be. I was hoping I would go back and be how I used to be. Time has passed. It didn't happen. Just like those who eat too much chocolate get indigestion and ever since can't stand, ever again, even a whiff of cocoa, I can no longer smell her without being overcome by a certain nausea. I feel full of acidity, just like after indigestion. A frustration that is eating my soul and gives birth to an anxiety, a strange urgency, as persistent and annoying as an itch, as absolute and imperative as piss. The urgency to ruin everything.

***

Giovanni rarely receives clients on Saturdays. His clients follow his own pace and make appointments in the weekends only in urgent cases. Today it's different. Uncle Maurizio, the only relative Bianca has, died suddenly last week. The whole family attends the funeral, on Wednesday. All have returned to Castel San Gerolamo after two days, but Bianca had to remain, to decide how to arrange things and divide assets with her sister. Massimiliano has stayed behind with her; they will return as soon as they have solved everything.

Giovanni finds himself alone for only the second time since he got married. It's Saturday, he has nothing to do; it feels odd to be alone, but it's not a heavy loneliness; on the contrary, he's enjoying it. He had a late breakfast, pottered around, watched Pablo piss against the flower pots that Bianca cultivates with passion and patience. He would like to work in the vineyard, but it has rained for days, and the vineyard is a muddy swamp. It's not cold; the air is humid. He decides to wash, dress, go into town. At Pier Vittorio's cafe, he stands at the counter for a quick coffee. It takes no longer than twenty minutes to reach his office, by car. He walks in, doesn't even pull back the curtains: he reads the newspaper, tidies his papers. The bell tower clock strikes twelve times. Almost lunch time. He thinks he should go and see his parents. Yes, that's it; he'll call them in a minute. He has nothing else to do. As soon as the bells stop ringing someone knocks at the door. Irritated, annoyed, interrupted in the contemplation of his boredom, Giovanni gets up from his desk, walks down the hall, opens the door. With hair as black as a crow's wings, pale skin, cheeks and lips as red as blood, the woman standing in the doorway looks like Snow White. A Snow White in her thirties, a little heavy.

"Good morning."

"Good morning."

"I'm sorry to ring the bell out of the blue. Are you Mr. Ferraro?"

"Why, yes. I'm Giovanni Ferraro."

The woman holds out her hand. "Michelina Dalmasso, nice to meet you."

"Nice to meet you, too. Do you want to come in?"

The woman follows Giovanni along the corridor, apologises for daring to disturb him on Saturday, but: "I'm not from here, I come just once a month to visit my father who is in Mombello's nursing home. I asked around and everyone talked so highly about you. They said: you must go and talk to him, he's the right person. So here I am," she says, sitting down, fanning herself with her hand. She tells him about her business: the purchase of a café in a neighbouring village, the debts accumulated by her husband from whom she is separated, the mortgage payments unfulfilled.

Michelina puts her hands to her red face. She is wearing a low-cut dress. Her chest shines like ice.

"I'm so sorry to disturb you. Maybe I'll call your secretary on Monday and make a proper appointment."

"Not at all. I am rather free, today," Giovanni says. "Happy to help."

"I don't know how to thank you."

"Don't worry. Honestly," Giovanni says.

"Let me show you all the documents."

"Yes, I do need to see them," Giovanni says. Michelina's bag is on a chair next to her, three bulging folders are balanced precariously on top of it. She moves too quickly; she hits the chair with her foot; it wobbles, then falls over. The folders fall onto the floor.

"Goodness - I am so sorry, I'm so clumsy," she says.

"Don't worry. It happens. You're nervous. Let me help you," Giovanni says, standing up and walking around the desk. He kneels beside her. On all fours, her hair over her face, her skirt raised up over her thighs, Michelina nods, her lips parted and wet. Giovanni hears the sound of his heart in his ears: woosh, woosh, in a chorus with the rain outside. He tries to get up. He puts his hand out to seek a support, but he finds the woman's body. He stops moving, squatting, his legs bent, his back curved. He feels light-headed. His fingers fumble until they rest on the thighs of the woman who exudes a soft breath and opens them slightly.

THE HEART OF THE OCTOPUS

PART V

"Everybody does it" could be one of the phrases that best represents the Nash Equilibrium as conceived by John Nash, American mathematician and economist, known for his contribution to the application of the theory of non-cooperative games to the economy. In the so called *Nash Equilibrium*, each player's strategy is optimal when considering the decisions of other players. Every player wins precisely because everyone gets the outcome they desire. "I refuse to be the first Prince of Wales without a mistress," Prince Charles apparently told his first wife Diana. In short: "Everybody does it." Exactly.

The Belgian therapist Esther Perel recently gave a Ted Talk on the subject, urging the audience to rethink infidelity: according to her, although often extramarital relationships end up covering profound emotional crisis, deception and betrayal aren't the main motivation. "Becoming parents," she says, "Is the final blow to eroticism." Perhaps, she suggests, one should consider infidelity in terms of growth, of autonomy; as a desire to reconnect with lost parts of ourselves. Perhaps infidelity is also an expression of desire and loss.

Giovanni no longer desires Bianca; he's lost her. But he is a man of passion. He needs it like air.

***

It is a truth universally acknowledged that a married man, of beautiful presence, and with a job that bestows him a good fortune, should need a mistress. There you are: I wasn't even looking for her; I didn't even know that I needed one; and to tell you the truth and nothing but the truth: she doesn't satisfy me either. But what she does do, and well, is that she distracts me from the tedium in which I have sunk.

Michelina is different, in everything. If I still had a little sense of humour, that I've lost along the way, together with so many other things (self-love, sincerity, optimism, hope), I would burst out laughing: *tu quoque,* Giovanni? What the hell are you doing with *that* woman? Come on; it's not true; you're making fun of me. You? Such a nice young man? Yes: I really see myself this way, from the outside: a nice, commendable, well-mannered young man. Because I'm worth it, as the ad says, and there you are, shaking one's head full of lusciously shampooed hair, there you go with wrinkle-free skin – all thanks to a miracle cream. Yeah: me, Giovanni: I'm worth it! I'm respectable. No, wait, I want to choose an even more suitable adjective: *decent*, as I had been addressed a long time ago. Michelina is – well, she's just too much. She's fleshy, a fleshy flesh, flesh that needs other flesh. Her big tits her big belly her big ass her big lips. So much hair all puffed up, and then down below, a hairless sex like in porn movies, wet and hot - I sink into it like in quicksand.

My wife makes me sick; she disgusts me. The smell of her hair and her neck, the smell of her breasts and legs, the smell of her breath - revolting. I dare not tell her openly; she just wouldn't understand; but how can she not – it's so obvious. Every time she gets up close. Whenever she caresses me, I shake. I move further away. We go to bed: I turn onto the other side, pretending to fall asleep right away. The worst is when she becomes persistent and tries to kiss me, sticking her greedy tongue between my dry lips. I turn my head, I wipe the damp traces of saliva from my cheek, like I've seen Massimiliano do after a sloppy kiss of my mother's.

***

September 6th

Dear Diary,

it's Friday night. I'm about to go to bed. Bianca is in the bedroom, in front of the mirror. She wears her hair long, now. One by one she removes the clips that hold up her beautiful, shiny hair; it falls in soft waves over her shoulders. She brushes it for a long time, her white eyes fixed on herself, her chin raised. She massages cream on her face and neck, on her dark-nippled breasts. I write my diary, I put it away (well locked, with its own key, and then I hide the key in my wallet). I slip between the fresh sheets; I'm nervous, anxious.

It happens every week. Every Friday night, before falling asleep, and every Saturday morning, when I wake up, I am restless, excited. Impatient, full of expectations. Something is going to happen. An event that, as in fairy tales, will have the power to transform my life.

The fairy tale began a few months ago. It hasn't changed since. I know it in all its most minute detail. It begins with my impatience, on Friday night. A night full of dreams, of desires at hand - just a few hours (it makes me think of Rilke's Admetus: weeks, a few days, oh, not days, for nights, for only one, for one night, for just this one, for this), and I say: a few hours, and then only three more, two more, and a few more minutes, and then: here it is: it's Saturday. At around ten o'clock in the morning I remind her I am going out for a game of tennis. I say goodbye to Bianca and Massimiliano, lined up on the doorstep waiting for my kiss on the forehead or on the hair. I drive slowly, carefully, down the hill, I stop for a coffee, I greet some acquaintance. When the church bell rings eleven times, there is a knock at the door. I open it, and before me a maiden appears, her skin as white as snow, her lips as red as blood, her hair as black as coal. I tell her to come in; she follows me. We do not talk; there is no need for words; we both know why she came here. She slips off her shoes, takes off her stockings. Like Prince Charming with Cinderella: I pick up one of her beautiful feet, whiter and softer than butter, more fragile and precious than crystal. My hands travel up her thighs.

With the midday tolling, the spell suddenly ends. The princess disappears, evaporates. She's replaced by an ordinary woman, stout, commonplace. A woman like any other, with no magic, without charm, with smeared lipstick around her lips. She fastens her bra, she readjusts her displaced garments, she puts her shoes back on, she smooths down the vulgar cloud of her hair. I walk her to the door; she leaves. I get dressed, I lock up the office, I join my friends at Pier Vittorio's for a glass of wine. I drive up the hill. Upon returning home, with the excuse of needing a shower after my tennis match, I carefully soap Michelina's scent off my skin. I get changed. I go back downstairs to join Bianca, Massimiliano and my parents who are already sitting at the table, ready for lunch. Within two hours the euphoria of my petty secret vanishes. Ennui sits at the head of the table. Everything returns as before. Saturday mornings are nothing more than a new piece in the banal game of my life. A dangerous game, that leaves me exhausted, worn out, and: ultimately: disappointed. It gives me so little relief. It's not even worth the effort.

Bianca has no idea. She will never know.

Sometimes she still looks for me, but less and less often. She no longer mentions having another baby. I sit in front of her, but she doesn't see me. She smiles. It's a smile with tight lips, as tender as a Madonna's. Like her, Bianca sees only the fruit of her womb.

***

I am in a constant state of feverish excitement; I can't wait for the weekend, to see her, to touch her: my lover. The taste of that word turns and turns in my mouth like a hard candy; like the Rossana candies I ate as a child, with a red wrapper enveloping a crunchy shell; sucking it slowly, they'd reveal the creamiest, sweetest heart: mmm: my lover.

And at the same time, absurdly, I know that the most exciting moment is just and simply and only *waiting* on the Friday night. As in the *Sabbath of the Village* by the poet Leopardi, where the description of the inhabitants of the village, caught in the preparations for Sunday, is the starting point for a general reflection on happiness, which can reside only in expectation. Saturday is the best day of the week; Sunday will actually not bring the longed-for joy. Well, it really feels the same, here: the act of fucking Michelina is not that great a thing. I do like it; I do enjoy it; I do come. But having an orgasm in itself – fucking her on the floor, leaning against a wall, on my desk, on a chair in the waiting room; standing, lying down, sitting down; from behind or in her mouth – well: an orgasm is an orgasm is an orgasm. In fact,

"And what does this lady do with you on Saturday morning, Dr. Ferraro? Shouldn't you be playing tennis, right now?"

Inexplicably, I also cherish and get a kick out of this sense of insecurity, of danger; the possibility of being discovered. I like to know I have a secret lover; I like to hear the ping of her message confirming the weekly appointment; I hear the ping, I take the Blackberry out of my trouser pocket. Bianca looks at me. "Everything good? Something about work?" she asks, and I reply with a shrug, my ears red like a kid's, my heart beating hard. She could find out! But no, she loses interest after three seconds.

The weekend goes by; and from Monday afternoon I start to want her again. I am tense and in a bad mood and prone to outbursts of rage for the rest of the week; Bianca, with her feigned care, begs me to play more tennis. "Darling, it relaxes you, it is so good for you" ...

I would slap her. Bianca, Michelina, these women who do not understand anything about masculine psychology, about our desire, which comes on suddenly and goes off just as quickly. Bianca doesn't know, that if she prevented me from going out, one Saturday morning, I'd kick her, I'd slap her, I'd hurt her. Seriously. Nothing and nobody could prevent me from going out. I can't do anything about it. It's stronger than me. It's a need: like thirst. A need that I have to satisfy even if it does not satisfy me.

***

THE HEART OF THE OCTOPUS

Giovanni's clandestine relationship continues; he meets Michelina every week; a couple of times, unable to resist, he suggests they meet along the road that leads to Rocca delle Donne. He sees her from a distance, standing on the edge of the road, like a whore. Michelina tells him to park in the woods. She brought with her some wipes, to clean herself with, and for a moment the smell of talcum powder makes him waver - if he closed his eyes, he might think he's home, within reach of his son's diaper change.

Michelina lies down on the back seat, legs apart, feet on the headrests of the front seats, as if she were at the gynaecologist's. He grabs her, pulls her hair, slaps her, brutally takes her. Sex with Michelina becomes like a drug: the only thing capable of making him endure his wife, his son, the claustrophobic quiet of home. Like a vent valve. In mechanics, this is the valve that provides a way out for steam, pressure and similar overloads. In a figurative sense, it's that which allows the release of the tensions and instincts of an individual or of a group, allowing the reestablishment of a situation of equilibrium. Exactly: having a lover gives him that sense of freedom and transgression he needs. He does not care about Michelina; he does not want a true relationship; it's just sex. Intense, brutal, passionate, but sex. Nothing to do with a relationship. He wants to make it clear even with her, and finds a way to do it, starting to pay for it every Saturday morning. She pretends to be offended, the first time Giovanni opens his wallet and offers her two bills.

"Come on, take it. Buy something nice. Something you can show me, next week," he tells her. And she, she takes them.

It is he who decides when to see her (one week he has even managed to resist the temptation, telling her not to come), whether to respond to her messages, how much and if to pay - not every time. This new sense of control makes him feel good, taller, more powerful. He is the boss, the master, he dictates the rules; she is a tap he opens and closes whenever he wants. He decides to use the same tactic with Bianca; he asks her to give him the debit card and her Visa – recently there have been several cases of credit card cloning.

"We must be careful." From now on, he'd like her to make all of her purchases using cash only. He studied the bank statement, knows exactly how much and on what they spend each week; every Monday he puts money on the kitchen table: a few bills, never enough to cover the whole week. Bianca is forced, every time, to ask again. How he likes to look amazed, almost worried. "But honey. Of course I'll give you more. Tell me how much you want," he tells her. But on Monday he's always short of cash. "I'll give you some more later. Will you please remind me?" he tells her, knowing how much it annoys her to ask him. Yes, Bianca is annoyed, but she does not suspect anything, committed as she is by housework and by Massimiliano, who is going through a difficult phase, suffers from separation anxiety and does not leave her a minute. It seems to her that her husband alternates inexplicable kindness to equally unmotivated outbursts of anger;

he's distracted; but they spend so little time alone, they rarely have the opportunity to really talk. Bianca is not worried; she is a practical girl; mindful of the irascible and lonely mood of her father, she knows that the best reaction consists in ignoring him, concentrating on the garden, the house, the child. Bianca considers Massimiliano as something of her own, not theirs. It is her creature, her project: not so dissimilar to how Marieke always thought of Giovanni.

Marieke also noticed her son's mood swings.

"Have you seen what a dreadful mood he was in, today?" She asks Luigi. "Awful. He blew up as if something had stung him. I wonder why. Maybe it was Bianca. Yes. She must have made him angry. But she seemed normal to me, as usual. Maybe something wrong with the office. Did you ask him anyhing?"

"No."

"Ask."

"No."

"But come on, something is wrong. I sense it. I know it."

"Mind your own business, Maria," Luigi advises her. "No one loves a nosy mother-in-law."

"Are you accusing me of being a busybody? Me? Really. But I only worry about my son."

"As Kierkegaard said: "Cast an inquisitive look on men and you will not find anyone whose wisdom is essentially not reduced to this: keep as far as you can from nosing into other people's affairs."

THE HEART OF THE OCTOPUS

Marieke can't help sticking her nose into his business.

***

Giovanni wakes up and finds his wife is up already. When he goes downstairs to have breakfast, she is busy in the vegetable garden. On the table in the kitchen there is a teapot, two slices of toast with butter and the plum jam that Viola prepares every year. He doesn't eat much; he washes his hands, he puts his jacket on. He strokes Pablo's back, says goodbye to his wife with a nod, kisses his indifferent son, gets in his car, sets it in motion, leaves. Inside the office it's cold. The shutters are closed, it's dark. Giovanni turns on the electric heater and remains at its side until it warms up. The church bells ring eleven strokes. Michelina knocks on the door. Giovanni moves aside to let her in.

"Good morning."

"Good morning."

"Do you like this colour?" she says twirling. She is wearing a saffron-coloured raincoat and a dress of the same colour.

"Yes."

Michelina walks in front of him along the corridor leading to his office. Giovanni follows her. She sits down, takes off her shoes that are wet from the rain. The feet of the woman exhale a slight hint of moisture. Giovanni takes them in his hands, one at a time. They are cold. He massages her toes, her sturdy ankles. He lifts up her dress. He slips off her silk stockings. Michelina stops him,

"Wait. Wait," she whispers. She unbuttons his trousers. She kneels down. They don't hear the door that opens and closes, they don't hear her footsteps in the hallway. Marieke walks in and stands in the doorway, watching the unknown woman kneeling on the floor with her mouth open.

"Oh. *Godverdomme*."

Giovanni opens his eyes, pulls up his trousers to hide his erect penis. They stare at each other for a second, then Marieke starts to run – it's difficult, she hasn't run for years, she's short of breath, her flabby flesh dances freely inside her dress, sobs break out in her throat. Her footsteps echo like thunder. The door slams shut. Michelina gets up, panting, red in the face and chest, smooths down her dress. Giovanni zips up his trousers, buttons up his shirt.

"Who was that?"

"Shut up. Get dressed."

"Who was it, Mr Ferraro?"

"Get dressed. Quickly."

Michelina readjusts her clothes, puts on her shoes. Giovanni opens the door. Michelina gets out. He closes the door behind her without a word.

***

At the bottom of the hill, there where the road bends onto the right, hiding the vineyard, Giovanni parks his car and proceeds on foot. He walks past the *Willow*, continues to walk, reaches his parents'. The door is not locked. He's about to knock, but has second thoughts, lowers the handle and the door is open, as always. He goes in. His mother is sitting at the table, alone.

"Why did you come? You've never come, before."

"Why, Giovanni? You tell me," Marieke says. "Don't you love Bianca anymore?"

Giovanni doesn't respond. She carries on. "Your strange behaviour, lately. That bad temper. Was it for her?" Giovanni doesn't reply. "And who is she?" Her son draws a vague gesture in the air as if to say that it doesn't matter. "A whore." Marieke lowers her head, swings it left and right. "You disgust me. My good Lord: you disgust me. You men. You're all the same. All you want is that. And in order to get it, you do anything. You don't care about your wives; you don't care about your children. You don't care about anything."

In Marieke's voice there is a desolate coldness. The chignon on her nape is undone, some grey locks hang down between the folds of her neck.

"I was coming over to surprise you. Like a mother who goes and visits her son." She pauses. "I really thought you were different. I wanted you to be different. I've raised you, to be different."

"I am."

"No. Look: you're like everyone else. You just want what's between a woman's legs. And that woman. I saw that bitch. She sniffs and licks and sucks, like a bitch." She lifts her skirt up. "It's all here. Not that nice. Look: it's just a hole, Giovanni." He averts his gaze quickly. "A hole. You've ruined my life for a hole. Shame on you." Marieke shows him the door. "Go away. Go away." Giovanni leaves the room. Marieke's voice reaches him. "Go away."

Giovanni is in the hallway. He opens the door, runs out. Outside, it's thick with darkness. It's still raining. Giovanni isn't wearing a coat; his clothes are wet before he manages to reach the main road. He slows down but doesn't stop, he keeps walking, he doesn't know where he's going, he just keeps walking, and cries, cries without drying his tears, cries and moans like a wounded animal, he cries and cries and even the night cries, and the grass, and the crickets, and the vineyard.

***

Giovanni is already sitting in his robe by the fireplace, his knees covered with an orange blanket crocheted by Marieke. He shivers, has waves of nausea, a terrible headache. He holds in his hands a cup of warm milk. Bianca is sitting on the leather chair in front of him, embroidering. Massimiliano's upstairs, asleep. The quiet of the evening is interrupted by a sudden clamour coming from the courtyard. Husband and wife don't have time to get up before Luigi, panting, wet, enters the room.

"Luigi! Why - do come, come on in," Bianca says. "You're all wet. What happened?"

"Maria's not well."

"Giovanni, too. He caught a ..." Giovanni interrupts them. His father is pale. Luigi is never pale, not even in winter.

"What's up?"

"I don't know. She's all sweaty, she says her heart hurts. I don't know whether to call an ambulance. I tried to call you, but your mobile was off." His father shudders. "When I came home, she was in bed. She kept complaining she was cold; that her stomach ached. It's so cold and humid, today. I thought that was that - her usual pains and aches. But it doesn't stop. She tells me not to make a fuss, to just wait, it'll get better, just wait. I can't. I can see she's in pain."

Giovanni throws the blanket and his dressing gown on the sofa, quickly. "Let's go. No, I'll go. You stay right here, drink something warm." Giovanni rushes off, walks quickly, as fast as anger. He starts to run, crosses the village over to the other side, arrives breathless. The door is open wide. "Mamma?" Giovanni calls out loud. "Marieke?" Louder.

He climbs the grey stone stairs, stops on the first floor landing. He jumps the next three steps all together. He lingers for a moment in the hallway. He can't hear any noise. He's about to enter the room immediately to the right, then recalls that for some time his parents have taken to sleeping in separate rooms. His father's remained in the master bedroom, his mother's moved to the next, the guests', that has twin beds. He knocks.

"Mamma? Can I come in?" There is no answer. "Mamma. Please."

Giovanni enters. His mother is in bed. Her half-closed eyes are fixed on a point above the fireplace. Her mouth is tight. Giovanni approaches the bed. "How are you? Are you better, now?" His mother doesn't respond. "Oh, I'm sorry, mamma, I'm so sorry." Marieke doesn't respond.

She's not breathing. Giovanni realises he screamed only when he stops. He stops, and all is silent. Only then he starts talking to his mother with a little voice like a child's, to tell her that he loves her, oh, sorry, Mummy, I'm sorry, really, I love you so much, so much, so much the words never came, were never enough, words are not as big as my love, my darling, my angel, I can't live without you, oh my mum, my guardian angel.

He lifts up Marieke's limp body, his arms under her armpits, his mother's inert head slumping over his chest like a Pietà in reverse.

"Mamma, what will I do now, what will I do without you, you can't, you can't do this to me, my darling, my *mammina*, oh, I'm so so so sorry, sorry, Mummy, my angel, you can't leave me alone, do not leave me, no, no, No. Please. Please. No."

***

to be honest, immediately after coming I am horrified, by her and by myself. She tries to talk, the idiot: yes, I swear: she would like to have a conversation. She asks me about my life, about my family. Last time, she even brought a small tray of pastries to share: "You must be hungry after all that effort!" she said, looking at me as if I were her famished hero. She would like to get to know the real me, she tells me. I have nothing to say; I treat her badly, I call her a whore, I slap her - and she comes back every time, more loyal than Pablo. I can't wait to get her out of my office, away from my territory, to clean up and remove any trace of her from my body, from my hair, from my mouth. Like when you watch porn and have a quick wank: you are lying there, still dishevelled, panting, holding in your hand a tissue soggy with semen; then you open your eyes and see - at the computer, on the television screen - those same images that turned you on just a few minutes ago; inexplicably they now make you sick, disgusted.

I love Michelina's abundant flesh, I love to be able to feel – how to call it? Yes: passion. I would like to tell someone about it, about her - but whom? My father is too decent. Filippo would laugh, and then he would start asking too many questions: and what will you do, and how will you do it, and what about your family; he would not be able to keep it secret. I don't think about the future. I think only of next Saturday. What if someone sees us? Sometimes, when I open the door, I expect to see a familiar face, someone who could ask:

The bouquets have invaded the house with their fragrance. A sticky, rotten stench. With the passage of time, the smell has become from unpleasant to unbearable. The day of the funeral they are taken away with the coffin - bunches of daisies, chrysanthemums, a wreath of yellow roses Luigi ordered.

On the first floor, in Marieke's bedroom, Luigi lays another bouquet on the bed. Carnations: her favourites. "Just like lace," Marieke used to say. He lingers a little longer in the room – he can hear, downstairs, the murmur of relatives and friends who've arrived. He goes to the window and looks down into the yard where the hearse is waiting. He blows his nose; he looks at himself in the mirror. He runs a hand on the bedspread to smooth it well. Before going out, he lifts his right hand to his lips as if to send a kiss. He descends to the lower floor, where they are all waiting for him, gathered around the still open coffin placed on trestles in the middle of the beautiful drawing room, the blue one.

"She looks as if she was asleep," someone says.

Luigi arranged everything himself. He's chosen the coffin, he's written the notice for the local newspaper, he's spoken with the priest to decide the date of the funeral. He had a prayer Vigil the night before the funeral, in the small Santa Liberata's church, which was more crowded than when his son had got married.

A long procession of carriages descends from the hill, across the village and drives all the way to Trino, where there is the family tomb. There are relatives and friends in mourning clothes, all numb, cold, sad. They listen to Don Gianni speak of Marieke as a mother and a wife and a grandmother – even if she wasn't Catholic, her faith mattered to her. He recites the rosary. Luigi holds Giovanni up, and vice versa. The priest gives the order to close the tomb.

Luigi invites the family to tea, afterwards. He needs to be comforted. He doesn't want to be left alone. Giovanni goes into his parents' house, runs up the stairs, opens the door of Marieke's room. It's as if her bed still bears the imprint of her body; the bouquet of carnations sits level with where her heart would be, in the middle of the bed. He rips one and puts it in his jacket's buttonhole. In the evening, he places it delicately between the pages of his diary, where it dries and falls apart.

***

Like Barthes in *Mourning Diary – a Son's Grief*: "The locality of the room where she was sick, where she died, and where I now live, the wall against which the head of her bed rested where I have placed an icon—not out of faith—and still put flowers on the table next to it."

***

With the rise of contemporary life expectancy in most developed countries, nowadays it's normal to experience the death of one's parents in adulthood, rather than during childhood or adolescence. Even the children of the old are old; some lose their parents at seventy-plus. To feel sadness for the death of a parent as adults falls into the natural order of events although what one feels might be of contradictory nature, easily switching between states of pain and sadness to anger, helplessness and guilt.

In recent years, it has been suggested that the concepts of attachment theory could continue to be relevant applied to adults in relation to their elderly parents. As we have seen a little earlier in my narration, this theory postulates that children, in the first months of life, look for a bond and a sense of security through the primary attachment figure, who is, generally, the mother. Given the importance of this person, it is a given that the child wants to protect her. Then as an extension one could suggest that adult attachment carries on in a similar form, with *looking after* one's aging parents: and by doing this – with the act of caring after them - we continue to maintain a sense of emotional security. In the case of the loss of a parent, the same theory might suggest that the sudden absence of the attachment figure may lead to terrible unhappiness: the very foundations of our sense of security are missing, have gone: who is going to protect us, now? Who are we, without them?

With the death of a parent, we lose part of our history, of our past, and as a consequence a part of ourselves, of our roots: we lose a confidant, a friend, a vital emotional bond. It is easy to feel "lost": we may feel like an abandoned child, even if we are adults, often with a job, our own family and our own life.

Marieke was Dutch, not Italian; independent, a free spirit, she had chosen to live away from her family of origin; to spend her life in another nation, speaking another language, surrounded by people who did not share the same customs and traditions of food, religion, of general ways of doing things. Italian mothers are often accused of creating mummy's boys: sons who lack autonomy, totally dependent on them or on another woman. It is said that these mothers have a unique moral imperative: to take care of their children in an obsessive and relentless way: overfeeding them, protecting them, helping them financially as adults, thus developing an inextricable bond that is a dependence, a form of morbid addiction. Marieke, in a very Italian way, has spent her life obsessed with creating, in Giovanni, the perfect child: perfect because formed by and on her desires and ambitions. A child grows and separates as an individual from attachment with his/her mother (and father) when he/she chooses his/her own life without expecting or seeking approval of his/her parents, when the umbilical cord is cut not by an act of pride, but because this son or daughter grew up, is doing well, knows he or she can make important decisions alone.

Giovanni - married, father, head partner in his office, with ten employees - has never cut the umbilical cord. Marieke has held him close to her, part of her, all her life.

Marieke is dead.

THE HEART OF THE OCTOPUS

Giovanni is lost.

***

In *Mourning and Melancholy*, Freud analysed mourning as a model for an interpretative theory of depression linked to the death of a loved one. Giovanni's reaction (which is the reverse of the manic one) leads to melancholy: in the paradoxical impossibility of forgetfulness. The lost person is seen as irreplaceable, impossible to forget.

Giovanni does not follow the stages of mourning; Giovanni does not elaborate; Giovanni is still, motionless, stunned by his unbearable pain, as if Marieke had died only a few hours ago. Bianca - healthy, naive, young Bianca - does what any young and naive person would do: she puts her trust in medicine. She calls the family doctor, asking him to come to visit her husband. He will know what to do, how to treat him. Dr. Gamba has always known the Ferraros - he went to school with Luigi, he also knew his grandfather Ludovico. Without promising miracles, he goes to the *Willow* to see him. Physically, he confirms, Giovanni is fine, but his reaction to Marieke's death worries him. Of course, he explains, the reactions to a loss change according to whether the death follows a long illness or if it is sudden. In the first case, it sometimes happens that the process of mourning begins even before the sick person dies; on the other hand, if the person participated in the event that caused the death, even if in the absence of specific responsibilities, he can develop a deep sense of guilt. It may be that Giovanni feels guilty for some reason.

"Marieke died of a heart attack," says Bianca. "You can't feel guilty about a heart attack," she says.

Giovanni listens to the conversation from the bed, his eyes closed. He knows the truth: he does not know that it has a name, but he knows it was him. Takotsubo syndrome, or stress cardiomyopathy, mainly affects women and predominantly after emotional stress. Usually, a heart attack is caused by a thrombus in a coronary artery. In Takotsubo's syndrome, although the symptoms are similar (chest pain, sudden breathlessness) the arteries are normal. Instead, the heart presents an anomaly: the swelling of the lower part of the left ventricle. The term was coined by a group of Japanese cardiologists in the nineties, because during contraction this protruding ventricle resembles the basket trap (tsubo) used by fishermen to capture the octopus (tako). The precise cause of this new syndrome is not known, but experts believe it is stress, or a situation that the individual can't handle or to which she can't react. Basically, the effect is similar to a heart attack, even if the causes are not the same.

Takotsubo syndrome is also called heartbreak syndrome. There again, once more: the heart of the octopus.

***

THE HEART OF THE OCTOPUS

It's ten-thirty in the morning, Giovanni is still in bed. He's not sleeping. He keeps his eyes open. The room is dark. Bianca got up an hour earlier, opened the windows, went downstairs. Giovanni got up, closed the windows, returned to bed.

It's Christmas day.

Luigi asked them to go and celebrate at his. Bianca has been in charge of organizing the festivities, and with Massimiliano they have made decorations, bought and wrapped up the presents, prepared homemade ravioli. The child is very excited for the upcoming holiday, for the treats and gifts that await him. Bianca worries about the influence that Giovanni's depression might exert over him. She is surprised: she'd never guessed that mother and son had such a strong bond. He was always criticising her; such a controlling parent, he used to complain. A mother that would never give him even a tiny bit of freedom – he had to fight for each crumb, every day. And: in reality, he was still dependent on her. Look at the state of him. Luigi has reassured her, told her that it's just a temporary crisis. It often happens when a single child loses his mother. It's normal. Have faith in him.

A beam of light sneaks in through the shutters, rests on Giovanni's sleeping face. He gets up again, closes the curtains tight, goes back to bed. At eleven o'clock, Bianca enters the room, switches the light on. Her husband buries his head under the blankets.

"Come on. You have to get up, today." She helps him wash and dress, holds his hand - Giovanni is weak, thin, his dark suit seems to be what holds him together. Bianca insists on walking to Luigi's house, on the other side of the village - a walk will do him good, she thinks; a bit of fresh air. He holds Pablo's leash, who's whining in a delirium of joy. They walk down from the hill, slowly, Giovanni clinging on to the pushchair as if it were a zimmer frame. They walk downhill, then across the village, and slowly start the climb up; Luigi, all dressed up, is waiting for them in the yard with his brother and sister. The corners of his mouth tremble.

"Merry Christmas, Luigi."

"Good Christmas, Grandpa!" Massimiliano shouts from his pushchair.

The first thing Giovanni meets, when he enters, is her perfume. Nothing is more powerful, in order to remember, and nothing awakens memory quite like the sense of smell, which is at first processed by the olfactory bulb, that starts inside the nose and runs along the bottom of the brain. The olfactory bulb has direct connections to two areas in the brain that are closely linked with both emotion and memory: the amygdala and hippocampus. It is interesting to note that visual, auditory and tactile information do not pass through these brain areas. This might be the reason why olfaction is so successful at triggering a variety of feelings as well as old memories. It is through this sense that past and present converge; temporality, instead of being abolished, is doubled. Giovanni slams his nose against the scent of his late mother - a scent of roses, powder, dry skin; a material, solid smell. Of course, they'd just need to open the windows, to wait until the other aromas that linger - the turkey that sizzles in the oven with the potatoes, the chocolate cake – prevail and win over this. But there's no time: her perfume has reached Giovanni's brain, and the horror and fear and loneliness and a kind of disgust overwhelm him. And then an impulse for violence that explodes inside him like a dry branch catching fire quickly; it burns everything: a remnant of nostalgia, the resurgence of all kind of memories, and time. The smell and the past vomit over him in slimy, sticky lumps and it's not enough to close his eyes and mouth, this viscous warm material gets inside him through his breathing, which he can't stop, travels down to his heart. Giovanni runs into the yard. His lean body is shaken by retching. Vomiting consists of an involuntary, unnatural movement, which acts in the opposite direction to the force of gravity. It is a catharsis with a strange anodyne effect; one comes out of it free and pure. Purged. Redeemed. Instead Giovanni trembles like a baby and cries like a baby and shakes his fist like a baby and feels that his brain is empty, completely empty, only full of pain, fear, and anger.

***

Giovanni spends his days in bed, lying under the warm sheets, looking at the red walls of the room. He goes into the bathroom to wash – to be standing under the hot water, in the shower, is the only action that brings him some sort of relief. He listens to Maximilian and his wife's voices; he listens to their steps; the smell of cooking travels upstairs at regular intervals.

Luigi arrives to the *Willow* in the afternoon before dark; he takes Massimiliano and Pablo for a walk; he helps Bianca prepare dinner, bathe the baby; he looks after the vineyard. After the harvest, during the winter, the vine slows down its metabolism; the leaves fall, the plant falls asleep, goes into a sort of hibernation. All that is needed is a little pruning.

"It looks as if nothing is happening, now," Luigi explains to Bianca as they walk along together. "In fact, this is a crucial period for the plants, which need to be ready for shoot and fruit growth once spring finally arrives. Every vine requires individual care. In late February, we'll need to plant new ones." The winter so far has been rather unusual; there has been little rain, temperatures have remained low, the ground hasn't frozen over. "And this is not good; snow is actually very good: not only because it ensures a water reserve for the vineyard but also for its phytosanitary value for the prevention of diseases. Parasites hate snow; and it is snow that forces it to a beneficial rest."

"Doesn't it die, in the cold?"

"Not at all. It can resist all the way to minus 18°C. Look," he says, pulling out a penknife from a pocket. He makes a cut into the vine. "See this? It is green, inside; this means that it's trying to start again; the branch is soft whereas normally it should be drier. If now the temperatures start to go up again, the vine will begin to produce sap. Then it wouldn't be sleeping any longer; it would wake up."

"You know what? We'd need to perform a little surgery on my husband," Bianca jokes. "Just a little cut on a leg. If there is green sap inside, he's about to awaken."

"Give him time, Bianca. He just needs time."

They walk back home, put Massimiliano to bed and have dinner together, like an old married couple, Luigi and Bianca, in silence. Sometimes they watch television together. They can hear water running upstairs.

"Another shower," Bianca whispers. "He'll end up losing his skin."

Later, when Luigi goes home, Giovanni gets up. He puts on his robe and slippers, lurks at the top of the stairs and listens carefully, to make sure there's no one else, in the living room. He walks slowly down the steps, dragging his feet like an old man. He falls over on the sofa, in front of the fireplace. That's where Bianca brings him dinner, on a tray that Giovanni balances on his knees, a napkin tucked into the collar of his robe: a little rice; a spoonful of soup; a slice of polenta drowned in milk. A quarter of an apple. Bianca doesn't say a word, pretending to be busy with her knitting. She spies stealthily the still full plate, the food pushed into a corner, hidden under the fork, as some children used to do at her nursery. When he's finished (he hasn't finished, but has stopped trying) Bianca takes the tray away to the kitchen. After every meal,

Giovanni has to lie down - even the weight of the cutlery exhausts him. Pablo lies down next to him.

Giovanni lies down on the leather sofa, his eyes closed. Bianca leaves the knitting on a chair, takes a book and sits down at the other end of the sofa, next to her husband's feet. Her right hand holds the book, her left strokes his feet. Giovanni keeps his eyes closed, his face turned to the fireplace, his head resting on the pillow crocheted by Marieke, while Bianca reads aloud. Her hand on his feet consoles him. Mummy used to do it. He loved that. Marieke's soft hands would take his socks off, she'd pull his toes, tickle him, made him sleep. How warm he was, and soft, and happy.

"I feel awful." Bianca doesn't stop reading. "I'm so tired," Giovanni says.

Bianca looks at him without being seen. Perhaps if he thinks she's not watching, he will stop; maybe he just wants her attention. Maybe he'll wipe away the tears with the back of his hand and will turn towards her, and smile. Maybe everything will be fine, yes: finally: and she'll be able to go upstairs and check on her son, to make sure he is tucked in, that he's sleeping peacefully. Giovanni continues to cry, and the tears don't fall in silence, but are accompanied by his sobs.

"What have I done, what have I done," he says. Bianca keeps reading. Perhaps he'll stop, now. Maybe if she keeps quiet, if she doesn't say a word, he'll stop, and she'll be able to go upstairs and check on Massimiliano.

"Stop touching me."

"What is it, Giovanni?"

"What is it? I tell you what. I want to be left the fuck alone. You don't understand, do you? Don't you understand that I want to be left alone? That I want to be alone? Leave me the fuck alone."

"Shh, Don't shout. Don't wake the baby up."

"You and your child," Giovanni says with disdain. "I'd strangle both of you. You and your child," he says. Bianca stops stroking his feet, puts the book away, picks up her knitting. Giovanni fastens his robe, and leaves the room, dragging his slippers inside his feet up the stairs.

***

Giovanni's voice echoes on the stairs.

"Bianca?" Silence. "Where are you? Bianca?"

Nobody answers. Giovanni is barefoot, in his dressing gown, on the landing. He leans over – his torso reclining on the iron railing - and looks down. He can see the clock in the living room, showing it's nine o'clock. Nine in the morning. He must have fallen asleep. He runs a hand through his hair, walks down the stairs. The house is shrouded in silence - if his wife and Massimiliano were at home, or even in the garden, he'd be able to hear them.

"I better check anyway," Giovanni whispers. He opens the kitchen door. On the table there's a cup of coffee - now cold - that

Bianca has left on the table, next to a plate containing some bread spread with a layer of orange marmalade. Giovanni decides to ignore them. He rinses the cup and puts it on the counter, face down, to drain. He drinks a glass of water. He washes his hands, once, twice. He lets the dog out. His heart is pounding. Up to the first floor, quickly. He walks along the corridor, goes up the other five steps leading to a room, used as storage; there are old games piled up in a corner, rugs, trunks containing his and Bianca's old clothes, boxes of various sizes filled with stuff, unpaired shoes ("we should throw them away," Bianca says every time she comes in here, without ever do it), coats, bags, blankets. Giovanni closes the door behind him.

    He moves a chair out of the way, a couple of boxes, a broken mirror, slips between two trunks and stops in front of the largest one. He lifts the lid – there is a cast with his fingers on it, on the dust – he was here twelve days ago, new dust hasn't been able to cover his handprints. He crouches beside it. Inside the trunk there are Marieke's clothes. Giovanni extracts the garments, one at a time, examining them carefully. Nightgowns, a robe, two wool dresses, many silk dresses. This turquoise one, yes: he remembers it well: she used to wear at the beach. Here is the one she wore at his wedding, and her old tweed jacket, and the Burberry raincoat she loved so much even if it was tight for her; a series of bags – small big, made of leather, a pink plastic one, in which she used to carry beach towels - her beloved white blouses. She's got (she had, he corrects himself), twelve; and just like when he was small, he is impressed and overwhelmed by a sense of pride for those twelve shirts. They are immaculate, pure white, some made of silk and others of cotton, with smooth or puffed sleeves, some with a pointed collar, others with a round one, one scalloped: all different, all recognizable. Giovanni takes one and rubs the fabric between thumb and forefinger, he brings it to his face – he thinks he can still smell her, just a whiff of her scent. He slips a blouse on (it is short, but wide enough for him), he buttons it up to the neck. He tries on one of her jackets. It smells of humidity, and of the soap his mother used to perfume linens. He dives once more into the trunk to retrieve one of her scarves; there are many, and handkerchiefs, hats, gloves of all sorts. He lifts the shirt collar and knots one of the scarf around his neck. He looks in the mirror and crosses his arms over his chest, and holds tight.

***

February 3rd

Shall I write how I feel? I feel sick.

Shall I write what I do? I can't sleep. I spend all day in bed, waiting for time to pass. I don't sleep, I don't turn over, in my bed - I remain motionless, my eyes open, fixed on the bureau. I wash. I don't eat. I don't sleep. I wash. I don't eat, I don't sleep. I don't eat, don't sleep. I wash. Water cleanses me. I am sick.

THE HEART OF THE OCTOPUS

My dear diary: I have written pages and pages: all that I have done, all that I have thought. For so long I can't remember when I started. It's as if you were a person – a relative, a friend – who has seen me grow into a man. You have witnessed my highs and my lows, my battles, my wars. I feel defeated; beaten; lost. My father says I'm depressed. I don't know if I am; I feel sad, yes, but that's normal, isn't it? I am sad and angry and scared. Scared of what I could do. I'm afraid to hurt her. It would be so easy. It scares me, it's so easy. It just takes a bit of hatred, and I am full of it - it's licking my heart with its sharp, poisonous tongue. I'm afraid to hurt her, I will do it and I'm afraid. I want to hurt her, and it scares me. I wish she died – god how do I wish it. She is the cause of everything. She's guilty. It's her fault.

***

Guilt is a psychological mechanism that rebukes us when we do something that goes against our code of conduct. It manifests itself with getting angry with ourselves, something that torments us until we do something about it. Giovanni is tormented by recurring unpleasant thoughts and is pushed to enact ritual behaviours, such as washing frequently. He keeps thinking of the past, he keeps revising it, brooding over it. He keeps thinking about Michelina, the sex they had, about his mother. Marieke. Michelina. Bianca. If only Bianca had been more present. If only she had loved him more. His mother would still be alive, he would never have met Michelina. If Massimiliano had not been born. *If.*

***

Do you believe me?

I tell you what happened. It's the truth. We were sitting in front of the fire, mid-afternoon. Massimiliano still asleep upstairs. Bianca is reading. I am looking out of the window; looking at nothing. It's all quiet. I'm enjoying it. And then the fucking dog starts barking; it wants in, it wants out, it never stays still. Bianca gets up to open the door, again. I'm annoyed. I watch Pablo enter the room– self-confident; almost: swaggering. I swear. It walks in, rolls over on the rug, gets up again, comes to me, and I ignore it, willingly. Wilfully. It walks around the room for a while, unsettled, unsettling. I close my eyes. I breathe slowly. I'm annoyed. I open my eyes, and it's right in front of me, and it barks once, twice.

Bianca walks to the door and opens it, and stands waiting, whilst Pablo goes out, pisses against a flower pot, and comes back in. I'm annoyed. Bianca sits down again, picks up her book. Pablo lies on his back and Bianca rubs its exposed belly.

"Good boy, Pablo. Good boy," she repeats. Pablo lies there panting, then gets up again, walks around the room again, and comes to me: not to have its belly rubbed, though. It looks at me directly, as if to say: "Watch, now," and I watch. He goes up to my wife and starts humping her leg like crazy. She laughs, pushes him off. Pablo looks at me again – I swear – and off he goes again, against her leg. Bianca laughs. This happens three times.

If I told you that I'm not sure what happens next, would you believe me? If I told you that there is a blank, in my brain, would you know it's the truth? I honestly can't remember. I remember breathing hard. Harder. My ears whistling. My annoyance becoming anger, catching fire quickly, like phosphorus. I remember standing up, straight. Walking over. Seeing his thing against her smooth leg. And then – after – the pain in the front of my ankle, a whimper. Pablo on the floor, and Bianca kneeling next to his body, blocking my foot from kicking again, screaming, begging me to stop.

"You could have killed him."

The look in Pablo's eyes: fear. And respect.

Yes. Respect. From a dog.

***

She. She, who has ruined me with her purity. Bianca, a woman to die for – one could kill, for her. One could kill her. Bianca, my pure whiter than white Bianca. Bianca doesn't want to see, doesn't want to understand. How could she see, how could she understand: she is pure and white and as perfect as a magnolia blossom. But it's all her fault.

It is your fault.

THE HEART OF THE OCTOPUS

Bianca,

Bianca,

My whitest darling if only you could guess my hatred. Can't you feel it on your skin, acrid like sweat? Can you guess this bud of violence that keeps growing inside me that is writhing and sliding and inching away to come near you? Each day it's getting closer. It's almost reached you. You wake up next to me every morning, White-eyes, you wake up and glare at me and do not understand, White-eyes, White-lily. White-lamb. You are my lamb. My sacrifice. *Agnus dei.* You raise your chin, a little higher, White-eyes, you cross your arms in front of your chest, tight, like you're hiding something. But you've never hidden anything in your life, have you, my white darling? It was me. It's only my fault. My fault. I'm guilty. If only you had been more present. If only you had loved me more. More. You. You alone can grant me peace. *Dona nobis pacem.* You are my sacrifice. You. It should not have happened. It was not supposed to happen. It is you. You.

My White Lamb: *Dona nobis pacem.*

***

It seems to him as if Bianca was spying on him; yes, look: she keeps following him; she's always appearing in front of him, beside him, behind him, watching his every move, his every sigh.

He remembers seeing, in a book, photographs of a temple in Cambodia, where the head of a god or a king appeared in

THE HEART OF THE OCTOPUS

hundreds of stone sculptures, scattered in the jungle. One night Giovanni dreams about that scene, as if it was himself in the photograph. He found himself somewhere hot and humid, and he had an uneasy sensation, he felt uncomfortable, as if someone was watching him, but he couldn't understand where from, who it may be. And then he looked around; a pair of eyes fixed on him, two, and then fourteen and then seventy and a hundred pairs of eyes. He had counted them: there were fifty-four towers with four faces each, masks carved in stone, each the same and yet different, motionless yet alive, faces of a good God, infinitely tolerant and kind. A god who appeared in every corner; you just needed to open your eyes and there he was, again, omnipresent and obsessive, he wouldn't leave you alone, ever, he followed him everywhere, as ironic and mysterious as his smile, his lips upturned with the mildest of curves, just a hint, not even that, only a sigh. These parted lips were not uttering a single word; they seemed to be waiting, like a snake that is still considering his prey, his mouth open but just barely, only just enough to let out his tongue, ready to strike and kill. And then, suddenly, the god-king was changing features – his eyes were growing rounder, and he was turning into a she, with long hair and black eyebrows and empty eyes, and behold, it was not a god nor a goddess, but Bianca: his wife. She is the one that was staring at him, again and again and again, from a thousand towers, a thousand times, with a smile full of dignity, gentleness and detachment, full of patience. Giovanni had never before seen her like this, serene, composed, confident, satisfied, quietly in contemplation of her own peace of mind. And he, Giovanni himself, standing before her, naked. Her victim.

***

Can't you just leave me alone. Leave me alone, let me cry, let me live. Let me die. Leave me. Leave me.

Agnus dei.

Leave me, leave me, leave me, leave me, leave me, leave me, leave me. You don't leave me, ever. As soon as I turn to see what you are doing, I catch you - you're always there and you stare at me with your eyes the colour of milk. And you smile! Your smile is dangerous and slippery and I don't know what to do with it. There are nights when you're in front of me, my Bianca, my lamb, and I move my hands on your white shoulders - like marble, like snow, like ice; and I sense you relax, I can sense, under my fingers, the muscles of your back, and they are releasing their tension, that you are relaxed, and I move my hands and I want to tighten my grip on your white neck. Your swan-like neck, long and white and pure. I want to unroll my fingers around it, I want to hold it tight and tighter and break it like I would break the stem of a flower.

Lamb of God, Lamb of God,
You take away the sin of the world,
Have mercy on us
Have mercy on us

Lamb of God, Lamb of God,

You take away the sin of the world,

Have mercy on us

Lamb of God, Lamb of God,

You take away the sin of the world,

Grant us peace

Grant me peace.

***

Oh my Penelope, my Penelope whose hair is shiny like silk, my white-eyed Bianca, precious like a goddess. You look at me with those eyes of yours that have the colour of the sky. I close my eyes and wrap my hands around your swan-like neck.

So white, Bianca, so white.

And then I hear you.

***

Giovanni is sitting of the stairs. He's listening to the conversation between his father and his wife, downstairs. They're in the kitchen; Bianca is preparing dinner for Massimiliano, who eats before them. The windows are closed, the doors open, the table is set, the oven on. He can hear everything, word for word.

"This baby has a good appetite, hasn't he?"

"Please don't give him any more bread, Luigi, otherwise he won't eat my lasagne."

"All right, then. Enough, Max. Bravo." Massimiliano tries to protest, but weakly. "Bravo. Just like your daddy. Did you know Giovanni was a great little eater as a child?"

"Really?"

"Oh yes. Marieke fed him continuously: pasta, bread, cakes, chocolate. It was enough for him to ask her, and she'd open her bag, which was like that of Mary Poppins, with an infinite capacity, and pulled out candy, bread sticks, cookies. Incredible."

"She couldn't say no to him ..."

"Exactly. Like all mothers. Fathers manage to be more severe because they see their children less. But if you're with them all day, how can you say no?"

"Maria adored him."

Noise of crockery.

"Here, darling, open your mouth. There. It's mummy's lasagne. Bravo. Where's the bib? Here it is."

Bianca is feeding Massimiliano. There is a bit of silence.

"Marieke loved Giovanni so much," Luigi resumes.

"You say it as if you were almost jealous of him."

"I was. Really. Do you know, once we had a terrible argument," Luigi says.

"Tell me."

"Well. We had gone skiing. We had skied all morning since rather early on. It was about two o'clock, we were tired and ready to go to lunch; we had decided to try a little restaurant at the top of the mountain – we queued and took the ski lift. After a few minutes, there was a power failure, and we were stuck on the cable car for hours."

"Oh my goodness. I'd have been terrified."

"Yes. But also: hungry. Maria had, as usual, a backpack full of goodies, snacks, a juice, some crackers - I remember it all so well: a little box of crackers: and you know what? She wouldn't give me any. Not one. Not a candy, nothing. Everything was for Giovanni, only for him."

Bianca laughs. "Poor Luigi! And were you angry?"

"Yes. You can say that. I'm ashamed, you know. I remember pleading, with her – my tummy was rumbling, my throat dry. She gave me nothing. Not a crumb. And she said, I remember it word for word: "Well, now you know it. I love Giovanni more than you. Like all mothers ." She floored me."

"Really?"

"Really."

Silence.

"Do you think so too, Bianca?"

"What?"

"That mothers love their children more than they love their husbands. Marieke said that they all do, but that nobody admits it. That even when a woman is madly in love with her man, as soon as a child is born, it all changes. It's as if she's transferred all that love to her child."

Giovanni is still sitting on the steps. He holds his breath. Bianca responds immediately.

"Of course," she replies. His wife. His wife. "It's a different type of love. Protective. But for - well, I would do anything; I would jump into a ditch; I would take a bullet; I would die: yes, I would happily give my life for him. I wouldn't even need to think about it."

"And Giovanni?"

A sigh. "Luigi: I do love my husband. But if things continue like this if this depression keeps persisting. If this keeps going on. I don't know. Sometimes I think he'd be better off alone. I seem to bother him."

Giovanni stands up and goes back into his bedroom.

***

Dr Gamba prescribes Giovanni an antidepressant, assuring him that within six weeks it will begin to take effect. One morning, he walks downstairs dressed, sits down at the table for breakfast. Bianca and Massimiliano look at him. He smiles the sweetest smile. Relief floods his wife's delicate face.

He is precise; methodical. He enjoys planning. He knows what he's doing. He's done it before.

***

THE HEART OF THE OCTOPUS

But if there is harm, then you shall pay life for life, eye for eye, tooth for tooth, hand for hand, foot for foot, burn for burn, wound for wound.

***

On the afternoon of Friday, March 9th, Bianca has an appointment at the hairdresser's - Giovanni has booked a restaurant in Moncalvo for the next day, on Saturday, to celebrate his birthday; he told her to leave. To get out. To go and spend some money: to have a haircut, to buy him a present, and a cake. Luigi offers to accompany her; Giovanni will look after the child, and Pablo.

Massimiliano says goodbye to his mother and grandfather, waves as Luigi's Fiat Uno slips off along the road lined with cypress trees. Giovanni holds his sticky hand and accompanies him into the kitchen. The boy plays with his plastic toy cars, his favourites. He makes them run along the edge of the table. Giovanni opens the fridge, takes out a bottle of fruit juice; he pours a glass. From his trouser pocket he extracts the Rohypnol he had used, so many years ago; it has expired, but he is well prepared. He took a quarter of a tablet, a few days ago. Yes: it's still active. It will work.

He puts four tablets in the mortar that Bianca uses to make pesto. He grounds it until only a powder remains, as fine as sugar.

"Yes: sugar," he whispers, pouring it into the juice. He stirs slowly, meticulously. He offers the glass to the child. "It's nice and cold. Drink up."

Afterwards, he picks up his small warm body and takes him into the garden. It is three PM. The countryside is silent; even Pablo has calmed down. Massimiliano is light. He breathes with his mouth open. Giovanni sits on the edge of the fountain, holding his son. He looks at him. He strokes his cheek, his hair. He lets him go. A baptism; a sacrifice. "Take your son, your only son Isaac, whom you love, and offer him there as a burnt offering on one of the mountains of which I shall tell you."

Massimiliano slides into the water, still holding the two plastic cars in his hand.

EPILOGUE

October morning, Castel San Gerolamo.

The house stands on top of a hill. It is robust, has thick walls, and it's yellow. There is a chestnut tree in front of it - its branches skim the upper floor windows. It has been uninhabited for a long time – the windows are barred. The interior is dark.

There is a fountain, in the middle of the garden. It is accessed via three steps; on the top is the statue of an angel. Giovanni, Bianca and Massimiliano had spent entire afternoons sitting on those grey stone steps, fingering the water, catching tadpoles in transparent glasses, watching them go crazy.

A sweet scent rises from the fountain; a smell of rotting leaves, which mixes with that of ripe grapes that fills the air and of the wild mint Giovanni has crushed underfoot. The water is still. Giovanni walks slowly. His hair is grey; his face is lined, hard. His steps are cautious – because of his age, and because of the pain that is flowering in his heart. It's the first time he has returned to the

Willow after almost thirty years. He sits on the edge of the fountain. At its bottom lie the carcasses of two toy cars, abandoned long ago.

ABOUT THE AUTHOR

Mariateresa Boffo was born in Italy where she studied Law and published her first novel (Senza Mani, La Tartaruga edizioni). In 1996 she moved to the UK to complete a MRes followed by a career in publishing, working as senior commissioning editor for Penguin Classics. She is now a freelance editorial consultant based in Hove.

IL CUORE DEL POLPO was first published in Italy in 2019 by Enrico Damiani Editore. For Press Review of the Italian edition, please see: https://www.enricodamianieditore.com/il-cuore-del-polpo-rassegna-stampa/

Printed in Great Britain
by Amazon

56238941R00249